Selected Stories

Maurice Shadbolt

Also by Maurice Shadbolt

FICTION
The New Zealanders
Summer Fires and Winter Country
Among the Cinders
The Presence of Music
This Summer's Dolphin
An Ear of the Dragon
Strangers and Journeys
A Touch of Clay
Danger Zone
The Lovelock Version
Season of the Jew
Monday's Warriors
The House of Strife
Dove on the Waters

AUTOBIOGRAPHY
One of Ben's

DRAMA
Once on Chunuk Bair

NON FICTION
New Zealand: Gift of the Sea (with Brian Brake)
The Shell Guide to New Zealand
Love and Legend
The Reader's Digest Guide to New Zealand (with Brian Brake)
Voices of Gallipoli

Selected Stories

Maurice Shadbolt

Selected and Introduced
by Ralph Crane

𝔇𝔏

David Ling Publishing Limited
PO Box 34-601, Birkenhead, Auckland 10

Selected Stories

First Edition

ISBN 0-908990-56-1

First published 1998

Selection and Introduction © Ralph Crane 1998

Stories © Maurice Shadbolt 1959, 1963, 1967, 1993, 1996, 1998

The cover features a detail from a pastel by Eric Lee-Johnson,
Coromandel 1989/90. Reproduced by permission of
Elizabeth Lee-Johnson.

Typeset by ExPress Communications Limited
Printed in Australia

Contents

Introduction 7

from *The New Zealanders*

After the Depression .... 19 —

The Strangers .... 35 — ✗

Play the Fife Lowly .... 55 —

Thank you goodbye .... 73 —

from *Summer Fires and Winter Country*

Ben's Land 79

The Wind and the Spray .... 101 — ✗

Homecoming .... 131 —

The Room 161

Neither Profit nor Salvation 181

The People Before 223

from *The Presence of Music*

The Voyagers 245

Figures in Light 281

from *Dove on the Waters*

Dove on the Waters 319

uncollected story

The Simple Life 345

Introduction

There is only one reason to write, and it is not to serve literary fashion or scholarly fads. It is, as it was in the beginning, to get a grip on our existence.

One of Ben's

The world belongs to the imaginative.

'Dove on the Waters'

Maurice Shadbolt is without doubt one of New Zealand's major writers, perhaps our greatest storyteller. In a writing career that now stretches back over forty years he has published short stories, novels, a play, and various works of non-fiction. And during that time Shadbolt has won almost every major literary prize and writing fellowship New Zealand has to offer, some on more than one occasion. His enormous contribution to New Zealand literature was recognised in 1989 when he was awarded the CBE for services to literature, and again in 1990 when he was awarded the New Zealand Medal. In 1997 he received an honorary doctorate from the University of Auckland.

It may well prove to be the case that Shadbolt will be best remembered for his novels, particularly his historical trilogy of the New Zealand Wars. Yet it is nevertheless difficult to overstress the importance of the stories. Without the stories, there would have been no novels. But the importance of the stories stretches well beyond their significance to the longer works of fiction. Maurice Shadbolt's first collection of stories, *The New Zealanders*, was published in 1959. It was followed, in 1963, by *Summer Fires and Winter Country*, and then in 1967 by *The Presence of Music*, a triptych of novellas, which was to be his last collection of new stories for almost thirty years—though a collection of selected (and in some cases slightly revised) stories, *Figures in Light*, (drawn from *Summer Fires and Winter Country* and *The Presence of Music*) was published in 1978. Then in 1996 *Dove on the Waters*, a sequence of three skillfully linked novella-length stories, marked

Shadbolt's return to the short story form. Together these many stories represent a portrait of a colonial society in transition; in particular, they offer perhaps the most outstanding vignette we have of the New Zealand of the 1950s and stretching back to the inter-war period. Collectively and individually Shadbolt's stories give voice to ordinary New Zealanders.

It is apparent that Shadbolt intended his first volume of stories, confidently—even grandly for an author then living in England—entitled *The New Zealanders*, to be more than an arbitrary gathering; only two of the stories 'Play the Fife Lowly' and 'After the Depression', had been published previously, both in *Landfall*. The book's subtitle, 'A Sequence of Stories', suggests that Shadbolt was conscious of an organising principle, further emphasised by the division of the book into three parts, each of which takes its title from an excerpt from James K. Baxter's poem 'Homage to Lost Friends', which serves as the first of the book's two epigraphs. The first section, 'Wave Walkers', focuses on what Shadbolt has referred to as 'rural and small-town New Zealand'; the second, 'Cloud Riders', concentrates on 'urban society, or such of urban society as existed in New Zealand in the 1950s'; and the third, 'In the Blind Canyon', 'is tinged with the colour of the larger world'.[1] The settings of the stories range from pioneer farms to European cities; the characters include farmers and artists, Maori and Pakeha, men, women, and children, New Zealanders at home and abroad.

I have chosen four stories from this first collection: 'After the Depression', 'The Strangers', 'Play the Fife Lowly', and 'Thank you goodbye'. The first two, from 'Wave Walkers', the first section of *The New Zealanders*, look back to the 1930s and highlight various social and political issues of that decade. 'After the Depression' recounts the early morning arrival at a lonely railway station of a man, a woman, and a child, and their long walk to the mining settlement where the man has been promised work. The hope that briefly flickers as the wife looks wistfully at one of the empty cottages she imagines may be their home, is cruelly dashed in the climax of the story. A heated argument takes place between the man and the mine manager, who has withdrawn his offer of a job after finding out about the man's three-year jail sentence for sedition—no doubt for involvement in trade union politics, perhaps for his part in the Auckland riots of 1932. The story concludes with the man and woman attempting to distribute radical leaflets to the miners at the end of the day's shift before slowly retracing their steps to the station. As in Denis Glover's poem 'The Magpies', the all-pervading sense of hopelessness at the end of the story is a damning indictment of the times, all the more effective for its refusal to lay the blame for the family's problems at the feet of either the man or the mine manager.

'The Strangers' is narrated by the son of an unnamed pioneer farmer. It is a complex and sympathetic portrayal of the struggle of the widowed, lonely, obstinately self-reliant father to bring up his rather imaginative and sensitive son. The son's unquestioning acceptance of his father's puritan work ethic is challenged by the arrival of Tui, a Maori farm-hand who befriends the boy and takes him hunting and fishing in their spare time. Tui's warmth and his values operate as a contrast to those of his employer, and offer the son a glimpse of an alternative vision of life.

'After the Depression' and 'The Strangers' are complementary stories which would later be reworked to provide the foundation for Shadbolt's 1972 novel *Strangers and Journeys*. The radical Bill Morrison of 'After the Depression' and the pioneer farmer of 'The Strangers' would be reincarnated as Bill Freeman and Ned Livingstone in the novel, while their sons, Ian Morrison and the narrator of 'The Strangers', would become Ian Freeman and Tim Livingstone.

If the first section of *The New Zealanders* can be said to deal with the New Zealand of Shadbolt's parents' generation, the second and third sections deal with his own generation, focusing particularly on the 1950s. 'Play the Fife Lowly', taken from the second section, 'Cloud Riders', shared the 1957 *Landfall* Prose Award with John Caselberg's 'Eli Eli Lama Sabachtani'. The story is interesting for the fact that it is told from a woman's point of view. On the surface it is a brilliantly-realised sketch of a typical 1950s, male-dominated, Saturday-night student party. At the centre of the story are two couples, the hard-drinking, boisterous host Mike and his fiancée Sylvia, and Gerald and his girlfriend Helen, from whose point of view the story is told. The other major character is Tom Anderson, an ex-college friend of the two men who 'went all arty after college'. But what makes the story so compelling is that Shadbolt scratches away at the surface he creates. What is carefully not stated, but always clearly evident, is that Tom is homosexual, and that he has been invited to the party by Mike to provide entertainment at Gerald's expense. As a result of Mike's teasing insinuations and the presence of Tom and his friends, Helen recognises that Gerald is a closet homosexual, and is able to escape the marriage of convenience that she seemed to be slipping towards.

The final story from *The New Zealanders* is taken from 'In the Blind Canyon', the third section of the book. The inclusion of 'Thank you goodbye' is in some respects a personal indulgence on my part, a story I greatly admire for is economy and for its enigmatic nature. It perfectly captures one of those fleeting episodes which are of such importance in our lives. Like 'Play the Fife Lowly' this story is also told largely from the woman's point of view. A man, who we presume is a New Zealander, and a woman, a native of an unnamed East European city (which could easily be Sofia, the capital of Bulgaria), meet for the last time before the man leaves for the West. The ritual they play out—the man regretting that he must leave, while the woman replies that something could be arranged which would allow him to remain—is mocked by the only English words the waiter knows and which he proudly displays: 'How you do. I love you. Thank you goodbye.'

Soon after the publication of *The New Zealanders* Shadbolt returned to New Zealand, where he had to contend with the distinctly cool critical reception his first book received, a task made all the more difficult by the high praise the book had attracted in England and elsewhere. A novel he had been working on had to be discarded, and instead Shadbolt answered his critics, first with 'Ben's Land' (in 1961) and then with *Summer Fires and Winter Country*, published in 1963, some four years after *The New Zealanders*. In 1978 Shadbolt claimed that 'Ben's Land' was still his 'most satisfying story personally' and that *Summer Fires and Winter Country* was his 'most personally satisfying book', one which proved 'that *The New Zealanders* wasn't after all to be a solitary book, a tombstone under which a tiny talent rested'.[2] The pattern of the book is rather different from that of *The New Zealanders*. The title suggests oppositions: between youth and age, innocence and experience, energy and inertia, past and present. And indeed the stories explore all of these. Informing each, and offering a unifying theme, is a sense of return: to New Zealand, in many and various ways to the land, and to the past as a journey towards self-discovery. I have included six stories from *Summer Fires and Winter Country*: 'Ben's Land', 'The Wind and the Spray', and 'Homecoming' from the first section of the book, 'Summer Fires'; and 'The Room', 'Neither Profit Nor Salvation', and 'The People Before' from the second section of the book, 'Winter Country'. Personal preference has, of course, again played a significant part in my choice; so too has a desire to include Shadbolt's prize-winning stories: 'Homecoming' was a Katherine Mansfield Prize winner, as was 'Figures in Light' and 'Dove on the Waters'. But more importantly, an overall scheme is at work: these six stories, with their shared interest in the idea of return, seem to offer a logical continuation to the sequence established in the three sections of *The New Zealanders*. That I have chosen to include six of the nine stories which make up *Summer Fires and Winter Country* and only four of the eleven stories which make up *The New Zealanders* perhaps needs some explanation. It is simply this: reading the stories now, close to forty years after they were first published, it seems to me that the stories in the second collection have in many cases dated better than those in the first.

It could be argued that 'Ben's Land' has to some degree been overshadowed by the author's later autobiographical excursion, *One of Ben's*. On the contrary: the relationship between the story, Shadbolt's first novel *Among the Cinders* (1965—Hubert Flinders clearly grew out of grandfather Ben in the story), *The Lovelock Version* (1980—where ideas which first surfaced in the story are further developed and expanded), and the autobiography (by which time Shadbolt had discovered his convict ancestry) is a fascinating one which rewards pursuit, and if anything adds interest to the story. 'Ben's Land' spans four generations of Ben's tribe: those of the three Benjamins—great-grandfather Benjamin, grandfather Benjamin, and Uncle Ben—as well as the first-person narrator's own generation. The story hinges, however, on Uncle Ben who, fuelled by a mixture of nostalgia for the utopian dream he believes is the pioneer past of his grandfather and a need to make sense of his own generation, turns his back on the sterility of suburban middle-class life and attempts a return to the land by clearing a few acres of scrub he manages to buy. His attempt predictably fails, and this is underlined by his death in a fall from his crane on the waterfront after family pressure forces him back to the city; but the significance of the tale is that through Ben's story and the myths it explores, the narrator is able to make sense of *his* life.

Mark in 'The Wind and the Spray' also appears to fail in his bid to make sense of his world, in his search for identity. Early on he turns his back on his pioneer history and moves to the city, only later to return to the land, to the remote Hokianga farm he inherits from his parents. His initial rejection of his past and his subsequent failure to find anything meaningful to take its place is played out through his relationships with two women: the rapacious Susan, who operates as a symbol of the city and its values, and the Maori woman, Huia, who is a symbol of the land and all that it represents. His failure to make sense of his own identity is emphasised when he finds himself married to Susan, a woman he doesn't love, and father to a child that is not his own, while Huia, the woman he does love, has given up his child for adoption in the city. The strong relationship that develops between the two women further isolates Mark, and leaves him dislocated in his own land. It is only as the story closes, as he steers his boat out into an enormous sea, and feels 'the wind and the spray sharp and exhilarating on his face', that Mark finally makes sense of his life; Shadbolt deliberately leaves unresolved the question of whether he survives the discovery.

'Homecoming' is the story which most obviously continues the sequence established in *The New Zealanders*, and like the stories in the final section of that book it clearly draws on Shadbolt's own experiences. 'Homecoming' is told from the point of view of Eve, a New Zealand writer (a journalist) whose considerable success in England is the cause of the petty jealousies which greet her on her return to Auckland and deny her a sense of belonging. It is only when she completes the last stage of her journey, to her parents' farm in the Hokianga, that she begins to experience a sense of New Zealand as 'home' again. Belonging in this story, as in 'The Wind and the Spray', is clearly associated with the Maori; first through the presence of the young boy who takes her up the river to her parents' farm, and then specifically through Muru (whose attitudes towards Pakeha society anticipate those of later Maori radicals). Throughout the story what might now be read as essentialized Maori values are juxtaposed with those of the Pakeha. It is ironic that the successful Eve should become jealous of her Maori friend Sarah Arapata, who has left her liberal Pakeha husband (who would preserve Maori culture in amber) in the city and returned to the Hokianga where she now lives in apparent squalor with Muru, but comfortable in her sense of identity. Echoing the scene in John Osborne's *Look Back in Anger* where Helen, having persuaded Alison to leave Jimmy prepares to take her place, the story closes when Eve successfully manages to persuade Sarah to return to her husband (and Pakeha values) while she herself remains behind, apparently ready to slip into the gap left by her friend's departure, to live with Muru and use him in an attempt to anchor herself to her native land.

'The Room' is a highly symbolic story, a movement from innocence to experience, which operates on two distinct levels. On a cultural level it pits the pioneer vision (represented by the family homestead) against the modern reality of the city (represented by the lonely room first Margaret then Sonny inhabits). And simultaneously, on a personal level, it is a further exploration of the theme of self discovery which Shadbolt returns to again and again in the stories gathered in *Summer Fires and Winter Country*. In some respects Margaret's and then Sonny's shift to the city and university is presented as an ironic echo of the earlier journeys of their pioneer forbears. And like those earlier journeys, this one is fraught with dangers, which prove too much for Margaret, who dies after a back-street abortion. As Sonny sorts through Margaret's possessions as he prepares (in a rather macabre twist) to move into her old room, he makes a series of discoveries about his sister and himself. As he reads her letters and an unfinished poem he is forced to recognise the jealous, almost incestuous nature of his love for his sister. He discovers, too, that she worried about his innocence and how he would cope in the city, and that when she died she had been in the process of searching out a room for him. With his sister's experience, the innocent Sonny will be better equipped to survive. The room, then, becomes for Sonny both a doorway to the city, and a doorway to the past; the Maori symbols of burial cave and tiki which Shadbolt introduces become in turn the keys to an understanding of that past and a discovery of self.

A return to the land is also the central theme of 'Neither Profit Nor Salvation'. With two failed marriages behind her, and dissatisfied with

her life in the city, Diana buys an orchard in a the far North. She takes
with her a young female companion, Merlyn, another casualty of city
life. Their idyllic existence—working, swimming, and sunbathing
together—is interrupted by the arrival of Diana's husband, George, the
ubiquitous serpent who invades their garden of Eden. After Merlyn
falls pregnant by him Diana persuades her that if they can be rid of
George their state of paradise will be restored and they will be able to
bring up the child together. Her wish is fulfilled when she calmly
watches George drown after his dinghy sinks out at sea. With evil
expelled, harmony returns, with the added promise of the child who
will be born to Merlyn, and the possibility of a comfortable lesbian
relationship. The sense of hope invested in the relationship at the end
makes 'Neither Profit Nor Salvation' unusual amongst Shadbolt's
stories. It is also well ahead of its time in its suggestion of a satisfying
lesbian family unit.

Most of the stories in *Summer Fires and Winter Country* focus on the
1950s; 'The People Before', like 'Ben's Land', looks back to an earlier
period. In this first-person narration the son of a farmer (and there are
similarites between this farmer and the farmers in 'The Strangers' and
later in *Strangers and Journeys*) looks back on his boyhood on the family
farm in the years following the First World War and through the
Depression. A further historical framework is established through
references to the New Zealand Wars and the confiscation of Maori land
which followed. The family's gruelling routine is interrupted by the
arrival of a group of Maori—'the people before' of the title—whose
tribe had lived on this land prior to the nineteenth-century
confiscations. They bring with them an old man, the son of a chief and
the last Maori to be born on the land. When they return from the site
of their hilltop *pa* a few days later, they leave behind the old man who
has died. This visit is the catalyst which causes the farmer to sell his
land. While he may have won his battle to survive economically, the
story implies that he cannot win his battle to possess the land spiritually.

In their portrayal of Maori-Pakeha relations, their embracing of
feminist perspectives, and their treatment of such issues as abortion,
incest, and homosexuality, the stories published in *Summer Fires and
Winter Country* display an awareness of aspects of New Zealand society
that few were then willing to confront.

After the publication of his first novel, *Among the Cinders*, and before he returned to the task of completing *Strangers and Journeys*, Shadbolt wrote a triptych of novella-length stories which were published under the title *The Presence of Music*, the title of the central panel in the triptych. I have chosen to include the two side panels of Shadbolt's literary triptych in this collection. Not surprisingly, the stories share common themes—particularly a concern with the position of the artist in society, in the 1950s in 'The Voyagers' (and in 'The Presence of Music') and then in the 1960s in 'Figures in Light'.

'The Voyagers', set in Auckland and the King Country, contrasts the life of Mike, a rebellious, bohemian artist who deserts New Zealand for Europe in a bid to discover his talent (who would later re-emerge as Tim Livingstone in *Strangers and Journeys*), with that of the narrator, a more conservative figure, content to remain in New Zealand. A newspaper article announcing Mike's return to New Zealand prompts the narrator to tell the story as he considers the meaning of his friend's voyage and eventual return. The two men grew up together in a small King Country town, and then shared a room in Auckland until Mike leaves to work his passage to England on board a merchant ship. Mike's voyage to England is contrasted with the voyage of a few hundred yards the narrator and Mike's girlfriend, Betty, make in a stolen yacht on the Waitemata harbour. By later marrying Betty the narrator accepts the security and middle-class values that Mike rebelled against.

'Figures in Light', which shares its title with a series of painting by Pat Hanly, to whom the story is dedicated, is another look at the artist figure in New Zealand society. The artist here is the narrator's sister, Ruth, who is contrasted with her solidly middle-class brother in much the same way as Mike is contrasted with the conformist narrator in 'The Voyagers'. The relationship between Ruth and her brother is explored when they travel up to Northland together for their father's funeral. That journey serves the purpose of drawing the narrator away from his wife and children in Wellington and Ruth away from her artist friends in Auckland, and gives each the opportunity to come to terms with what the other means to them (and Shadbolt the opportunity to explore the boundary between incest and sibling love). The story doesn't share the public concerns evident in many of Shadbolt's stories, but instead focuses on the private relationship between the narrator and his sister. If there is a wider concern in this story it is carried in the fact that Ruth has a place, however marginal and shadowy, in New Zealand society, and unlike Mike in 'The Voyagers', does not feel compelled to leave New Zealand.

In an article published in *Landfall* in 1973 Shadbolt claimed that 'Figures in Light' was 'the most near to perfect story [he] was ever likely to write',[3] and gave that as the reason behind his decision to abandon short fiction in order to concentrate on the novel. He was not to publish another story until 'Dove on the Waters' appeared in 1995, twenty-eight years after the publication of *The Presence of Music*, and thirty years after the triptych of stories were written (in 1964-65). 'Dove on the Waters' challenges Shadbolt's bold claim. Not only is it a 'near perfect story', it was also to become, with two other stories, a 'near perfect' novel, *Dove on the Waters* (1996).

Most obviously, 'Dove on the Waters' is the story of Walter Dove, an eccentric and enigmatic Auckland lawyer who, in 1902, turns his back on wife, career and society, supposedly to sail solo round the world. In fact he voyages no further than a few miles up the Waitemata harbour before beaching his boat in tidal shallows where he and it reside undiscovered for eight years, and will remain, self-sufficient, until his death in 1938. In Walter's story themes explored in earlier stories—such as the return to the land, the necessity of voyage, and the need to make sense of our past—are freshly encountered. On another level the story is magnificently about love: the love between Walter and Alice, whose admission that she has spent a 'splendidly libidinous week in the Caribbean' aboard Walter's marooned boat ends the story, and the love shared by Alice and her great-nephew, the author. Along with the other two stories which together form the novel *Dove on the Waters*, this story is also one of Shadbolt's most evidently metafictional short fictions. Walter's story is framed and interrupted by the ninety-year-old Great-Aunt Alice (a character who owes much to Shadbolt's grandmother Ada Shadbolt and his Aunt Renee—or Sis—as they appear in *One of Ben's*) telling her nephew the tale in the 1960s, and by references to the author, who makes a cameo appearance in the main tale, circumnavigating the globe as a young boy aboard Walter's boat, writing the story in the 1990s. 'Dove on the Waters' is a particularly fine story which spans the entire twentieth century and celebrates the human spirit, nonconformity and, above all, the imagination.

The final story included in this selection is 'The Simple Life', the only previously uncollected story in the volume, first published in *Metro* magazine in February 1998. Like many of the stories in *Summer Fires and Winter Country*, 'The Simple Life' is a story of the 1960s (albeit one which is carefully framed by the consciousness of the 1990s), and like 'Ben's Land' and particularly 'Neither Profit Nor Salvation' its central theme is a return to the land; what makes it different from the earlier stories is the added assurance with which Shadbolt approaches his theme and the different conclusions he draws. Initially the idea of a return to the land is promulgated as a weekend retreat from the city for Don Fox, an art dealer, and his arty friends, a place where they could 'kick ideas around informally', perhaps even make sense of themselves and connect with their pioneer beginnings. While they lack the necessary commitment to succeed in either making sense of themselves or connecting with their pioneer past, their project does provide the platform for Eddie Moorehouse, a faltering artist, to do just that. After being invited to caretake the property following a burglary, Eddie slowly begins to establish himself on the land, planting a garden, running sheep, and clearing scrub, and eventually, following a stand-off with a shotgun, he drives Don and his friends off the land and back to the city. In this story Eddie's relationship with the land is valued for its commitment—which links him to the past, and provides, in the closing lines, a pattern for the future.

Perhaps, finally, I should justify, or at least explain, the need for a new selection of Maurice Shadbolt's stories. It is this: if we are to make sense of our present, we need first to make sense of our past. Through the New Zealand he invents in his stories Maurice Shadbolt helps us to do that; which is reason enough for this selection.

Ralph Crane
Hamilton, May 1998

NOTES

[1] See 'Author's Note', *The New Zealanders* (Auckland: David Ling, 1993) 10. Baxter also provides Shadbolt with an epigraph for *Summer Fires and Winter Country*, and *The Presence of Music* carries the dedication 'FOR JAMES K. BAXTER'.

[2] *Figures in Light: Selected Stories* (Auckland: Hodder and Stoughton, 1978) 238.

[3] 'The Making of a Book', *Landfall 27* (1973): 288.

* * *

Ralph Crane is Senior Lecturer in English at the University of Waikato. He has published a number of articles and reviews on Maurice Shadbolt's fiction, and is the editor of *Ending the Silences: Critical Essays on the Works of Maurice Shadbolt* (1995).

After the Depression

The night had come and almost gone again; now, when the rough sweep of his large hand gashed the mist of the carriage window, he was able to see, beyond steep yellow clay-cuttings crested with damp green bush, the brightening grey of the morning sky. His view was obscured for a moment as steam from the engine, shredding and spinning, gusted past the window. But he had seen enough: he sighed, stretched, yawned, and sat back in his seat.

The guard, his cap awry, picked his way through the swaying second-class carriage, carefully avoiding the pillows, heads and legs which jutted into the narrow, dirty aisle. He called the name of the next station, a one-minute stop. His voice in the dim, sleeping carriage was loud, without apology for intrusion. There was an angry mutter from one awakened passenger; but the rest, apart from the tall man stiff in his seat, stirred sleepily, adjusted their pillows, and slept again. The guard left the carriage, slamming the door after him: and once more there was only the sound of iron wheels racketing on uneven rails, and teacups and saucers rattling beneath the seats.

The tall man, who had sat sleepless through the night, gashed the healed mist of the window again. But his view of the dawn sky was gone; in its place was a swift, gloomy blur of thick bush tangling close to the track. Weak spots of light flickered on his face: a face with a coarse, grainy quality; the spare flesh bleak and unhealthy. The features, though, were firm, the eyebrows dark and heavy, the eyes sharp blue, the nose slightly hooked, the lips dry and pale; there was a faint blackish stubble on his thin, pointed chin. He wore a tight black suit that had probably been too small even when it was purchased from a cheap ready-made store six years before; it was frayed at the cuffs and food-stained on the lapels. His thick, broken-nailed fingers and flattened thumbs had by degrees loosened his brown, imitation-silk tie: it hung askew, proclaiming its unfamiliarity with his sinewy neck. The top button of his shirt was undone, and the twisted collar grubby with travel.

He occupied a double seat, his back to the engine. He hesitated a moment before waking the woman and child who slept in the seat opposite.

The woman was upright, her head against the window: a woollen jersey packed between the window and her head served to cushion her from the monotonous violence of the train's motion. Her face was young and pale, verging on plumpness; it quivered with the movement, and her mouth had fallen open. The lapels of her shabby grey coat were drawn up to cover her white throat. Her figure was short and mannish, and her dumpy legs barely touched the floor. The child, cocooned in a faded tartan blanket, slept with his head against her thigh. He had the fresh, sexless face of a three-year-old; the features girlish and delicate, like those of the woman. A cream beret had slipped to the back of the head, releasing a small cascade of uncut crinkly blonde hair, streaked with brown.

The man reached forward, finally, and touched the woman gently on the arm. She woke with a jerk, her eyes fluttering open: finding herself in the gloomy, jolting carriage, she was, for a moment, bewildered. Then she saw the man and smiled sleepily.

'Nearly there,' he said. 'We're nearly there.'

'There?' said the woman, vaguely. 'Already?'

'It's morning,' he said. 'Look out the window.'

'Ian,' the woman whispered. 'Ian, wake up.'

The child woke and murmured. The woman stood, replaced the lapels of her coat, shook out wrinkles, and bent to the child. Uncovering him, she folded the blanket and put it away.

The train, hammering along a flat stretch of track now, had begun to slow. Whispering soothingly, the woman fastened shoes on the child; the man removed luggage from the rack above their heads. There was a hoarse whistle: the train shuddered with a prolonged clashing of couplings, and was still.

The three descended from the stuffy warmth of the carriage into the chill of a sunless, misty morning; they were the only passengers to leave the train. His thick dark coat flapping obstinately about his legs, the man carried two heavy suitcases alongside the stationary, hissing carriages. The woman followed, carrying a small case in one hand, and guiding the slow child with the other. Their feet made crunching sounds on the raw gravel.

The station consisted of a square, broken patch of concrete, a set of hand-operated signals; and a dully reddish waiting-room, an uninhabited box of feeble yellow light. The buildings of the settlement around were dark and obscure in the mist.

'It's early yet,' the man observed, as he set down the suitcases in the waiting-room. 'We can wait here.'

The room smelt of soot and urine. They sat on hard wooden seats, the child's feet dangling above the filthy, paper-strewn floor. The woman blanketed the child and drew the coat-lapels over her throat again. The man sat hunched forward, his large veiny hands dangling fidgety between his knees: he looked at his hands, turning them over for inspection, as if seeking some answer there.

'It'll be all right this time,' he said at last. 'I know it will.'

The woman was silent.

'I got a good feeling about it,' he said, still looking at his hands.

The woman remained silent. The child was again asleep against her thigh. The man became annoyed with looking at his hands, and suddenly thrust them deep into the pockets of his coat. He discovered, as if by accident, a tin of tobacco and began, laboriously, to make a thin cigarette.

The engine whistled: the shrill, imperious sound echoed and re-echoed against hills hidden in the mist. There was a renewed hissing and lurching, and a long line of unlit carriage windows steamed past the waiting-room.

A solitary railway employee, walking homeward, looked into the room. He was puffy-eyed; and under his railway uniform a pyjama-top showed. 'Anything I can do for you people?' he asked.

The man looked up. His eyes were sharp and hostile. 'We're just waiting here,' he said aggressively. 'No law against waiting, is there? That's what this place is here for, isn't it?'

The railwayman was startled. He blinked. 'Don't get me wrong, mate. Just wondering if I could help, that's all.'

'You can't,' the man said.

'Strike me dead,' the railwayman said. 'No need to bite me head off, mate.' He retreated, still astonished, and strode off; his feet crackled away into the quiet, grey morning. They were alone again.

'He was only trying to be helpful,' the woman suggested timidly. 'You could of been nicer to him.'

'Helpful?' The man laughed. 'Nicer?' He stopped laughing suddenly. 'I pick his sort a mile. Bloody snoopers everywhere.'

The woman shrank from him. The child stirred and murmured.

'Sorry,' the man said. He seemed dismayed. 'You're right. I don't know.' He shook his head. 'There wasn't no need for me to go crook like that. I'm just a bit jumpy about everything. I didn't sleep. I suppose he might of been all right.' He drew hard on his cigarette, but it had burnt out. He threw it away in disgust, then reached in his pocket, took out a soiled paper bag, and tore it open. There were three stale-looking refreshment room sandwiches inside. He offered them to the woman. 'You hungry?'

'We can wait a while,' she said. 'You eat.'

'I'm not hungry neither.'

The woman looked sick with tiredness; she touched his arm hesitantly. 'Where are we?' she asked softly. 'Do we have to go far?'

'This place here's a timber-milling outfit,' he said, pointing out the door to where mist still curtained the landscape. 'The mine's a couple of miles or so from here There's a road down to the mine, and a railway track. Don't know how the loco runs from here down to the mine. That's what we got to find out.'

'You could of asked that man then,' the woman pointed out cautiously. 'He could of told you how the loco runs.'

The man sighed. 'I could of,' he agreed. 'I just wasn't thinking. When I seen him come along I was thinking other things.'

The woman seemed altogether satisfied by his reply, by his admission that he had been wrong. It was an event of a rare kind, and she could afford satisfaction. He sat forward, looking out the door, thinking his other things again.

The light outside was now quite bright. The mist, retreating from the settlement, fled up the sunlit flanks of the hills. In the waiting-room, the child slept against the woman, and the woman against the man; the man was awake. He at last reached for a sandwich and began to eat it slowly and thoughtfully. His movement woke the woman, then the child.

She took the child to a tap outside the waiting-room and washed his face with a dampened handkerchief. Then she set the beret squarely on his head and led him back into the room. She took a bottle from her case and poured some cream-flecked milk into a peanut-butter jar that now saw service of a different kind. She gave the child the milk and a sandwich. There was one sandwich left. She looked at her husband, then at the child; and her hand darted out, as if of its own volition, and carried the sandwich quickly to her mouth. She ate almost guiltily.

The man stood. 'I'll find out what time the loco runs down to the mine,' he announced. He went out of the room, across the tracks, and into the settlement, walking with an abrupt, jerky stride. Presently he returned.

'There's a loco comes up about ten,' he said. 'It don't go back again till about one. That's five hours yet.'

'We can wait,' the woman said patiently; she fingered back her limp hair.

'Wait?' he said. 'I'm sick and tired of waiting. It drives you up the wall. We can walk to the mine. It's not far.'

'Walk?' the woman said faintly.

'All right?' he said briskly, but gave her no time to answer. He took up the two large suitcases. 'Let's go.'

They walked over the tracks and through the settlement. Along a single stony road, pooled with rainwater, there was a store and post office combined in an ungainly wooden building with unpainted weatherboards; one or two early-morning loungers watched the three strangers go past. Further along there was a string of old houses, knotting at the end into a cluster of ramshackle single men's huts. The timber mill, which stood at the end of the settlement, was already alive with grinding, tearing noises.

'Hell-holes, them places,' the man observed.

'They couldn't be much worse than mines,' the woman said; but he didn't seem to hear.

An articulated timber-truck, unloaded and jerking, rumbled past, splattering them with mud. The man spat after it. 'Could of given us a lift,' he said.

'He mightn't of been going the same way as us,' the woman

observed.

'How does he know till he's asked us?' he demanded. He spat again, at nothing in particular this time.

'Anyhow,' she said, 'there wouldn't of been room for the three of us in it. Not in the cab.' She was right in defending the driver; she knew she was right. But this time, she knew also, he would not admit it. So she added appeasingly, 'It doesn't matter much, does it? You said it wasn't far.'

'No. It's not far.'

They walked in silence. His pace, even with the two heavy suitcases weighting him, was too brisk for her and the child. Soon he was several yards ahead.

'Wait,' she called, her voice mild with an old despair.

He sat on his cases and waited. She expected irritation in his face, but found only concern. 'I'm sorry,' he said. 'I keep forgetting him.' He pointed to the child. 'Let's have a rest.'

The child's face was still sleepy, and bewildered; the woman sat him on her case. 'Where we going?' he said.

'I told you before, sonny,' the woman said, sighing. 'We're going to a new place.' She was tired of the question.

'Why?'

'Shush, Ian,' she said with annoyance. Then, repenting, she straightened the cream beret on the small head.

'Why?' the child repeated.

'Because,' she said, raising her eyes in appeal to the man. 'Because Daddy's taking us.'

'Why Daddy taking us?'

The woman didn't answer: she didn't look at the man. He knelt beside the child; the child surveyed him gravely. 'We're going to a new place because it'll be a better place,' he said simply. 'That's why.'

The sun warmed the pale sky, lighting a landscape stripped and harsh. On the upper slopes of the hills, where limestone outcrops stood gaunt against the sky, were long-dead trees, tangled and whitened, and giant ulcers of erosion scabbed with weeping crusts of clay and papa; on lower ground lank wire fences straggled about small, pine-sheltered farmhouses. The pasture was a dead green colour, and loose-bellied cows grazed. The road unwound slowly, a thin strip of clay and bluish metal edged with ti-tree and gorse. They came, at length, to a crossroad, and a signpost which said: FERNDALE MINE $2^1/_2$ M.

'I thought you said it wasn't far,' the woman protested.

The man didn't argue. 'It was a bit further than I thought, that's all.'

'We should of waited. We should of waited for a loco.'

The man seemed to agree. 'I just wanted to get there. I just don't like hanging round.' He paused. 'I didn't think it'd of been so far. I'm sorry.'

She was placated; she nodded, as if she too well understood his impatience. 'I don't like hanging round neither,' she said. 'But we should of waited.'

They came to a rise. The man, walking ahead, met the rise first. He stopped and set down his suitcases. 'There she is,' he said, pointing as the woman and child came up beside him.

The mining settlement discoloured the end of a tawny valley; the hills around were lacerated with black weals. Two groups of buildings made the settlement, one group large and dark and tightly gathered, the other small and white and more scattered. The large dark buildings belonged to the mine; the small white ones, a little distance removed, were the miners' homes. Above and beyond the valley were hills tall and blue and remote.

'What that?' the child said.

'That's where we're going,' replied the man. He said it almost with pride, sitting on a suitcase and rolling a cigarette. 'Might as well have a rest now,' he announced. 'It looks pretty good to me.'

Sitting beside him, the woman looked down the valley with a pensive expression. He touched her playfully under the chin, tilting up her face. 'What do you think, mother?' he said. 'Look good to you?'

'Any place,' she said. 'Any place looks good.'

'I think you'll like it here. I just got a feeling.'

'I'd like it anywhere. It doesn't matter where. Just as long as it's somewhere.' She continued to look thoughtfully down valley.

'I don't want to go,' the child said. 'I want to go back.'

'We can't go back,' said the woman, softly. 'We can't ever go back.' She didn't look away from the distant settlement.

'Why?'

She didn't seem to hear.

'Why?'

'Shut up,' she hissed suddenly, jerking her eyes to the child. Astonished, he began to whimper; she softened. 'Shush, Ian,' she whispered. 'We're going to a new place. A nice new place.' She pointed. 'See?'

But the child couldn't see; his eyes were filled with tears. 'My feet are hurty,' he complained.

The man picked up his suitcases. 'Let's go,' he said jubilantly. He set off with a jaunty stride, humming a tune.

The sun grew hot in an empty sky. A few hundred yards down the road they came to an old wooden bridge which spanned a clear, glittering stream. Upstream a little they could see a sandy place, like a miniature beach, strung around with toi-toi and flax, and shady with willows.

They made a halt on the bridge. 'It's a pretty place,' the woman murmured. 'A pretty place.'

'That'll be nice in summer,' said the man, pointing across the glittering water to the place of sand and shade. 'We could have picnics there. And swim. And eat our lunch under the willows.'

'Yes,' said the woman doubtfully. She had heard all this before. But there had never been picnics.

Their halts along the last stretch of road became more frequent. The child whimpered with hurting feet while the woman became tired and ill-tempered. The man, however, only seemed to increase his pace as they neared the settlement.

It was late in the morning when they came to it. The white miners' homes, attractive from a distance, were now small square boxes, crudely built and ugly, crammed together as closely as houses in a city suburb; they looked as if huddled for protection in the bare valley under the colourless sky. Each had a black strip of garden and a green patch of lawn.

The man nodded towards one of the homes. No curtains showed in the window; no smoke wisped from the chimney. The lawn was long-grassed and unkempt, and weeds grew in the garden. 'That one's empty,' he said. 'That might be the one we get.'

The woman looked at the place wistfully.

'Like it?' he said.

'There'll be a lot of work to do,' she said. 'I expect the inside's a mess. And the garden.'

'I knew it was going to be good,' he said with satisfaction, spitting on his parched palms and gripping the suitcases again. 'I knew it was going to be pretty good here. I had a feeling we was going to like it.'

This too she had heard before. Reluctantly, she turned her eyes from the house, took the child's hand, and followed the man.

Beyond the store and post office they found the settlement's most imposing structure, the mine office; a squat grey building. 'Wait here,' directed the man. 'I don't think I'll be long.'

The woman and child sat outside while the man went into the office. She removed the child's shoes and massaged the small, blistered feet. 'We'll be all right soon,' she said.

'Why?'

'I know,' she answered, confidently.

The reception office was a small, gloomy room. Beyond a dark counter were two desks. At one a grey-haired woman sat typing. At the other was a clerk, a slight mousy man of about fifty. He had a shiny bald head with a slender periphery of silver hair; steel-rimmed glasses sat on a thin, bony nose. His face was dried-up and humourless. He worked in a limp black smoking jacket. Just beyond him was a door displaying the sign Mine Manager.

The clerk looked up from his papers, apparently to ascertain that the visitor was of not much account, and then bent to them again. His pen scratched briefly, and he rose without haste, fastidiously flicked a spot of dust from his papers, and minced slowly to the counter.

'Yes?' he said. 'Anything I can do for you?'

'I'm here about a job. I wrote a letter—'

'The name?'

'Morrison's the name. William Morrison.'

The clerk screwed on the top of his fountain pen; he began to twirl the pen slowly in his fingers. 'Ah, yes, Mister Morrison,' he said. 'I remember.' His expression was pained; the pen twirled.

'It's all right, isn't it?' the man said. 'You said in your letter—'

'There were two letters actually, Mister Morrison.'

'Two letters? I only got one. You said there was a job for me here.'

'It's apparent you couldn't have received our second letter. We only posted it two days or so ago. We hardly expected you would turn up here so soon. You see, there was some mistake.' The clerk smiled blandly.

'Mistake?' His voice trembled. 'What do you mean a mistake?'

'About the job. An error in the office here. Really most unfortunate. What it amounts to is that there isn't a job here for you at all.'

'But you said—'

'As I explained, Mister Morrison, there was a mistake. We tried to tell you in our second letter. Unfortunately you set off before that letter arrived.' The pen still twirled between nervous fingers. 'The whole thing is really most unfortunate.' He shook his head. 'I'm so sorry.'

The man's eyes flickered, and were suddenly sharp. He slammed his fist on the counter. 'Don't lie to me,' he snapped.

'Really, Mister Morrison. Please.' The clerk retreated from the counter; he gave a small, despairing shrug.

'I don't want none of your bloody lies.'

The grey-haired woman, startled, looked up from her typewriter. The clerk appeared to wither before the prospect of further violence of language. 'Please, Mister Morrison. Please. There's a lady present.'

'Tell me the truth,' the man demanded.

'I'm afraid I don't understand,' said the clerk weakly. 'I've explained all there is to explain.'

'Let me see the manager.' The man pointed to the door beyond the clerk's desk. 'Maybe he'll have some truth.' He went round the end of the counter, but the clerk blocked his way.

'He's a busy man. He wouldn't want to be disturbed. He really—'

Shoved aside, the clerk fell back against the woman with the typewriter. She gave a cry, and saved her typewriter.

Without knocking, the man pushed open the door of the manager's office. This room was bright after the gloom of the other, too bright. He could not see at first. Sunlight fed through a long window in the opposite wall, silhouetting the desk and its occupant. The walls were cream-coloured, and there was now a thick green carpet beneath his feet. This room was not only brighter; it was luxurious by comparison. There were leathercovered chairs and light-varnished filing cabinets.

'My name's Morrison,' he announced.

He could see the occupant of the desk now, as he rose slowly to his feet, removing his thick tortoise-shell glasses. A short stocky man, moon-faced, in a pepper-and-salt suit; a gold watch-chain was looped across his waistcoat. He was a man with every appearance of assurance. He looked mildly puzzled.

'I beg your pardon?' he said.

'I said my name's Morrison. William Morrison. I want to know why I can't have a job here. After you people said I could have one. And I don't want none of your bloody lies.'

'A job?' the manager said. He resumed his seat and began, methodically, to clean his glasses with a white handkerchief.

'The job you people promised me. Now your bum boy out in the office tells me I can't have it. I want to know why.'

'Why?' the manager repeated. He seemed amused. 'You want to know why?' He coughed significantly, and added, 'There was a mistake. No doubt you've been told that.'

'I told you I don't want no lies. I'm sick of these kind of lies.'

The manager replaced his glasses and studied the man before him. The glasses seemed to give him added assurance.

'Well, Morrison,' he began casually, 'if you must know—'

The clerk put his head cautiously around the door. 'I tried to stop him coming in,' he started to apologize.

'Get out,' the man said. 'Leave us alone.'

The manager appeared to agree: he too irritably waved the clerk out. The head vanished and the door closed softly.

The manager straightened a file on his desk and closed it. 'Now,' he said slowly, fingering his lower lip. 'Your name is Morrison. William Morrison.'

'That's right. And I'm proud of it.'

'I daresay, Morrison. I daresay.' He slipped the file into a wire basket and drew out another one. The item he wanted was near the top of this file. He coughed before he spoke again. 'You're the Morrison who was gaoled for sedition three years ago, aren't you? You seem to get around quite a lot. And everywhere you've been there seems to have been trouble. Strange how trouble follows you around, isn't it?'

'I'm not ashamed of it. None of it. I've never caused no trouble. It's you people make the trouble. No, I'm not ashamed of nothing.'

The manager coughed tactfully. 'That, of course, is no concern of mine, Morrison. My concern is that we don't have trouble here, or trouble-makers. Up till now we've been free of trouble. The management's on excellent terms with the men. We wouldn't like any change. We want to keep things pleasant here.'

'Keep them down, you mean. I know your kind. I suppose you run the union too, eh?'

'I don't want to hear speeches. Speech-making might be part of your business. Listening to them is not part of mine.'

'You won't get away with this. You can't victimize—'

'No one, to my knowledge, is being victimized. No one is being discharged from employment here. There was just a mistake, as I told you. In any case, I'm sure if I discussed this thing with the men they would certainly prefer to be without your company.'

'Or else,' the man said with sarcasm. 'I know your stunts.'

'They would,' the manager repeated, 'certainly prefer to be without your company.' With an expression of innocence, he held up his hands. 'The clerical error which led us to advise you that we had a job offering is, of course, most regrettable.' He laid his hands flat on the desk, as if to signify he was finished with the subject.

'Bloody lies.'

'If you persist in seeing things in that light, Morrison, then of course there is simply nothing I can do about it.'

'If everything's so sweet here, what are you scared of? Eh?' He didn't give the manager time for reply. 'You know as well as I do. This place is known right up and down the country as rotten, isn't it? That's why.'

'If it's as bad as you say,' said the manager calmly, 'why did you come here, Morrison? Why don't you,' he added deliberately, 'go to Russia?'

'You really want to know. Because I don't like the likes of you. Because I got a kid I want to bring up decent here. Because I'm not a Russian.'

'Just as well for you,' observed the manager. 'They'd shoot you.'

'And you.'

'I've a considerable amount of work to do today,' the manager said abruptly. 'I'm sure we could have a most interesting discussion some other time.'

'Like hell. Scared, aren't you? All your kind.'

'If you'll excuse me, Morrison.' The manager opened a new file. 'I have work to do.'

'Take a good look around you sometime.' The man pointed out the window. The colliery workings, the mine shaft, blackened sheds, rakes of coal-trucks shunting, were all visible against scarred hillside. 'One day that's not going to belong to you. Or any of your kind. One day this country will belong to the people who sweated into it.'

'Get out,' the manager said.

He strode out of the mine office into the street; a door slammed behind him. He went past the woman and child, as if he had not seen them. The woman ran after him and caught at his sleeve.

'Where you going?' she said. 'It's all right, isn't it?'

He stopped to look at her; but his face was remote and expressionless. He hesitated, turned, and walked silently back to the suitcases. He lifted the sitting child aside, and took up the two large cases again.

'It's all right, isn't it?' the woman said, still plucking at his sleeve. He shook her away and began to walk. She picked up her small case, took the child's hand, and hurried after the man. 'Where we going?' she pleaded. 'It's all right, isn't it? There's nothing wrong? You got the job, didn't you?'

He stopped walking and let the cases fall heavily. 'No,' he said. 'They knew. They found out.'

Her eyes trembled. 'But the letter,' she said. 'The letter. They said you could have—'

'They must of found out after they sent the letter.' He was not looking at the woman now. 'They said it was a mistake. All a mistake. Bloody liars.'

Her shoulders quivered; the child began to whimper in sympathy. The man took her by the arm. 'Stop it,' he said. 'Not here.' He looked up and down the deserted street, but there seemed, at that moment, no onlookers. 'Not here,' he repeated.

'Where we going?' she whispered. 'Now?'

He avoided the question. 'We'll wait,' he said. 'Until the men come up from the pit. The day needn't be wasted.'

The woman gave her attention to the child. 'Shush, Ian,' she said.

'He's hungry,' she appealed to the man.

He wasn't listening: he had taken a letter from his inside suit pocket and was shredding it. 'Liars,' he said, more quietly now. A light breeze fluttered the torn paper from his hands; it whisked a little distance along the street and then lay still. 'Well?' he said at last. 'What are you waiting for? You can get something to eat from the store, can't you?'

In the late afternoon a low siren moaned: echoes circled the valley. Thick wire rope strained against turning winches: the cage from the pit screeched and rattled to the surface. Presently men emerged, dusty and blackened, in scarves and helmets, with eyes negro-white, through the colliery gate. They carried lamps and lunch-boxes and blinked against the bitter sunlight.

On one side of the gate they saw the short woman, drab and pale, with a child and some suitcases; on the other, the tall gaunt man in evangelical black. They were distributing leaflets with huge, exclamatory headings. The woman gave out her leaflets almost apologetically; the man was confident, entirely without apology, and called friendly slogans to the miners as they passed. 'The truth,' he said. 'Get the truth, comrades.'

Puzzled, most of the miners accepted the strange, rustling sheets of paper with urgent words; though some, as if fearing infection from a malady which they themselves could not properly define, side-stepped the outstretched hand, the humourless slogan, and hurried away. Some accepted only to repent, crumpling and discarding the leaflets as they walked with quickened step towards the safety of their homes. One or two stopped to talk briefly with the gaunt man in black; one pressed money into his hand. And then they were gone, all of them, into their square ugly homes with strips of garden and patches of lawn: the streets were empty again.

The man, moving slowly now, gathered up the remaining leaflets and packed them into a suitcase glutted with pamphlets, books, and other leaflets.

'How we going to get back to the station?' the woman said, as though waking from deep, dreamless sleep. 'Can we catch a loco?'

'Walk,' said the man. 'The way we came. There's no loco back now. It's too late in the day.'

'Walk?' the woman said.

They walked. The sinking sun coppered the land; the valley was still and quiet, dry and dead. The road had whitened, and their footwear grew dusty.

'Where we going?' the child said.

'Shush,' said the woman. 'Daddy's taking us.'

The sun sank; the valley was shadowed. In the east the clouds were pale and curdled; in the west they were gold and pink.

'Why?' said the child.

Dusk smoked from the land. When they reached the rise in the road from which they had first seen into the valley, they paused and looked back. An island of weak lights had grown under a lone star. The child was tripping and crying.

'Why Daddy taking us?'

'Shush,' said the woman, patiently.

The man set down his suitcases and took up the child. 'He's tired,' he said. 'Poor kid.'

'Why?' the child said, stubbornly.

The Strangers

The sun of a hot summer cooled in lightening blue skies. Along the
trees of the front driveway the leaves withered and twisted into their
autumn colours. Sudden breezes showered them down, chasing them
across the grass; afterwards, in the calm, their browns and reds and
golds speckled our paddocks brightly.

Sometimes, feeling the new chill in the air as I walked back to the
house after putting the cows to pasture for the night, I would see the
yellow light from the kitchen window slant out into the blue twilight,
and I would consider, almost with surprise, how tightly the nights were
gathering about the days: I was still young, and had yet to learn by heart
the farmer's story of changing seasons, birth and death, growth and
decay; of the fluent dance of natural things.

And with our household milk slopping noisily inside the billy which
swung from my hand, I would hurry to get inside. Already the dusk
song of birds would have thinned and faded; there would be the rattle
of cicadas and perhaps from far back in the bush a morepork uttering
a single, plaintive cry. My gumboots swished quickly over dewy grass
and made small rubbery clumps up the steps to the back porch. Always
I remembered first to strip them off and wipe my bared feet on the
doormat, as Mother had taught me. Then, opening the door, I moved
swiftly inside, clicking it shut against the cold and dark and damp of
evening. The house was always filled with the fragrance of cooking
food, stew bubbling or sausages frying. Padding through to the warmth
and brightness of the kitchen I came upon my father stooped over our
huge old iron stove, feeding wood into its mouth; or turning and stirring
food with a fork folded into his large, worn hand. And while he worried
and muttered I made haste to prepare the table before he put out
steaming meat and vegetables on two warmed plates.

But of all those autumn evenings there was one to remember
clearly, a different end to a different day. Since morning there had been

the promise of rain; grey clouds built on the hills, growing darker and finally smothering the weak sun. We hurried through our evening jobs. But it wasn't until we were about to sit down to the meal that we heard the falling patter of rain on the iron roof. Shortly afterwards there was a faint rapping on the door. Looking surprised, Father rose to answer it.

—I didn't hear any car, he said.

We were out in a lonely part of country and didn't often have visitors. At that time it was an even more pleasant surprise to have them, because Father didn't always know quite what to do with himself in the evenings the first year after Mother died. Most nights, if he couldn't find something to keep him busy, he'd fall back in his favourite easy chair, put up his stockinged feet on another chair and balance his steel-rimmed reading glasses on the tip of his nose. There would always be a big pile of newspapers for him to read; always too many, for all the time new ones arrived at the farm. Now and then, with sudden resolution, he threw out all those unread and began again with the very latest issue. But the pile grew again. Because some nights, too tired to work or read, he just rested in his chair and looked up at the ceiling through half-closed eyes. If I asked him anything, while I read or puzzled over homework, he answered only with effort.

And, after he'd sent me to bed, the living-room light would burn till late: from the warmth of my blankets I saw its reflection under the bedroom door. Sometimes, when I was awake longer than usual, I slipped from my bed, opened the door quietly, and tip-toed over the cold floor down the passage to the living-room. Often I found him still in his chair, sprawled asleep, the glasses balanced precariously on the tip of his nose while he made loud snoring noises in his mouth. Timidly, I moved closer and touched him lightly on the shoulder: he always woke with a jerk, and stared at me with wide-open tired red eyes as if I were a stranger, as if he had expected to waken somewhere other than under the cold glare of light in the living-room, with me standing before him small and frightened in my outgrown pyjamas. Presently he seemed to recognize me. Then, slowly and deliberately, he removed his glasses and said:

—You ought to be in bed. Asleep.

It was a stern voice, one that made me scurry back to bed. In a little while I heard the jangling of easing chairsprings as he lifted himself up. He went through to the kitchen, and presently the kettle hissed for his suppertime cup of tea. And suddenly my door swung open and the light behind showed him tall and upright. Bending, he gave me my glass of milk and a thick slice of fruitcake.

—And after this you better go to sleep.

And before he left he reminded me:

—Early to bed and early to rise makes a man healthy, wealthy and wise. Goodnight, boy.

—Goodnight, I murmured through my mouthful of cake.

And after a while I'd hear the rattle of his cup and saucer as he finished his tea, the splashing of water as he washed himself, the lights clicking out one by one, his feet whispering up the passage to his bedroom; and, finally, the slow grating as he wound his shrill-voiced alarm clock, and the wirewove of the big double bed straining as he eased his weight on to it. But I rarely heard him begin to snore, for I was tired too.

—I'm damn sure I didn't hear any car, Father repeated.

I followed him from the table. He opened the back door, and light played faintly on the damp face of a young Maori with a swag on his back. He smiled cautiously, as though uncertain of his welcome. The rain whipped under the porch roof and stung our faces. Father quickly invited the young man inside and closed the door. Still surprised, he asked:

—How'd you come?

—Walked from town.

The stranger spoke as though there was nothing interesting in the fact that he'd walked fourteen miles. He hastened to explain:

—Heard you might have a job going.

—Well, Father said. Well, yes, I might have.

He paused thoughtfully a moment.

—Well, dump that swag of yours. Tim boy—run and get the young man a towel to dry himself.

The stranger eased the load from his shoulders.

—It don't matter. Don't fuss me. I don't want to be no bother.

As I fetched the towel, Father said:

—Don't suppose you've eaten.

—No. I was walking to beat the rain.

—Well, you can eat with us then. You're pretty lucky. We was only just starting on the tucker.

Father spooned out stew and potato on a new plate while the stranger dried himself. I set another place at the table, and we all sat down.

—My name's Tui, he said. Tui Waritene.

—I expect you know mine already, Father said. Anyhow I'm Ned Livingstone and this is my boy Tim. We run this place between us, Tim and me.

—Yes, Tui said. They told me your last man left quite a while back.

Father frowned. Just as if nothing had been said, he asked:

—What part of the country you from?

Once that question was asked he could talk for hours, contrasting different places. Tui explained that he'd come up from the south lately, and liked the look of our district. When Father began to talk my eyes stayed on Tui. Even to me he didn't seem very old. His skin was the rich brown full-blooded colour, clear and smooth; different to Father's wrinkled, weathered face with its greyish stubble of beard which he never seemed able to shave. He smiled with brilliant teeth and a friendly twinkle in his eyes; his voice was soft and pleasant and made me think of restful places with cool shadows, deep grass, and running water. He was careful with his table manners and listened attentively to all Father said. It didn't seem Father would stop talking. And the more he talked, the more carelessly he ate. Stew splashed off the plate and soiled the table-cloth; little bits of food clung to the corners of his mouth. When he tried to eat and talk at the same time he never had good table manners: when Mother was alive she often reproved him for them after visitors left the house. Now, seeing his bad manners, I felt embarrassed and uncomfortable and responsible. I shifted in my chair, trying to catch Father's eye while I rubbed industriously away at the corners of my own entirely clean mouth. I desperately hoped he would see my meaning. When he at last took notice he regarded me sternly, the food still clinging to his mouth, and demanded:

—What's the matter, boy? Eh? You got St. Vitus' dance?

He glared as though ashamed for an idiot son. Tui was smiling at me in a friendly way, but I wasn't prepared for that yet, and lowered my eyes.

After dinner Father went out and Tui helped me with the dishes, drying while I washed. He wanted to know how I liked living on the farm. I told him I wouldn't ever want to live anywhere else. Did I like school? Not much, I said, because I'd sooner be with Father than sitting in class. And Tui said it was a great change to hear a boy talk that way. After a while Father came inside the house again, his clothes spotted with rain, and took Tui through to the living-room and said for him to make himself comfortable while they had another yarn.

I was sent to bed early. They talked till late. Or at least Father talked. I could hear his voice rising and falling, like the sound of sea, as he told Tui about the farm. One of the last things I heard was Tui asking about the job again. Father said, well, they could sleep on the subject and see about it in the morning. I was sure then, by the tone of his voice, that he already intended Tui should have the job. But it was Father's belief that you should never make things too easy for anyone. They never appreciated it, he said. And before I fell asleep I thought about the last man.

He was a Mr Smith. He arrived in winter, not long after Mother died, and left just before Christmas, staying nearly six months altogether. He was a young man too; but pale and thin and awkward in movement, much different from Tui. He was very quiet; he spent most of his spare time reading in his small bedroom and smoking cigarette after cigarette, so that for a long time after he left the stale nicotine smell haunted the room; and the smell, together with the tattered jumble of detective novels in the corner, infected it with the memory of his presence. Mr Smith rarely spoke to me; often he didn't acknowledge my existence. Father liked him, though, and slapped him on the back and called him Bill; I wasn't sure whether to like him or not. And it wasn't just because he passed me by without a flicker in his bleak eyes; or because of the times when he threw stones at friendly birds or kicked and growled at the cows when Father wasn't looking. I was always noticing things about him, like the way his lips trembled and his eyes shifted when someone spoke suddenly; or the way he sat out on the porch looking at nothing, his eyes growing big and watery while he smoked a damp-ended cigarette. They were things Father didn't notice. Though Mr Smith never said much, his clumsiness let Father make up his mind that he was a city man seeking a clean and decent way of life by working in the country. He was pleased to have such a sensible chap; he was very pleased with Mr Smith. Until one day, when we went to town, we returned to find that Mr Smith had left suddenly, stealing thirty pounds. Father stood in the kitchen, bewildered.

—No. It can't be. It can't.

A ripple of looseness went through him, and he slumped to the kitchen table, his head in his hands. And he said the words I could remember him saying, over and over, from the time I began to remember.

—There's no one you can ever rely on. Only yourself.

And, in a voice a whisper:

—Don't you ever forget that, boy. Don't ever forget it.

A little while afterwards the police called at the farm; they had been seeking Mr Smith for some time, under his real name, and for reasons of their own.

I knew how difficult the stolen money made things. Though we'd been working hard, the cream-cheques were poor, and there had been all the expenses for Mother's funeral. Not to speak of the thing called a mortgage which worried Father so much. And it was nearly Christmas.

—It's a day for those with money, boy. Not for us.

But it seemed to make no difference, for when I woke in the grey early light of Christmas morning I found at the foot of my bed, brightly wrapped, the model railway set I'd wanted. I began to play with it. Then I saw his bare bony feet splayed on the floor. He was still in his sleeping shirt, his legs pale and hairy, the sleep clinging to his eyes, the rumpled hair falling over his face, and the faintest of smiles playing about his lips. Presently he squatted on his haunches, farmer fashion, and while he rolled and lit his first cigarette of the day advised how to lay the rails properly and wind the toy engine.

Later in the morning he went to a cupboard and removed a single bottle of beer. It had gathered dust with time, and he polished it against his shirt and uncapped it with ceremony. He poured a few drops into an egg cup for me, and filled a large glass for himself. The beer frothed a cheerful smell.

—And go easy, boy, he said, raising his glass. Learn to be moderate. Cheers, now.

He drank while he prepared dinner, and presently he even began to whistle tunelessly. I couldn't remember having heard him whistle for a long time, not since Mother died.

When we were about to sit down to the meal, he suddenly remembered something. He went from the room and returned with three coloured-paper party hats. They were hats we'd used for Christmas dinner for years; Mother had always carefully folded them each year and put them away for the next Christmas celebration.

Standing before the laden table, he peeled off one of the hats and gave it to me; he watched with a smile as I put it on my head. Then he lowered his eyes and the smile slowly went from his face as he separated the two others in his hands. He took one for himself, then seemed to become rigid as he looked at the other. With a queer expression, he crumpled it in one hand, and threw it away. He sat down heavily, and I could see the big vein at the side of his temple beginning to throb.

—Eat, boy. Eat. Go on. Don't sit there like a ninny.

He forced the hat on his head: it ripped. Obediently, I began to eat. There was a fowl which he had killed, cooked, and dressed; it had somehow burnt in the oven, but there was still enough of the novel poultry taste to be enjoyed. And Mrs Fletcher on the next farm made a Christmas pudding as a present for us, filling it with surprise threepences. Father ate in silence. Astonished at my own boldness, I said:

—I bet I can find the most.

—Most what? he growled.

—Threepences, I said timidly.

He looked at me, startled.

—You do, eh?

—Yes, I said.

He seemed almost to smile. In no time at all he discovered four threepences. I found only one.

—What happened to you, eh? he grinned in triumph. You swallow all yours?

He stood up and looked at himself in the mirror. The torn hat was askew on his head.

—Don't I look stupid?

He grinned, and we laughed. For the rest of the day everything was all right. We spent the afternoon chopping out a rebellious patch of scrub and gorse. Father said people like us couldn't afford to be idle, not even on Christmas day. Besides, he added, idleness led to the habit of slackness, and if there was any such thing as sin, then slackness was the worst sin of all. He explained I should be glad to learn this so early in life. Some people went all through life without ever learning it. So many in fact, he hated thinking of them all. It wasn't, though, that he was afraid for their souls; he said he wasn't worried about nonsense like after-life. It was just that he didn't like the thought of them going into the darkness without ever knowing.

The sun baked the sky, and stung the sweat from our faces. We worked all afternoon, till our backs ached and hands chafed, and then it was time for the evening jobs. After tea he took me to the living-room, where he spread the railway set on the floor. But soon I wilted and fell asleep when I should have been watching him explain something. He must have taken me up gently and carried me to bed, for I remembered nothing more until I woke with the morning sun shining through my window.

One night not long after Christmas he jumped from his chair, waving a newspaper.

—My God, he said. They got him.

—Who? I said.

—Him. That Smith joker. They got him.

He pointed to a news item.

—Two years they give him. There, he said with satisfaction, they got him all right.

He fell back in his chair, reading the item again.

—Yes, he said. No doubt about it, eh?

He was silent a while. The newspaper rustled to the floor. Then his voice was changed.

—The poor young devil. Two years.

Presently he added:

—He probably didn't have a chance. It's just the way it is in them cities. It's the way people get.

He rose and paced about the room.

—I liked that young joker. I had faith in him.

He paced about for some time. Then he halted, stiffened.

—But there's no one you can ever rely on, he said. Only yourself.

He turned to me, and his face was hard.

—Remember that, boy.

2

Now the cold wet night of the young Maori stranger had come and gone, receding beyond the days of deepening autumn and approaching winter. Tui slipped so quickly into our life that it was hard for me to remember back to the time when he was not on the farm. One day Father took me aside and told me how pleased he was that Tui fitted in so well. But that day too had come and gone, merging into the grey twilight of the season. And there was only the present, the cold morning awakening, the beginning of each day. When Father and I stepped out on the back porch, Tui would emerge from his little room, washed and dressed and ready for work. There were brief morning greetings and Father and he talked as they walked down to the cowbails with me trailing behind. Sometimes the farm was under a slow-dissolving fog, which might in time lift to reveal a sullen, weeping sky. Other times, those which fastened on my memory, a heavy white dust of frost covered hillside and flat, icy grass crunched under gumboots, and warm breaths bloomed steam in the clear air as sharp voices crackled through the brittle silence. Above, beyond the eastern hills, there was the first glow of sunrise. Threads of mist hung in hollows and folds, soon to be warmed away by the risen sun. But always, rain or fine, there was that brisk morning mingling of awakened voices; and, later, while Father brought our antiquated milking machine racketing and chugging to desperate life, Tui's voice bursting into song above the noise. He had a good voice, and I loved to hear it. He said he reckoned the cows gave up their milk easier when you gave them a little song. Though Father never said anything, he liked the changed atmosphere too, in his own way. Afterwards Tui was left singing by himself while he cleaned the separator. Father cooked breakfast and I got ready for school. Every morning after breakfast I had to excuse myself, pick up my schoolbag, and hurry to the door while the two of them still relaxed at the table, lingering over steaming cups of tea, rolling cigarettes and talking. I felt badly about leaving them, but there was nothing I could do about it, and so I'd be walking quickly down the driveway, turning now and then to look back at our old unpainted house, tiny behind the trees, with its chimney and faint blue wisp of smoke. Father and Tui usually came to the window to wave goodbye. Satisfied now, I'd run the rest of the way to the gate, where presently the school bus would call to take me the long miles to the classroom.

I liked being with Tui. Towards evening, while the shadows merged and deepened through our valley, we winterfed the cows with hay from the barn while Father cooked a meal inside the house. Sometimes we chatted as we forked.

—Your Dad's a great man, eh? Tui said.

—Yes, I said, pleased.

—Yes, Tui said, he's a great man on the work. He never stops. All day and half the night. He's a great man on the work all right.

—He works pretty hard, I said proudly.

—Too much work's no good. What d'you think, eh?

Surprised, I only said:

—It makes you pretty tired.

—Too right, Tui said. Too right it makes you pretty tired. All work, no play, eh?

—Yes, I answered; though I still couldn't see whatever it was he meant.

—You got to have fun sometime, eh? You're a long time the corpse.

Paused in his work, leaning on his fork, he looked down at me as if he expected an answer. But I didn't know what to say.

Through autumn and winter, as the cows dried off and things became easier, Tui and I shared our spare time. On fine days we went for walks. Climbing the hills which rose steeply from the back of the farm, we came upon the sight of bushland tumbled out in a carpet, blurred and crumpled, of brilliant browns and greens. In the distance, greys and blues washed the purple line of the horizon. It would be strange then to look back and see the valley so naked where Father had burned and axed to sow pasture. As if flung back by storm, the bush hung ragged on the hills around. Burnt stumps jutted from the grassed earth; second-growth manuka strung itself weakly on erosion-veined slopes; bracken, fern and toi-toi clung weakly to weatherworn limestone cliffs. Thickening, the bush fell back over the hill-crests to flourish, lush and tall-treed, circling the valley. When an inflamed winter sunset lit the valley, it seemed an island in a wild sea.

While I skipped and scrambled along beside him Tui told me the names of trees and birds, and old Maori legends and tales about them. Guiding me by the hand, pointing things out, he explained how easy it was to live off the bush if you wanted, eating eels and birds, fernroots and berries and the juicy white insides of nikau palms. He told me his own adventures in the bush. And one day he let slip that his great-grandfather was one of the old chiefs who fought the pakeha in New Zealand's wars. After that I made him tell new stories, stories he had heard from old men. The thing that caught my imagination was not so much the actual resistance to the pakeha, but the picture of the brown men after defeat, fleeing through the bush before the clumsy advance of Britain's troops. And his slow voice made the picture come alive, so that sometimes I could almost imagine that these things were still really happening, so that I could see the long-dead tattooed men fleeting softly and shadowy through high fern, never to be glimpsed warring again.

He would tell the stories reluctantly. At times like these we would have halted our walk. I would sit on something, perhaps a fallen treetrunk, while he stood and talked before leafy curtains of evergreen. Sometimes startled wood-pigeons flapped heavily away at the sound of his voice. The sun, shafting thinly through the trees, streaked the fern and moss and maidenhair of the bush floor; and touched him, here and there, with its dusty pale lemon-colour as he moved talking, somehow sad and solitary, in and out of shadow.

Father didn't mind Tui spending time with me. He seemed pleased with everything Tui did. He said he was a pretty good sort of Maori. He worked hard, never complained; he was a big help around the farm. Pretty educated too, and sensible. Not like some of the Maoris who went gallivanting round spending all their money and having a good time. No, Tui worked hard and saved his money. He expected Tui was doing it with the idea of getting married, or something. Anyhow, whatever it was, he hoped Tui wouldn't leave us too soon; even a couple of years would be too soon.

The idea of Tui getting married interested me; I remembered it one mid-winter day when we were out fishing. The frost had melted from the grass, the sun was warm, and long white clouds feathered the sky. Below us the cold-running creek sparkled as we waited for eels to swim into the trap Tui had shown me how to make.

—When you going to get married, Tui?

He laughed.

—Married?

—Yes.

He laughed again.

—You get some funny ideas, he said.

I thought of when Tui and I went down to the town together. Maori girls, shy and hopeful, or haughty and proud, would often look at him as he walked the street. And I remembered that Tui never seemed to notice them at all.

—Aren't you going to? Not ever? I said hopefully.

—Sometime I might. No big hurry, eh?

—I just thought you might be going to.

—No fear. Not me. Not yet for a long time.

—Dad thought you was going to.

I spoke as though that somehow proved he really should be getting married.

—Hah, Tui said; his smile was big. Why, eh?

—Because you save up your money.

With his hands behind his head, he lay back and closed his eyes.

—Well, he said, you both thought wrong, eh?

There was a silence.

—Then why do you save up?

—To get money.

—What for?

—So I can do things.

—What kinds of things?

He rolled on his side, took out a tobacco tin, and began to make a cigarette. After a while, reluctantly, he said:

—Things I want to do.

—What kinds? I persisted.

—Well, he began. Then he fell silent, licking the tissue paper around the tobacco, and lighting the finished cigarette.

—Well, there's lots of things I want to do. Around the country. Like a bit of shooting. I need a good new rifle.

—That'll be good fun, I said.

I began to get excited at the prospect of all the good times we'd have together. But he didn't seem to hear what I said; he was still talking about the other things he wanted, for hunting and fishing.

—Gosh, I said. You want a lot.

—I want things like that. And money to keep me going. For clothes and food and smokes and stuff. I'm spoilt now, eh? I can't go living off the bush for everything.

I was slow to see his meaning. Bewildered, I asked:

—Then won't you be stopping at our place?

—No, he said. Think I'll have to be moving on for that. For what I'll be going to do. Don't think your Dad would like me spending all my time having fun, eh?

There was a long silence. The creek rippled, and a bellbird sang. I looked at Tui.

—You never ever told me you'd be going away.

—Not right now, he said.

—Don't you like it here?

—I like it all right. I like you and your Dad all right.

—Then what d'you want to go away for?

He sat up and folded his arms around his legs.

—I just think I'll have to be moving on one day.

Then he rose to his feet.

—We better have a look at that trap.

We raised it. There were five eels; three big, and two little. Tui let the little ones wriggle back into the creek.

—They'll be big next year, he said.

—Will you be here next year?

He shrugged.

—It depends, he said.

Things I'd been about to say fell back into my mind, like drops of

water into a brimming pool; I was sad. Tui, singing, dropped the
threshing eels into a sugar bag and slung it over his shoulder; as we
walked home, I wondered if he might stay long enough for me to leave
school and go away with him. But then I thought of Father lonely by
himself on the farm: and I didn't know.

Presently we mounted a ridge and saw the trees and buildings
clustered tiny on the green valley floor. We could only just distinguish
Father's distant, solitary figure as he moved about the backyard, close
to his workshop. He began to hammer at something; the hard, rhythmic
sound rose up to us.

—He's a great man all right, Tui said. A great man on the work.

He paused, and added:

—You better not tell him what I been telling you. He mightn't think
it's a good idea, eh?

3

Spring slipped behind us: the stirring and change, the swampy paddocks
drying, the cows coming into milk, the calves tottering spindle-legged,
the awakening green of the bush, the flash of rata blossom, the pink of
puriri, the sharp new clamour of birds. And there was Tui, restless and
alive, moving abruptly away from his work to stare at the bush along
the horizon: staring, and then walking away, quickly, with me following
until he tired and sat in silence. If we talked, the conversation circled
slowly to alight on the things he would do when he left the farm, while
his eyes lit and I wondered.

Then summer was upon us. Ahead were rainless months while the
sun browned and killed the grass and dwindled the creeks to trickles;
while fire crackled through the hills to bloom blue-grey smoke and
send cinders falling like rain. Father would afterwards recall that we
only came through that summer by the thinnest skin of our teeth.

—If that much, he'd say.

But the future was still pushing through the present into the past;
and at night Father, settled comfortably in his chair, talked to Tui about
this summer, next autumn, next winter, and about bigger cream-
cheques and a smaller mortgage.

—It'll be a great thing, he said, when a man can go out there and plant his two feet down and look around and tell himself it's all his, eh?

—Yes, Tui said. It'll be a great thing, all right.

But he would seem uncomfortable in his chair; he shifted, and rolled another cigarette.

One evening after milking, while the farm was alight with a cool orange sunset, Tui came into the kitchen and told Father he wanted to leave.

Father was bent over the hot stove. He turned stiffly at the sound of Tui's voice. In a slow, bewildered way, he drew the back of his hand over his sweaty brow. Tui's eyes were dark and apologetic.

—Well, Father said at last. I'm sorry to hear that, Tui. I am sorry.

Tui was silent.

—I thought you'd be with us a bit longer.

—I think I'll have to be moving on, Tui said quietly.

—Well, I don't expect there's anything can be done about it. If you want to go, you'll go, and that's flat. I couldn't make you change your mind, eh?

Tui shook his head.

Father turned awkwardly to the stove again.

—I knew you'd be pulling out one day. The only thing is I didn't pick it'd be this soon.

Tui went to bed unusually early that night, leaving Father with his newspapers. Sitting near him with a book, I looked up suddenly at the sound of his voice. Then I realized he wasn't talking to me, but to himself.

—He must be going to get married. It's the only thing. That's why he's been saving so careful. Been putting away every penny. Probably counts on getting himself a bit of land one day too.

He was silent, and I began reading my book again. Presently there was a small rustle of paper and, looking up, I saw a newspaper slide from a limp, dangling hand. He slept with his mouth fallen open, and the deep lines on his brow relaxed. Moving quiet towards him, I saw his face as older than I had ever seen it before, and I noticed the new grey hair patching the side of his head. Gently I removed the glasses from his nose and set them on a table. Then I switched out the light and went to the kitchen. With the least possible sound, I set the kettle to boil for his suppertime cup of tea. While I waited I opened the window and, resting my arms on the sill, looked out into the mild summer evening. Stars peppered the sky above the dark hills, and from somewhere deep in shadow a morepork called, its cry long and lonely.

It was another clear day, that Saturday, and I was home from school. The sun, climbing clear of the hills, had still to smother the clean smell of morning. I sat on the porch. Tui was singing as he packed in his room; Father was out in the backyard, tinkering with the engine of our battered old Ford. He had promised to run Tui down to town, but the car had broken down earlier in the week and he wasn't able to get it running again. He made a lot of apologies to Tui, but Tui just said not to worry, he was used to hiking, and anyhow he really liked it better that way. It made no difference, though, because Father kept apologizing and making Tui more embarrassed.

Father was still swearing and muttering at the engine when Tui came out of his room, his swag dangling from his hand. He set it down, took out his tobacco tin, and began to make a cigarette.

—Well, he said, looking around and breathing the morning. She's a great sort of day to be starting off, eh?

—Yes, I agreed miserably.

Father came over and spread himself, large and loose-jointed, at the foot of the porch steps.

—Well, it's no go with the car, Tui. I'm sorry.

—She's right, Tui said. Don't worry.

There was a silence.

—She a nice girl? Father asked suddenly, twisting his head to look up at Tui.

—Girl? Tui said.

—Don't you think we can guess? Father said, smiling.

—There's no girl, Tui said quietly.

—We can guess.

—No, Tui repeated. There's no girl.

—Then why you going?

—It's just time to be pulling out, Tui said. Time to be moving on.

Father rose stiffly. He looked at Tui.

—But the money you been saving up. Aren't you going to get married? I thought you might of been thinking about settling down on your own bit of land or something.

—No fear, Tui said.

—But what about the money?

—That's for me. To keep me going through the summer. And for things I want, like a rifle and stuff.

—And that's all you worked for?

—Sure thing, Tui said.

He tucked the cigarette in the corner of his mouth and deftly swung the swag up on his shoulder.

—Well, I guess I better be starting off.

But he didn't move. He and Father stood quite still, looking at each other. And I saw it wasn't just Father who didn't understand; Tui couldn't understand Father either. There were the two of them there, neither understanding the other, and I stood between, only knowing that of all the hurtful things in life the most hurtful was two people not understanding each other. I knew that it was important that they should come to understanding, though I didn't know why and would never have been able to explain. I wanted to jump up and down between them, shouting words that would make them understand. But I knew no words, and was silent.

—Gee, Tui said. I almost forgot.

He went back into his room and returned carrying two parcels. He handed one to Father, the other to me.

—Presents, he said.

Father's face looked queer as his thick fingers fumbled with the string and paper; his parcel was small, but mine was long and thin.

—A fishing rod, I guessed, grinning at Tui.

But he just smiled, not saying anything.

And it was. Then wrapping fell from Father's hands to reveal a combination spanner. The bright, new steel glinted in the sunlight as he turned it over.

—You shouldn't of done this, he said, and his voice was as queer as his face. You shouldn't of—

—Forget it, Tui said.

—Thanks, Father said. But there wasn't no need—

—Well I better be starting off, Tui said, patting me on the head. You be able to have fun now, eh?

I nodded. My tongue was stuck dumb in a dry mouth.

—Oh yes, Tui said, taking an envelope from his pocket. I almost forgot this too. That's my sister's address. She usually knows where I am. If you have any troubles getting a new man you better tell her and maybe I can come and give you a hand for a while next year. O.K., eh?

—Thanks, Father said. That's real good of you.

He was not looking at Tui now. We followed him down to the gate. He shook hands and gave me another pat on the head. Then Father swung the gate shut while Tui walked away down the long white road. Dust puffed out under his shoes, leaving tiny clouds behind him.

Father leaned on the gate and I sat, my legs dangling, on the top rail. Tui's figure grew smaller with distance. Now and then he would turn to wave. Presently we heard his voice rising into the morning, the faint song receding. Then he was gone; his voice too. Father thumbed his hat back on his head and began to roll a cigarette.

—Well, he said.

The sun was hot now, and the cool shadows of the trees splashed over us as we walked back up the driveway to the house, our feet brushing over the parched grass. A friendly fantail twittered round us, then wheeled away.

I expected Father to go directly to his car and begin tinkering again. Instead he came to sit beside me on the steps of the porch. While I fingered my fishing rod, he sucked at his cigarette, puzzling and frowning.

Presently he rose jerkily to his feet. He picked up the spanner and envelope together, turning them over in his hand. Then he lifted his eyes.

—There's no one you can ever rely on, he said. Only yourself.

He spoke in the same way as I might repeat some school lesson; mechanically, without conviction. Bewilderment had settled on him now, and he was saying the only thing he could find to say.

He looked down at the spanner and envelope again. Then, as though they contradicted him, he flung them away. The spanner fell with a dull sound; the envelope fluttered down limply.

—Only yourself, Father said.

Standing tall and straight above me, his brow puckered, his hands curled into tight fists, he considered what he had said. Then, breathing deeply and uncoiling, he moved loosely, almost shamefaced, to retrieve the spanner and envelope before he crossed the yard to where the rebellious engine waited for him.

Play the Fife Lowly

1

She ran, her legs jerking steadily forward, her feet striking echoes from the moonlit streets. Quick swallows of air rasped her throat and stung her lungs; her coat slapped back and forward, as though trying to impede her progress. She still called his name. Once she thought she heard an answer; once a voice in faint, mocking song.

But there were only deserted corners where the wind sidled through rustling papers, and streets leading to more empty streets: and these with the same decayed shops and secretive houses.

She paused and, in the moment the echo of her own footsteps died, she heard the other feet ringing behind her.

2

They were not the first city feet Helen had fled. Earlier there was the night when other girls in the flat rustled away with their sleek boy friends; when she forsook her fireside chair.

It had been pleasant at first: her heels clipping over pavement, the rain-cooled darkness, the harbour lights. And there was the shabby wharfside milk-bar where, from a rainbow juke-box, a thin masculine voice wheedled for the return of lost love. Sipping her milk-skinned coffee, she watched the Saturday-night drifters: sad, shuffling old men; middle-aged women with dusty furs and shapeless hats; sallow young men with pin-stripe suits, nicotine-yellow fingers and tragic faces. She felt an affinity with them: she was like them, she told herself, one of the harmless strays of the city. When she walked home, that proposition fell apart. A figure lurched out of shadow, a bottle smashed and a slurred voice called. She began to run: unsteady feet hammered behind her. Once she fell, shredding her stockings and skinning her knees. But she was running again, not stopping until she slammed the door of the flat and leaned limp against it, listening, for the footsteps that never quite came.

Sometimes, waking from a dream of smothering, she thought she heard the feet again: it was almost as if the quick, ringing footfalls were always there, always ready to burst into earshot. She remembered them more calmly at other times. Then she would put down her book, silence the radio, approach the mirror, remove her glasses, and tell herself: I am twenty-five, not pretty, and will never be married.

Such nights were before Gerald. Not that she could regard Gerald as more than a casual friend, a Saturday friend. He was mild, pleasant, courteous, but hard to take seriously. And when she realized she had aroused his deeper interest she was not sure what she should feel. Pleasure, she supposed, firstly: that was only natural. Then regret. She was already wording her rebuff.

Yet she was no longer sure she could once again face the nights in the flat alone; the nights when not even books or music could camouflage the truth.

Tonight, in the restaurant, as Gerald leaned intimately across the table, fingering his engraved cigarette case and exhaling smoke smoothly, she decided there was no reason why she should not, after all, marry him. As she half-listened to his murmured confidences, she avoided his eyes and, turning her head slightly, studied his reflection in a wall-mirror: he was even handsome, she supposed, in his boyish way. In his neat suit, starched shirt and college tie, he always seemed so much younger than herself. She glanced at her own reflection only briefly. He could be likeable enough: she would have to be content with that.

And then, leaving the restaurant, he ended her compliant mood. He spoke curtly to the girl behind the cash-register about a noisy drunk the girl had allowed to enter the place. He was needlessly unpleasant, and it brought back all she tried to forget: his pompous mannerisms, his opinionated monologues.

As they drove to the party, he sat stiff behind the wheel, his face impassive; and she knew he was examining a new approach, calculating her response. She was almost certainly in for another uncomfortable talk.

The street into which the car turned was broad and prosperous, with large white homes set back among well-ordered greenery.

Gerald silenced the engine.

'Well,' he said, speaking for the first time in minutes. 'Here we are.' He paused, fumbling through his pockets for cigarettes. She waited, tightening her coat about her neck, stiffening slowly.

'You know...' he began, inserting a cigarette in his mouth.

'Yes?'

'It ought to be quite fun tonight,' he added lamely. His fingers fidgeted with his lighter: the flare lit his face forcing a smile.

'Any particular reason?' She felt calmer: he surely wouldn't attempt to say anything now; his moment had escaped him.

'A bit of a joke, really,' he said, tilting back his head to exhale smoke. 'But Tom Anderson's been invited.'

'Tom Anderson?'

'You must have heard us talk about him.'

'Was he the one—'

'—the one that went all arty after college. Really went off the deep end. Everyone knew he'd come a flop. He did, all right. Hit the booze and got T.B. and God knows what else. Trailing round with all types. I hadn't heard anything about him for years. Mike met him in the street. Thought it might be fun to invite him along tonight.'

'Wasn't he your friend?' Helen said, remembering conversations where her interest had been lit.

'Just a friend,' he corrected quickly. Dismissing the subject, he slid his arm around her. He seemed about to make another attempt at serious talk.

'Tell me more,' she said evasively.

'About what?'

'About this Tom Anderson—and what he's like.'

'He's not all that interesting.' He drew her towards him. His hand felt clumsily at her face. 'Helen,' he began.

'But you still haven't told me—' she protested.

'I wish I hadn't mentioned him,' he said petulantly, jerking back into his part of the seat. He shot open his door. 'Come on. Let's go inside.'

Beaming, a glass wedged in a huge fist, Mike met them at the door and led them inside. Guests grouped and regrouped rowdily. Almost all the boys, like Mike, were friends of Gerald from college days; to Helen they all seemed to possess the same clean features and tricks of speech. She often had difficulty remembering names, telling them apart. Only Mike was distinctive: heavy and shapeless, lumbering and loud-voiced, but always the leader, the one who had held them together since college.

At the bar, as Mike poured drinks, she looked about foreseeing the nature of the evening ahead. First, tipsy but not yet drunken, they would conjure names and events from the past to hide lapses in conversation: 'I say, did you hear about Hamish?' 'They tell me Robin...' 'You remember that time?' 'I always laugh when I think back...' Later, as alcohol took effect, they would return from rumour and reverie to the present; to back-slapping, name-calling, boasting and high-pitched frolic pursued with vast seriousness, as though they desperately wanted, now the novelty of adult life had worn thin, to escape from themselves and win back their schooldays. The girls present—the limpid girl friends and affectionate fiancées—would appear shocked at first: it was almost necessary they show some measure of disapproval. But later, they would join with the boys in feverish dancing, stamping conga-lines and suggestive games. And at the end there would be illness and upsets, tears and flushing toilets, and frantic petting on the verandah, in the bedrooms, and in car back-seats.

In another room a radiogram played: through a doorway Helen could see couples scraping listlessly around the floor.

'Well,' Mike said, handing out their drinks. 'Anderson hasn't arrived yet.'

Gerald frowned. 'I'm rather hoping he doesn't.'

'Why?' Mike demanded, regarding Gerald shrewdly. 'Don't you want to see your old cobber?'

Helen, perplexed, saw colour show in Gerald's face. 'Anderson's—well, all right,' he continued to stammer. 'But, I mean—inviting him here...' He faltered, and began to sip his beer.

Mike laughed hoarsely. 'Gerry,' he said, 'you know something? You're getting stuffy in your old age.' He slapped Gerald roughly on the back. 'And you want to know something else? I should've thought you'd only be too glad to see your old friend Tom. You're the reason I asked him along tonight. That's a fact.'

Helen felt irritated: they were leaving her outside. Mike seemed determined only to hint, and Gerald to remain reticent.

'What's so terrible about this chap anyway?' she said.

'Ask Gerry,' Mike said with a malicious grin.

'For God's sake,' Gerald said sharply.

The situation was uncomfortable. Mike's head was cocked slyly and Gerald's eyes were downcast. Helen was relieved to see Sylvia, Mike's fiancée, swaying towards them. Sylvia always had some serenity, even when drinking heavily. Tall and blonde in blue, she was smiling warmly at Helen.

'One guess to know what you're talking about,' she declared tipsily; her large glass of iced gin slopped and chinked in her hand. 'My God, Helen did you ever see anything like it? You know something? I think this chap's only a rumour.'

'You're only a rumour,' Mike said. 'And a vague one at that.'

Sylvia frowned dully, slow to discern insult. 'Don't you talk to me like that,' she snapped finally.

Mike, mildly amused, turned his back on her. 'By the way, Gerry,' he said, 'did you hear about Tony?'

Sylvia touched Helen's arm. 'Let's get out of here,' she said.

She followed Sylvia from the room. Near the door they passed a group conversing loudly.

'I always said Anderson—'

'—but, really, the way all these so-called talented people think they own the world.'

'My God,' Sylvia said as they moved down a quiet passage to the rear of the house. 'You wouldn't read about it. Talk about fowls pecking one with a broken leg.'

'Are you and Mike having trouble?' Helen asked quietly, as Sylvia led her into a bedroom.

'Trouble?' Sylvia crowed. Standing before a mirror Sylvia began to brush her hair. Her voice was sibilant. 'When Mike finally got me to bed it hurt his hothouse feelings when he found out I already knew the routine. Thought he was going to be the conquering hero. Instead he turns out the lamest runner in the race. Now he's finding excuses not to get married. Funny, isn't it?'

Sylvia brushed her hair even more vigorously. 'I think it's absolutely hilarious,' she went on. 'Because the funniest thing is I don't even want to marry the randy clot anyhow. Stupid, isn't it?"

Helen didn't answer.

'Well—isn't it?' Sylvia demanded.

'I'm sorry it's gone wrong,' Helen said softly.

'Gone wrong?' Sylvia laughed without mirth. 'If I had any sense left I'd get out while the going was good. But, there comes a time when it's now or never. For me it's now—or else.' Sylvia turned from the mirror. 'Well, pet, and what about your trouble? How's dear Gerry? Still serious?'

'Still serious.'

'A stayer, isn't he? When d'you think he'll get sick of it?'

'I haven't the faintest idea.'

'Don't tell me you're weakening?'

Helen shrugged. 'Hadn't we better go back?'

'In a moment, petal,' Sylvia said, clicking open her purse. 'Just a wee daub of warpaint for a weary old warhorse.' She inclined towards the mirror, half-stooping and peering intently at her reflected face as she worked the lipstick. 'Funny,' she murmured. 'But I had an idea he'd get you sooner or later.'

'What do you mean?' Helen said.

'What I say,' Sylvia said primly. Satisfied now, she replaced the lipstick and clipped shut the purse. 'Anyway, just how ridiculous can we get? I ask you.'

'What's ridiculous?' Helen said.

Sylvia threw her arms wide. 'Every damn thing. Here's me fighting like hell to get married when I don't want to get married. And there you are fighting like hell not to get married when you really want to get married. If that's not ridiculous, what is?'

Sylvia glanced finally into the mirror; she pinched and smoothed her frock. 'Do I look all right now? My God—my knees still feel weak. You know what time I started tippling today? Eleven this morning. Had to—to face up to him tonight. Ought to feel weak, poor things, shouldn't they?'

Helen didn't answer; she was listening to loud voices at the front of the house.

'What's that?' said Sylvia. 'Don't tell me. This character must have actually arrived. We'd better have a look. Before they pick the meat off him.'

As they moved to the door together, she caught at Helen. 'Look, darling, before I forget. Perhaps I was shooting off my mouth too much just now. But you won't say anything to anyone, will you?'

'Of course not.'

Sylvia squeezed Helen's hand. 'I didn't really imagine you would. It's just that I'm in a big enough mess now without—' She stopped, frowning. 'Do you ever feel cramped up and suffocated?'

She jerked Helen through the door. 'Come on. It's all free.'

The commotion had shifted from the front door to one of the rooms. When they pushed into the room they found attention centred on a varied group. There were four Maoris, two boys and their girl friends, young and bewildered in the alien atmosphere. The boys wore gaudy shirts and had guitars strung round their necks; the girls were flounced and floral. With them was a delicate youth with thin feminine features; he wore a yellow turtle sweater, and curls of fair hair tufted from beneath a black beret. He was surveying the room with apparent unconcern. If he had been the only one with the Maoris, Helen would have mistaken him for Tom Anderson: he seemed more the fragile male she pictured. She hadn't expected the tall dishevelled figure which dominated the odd group: red hair flared above a squarishly attractive face set on broad shoulders. His unbuttoned wool tartan shirt peeled from the chest to reveal red hairs on pale flesh; his soiled corduroys were hitched askew, and a flap of the shirt hung out; bare feet were sandalled loosely.

'Give drink,' he commanded. 'And we give music.'

Mike stared foolishly, seeming to hesitate between hostility and obedience: he paused indecisively, then went to the bar. 'What do you all want?' he said from the silence. 'There's gin and vodka and scotch and—'

'Forget it. Beer.'

Helen was aware of Gerald standing beside her. 'Serves Mike right,' he said. 'He should have known there'd be trouble.'

'What trouble?' Helen said. 'There's no trouble.'

'No trouble?' Gerald laughed shortly. 'You're a bit innocent, aren't you?'

Sylvia, who had been listening, turned on Gerald. 'What did you expect him to do? Come creeping in on hands and knees? Or did you just want him to stand up against a wall so you could throw darts at him?'

'I was talking to Helen—if you don't mind,' Gerald said stiffly.

'All right,' Sylvia said. 'Don't get shirty.'

Helen moved away.

'What d'you think you're doing now?' Gerald demanded, lunging after her. He was flushed and panicky.

'I thought I might help Mike with their drinks. Someone could be polite after all.'

Their exchange had become an incident. People stared; and from the other side of the room Tom Anderson regarded them with amusement. She broke free of Gerald and went to the bar.

'Can I help?' she asked Mike.

He raised blank eyes; sweat beaded his upper lip. 'Oh—yes, thanks,' he said. 'Thanks. Thanks a lot. What a mess this is. What a mess. What would you do?'

Gathering up the filled glasses on a tray, she moved slowly across the room. Tom Anderson stood protectively before his friends; he intercepted her.

'And who do you belong to?' he said. 'Gerry?'

'To no one,' she said and sped away.

Gerald was with Mike at the bar. He ignored her, but she overheard him say, 'After all, Mike, it's only a question of squeezing them out, isn't it?' Near them a large group talked in animated staccato. 'What a hide, though—' 'Those tar-babies and that fellow in the sweater—if you ask me...'

'Well,' said Sylvia, coming to stand beside Helen. 'There's only one thing for it. Get tight and watch the fun. Like a gin?'

They sat singing in an alcove, a recessed window seat; the Maoris occupied the seat, the fair delicate young man was arranged languidly on the floor, and Tom Anderson squatted on his haunches. Around them the party continued weakly: voices were unnaturally high. Only the newcomers appeared to be enjoying it. Elsewhere there was determination not to acknowledge the disaster; and the guitars and Maori voices made the scene absurd.

'What's with your boy friend?' Sylvia said. 'He's a cat on hot bricks.' Helen looked towards the bar and saw Gerald still talking earnestly to Mike.

Someone carried the radiogram in from another room in an effort to drown the singing. Then, the fair young man, who had apparently developed a dislike for a rather elegant girl sitting near him, said something insulting. As if they had been waiting for that moment, Gerald and Mike sprang across the room to where the fiancé of the elegant girl now menaced the fair young man. Trying to pacify everyone, Tom Anderson moved into the argument. The radiogram roared unchecked, smothering voices: the six of them, the five boys and the girl, postured and grimaced like dumb characters in a tableau.

Tom Anderson managed to end the altercation. The gathering dispersed, with warnings and meaningful gestures.

'Pity,' Sylvia murmured with a click of tongue. 'I was just beginning to enjoy it.'

With a new rush of music, several couples began to spin about the floor. The group in the alcove did not attempt to sing again. After persuading the Maoris to join in the dancing, Tom Anderson spoke softly to the fair young man, who had sulkily taken a place in a shadowed corner of the window seat. The only response was a violent headshake. Then, ignoring the young man, he took up a guitar and began to idle his fingers over the strings while looking out over the room. He saw Helen: he winked broadly, grinning, and raised his glass to her: she moved her eyes away.

'Well,' Sylvia said drily. 'Don't tell me you've made a hit.'

Gerald came towards Helen. 'Dance?' he said, almost apologetically. She slipped into the crook of his arm and let him slide her away.

Over his shoulder, as they danced, she watched Mike approach Sylvia and say something. Sylvia hesitated, bracing herself, and then she hissed a reply. Mike backed away as though stung.

'I'm sorry things have gone wrong,' Gerald was saying.

Sylvia's blue frock flashed towards the alcove. Helen's view was obscured for a moment, and then she saw Sylvia dancing with Tom Anderson.

Gerald stiffened. 'Do you see that?' he said.

'What?'

'Sylvia.'

'I know,' she said calmly.

'The sooner Mike wakes up to her the better. I've been trying to make him see.'

'What's wrong with Sylvia?'

'Ask yourself.'

'I wish you'd remember that Sylvia's my friend,' Helen said in a small, even voice.

'Please yourself.'

There was a pause.

'And there's just one thing I'd like you to tell me,' she said.

'What's that?'

'Why are you so twitchy about Tom Anderson?'

'Look,' he said with irritation. 'Can't we just quietly forget about him? He'll be gone soon, anyhow.'

'Why?'

'Because we just got him to promise to clear himself and his menagerie out of here soon—that's why.'

Helen was silent. She knew what she had to do. There was only the one question to ask.

'Dear old Gerry's girl friend, eh?' Tom said. They were dancing. His voice was low in her ear. 'Friend, is it—or fiancée?'

'Friend.'

'Well, well. And when shall it be fiancée?'

'I don't know—that it will.'

'He's asked, I suppose.'

'He's asked.'

'Well,' he said with his friendly smile. 'Dear old Gerry.'

Close, his face lost its crude strength. In the eyes were webs of red. He regarded her quizzically.

'Why is he so afraid of you?'

'Who?—Gerry?' he asked, with affected surprise.

'You've seen him tonight.'

'Have I?' he asked.

'You were good friends at college, weren't you?'

'Excellent friends.'

'Then why does he hate you now?'

'Perhaps,' he suggested, 'he's just forgotten—that we were friends.'

'He hasn't forgotten—you know that.'

'Well, then—I can't understand it. Can you?' He smiled winningly again.

'Tell me what you and he were like at college.'

'Well,' he said, pausing briefly. 'He used to keep me company when I wandered the countryside with my sketchbook. He was never much of an artist himself, as I remember; not that I was either, come to think of it. Also he used to produce poetry of a rather badly written variety; a pastime in which I encouraged him, since there might have been something there. That satisfy you?'

He paused for breath: there was a wheeze in his throat.

'And Mike?'

'Ah, yes. There was Mike. The big bad philistine.' He wheezed again, and added, 'I was expelled. Mike informed on me. Liquor on college premises. Girls over the college wall.'

'And why did Mike inform?'

'Let's say that perhaps he wasn't a patron of the arts and would have preferred me to give my full attention to rugby, a game at which I sometimes excelled. Not a puritan, mind. Not Mike—I never did find out where he got his own liquor from.'

'And what about Gerald?'

'Yes—alas, poor innocent Gerald. Betwixt and between.'

He appeared, suddenly, to have dismissed the subject.

The dance was faster now. Faces twitched in and out of focus, points of light blinked. She was out of breath suddenly, leaning against him, his stubbled chin prickling her cheek.

'Enough?' he asked.

'Yes.'

'Then let's have a drink.' He steered her towards the alcove. 'You will drink with us, won't you?'

'Of course. Why not?'

'I'd hate to get you into trouble with Gerry.' Strangely, he seemed to mean it.

'You haven't met Derek yet,' Tom said as he led her into the alcove. 'Helen, Derek. Derek, Helen.'

The fair young man didn't rise from his seat; he raised cool eyes briefly, his face still pouting.

'Derek plays the violin,' Tom said. 'He's enchanting when he plays the violin.'

Derek didn't look up again.

'Excuse him, won't you?' Tom said, as though apologizing for a child.

The cough came without preliminary: one moment he was smiling at her; the next he was doubled up with the violence of it. And then, as quickly recovered, he smiled again. 'Let's drink,' he said.

She looked at him quickly. If there was distress she was too late to see it.

She realized, for the first time, that he was drunk, though his manner and speech did not show it. He tilted back his head and drank with a flourish, his neck-muscles rippling.

'Tell me something,' he said as he wiped his mouth with the back of his hand. 'Think you'll marry Gerry? Or shouldn't I ask?'

'You shouldn't ask,' she said lamely.

She remembered that Sylvia too had vanished from the room. Perhaps to be ill.

'Who are you looking for?' Tom said. 'Gerry?'

'Sylvia.'

'Sylvia? Ah, yes, Mike's fiancée. She danced very nicely.'

'I think I should find her,' Helen apologized.

'It's all right—if you want to go,' he said, touching her arm lightly.

'How do you mean?'

'I mean it's all right if you want to go. Everyone else seems to be leaving us.'

The room was beginning to empty: the radiogram had been disconnected and carried through to another room. Apparently Mike had decided to isolate the unwanted guests altogether.

The Maoris returned to the alcove; their brown skins were shiny with sweat from the dancing.

'I think we better go now,' one of the boys said, showing white teeth.

'Nonsense,' Tom said. 'Let's make more music.'

'I think we better go,' the boy persisted.

'More music,' Tom insisted. '*Kapai te* music.' He began to talk persuasively.

'Really, Tom,' Derek appealed in his thin, affected voice. 'Don't you think all this has gone far enough?'

'Everyone sit down,' Tom commanded. 'We're just getting started.' He turned to Helen. 'Aren't we, Helen? You will stay, won't you?'

And his eyes, hinting again, seemed to add: after all, there is no real need to say anything; we understand each other, don't we, you and I?

'I'll stay,' she said faintly.

'Really, I think—' Derek began to protest.

'Shut up,' Tom said mildly.

He drew up a chair for Helen and sat himself on the arm. The Maoris crowded back into the window seat, and Derek slipped unwillingly to the floor.

Everyone else had left the room, but at that moment Gerald returned to stand at the door.

'Helen,' he said quietly.

There was a silence. Sylvia wobbled into the doorway to stand behind Gerald.

'Helen,' he repeated more sharply.

He stood only a few yards away, at the other end of the misty room. It seemed a greater distance.

She shook her head. He stared with disbelief, then turned away.

There was the sound of Sylvia's high laugh; Mike came and Sylvia allowed herself to be led away, still laughing. The door slammed and there was silence.

Tom touched her arm lightly, gratefully; she did not look at him. The guitars were strummed.

It was after midnight: out in the passage goodbyes were said as another group of guests departed.

From other rooms came the subdued sounds of the diminishing party: its dying fall infected even those in the quarantine room. Tom Anderson plucked a borrowed guitar and sang alone.

Lights had long been turned out. Moonlight found chinks in the curtains.

> *When I walked out in the streets of Laredo*
> *When I walked out in Laredo one day*
> *I spied a young cowboy all wrapped in white linen*
> *Wrapped in white linen as cold as the clay*

For one moment it seemed the song would break off altogether; she felt the body beside her arch and quiver. But this time he smothered the cough quickly. His finger found the tune again.

> *'I see by your outfit that you are a cowboy'*
> *These words he did say as I boldly stepped by*
> *'Come sit down beside me and hear my sad story*
> *I'm shot in the breast and know I must—*

Moving her eyes slightly she met Derek's steady stare; moonlight and shadow met on his face. His eyes continued to regard her with contempt and distaste: she looked away quickly, trying to check her trembling. For one moment she was afraid she might cry out.

> *It was once in the saddle I used to go dashing*

The door sprang open: light leapt across the floor. Mike entered the room and, peering uncertainly into the dark, sought Helen out.

> *First down to Rosie's and then to the cardhouse*

Mike spoke quickly, slurring his words. 'Sylvia—she needs you. Says she won't talk to anyone else. I can't do anything with her. She's squiffy as hell. I can't—' He caught at her arm in dumb appeal. 'She won't talk to anyone but you.'

> *Get six tall cowboys to carry my coffin*

'Please,' Mike said. Please.'

> *Six purty maidens to sing me a song*

She needed to escape the room, the eyes, the song, the singer. Insistent and mocking, the voice followed her as she moved off with Mike.

O beat the drum slowly and play the fife lowly

'You leave me,' she said to Mike over-loudly. 'I'll look after her.' The voice pursued her still. It had taken on another and dangerous dimension.

When I walked out in the streets of Laredo

She slammed the door. She leaned against it, her hot cheek pressed to the cold panel. Then she turned to face the bedroom.

Faint smoke lingered towards the ceiling, and on the table beside the bed stood a depleted bottle of gin and two large glasses, one overturned in its own puddle. The bed was crumpled. Sylvia lay face down, one brown arm crooked out from her body, the hand clenching and unclenching a corner of the bedcover. Hair tented her face.

'Get out,' she said, jerking convulsively. 'Get out you bastard.'

'It's only me,' Helen said quietly. She went to the bed.

Fingering back her hair, Sylvia raised her face. The skin was puffy, the make-up smudged by tears; her eyes were bleak. 'I'm sorry,' she murmured. Her breath caught in her throat; she smiled, crookedly. 'I'm sorry,' she said again.

'Are you all right?' Helen said.

'I'm all right.' Sylvia tried to smile again. 'There's only one thing wrong with me. Too much thinking.'

'Thinking?'

'About how it's only a dirty cheat, the things they put in music and poetry.'

She gave Helen no pause for reply.

'No? You'll find out what a cheat it is. There's no beautiful things. Just randy bastards and chemists' shops.' A shudder rippled through her body. 'Where's your Gerry, anyhow? What've you done with him?'

'He's somewhere. I don't know.'

'Poor old Gerry. He doesn't know what to make of you. He thinks he might be in on a win if he had an intelligent wife. But you only get him all balled up. What he really needs is a decorative blonde like me. So you've been with them—with the others, all night?'

'Of course.'

Sylvia laughed. 'I knew you didn't understand.'

'What don't I understand?'

Sylvia's laugh rang again. 'Tom Anderson's not interested in you. He's playing a game with Gerry. Can't you see? He—' Her voice broke. Helen tried to force her back to the pillow. The hysteria subsiding, they fought wordlessly. Presently Sylvia lay silent. Helen drew back from the bed.

'I'm sorry,' Sylvia murmured. 'It's not true what I said. I didn't mean to say it—I don't know—' She sat up and pointed to the door. 'Go on. Before it's too late to try. Go back and find him.' She seemed to choke. 'And God help you.'

Outside, there were voices: a door banged; someone laughed. Helen ran from the bedroom. Along the passage Gerald and Mike blocked her way.

'It's all right,' Gerald said. 'They've gone. We got rid of them.'

'Where did they go?' she said.

'They've gone,' Gerald repeated. 'Gone.'

'Sylvia,' Mike said, as Sylvia came stumbling along the passage. 'You should've stayed—'

'What do you think you're doing?' Gerald said to Helen.

'Can't you see?' she said. 'I'm putting on my coat.'

He caught at her shoulders. She tried to burst free, but he held tight, beginning to shake her. 'Can't you see—can't you...' The words bubbled in his throat; his face quivered. She couldn't be angry. She could only be sorry.

There was not even choice now. Even if flight was futile, pursuit pointless, she might at least know her own face in the mirror.

Confused, struggling, the four were bunched in the narrow hallway. Sylvia's hand smacked twice across Mike's face. Mike, recoiling, lurched against Gerald, and Helen broke free of him at last: she escaped through the front door into a silent world laced with moonlight: trees, gardens, and then streets, pale, empty and echoing.

3

Somewhere she had taken a wrong turn. She was lost. The familiar city was behind her; ahead it was new and strange. Sagging and weed-tangled, rickety buildings lined the way; and unlit windows.

She ran still: she ran until the feet ringing behind her slowed and a voice called her name. She leaned against a wooden wall and waited until Sylvia, limping, came to stand beside her.

They looked at each other without words; their breathing sobbed. A loose shop-awning flapped in the wind. Sylvia moved nearer.

'I should have made you understand,' she said. 'It was no good. That boy and—'

'But I knew,' Helen said.

'You knew? Then why—'

There was a pause. They were clinging together as though in fright. The wind grieved through overhead wires: it slapped and rustled, nipping them with cold. Sylvia lifted her head and tried to speak.

'No,' Helen whispered. 'Don't say anything at all.'

Thank you goodbye

They sat in the large-windowed cafe at the corner of the square. Outside, empty tramcars banged, autumn wind scattered coloured leaves over yellow cobbles, strollers dawdled. The pale buildings walling the square were new and austere. Fixed above the tallest building, in the corner directly opposite the cafe, a five-pointed red star rose against evening sky. The couple had only just taken their seats. The man was thin and pale, dressed neatly in charcoal suit and pastel tie. He appeared nervous. Twice as they waited for service he glanced at his watch.

'There is time,' said the girl calmly. 'Much time. More than one hour. A taxi will take only five minutes to the railway station. If that is what worries you.'

'I'm not worried,' he said, without conviction.

'Your suitcases have all gone from the hotel to the station?' she asked. She spoke an unemphatic, almost accentless English.

'They've gone.'

'Good,' she said. 'Then there is nothing to worry about, is there?'

'No,' he said. 'Nothing.'

'You have only to remove yourself to the station now,' she said. 'It is quite perfectly simple. And this time tomorrow where will you be?'

'I don't know. Vienna perhaps. I don't study timetables closely.'

'But you should,' she observed. 'Travel is adventure. I should. I should study timetables all the time I travelled.' She paused. 'But then,' she added wistfully, 'I have never travelled.'

'No.'

'In two days' time,' the girl calculated, 'you will be in Paris. In three days, London. You will be among friends again.'

'Please,' he said suddenly.

She raised her eyebrows.

'Please don't,' he said.

Though there were few customers, service was slow. The girl glanced over her shoulder at the old grey-haired waiter who moved methodically among the tables. She caught his eye presently, and he ambled amiably over to their table.

'*Molya,*' he said. He stood ready to pencil the order.

'Cognac?' the girl said to her friend. 'Or *rakia?*'

'Anything,' he said.

'*Edna malka bofilka cognac, molya,*' the girl requested. The waiter went away.

The man began to drum his fingers on the table. The girl hummed a tune softly to herself; she seemed serene. She was petite, lightly built, with an expressive, delicately-boned Slavic face. She stopped humming suddenly and, as she reached out for his impatient hand, a chunky gold bangle slid down her arm. There was a moment's silence; they could have heard, if they wanted, the rattling of leaves in the street outside.

'Then we will not look into the future,' she said. 'Perhaps the past is the more satisfying. Two hours ago—'

'Not that either,' he said abruptly.

'You are very difficult.' She hesitated. 'And, besides, that reminds me. I left my cigarettes by the bed. Have you—'

He took cigarettes from a pocket and, after she had taken one, he rested the packet between them.

'You are difficult,' she repeated. 'If we cannot discuss the future or the past, then there is only the present.'

'Only the present,' he agreed.

'And the present,' she said, 'is always so difficult to fix. It always escapes before you can discuss it. Is that not so?'

He appeared not to hear.

'Everything escapes,' she observed quietly.

The waiter returned with a small bottle of cognac and two glasses. He set them down on the table, smiled at the girl, and nodded towards her companion.

'*Angliski,*' he said. 'Eng-lish I speak.' He paused impressively. 'How you do,' he said. 'How you do. I love you. Thank you goodbye.'

'You see,' she said. 'He is showing he can speak English.'

'Tell him he speaks well.'

'*Mnogo dobré,*' the girl said to the waiter.

He chuckled, performed a jerky little bow of pleasure, and withdrew. 'How you do. I love you,' he laughed to himself as he went away.

'His vocabulary is limited,' the girl remarked. 'But adequate and effective.'

The man looked at his watch.

'There is still time,' she said.

The sky was darkening. Lights winked about the square. Above the tall building the giant red star was suddenly illuminated. On one side of the square, screened by thinning trees, a theatre opened its doors and a queue formed. Lights picked out the words *Narodna Kultura* and the smaller word *Teatr.* The night came to life; people scuffed past the cafe windows, over the fallen leaves. The girl poured the cognac carefully. They took up their glasses.

'*Nez dravé,*' she said as they drank.

'*Nez dravé.*'

'You learn my language so quickly,' she said jestingly. 'It is a pity you go so soon. A few more weeks and you would be speaking as a native.'

He was silent.

'You are not amused,' she said. 'You are not amused at anything tonight.' She sipped the cognac. 'After all it is I who should be sad. Is that not so? My room will be the same. My streets will be the same. It is your streets which shall be different. It is you who are going away. Is that not correct?'

'I don't want it like this,' he said.

'No?'

'I mean I wish it different.'

'Different?' she said.

'Much different. I wish it weren't necessary.'

'It need not be necessary. You could stay. It would not be impossible to arrange.'

'Please,' he said. 'Be realistic.'

'Ah, yes,' she said. She looked out the window at the lights in the evening. 'We must be realistic. Always.'

'Please,' he said. 'You're just trying to hurt yourself.'

'Trying?' She laughed.

'You're making it worse. For both of us.'

'Can it be so worse?'

'I mean you must see the impossibility of it all.'

'Of course,' she said. 'Naturally.' Without haste, she reached for the bottle and refilled the glasses. 'I must see.'

'We can't persuade ourselves that it could be different.'

'It was not I who was just now wishing it different.'

'It was in a manner of speaking.'

'Naturally. I only suggested that if you meant what you said, it would be possible to arrange for you to stay. But I was not to know that you did not mean what you said, that it was only a manner of speaking.'

'I see you don't understand,' he said.

'There are difficulties. When you talk to me in a manner of speaking.' She studied a speck of ash on the table-cloth and rubbed it away with a finger. She was silent.

'Why does it have to be like this?' he asked.

'I am sorry,' she said. 'If it is I who make it like this.'

'You become so cold,' he said.

'Then you must forgive me,' she said.

'I don't think you really want to understand.'

'I understand you cannot stay. It is quite simple.'

'Besides,' he added, 'I do not belong here.'

'Of course. Now you say what you mean. Now you do not talk in a manner of speaking.'

'It's important,' he said.

'If you wish to make it important, then it is so. But you are not political?'

'If you mean in the shrill sense, no.'

'Then it is perhaps not so important. Many live here who are not political. Like you, they are indifferent.'

'You don't speak of yourself.'

'If I am, it is not important. I am a person.' She paused. 'If you mean—how was it you said it?—in the shrill sense, no.'

'And if I mean any other way?'

'If you mean that it has been necessary, yes. If you mean it has been necessary because otherwise I might have been illiterate and barefoot in my village, yes. For you it has not been necessary.'

'But now?'

'It is necessary also. But that perhaps you would not understand. If one suddenly discovers one is the parent of a bad child, one does not run away. One must take responsibility. Someone must take responsibility. It is necessary.'

'Rhetoric,' he said.

'Rhetoric is sometimes necessary also.'

This time he was silent.

'It seems to me that with all things it is more important to you not being something than being something. Would you not agree?'

'Whatever you say.'

'Please do not be hurt. I mean only that you always make the greatest importance out of not being something.'

'I understand you perfectly.'

'It is nice,' she said, 'to end on such a note.' She saw him glance again at his watch. 'Yes, it is almost time. At the station there will be people waiting to say goodbye. They will wish to shake your hand. You must give them time, and not disappoint them. I will not come to the station. After all, what is one goodbye among many?'

'You won't come?' he said.

'You will observe that there is almost one glass of cognac remaining in this bottle. I shall sit here and perhaps order a plate of peppers to eat with it. Then I shall walk back along the streets to my room. Perhaps I shall listen to the radio, or read a little, and then it will be time for sleep. If I sleep early, then tomorrow I will wake refreshed for work.'

'Are you sure?' he said suddenly. He reached across the table and touched her hand lightly.

'Now go,' she said, not looking at him. 'I will say only the correct things.' She began to recite in a flat voice. 'I hope you have liked my country. I hope you have found much to interest you, and enjoy. I hope you will write pleasant things about us, and that if you must write unpleasant things you will balance them with the pleasant. I hope—' She stopped. 'Politics,' she said suddenly. 'I hate politics.'

'We must write,' he said.

'If you wish,' she said. 'But it is not necessary.'

'I promise,' he said. He looked quickly about the cafe. 'I must pay,' he added. Just at that moment there was no sign of the old waiter. 'Before I—'

'But it does not matter. I will pay the bill.'

'I insist. I mean I—'

'But it is I who am in a position to insist. And after all have you not the saying—in jest, naturally—that it is always the woman who pays?'

He pulled on his coat.

'Now go,' she repeated. 'Go quickly.'

She did not lift her eyes to see his back vanish out of the door of the cafe into the evening. She did not even see if he looked back. She heard his footsteps.

After a while she raised her head. The queue had gone from the front of the theatre; the plate-glass doors were shut against the chill of night. The wind had dwindled, and leaves rustled gently. The lights were cold on the empty square. Above the tall building, above the red star, stars of an older kind were distinct in the sky.

She filled her glass and beckoned the waiter.

'*Piperki—edna chiniya piperki, molya,*' she said.

He looked at the empty chair, then towards the door. '*Zamina li toi?*'

'*Da,*' she said tiredly. '*Zamina.*'

Presently he brought a small plate of peppers. They were red-coloured and covered with a thin film of oil. She ate with a fork, slowly, chunking off the seedy tops and picking stray seeds from the flesh. She ate only a very small portion of flesh at a time. Occasionally she sipped from her glass. When she had finished she beckoned the waiter again.

'*Smetka, molya,*' she asked.

He stood above her to make out the bill, adding two figures in his notebook. He tore out the page and placed it down beside her. She fed out the money from her frayed leather purse carefully, several notes and coins to pay the bill exactly, and beside them a small heap of coins as a tip. He thanked her and helped her into her coat. It was a light, pale-coloured trench coat and she fastened it tightly about her slight figure. Then she went to the door.

'*Dovishdane!*' she called suddenly to the waiter, swinging back on her flat heels as she opened the door.

'*Dovishdane!*' he returned. Then he paused a moment, looked puzzled, and remembered. '*Da,*' he said. 'Thank you goodbye.'

The door closed, feet clipped away, and as he stooped to clear the table he talked to himself, repeating a long-ago lesson. 'How you do. I love you,' he said softly. 'Thank you goodbye.' Now and then, remembering something, he laughed quietly.

Ben's Land

There were three, in our family, with the name of Benjamin.

There was great-grandfather Benjamin, then grandfather Benjamin; and uncle Ben. By the time the name reached my uncle it had been shortened in easy-going style.

To account properly for Ben—and not just for his name—it seems I must account for the Benjamins, and for the country of the Benjamins.

Great-grandfather Benjamin left England for New Zealand in the early eighteen-forties. One version of the family legend—the respectable one—has it that he was the son of a county squire, from whom he inherited a modest sum of money; the other version claims he was in fact the bastard son of an English earl who gave him money on condition he got out of England. The two versions agree that he was, in his day, something of a radical, a Chartist and Shelleyan socialist; certainly, as if to confirm his regard for the poet, a scorched and leather-bound volume of Shelley capriciously survived the fire which, late last century, destroyed most of the family papers and turned our history into legend. He had ideas, apparently, of some utopia where Jack might be as good as his master: New Zealand, only lately drawn into the map of the world, seemed a likely enough place for such a venture. In any case he detested the spread of smoke and ugliness in the England of the industrial revolution; and was glad to say good-bye to London. ('Hell,' said Shelley, 'is a city much like London.')

With a thousand pounds or two in his pocket—inheritance or bribe—he set sail in a whaling ship for New Zealand, nearly three years a British colony. He travelled down the Atlantic, round the Horn, and across the South Seas at about the same time as Herman Melville was finding bliss with the Typee: the voyage took the best part of a year. He carried with him, as the ship rocked slowly across the Pacific, his version of a new Jerusalem, a true fraternity of happy men which might be built in the last, straggling corner of the New World.

Just where his plan went wrong is difficult to say. What is certain is that he settled in the South Island, near the village of Akaroa. A year or two earlier that village had seen the Union Jack hastily raised a day or so before the arrival of a shipload of French colonists. So it was, when great-grandfather Benjamin arrived, a mixed Anglo-French community. Most of the local tribe of Maoris had been slaughtered a few years earlier by a musket-bearing tribe from the north. There appears, then, to have been no native land problem: he quickly acquired property. Perhaps the uncertain young immigrant, with a raw country before him and money in his pocket, felt some need to establish himself before he embarked on his democratic crusade. Or perhaps—and this is more likely—he was perversely dismayed by the fact that in New Zealand, even at that early date, Jack was fast becoming master. Immigrant tradesmen went on strike for an eight-hour day almost as soon as they landed in the country; most of the imported gentry had fled, or were fleeing, home to England.

And he was alone; alone with several hundred acres of heavily-bushed country, an axe, a shovel, a rifle, a bachelor hut. I like to imagine him nursing a volume of Shelley—perhaps that scorched copy I have on my bookshelf now—in his blistered hands before the firelight at night, in the deeps of the bush. But probably it wasn't like that at all; probably he only had strength enough to roll himself into a blanket by the fire before he slept. Certainly it wasn't quite what a soft young man, fresh from London, could have bargained for; but he appears, in his way, to have salvaged something from the wreck as Jerusalem foundered.

For when next I encounter him, in family legend, he owns a large farm and an impressive homestead. The young idealist and socialist is also, strangely, a near monopoly capitalist. In the nearest village he owned the timber mill, the pub, the general store—that is, he owned the village; and most of the homes that went along with it. He paid his employees at the mill, and they spent their wages in his pub and store and paid him rent too. He married a Frenchwoman who bore him sixteen children, ten of them sons. She is supposed to have drunk herself to death. After her death, possibly as a result—the legend grows vague—he began, with apparent success, to gamble and drink his money away, though he had until then been something of a puritan. Perhaps in later years, wandering the polished floors of his candlelit homestead, he was haunted maliciously by some gaunt ghost of his yearning youth. I don't know; family legends seldom supply that kind of information.

By the time he died he had lost the mill, the general store, and a good part of the farm. He may have retained the pub for some sentimental reason; but it seems unlikely. After his death it was sold to pay gambling debts. The homestead was made over to the daughters who quarrelled bitterly and sold it, so that it went out of the family. With that anchor gone, they were all adrift in a perplexing country. The sons, taking up the search for the new world where their father had left it, travelled the length of New Zealand, from the kauri gumfields in the north to the goldfields in the south.

Grandfather Benjamin, who married a tender-eyed girl fresh and bewildered from England, went up to the North Island, into the King Country, where the followers of the Maori King retreated into the bush after the bloodshed and defeat of the eighteen-sixties; and where, until late last century, the pakeha trod lonely tracks carefully, if at all. It was just opening up to the white man. Grandfather didn't ever stay long in one place; he hacked one farm after another out of the bush. One farm was ruined by flood; another was too remote to prosper; a third was abandoned after a shipping contractor failed to take delivery of a thousand sheep, and they all died of thirst. This affair led to litigation and grandfather Benjamin, who liked to talk a good deal about British justice, carried lifelong grudges. He conducted his own court cases, and soon became a notorious bush-lawyer; one grievance after another went to the courts, and he dispatched petitions to Parliament in Wellington. His eruptions in the courtroom were always something of a sensation, and it is said his talent for invective and character assassination improved with age.

'Eighty cases, boy,' I remember him saying when I was young. 'Eighty cases I've fought in the courts of this country for elementary British justice. And, by God, I won most of them too. Did you know, boy, I even fought and won five cases against the Crown itself? And,' he added with pride, 'I never spent a day in no university studying law. The lawyers used to come along and watch me when I was in the courts. Thought they might learn something. And they did, by God.'

'Didn't you stand for Parliament too, Grandpa?' I asked.

At that, for some reason, he grew terrifyingly red in the face and began to bluster. Afterwards I learned what had happened. He stood for Parliament on the strength of some obscure personal grievance; his platform was doubtless British justice. He made no politician's promises to the electors. He simply harangued them, abused them, told them they were incompetent fools unfit for the vote. He withdrew his curious candidacy just in time to evade a fairly punishing defeat at the polls. He then wrote a book called *My Family and Myself by Land and Sea*. It was published in a limited edition of fifty copies, of which none appears to have survived: five copies sent out for review were received coolly, and the others are presumed to have been destroyed in his ensuing fit of anger. After sampling the political, and then the literary life, he gave himself back to bush-farming again and, just to keep his hand in, conducted the odd court case. If he ran short of grievances himself, he made do with those of others; once he is supposed to have had an innocent man unlocked from gaol.

My father's earliest memories are of the crude slab huts grandfather Benjamin built on his lonely bush-farms; these huts were always hard up against the bush, for shelter. Their most distinctive feature was the enormous fireplace, fifteen feet wide by eleven deep, with a seat around the inside. With a wealth of logs available as grandfather axed through the countryside, this blazed winter and summer—there was always plenty of space for cooking, clothes-drying, and ridding oneself of the damp chill of winter; the huts were, of course, seldom tolerable in the heat of summer. At night the bush was alive with the cries of moreporks; in the morning the great tangled hills and gorges above the Wanganui rose serenely from the river mists. On clear days, when out on the hills shooting wild pig, the three volcanoes—Ngauruhoe, Tongariro, Ruapehu—could sometimes be seen, glittering with fresh snow, or streaked and summer-hazy, off to the east.

Though he was to remember vividly, all his life, the lonely huts, the bleak winters and sweltering summers, and the sound of grandfather's axe chopping into the heart of the country, my father, the eldest son, did not long suffer those bush-farms. He was a premature child, sickly. If my grandfather wanted to keep the name in the family, it might have seemed appropriate to call his eldest son Benjamin. But perhaps—since my father appeared unlikely to survive—grandfather did not want to squander the name. For he named his second son Benjamin; and Ben he became. And Uncle Ben was soon, to most appearances, the eldest son anyway; my weakly father was rescued, early in life, from the rigours of the King Country bush by a horrified spinster aunt who carried him gently back to Akaroa to be reared peacefully in a colonial cottage by the sea. He was allowed occasional holiday visits back to his family.

Each new visit home had its surprises. Often, of course, he found his family on a new farm. Grandfather Benjamin would meet my father on Taumarunui railway station with the news. And my father would, after hearing details of the latest farm, save his most important question till last. 'Is there a new one, Dad?' he asked timidly.

'New what?' my grandfather would roar.

'You know—' my father said, his lips trembling, near tears.

'Yes, by God,' grandfather blustered; he knew perfectly well, all the time, what my father was asking. 'There's a new one. A girl.'

And my father wept tragically as he was lifted into the bullock-wagon and carried off into the bush; at the end of that rough ride, when they jogged through darkness and fern to the door of the latest hut, there always seemed to be a new sister, or brother. When his last tear had fallen, he was one of eleven children, one of seven sons.

None of grandfather's farms flourished. In search of a stake in the country, he travelled north, across the fertile Waikato, and after a good deal of wandering, and one or two new farms, settled finally for a few acres on the outskirts of Auckland, a city saved by gold and kauri gum, made prosperous by meat and butterfat, but still, between the old Symonds Street windmill and the overgrown colonists' graves of Grafton gully and the frilled wooden mansions overlooking the harbour on the slopes of Parnell, living lightly with a memory of its days as capital of pioneer New Zealand. He chose a pleasant enough spot to grow out of restlessness into old age, alongside the Manukau harbour. On his few acres grandfather Benjamin milked two cows, raised chickens, stabled racehorses; and began, in the autumn of his life, to shed his children to the Pacific winds.

My father left his aunt in Akaroa, and followed his roving family to Auckland. Reared separately and more gently, and in a way which would leave him ill-fitted for the fine detail of life, he was a contrast to his six sturdy brothers, all of them energetic footballers and boxers when young. He was as tall as they were—all my uncles seemed to me giants—but light and fragile in build; almost feathery by comparison. He sometimes served his brothers as a second in boxing matches; and often cheered them on from the touchline of a football field. Frequently his brothers came to him for advice; he was seldom able to give it. But they still came to him, the outsider of the family—as if that, in itself, gave him some qualification, rendered him fit to offer advice.

Already the sons, inheriting the restlessness which had deserted their father, had begun to scatter across the country; it seemed, for a while, that history was repeating itself.

One was felling timber in a southern forest; a second was chasing gold, in some wildcat scheme, near Thames; and Uncle Ben returned to work as a labourer on a King Country farm with a mind to acquiring a farm of his own. But the depression struck at them all; and dragged them, one after the other, back to the family home in Auckland. The unemployed marches were only just beginning. It was clear that something was over, something ended perhaps for ever; but none of them would have been able to name it precisely. Some great door, behind them, had rolled shut. Had they been able to look back, they might have found the country of the Benjamins gone; they discovered the futility of an older world. They loitered about the family home, yarn-spinning, rolling thin cigarettes, playing poker, kicking a football in desultory fashion over grandfather's back paddock—he had begun to sell some of his land now. Sometimes they fished to replenish the family food supply; sometimes they earned a few shillings from relief work. After a while they haunted city gymnasiums, out of desperation offering themselves as sparring partners to professional boxers; they would carry scars—and cauliflower ears—the rest of their lives.

Baffled, they carried questions to my father who, vague and bookish, finally asked why and found an answer of a kind. He had married the poetry-writing daughter of a militant Irish socialist; early in the depression he found a copy of a periodical called *The Red Worker* thrust in his hand. Soon afterwards he was involved in radical politics. When he lost his job, he helped organise the unemployed. The day of the Auckland hunger riots, a month before my birth, when angry crowds rampaged through the city to the sound of shattering shop windows, he appeared to have suffered, apart from a baton-blow on the head, some particularly unpleasant and disillusioning experience; or perhaps was afforded some ugly glimpse into the perversity of human nature which bewildered, or terrified him; something which he could not grip wholly with the rest of life. He did not turn his back, exactly; nor did he retreat, exactly. He was, for a few weeks, paralysed. Then I was born and he appeared to emerge from his trance. He searched and found a job in a southern gold town which was a small island of mild prosperity in the midst of desolation. Sometimes, with flagging fervour, he made speeches at union meetings.

When we returned to Auckland for a short time, after the depression and before the war, my father found his brothers settled in and around the city; they seemed thoroughly urbanized and worked on the railways, on the waterfront, in factories. Some were married and had children. My father didn't find a job to suit him in the city, so we travelled back into the country and we were living in a quiet rural town when war came; we remained there for the duration. Father was medically unfit for the army, but five of his brothers were away fighting; we heard, in letters, of Greece, Crete, Alexandria, El Alamein and the Solomons. Then they came home again from their deserts and Pacific Islands; the war was over when we returned to Auckland.

It was about this time that I first became aware of grandfather Benjamin as someone remarkable. I suppose it had to do with my not having seen him for some years; for he had begun to loom out of my memory like a great grey statue. Now, to my astonishment, the statue began to walk and talk; he came barking off his pedestal, unfrozen and very much alive. He was a tall fierce grizzled old man with stubbly hair, powerful shoulders and arms, and a tremendously loud voice. Great-grandfather Benjamin, dead, might have been a legend with his Shelley, his drunken French wife, his vast homestead and his gambling; but grandfather Benjamin, alive, was still preparing his place in mythology with his bush-farms and court cases. He distrusted electricity, the telephone and radio, though he had in fact all three in his home. He would never touch a telephone receiver, but allowed my grandmother to do so; when calls came for him she acted as intermediary while he stomped about the room delivering wild-swinging phrases which she then interpreted, softly, into the receiver. He was also prepared to allow my grandmother the risk of switching on and off lights and radio. This caused many domestic complications, it meant, for example, that he could never be left alone in the house with these contrivances. He had a terror of the telephone ringing endlessly, the radio roaring unchecked, while the house grew steadily darker. He bellowed at his sons as if they were still ten-year-olds, but liked them gathering round him at the family home on Sunday. If they dared argue with him, he threatened to lock them in the chicken-house. Alternatively, he kept beside him, at the fireside, a few light lumps of wood which, accurately thrown, could quickly settle any dispute. He seemed entirely unaware that a city suburb had grown up around his shrunken land in the past few years. Neighbours soon grew used to the sound of his voice booming over the roof-tops as it once had over King Country valleys; they no longer came racing to their doors.

Once he sent me up a tree to chase down an opossum which had been a nuisance to his chickens.

'You lily-livered coward,' he shouted, when timorously I kept my distance from the opossum's claws. 'You're no grandchild of mine. Go after it, boy. Go on.'

I braced myself, and climbed closer to the maddened opossum.

'Idiot,' he cried.'Brainless idiot. What do you think you're doing? Don't go so close, you fool. It'll scratch your eyes out.'

There was no pleasing Grandfather Benjamin.

At the family home we met most of my uncles back from the war. My father predicted darkly that they would find trouble settling down again, after all the excitement.

True, they were restless. Uncle Peter, who had been a pilot in the Fleet Air Arm, found his way to university, and trained to be a schoolteacher; he was the youngest, the least touched by the depression. Uncle Albert gave up his job on the railways and went to work as a taxi-driver. Uncle Trevor divorced his wife, shipped off to England and, for some reason, cleared bomb damage in London for two years before returning.

But it was Uncle Ben, unexpectedly, who developed as the problem child of the family; and it hadn't, as it turned out, much to do with the war. Quiet and sober, steady and unambitious, he was less of an extrovert than his rowdy brothers: he was closer, in many ways, to my father. He seemed outwardly to have no regrets at having been sucked back to the city from the country during the depression; he had marched unobtrusively among the landless and the unemployed, and still had faint scar-tissue about the eyes from selling himself in city gymnasiums. Married, he had three children by the outbreak of war; after the war the number grew to six. In the war he served a year or two on some remote Pacific island, but saw no action. He came out of the war, as he came out of most things, without apparent change. He went straight back to his job as a crane-driver on the city waterfront. His build was large and heavy, and he had a gentle unassuming appearance; his nose was slightly flattened; his deeply-tanned face, beneath his receding hairline, was puzzled with creases; and his eyes, a clear blue, seldom animated his face. He seemed to smile without his eyes, unlike most people; they were apart, and distant, living some life of their own. 'You never have the feeling,' my father explained once, 'that he's altogether with you.' Only in rare moments did those eyes become one with his face; and that was usually when Ben, lapsing from conversation, assumed an expression of vague, baffled melancholy. Still, no one expected trouble from Ben—even if, looking back, faint warning signals were there. He was a solid family man, had a pleasant and neat suburban home and garden, and appeared happy in his work—high up and tiny in the cabin of his crane, above the waterfront wilderness of steel and rigging and concrete, expertly swinging cargo from ship to shore, shore to ship.

Sometimes, in school holidays, I wandered down to the waterfront to find him. He would insist I share his lunch and we sat in the sunlight, on tangles of rope, watching the pale ferry-boats and white yachts on the harbour, and feeding crumbs to friendly gulls. We didn't talk much. I should be honest and say Ben wasn't really one of my favourite uncles. Greedy for vicarious experience, I found other uncles much more exciting; they had stories of dramatic escapes from Greece to Crete, for example, or of air-raids up the Baltic Coast. Ben would study something for a while veins of sunlight flickering on a shadowy shipside, or a pattern of rust on a battered hull—and then pass an opinion on it. He sometimes inquired from me how much family history I had picked up from my father; I told him I'd heard about the bushfarms, the slab huts, of which my father spoke often.

'He talks about it?' Ben said, with surprise.

'Now and then,' I said.

'But he only ever went there for holidays,' Ben observed. 'He never really lived there, like the rest of us.'

'Well,' I said, 'he talks about it, just the same.'

I had an idea Ben wanted to talk about something of the kind too; but, after making the quiet approach, he appeared to change his mind. Probably he decided I wasn't much interested; possibly he was right. After we ate and sat silent a while, and the gulls flew off in search of new crumbs, he took me up a long, dizzying ladder and planted me down on the seat of his crane, inside his high-windowed cabin above the noisy waterfront. I suppose it was for that adventure, chiefly, that I sought him out—though now I like to think differently, like to imagine that his cryptic observations, mixed with silences, made me more alert and responsive to the world than I might otherwise have been. He had a way of stopping you up short, to see something you'd never quite seen before; but at the time that knack of his disturbed, rather than interested me. Only in memory has it assumed importance; and memory has the same trick—a way of stopping you up short to see something you've never quite seen, to feel something you've never quite felt. For now, when I try carefully and honestly to examine my memories of Ben, I find dark colours seeping through the sunlit scenes.

The first hint of something unusual came about the same time as grandfather Benjamin fought one of his last great legal battles. He was fighting the government again. During the war, when the country was panicky about the prospect of Japanese invasion, huge tank-traps were ploughed across the back of his property. The Japanese were beaten, the war was over, and yet the ugly trenches remained. Grandfather pressed for repair without success; then he sued for damages. He won one of his more spectacular victories, and had his photograph in the paper. As usual after such victories several of the family called on him to offer congratulations. My father was among them; so was I. Ben wasn't there, but he commanded conversation.

'You've heard about Ben, of course,' Uncle Tom said to my father. Uncle Tom was a no-nonsense man. He had never approved of my father's radical behaviour in the past. Nor, though he called round with congratulations out of family habit, did he entirely approve of grandfather, in his old age, continuing to make a spectacle of himself in the courts of the country.

No, my father said, he hadn't heard about Ben. In fact, he hadn't seen Ben for some time.

'He's bought himself some land,' Uncle Tom said.

'Well,' my father answered, not quite knowing what to say. Perhaps, since he knew Ben better than most, it came as no great surprise to him that Ben should, in middle age, rush off and buy himself some land. 'That's interesting,' he added mildly. 'Where?'

'That's the bloody point,' Tom said with a wild look in his eye. 'About twenty miles north. Kauri Bay. You know it? You don't? Rotten, lousy gumland; manuka fifteen feet high. Scrub and fern, gorse and blackberry. The deadest, dreariest land you ever saw. And Ben's gone and bought himself a slice of it—three or four acres. You ever heard anything like it? Oh yes—he bought it cheap, all right; it's probably the only land you can still buy cheap in this country. It's a wonder it wasn't given away to him.'

'What's he want to do with it?' my father asked,

'Strike me dead,' Uncle Tom replied. 'How should I know?'

The three or four acres soon became known, in the family, as 'Ben's land'. What did he want to do with it? No one knew, exactly; no one ever knew, exactly. There was reason to suppose, after a while, that even Ben didn't know. No one saw much of him; not even, we discovered, his own family. We called at his place in passing one Sunday, my father and I, and found the place, as usual, noisy with my cousins. The two eldest boys and some of their leather-jacketed neighbourhood friends were tinkering with an antique motor cycle in the backyard; there was a revving and roaring, and explosions of exhaust. An infant systematically shredded books and newspapers on the veranda. Two other children, a boy and girl, savaged each other amiably on a strangely unkempt lawn in front of the house; then the girl began to cry and ran inside. It was an ordinary enough suburban Sunday; usually Ben appeared out of the chaos, fresh from putting his garden in order, to greet us when we arrived. But that day Ben did not appear. Instead his wife Beverley, a timid desperate-looking woman, emerged from the house, seeming even more distracted than usual, with the wailing girl clinging to her skirt.

'Ben?' she said, above the din. 'No, he's not here.'

'What's he doing?' my father asked.

'Doing?' she replied, in a voice as near to a cry as she would ever get. 'What's he doing? God knows. But he's up there, on that land of his. You've heard all about that, haven't you?'

Well, we'd heard about it, if not all about it; and she told us the rest. Some weeks before, Ben had started visiting his land one day each week-end; usually Sunday. But then it had become both Saturday and Sunday. He drove up there early Saturday morning, returned late at night, and set out again early Sunday morning. But this week-end he hadn't even returned Saturday night; he had been up there, on his land, all weekend.

'Well,' said my father, comfortingly, 'I dare say Ben's got something up his sleeve. You never know.'

'*I* never know,' she replied. 'That's the truth of it.' She looked tired and baffled. She had been young, only seventeen, when she married Ben, a taciturn lumbering twenty-four. I knew because I had seen their wedding photograph; my father was best man. But she wasn't the thin pretty girl of the photograph, not any more. My father was sorry for her; he kept trying to say comforting things. But Beverley refused to be comforted.

'Have you been up there?' he said presently. 'Seen the place?'

'You think I've had a chance?'

As if in answer the exhaust barked in the backyard; and the little girl, who had grown bored with us and escaped her mother's skirt, now began screaming obscurely from inside the house.

There wasn't much my father could say to Aunt Beverley; I saw he was troubled too. Before we left, we walked round the house, to say hello to my elder cousins, and we noticed Ben's garden beginning to run wild. Ben had always been an energetic gardener; it was unlike him to neglect his garden. But perhaps, as my father said, Ben had something up his sleeve; something to surprise us all. The two small squalling children battled their way out of the house into the garden and, when we left, were trampling down the plants. A couple of months afterward

Uncle Tom called on us. We hadn't seen or heard anything of Ben.
Father didn't even talk about him. It seemed he had tested the problem
in his mind, found it too complex to admit of solution, and, refusing
to concede he had no answer, had simply shelved it for the time being
in some remote place of his mind. I tried to get him talking about Ben,
once or twice, and so did my mother; but he always changed the
subject. Perhaps he guessed that sooner or later the problem would be
dumped at our door. And perhaps he knew the time had come when
Uncle Tom arrived. Tom strode straight into the house; he was never
a man for preliminaries. Huge and barrel-chested, he planted himself
squarely in the living-room and announced, in his resonant voice, 'You
know all about Ben.' It was like an accusation.

'Yes,' my father admitted.

'Well,' Tom said. 'What are we going to do about it?'

My father made a helpless gesture. 'What can anyone do?' he said.

'It can't go on,' Tom said aggressively. 'You know that.'

'What can't?' my father asked. 'What *is* going on? Do you know?
Because I don't.' His tone implied that he didn't want to know either,
if he could help it. 'And anyway, Tom,' he added, 'is it our business?'

'Of course it is,' Tom declared. 'If someone lets the side down.'
Everyone, in Tom's eyes, was at some time or another in danger of
letting the family down, except possibly Tom; even my father, so far as
Tom was concerned, had only lately regained a semblance of
respectability. Tom began to elaborate. He had seen Beverley; she was
very distraught. It seemed Ben had given no attention to his home, wife
and family for months now. Everything was going to pieces. Beverley
looked about ready for a nervous breakdown. The children were
running wild. The house needed painting, and the garden was a ruin.
Tom put great emphasis on the garden, since he was a keen suburban
gardener too; he made it seem a final and damning piece of evidence.
Ben was a dangerous case.

'Of course it's our business,' Tom repeated. 'If we aren't a family,
what are we?'

Father made no immediate answer. Never wholly one of the family,
ironically he had always been more involved with it than anyone.
Unwillingly he was being dragged into something new; I saw, now, why
he had been so reluctant to discuss Ben.

'All right,' he sighed at last. It was all over; he was harnessed back into his family again. 'So what,' he asked weakly, 'are we supposed to do?'

The plan was that Tom should drive my father up to Kauri Bay one Sunday, and that they should talk things over with Ben and find out exactly what he was doing there. I went along with them for the ride. We drove up in the afternoon, through the thinning ranks of Auckland's northern suburbs. When the city wound itself in, and the last ribbons of houses flapped away on each side, the main highway was flanked by rich pastureland, divided with slack-wired fences and spotted with pine shelters, where fat and heavy-uddered cows grazed. After a while we turned off the highway, off the asphalt and away from the green land, and along a rough stony road which dipped into hilly grey scrub country. Dusty cabbage trees rose up along the roadside; beyond stretched dreary acres of gumland laden with tall tough manuka and fern; there were patches of gorse like dimming yellow fire. Once we almost ran down a rabbit; it was the only sign of life we saw. We were silent as we rode across the derelict land. Now and then we glimpsed the sea through the hills; then quite suddenly iridescent water rushed out of the horizon, and we were cruising down into Kauri Bay.

Kauri Bay took its name from pioneer times. Whalers boiled blubber on the beach, and ships called there to plunder the kauri forest. Then some early and optimistic settler must have put fire to the hills and the remnants of the bush, in hope of making pasture-land, before he departed for other, more fertile soil. Last came the diggers from Dalmatia, spading and spearing in search of kauri gum, residue of long-sunken forest. They all had come and gone. Now Kauri Bay was given back to scrub and wind.

There was a long thin beach, with rocky fingers of land each side, a pale quarter-moon curve under the hills. It was pleasant enough; scraps of paper along the foreshore indicated that carloads of picnickers had begun to come there from the city. But there was no one about that day; the waves slapped up the deserted sand. There was a steady breeze off the bright Pacific and a smudge of ship-smoke far out to sea. The road ran parallel to the beach. We stopped the car and looked around. 'I know his land's up from the beach somewhere,' Tom said. 'Let's have a look.'

But we didn't look; we listened. The sound came like steady stones dropping into the silence; we heard, a little way up from the beach, the chop of an axe. For a moment, in that desolate and lonely place, the sound was uncanny. Father and Tom stood very still, shoulder to shoulder, their faces lifting towards the sound; it was as if it were calling them to another place, another time. But I was too young to understand why they should be struck so still, so silent, by the sound to understand why they should then behave so gently and strangely towards each other. Their voices were so quiet I could still hear the birds calling out of the dense scrub.

'Look, Tom,' my father said. 'Perhaps I'd better handle this, if you don't mind.'

'It's all right with me,' Tom answered softly. 'Whatever you say.'

I only wondered at them both, at the change in them, as we climbed from the beach up an eroded yellow clay road where we found Ben's little pickup parked. Then we took a narrow track which wound through the scrub. In places the high manuka grew thicker than a man's thigh; at the edge was matted fern. Presently we came to evidence of clearing: splintered stumps, and great heaps of shattered manuka. It was as if a miniature storm had raged back and forward through the scrub. And at the centre of it all stood a small hut. A little askew, it looked as though it had been knocked together from driftwood and the remnants of gumdiggers' shacks.The pale texture of its old warped wood gave it, already, an ageless appearance. It stood there beyond time and weather, like a memory.

We paused. We couldn't hear the axe any more.

Then a hammering began, not far away, around the side of the hut hidden from us. It was startling suddenly, from that static scene, like a sound emerging freakishly from an old and dusty picture on the wall. Then my father stepped into the picture, in search of Ben. Tom and I followed.

Ben appeared pleased to see us, if a little bewildered. He dropped his hammer—it seemed he had just begun some small repair on the hut—and wiped sweat from his face with the back of his hand. It was a humid day. He smiled unsteadily.

'Thought we'd just drop up and see you,' my father explained. 'And see how you were getting on with—well, with this land of yours.'

'Yes,' Tom said. 'That's right.' As an afterthought he added ambiguously, 'We've heard a lot about it.'

'Oh?' Ben said, surprised. Our pouncing on him so suddenly left him uncertain now; he looked from Tom to my father as if, at any moment, they were going to take him prisoner.

'Yes,' Tom repeated idly and unnecessarily, 'we've heard a lot about it.'

But they did not unravel that line of conversation.

'Well here it is, anyhow,' Ben said.'Or some of it. It's only half-cleared.'

'You're taking your time,' Tom observed. 'How long you been at it now?'

'A few months,' Ben said.'I forget.'

'Taking your time all right,' Tom said.

'Oh yes,' Ben said. 'I'm taking my time.' He fetched a tin of tobacco from his pocket and, leaning stiffly against the hut with an appearance of being casual, began to roll himself a cigarette. I could see he was concentrating on the cigarette out of unease; he made it slowly and carefully. When satisfied the cigarette was a craftsmanlike job, he lit it, let the smoke curl slowly from his mouth and looked more confident.

'You could burn it off quicker,' Tom said. He seemed to have forgotten he had agreed to let my father do the talking. 'This scrub's dry as hell. You could burn it off a lot quicker.'

'And half the hills,' my father added quietly.

'Yes,' Ben said soberly. I suppose I could burn it off quicker.'

'This manuka, though,' Tom went on. 'You could chop it up, sell it for firewood. There's enough of it here.'

'Yes,' Ben said vaguely, lost between Tom's alternatives. 'I suppose there is.'

Then my father took charge. 'What is it you're doing, Ben?' he asked gently.

'Doing?' Ben said. 'I'm clearing this land. That's what I'm doing.'

'Yes,' my father said patiently.'I know that. But—' He hesitated, looked away from Ben, and studied the distant sea. 'But, I mean—what are your plans?'

'Plans?' Ben said indifferently.

'You must have some plan. Or plans.'

'Well,' said Ben. 'I plan to clear this land. Later on I might knock up a better hut.'

That wasn't the kind of answer my father wanted at all, but that was the way the conversation went. They would talk about one thing and another, and then Tom or father would ask the question again; and Ben, with strange stubborness, would never get further than saying he planned to clear the land and maybe, later on, knock up a better hut.

I didn't find their conversation very interesting. I left them talking, and wandered away. I noticed tiny new green shoots of manuka beginning to grow again where Ben had first cleared the scrub. Perhaps Uncle Tom had noticed that too, before he said Ben was taking his time. If Ben wasn't careful, I decided, he'd soon have a whole lot of new scrub to clear. There wasn't much interesting to see around the land, so I studied the hut.

They were still, the three of them, talking away; they didn't seem to be getting anywhere, still saying the same things over again. And very quietly, as if afraid of themselves. Only Tom, now and then, appeared a little irritated. I expected, from all that had gone before, some wild argument when Tom and my father met Ben. Not this quietness, this gentleness. I couldn't understand it at all. And, outside their talk, under the hills, there was silence; the breeze carried the sound of the sea faintly up from the beach. It was late afternoon and the sun was striking yellow on the hills. I couldn't imagine a place more different from Ben's quarter-acre suburban section, noisy with children, crowded among houses, with its patch of garden. Perplexed, I gave my attention to the hut and went inside.

The floor was earthen. The bed was a couple of old blankets strewn on a mattress of green fern. Beside the bed lay a shovel, a pick, an axe and a rifle. In one corner there was a blackened kerosene lamp and a box of matches; near it a couple of tattered paperbacks, Western novels, with cover-pictures of lone riders in silhouette against vast sagebrushed landscapes. There was a fireplace, a heap of ash and charred stumps in a tin chimney; and near by, some food—one or two tins of baked beans, a lamb chop half-wrapped in paper, a loaf of bread. And a black billy, a chipped cup, an enamel plate, a knife and fork. And that was all. I stood there, in the dimness, trying to conjure some meaning out of them all. But those scattered objects obstinately remained objects; they didn't connect, they didn't make the music for which my mind was numbly searching. They brushed past me lightly, leaves in a wind, leaving me empty-handed, puzzled, and a little dismayed.

Feeling vaguely cheated, I went outside; I was irritated at myself for still being so much a child. Ben was hospitably offering to boil a billy of tea. But Tom, looking at his watch, said it was time for us to start back. Was Ben heading back for the city too?

'In a little while,' Ben said amiably. 'I'm in no hurry. I've got a bit more work.'

'I see,' Tom said tightly. I could see the afternoon hadn't been a success at all. Tom held himself in as if to prevent an explosion. My father kicked idly at a lump of earth. They both, after all their talk with Ben, seemed as empty-handed as I had been, a minute before, in the half-light of the hut.

'For Christ's sake,' Tom burst out abruptly. 'Won't you tell us?'

'Tell you what?' Ben said mildly.

'What it's all about,' Tom said. He gestured, despairingly, at the hut, the shattered scrub. 'All this.'

Father reached out and took Tom gently by the shoulder. 'Don't you see, Tom?' he said. 'It's no use. Don't start again.'

Angrily Tom shook away my father's restraining hand. 'No,' he agreed bitterly. 'It's no use.' He turned away, angry at Ben, my father, and himself at everything and everyone; at a world so absurd that you might find in it a man who, for no good reason, deserted his home and family every week-end to chop endlessly and pointlessly away at a few acres of scrub. He stumbled off blindly. 'What the hell's the use?' we heard him say. Then he was gone.

Father smiled wistfully at Ben; there seemed some flash of intimacy, of understanding, between them. He held up his hands hopelessly. Well, he seemed to say, that's Tom for you. But he appeared also to be saying something else—not only that he understood, but that understanding made him helpless; so there was nothing he could do or say. Ben might have caught the message; I don't know. His eyes had their distant look again.

We said good-bye to Ben and followed Tom. We looked back, once, and saw Ben standing by his hut, on his land; he seemed at home, part of everything. And, oddly, he looked happy. Behind him the hills were coloured with sunset.

I should like to end there, for what happened afterwards is confused. We didn't see Ben for months, perhaps a year; and Tom, despairing of my father, never came near us with any news. We heard Tom had elected to spend part of his week-ends keeping Ben's home and family in order. He painted the house and tidied the garden.

Grandfather Benjamin died. He dropped dead early one sunny spring morning after milking his last cow and going into breakfast. He was nearly eighty. BUSH-FARMER WHO FOUGHT INJUSTICE DIES, said the headline above one newspaper obituary.

The funeral was a family reunion. At the service his sons stood lined like heavy stone figures in the church. It came as a surprise to me that a man as immense as my grandfather could be contained, without protest, in so relatively small a box. His sons took the casket effortlessly on their shoulders and, large and dark, they trod the sunlit aisle out of the church. The rest of us, the wives and sisters, children and friends, followed along the aisle. But our grief seemed light and unworthy beside theirs. And this appeared to be acknowledged at the graveside; for, after the text was read, the last words spoken, the crowd eddied and thinned away, leaving the seven sons motionless together, as they had been in the church, seven dark sentinels beside the grave.

Afterwards the family fell apart. My grandmother was ailing; she could no longer have too many visitors to the family home, and that had always been the meeting-place.

We heard Tom had Ben under control at last. No one knew quite how he had managed it, or what pressure he had used. But somehow he had shamed Ben into abandoning and selling his land, and reconciled him with his home and family. I suppose we imagined Ben pottering in his garden again at week-ends, like a good family man. Perhaps he did, for a while; but that picture of him soon ripped down the middle before it could even fray at the edges.

Ben, who had always been moderate in most things, was drinking heavily. And one day, climbing up to the cabin of his crane, after a lunch-hour spent in a bar, he fell from the ladder to the wharf. He lived another week.

That was a dozen years or more ago. I had cause to recall it all last summer. Just back from a few years in Europe, I was on holiday with my wife and year-old son, passing through Auckland on our way to a remote beach in the north. Auckland, the sleepy city of my childhood, was changed. It had become busy, brash, a city of the Pacific like Sydney or San Francisco, complete with harbour bridge. New buildings pushed up the central city skyline; new suburbs strutted out across the land. The Symonds Street windmill was long gone, a wave of ugly warehouses washed the slopes of Parnell hill, and there were sentimental letters in the newspapers about clearing undergrowth from the colonists' graves in Grafton gully. The summer heat struck trembling off the long shiny cars crowding noisy Queen Street and bustling Karangahape Road; the old rattling tramcars had gone, and in their place trolley-buses glided. There were expresso coffee-bars instead of fish-and-chip shops, beatniks and American tourists, and television aerials sprouting like strange parasite growth from city roof-tops.

We drove through the city, across the bridge. Where we should, according to my childhood memory, have emerged into open country, we were riding through new suburbs, new shopping centres. I was vaguely impressed and then, as the city lengthened, depressed.

We had hardly reached the countryside when I saw the turn-off I remembered to Kauri Bay. I pulled the car over to the side of the road and asked my wife if we were in a hurry. She said we weren't particularly. My son was asleep. So we took the turn-off. I had the idea I might find Ben's hut, tell my wife Ben's story.

If I'd had any sense, I would have turned back as soon as I saw the change. The road down to Kauri Bay was no longer rough and stony; it was trimly sealed. The hills which rose dreary and scrub-covered in my memory were sleek and green with grass. I wondered if aerial topdressing, or perhaps some new fertilizer, had done the trick and turned gumland into good pasture. Otherwise the hills simply weren't the same hills, and I was on the wrong road. I was just considering this problem when a large, crowded bus lumbered up round a corner of a hill and nearly pushed us off the road. I concentrated on my driving and we cruised safely down to the sea.

We had arrived in Kauri Bay, all right; there was no doubt about it.

But the city had arrived some years before. First weekend cottages had felt out the land, like an advance guard; they ran the length of the beach and scattered up the hills each side. Some looked pleasant and modern, with large windows to trap a fine seascape. But behind them, climbing the easy slopes at the back of the beach, was a battalion of homes. Neat square houses on the green quarter-acre sections beloved of New Zealanders. There was even a chromed shopping centre, and the growing skeleton of some new building, perhaps a pub or cinema or just another store. There might have been a good deal more I didn't see.

I didn't even stop the car. I drove slowly the length of the beach, turned and, while my wife sat beside me in baffled silence, drove out of Kauri Bay. Odd and unpredictable herself, it seldom occurs to her to question strange behaviour in others. I was glad of it that day; glad she accepted it all, that strange and apparently pointless detour, without asking a question.

As we travelled north I found myself, after a while, wondering if somewhere in that pleasant new suburb, somewhere among those neat square houses and trim green quarter-acres, there existed still, on one forgotten or forsaken corner of land, an old leaning hut. I might have found it still there, somewhere, if I had looked. I suppose I didn't look only because I was afraid I might not find it.

The Wind and the Spray

1

When Susan's letter came, Mark was baffled and obscurely alarmed.

He had risen early, trying to clear away a hangover with hot black coffee. The letter was in a packet of mail and newspapers which Tommy Patu had dropped into the homestead on his way back into the hills from the village the previous night: it might have remained undiscovered if Mark had not, when reaching for a pack of cigarettes, knocked the packet with his elbow and sent it exploding across the floor. The letter from Panama, with its exotic yellow stamp, lay vivid on the scarred linoleum.

He read the first few lines, crumpled the crisp pages, balled them into the pocket of his shorts, and plodded barefoot out on to the veranda of the homestead. Across the harbour the hills already blazed with day. There was still a mild haze on the water, with flashes of silvery light beneath. The tide rose shining through the mangroves at the foot of the farm. Even out at the entrance of the harbour, where westerlies had sent white horses galloping across the sand-bar for three days, the sea was calm.

He sat in shade, blinking and rubbing his eyes. The coffee was bitter in his mouth and the first cigarette smoke acid on his throat. Presently he took the pages from his pocket and smoothed them on his knee. He began to read slowly.

You never know anything, he thought. You never know anything at all.

The truth was that if it hadn't been for Susan, Mark might never have returned to the farm.

He had, after all, fled the farm and the dour ghosts of his ancestors, like his brother; but, unlike his brother, who felt at a sufficient remove in a suburban garden, Mark wished eventually to put an even greater distance between himself and childhood. He saw scholarship as his salvation; he imagined himself gowned and cloistered securely as a monk, buried among tomes behind ivied walls—in Oxford perhaps, or Cambridge, though it didn't really matter where. That was why he applied himself to university with such devotion; and it was then he first met Susan, at a time when he still considered himself a student of a serious kind, one who could not easily afford the luxury of university romance. He was in his second year, Susan in her first. She too was indulging in rebellion, rather more spectacularly than Mark. Quarrelling with her modestly wealthy parents, she had just switched from the Student Christian Club to the Student Socialist Club; and given herself over to gipsy ear-rings, gaudy head-scarves, and sweaters of plummeting neckline. Though actually rather unremarkable, moderately attractive and naively ambitious, she touched and almost overwhelmed Mark— himself so slow, heavy and thoughtful—with her marvellously aggressive innocence. But his enthusiasm for innocence, like his enthusiasm for study, soon flagged.

Two or three years afterwards, at the time he met her again, university dragged at him like a dead weight of sickness. He had simply lost interest. The farm, grown so remote, seemed no longer a menace; the city had captured him. Students he once knew were either overseas, perhaps studying at Oxford, or settled in suburbia, unhappily married, and avoiding him in the street. He drifted into bohemia and wrote, like a pledge of membership, unpublished verse; he wandered the waterfront, yarned to the old men sunning themselves, and watched the seagulls and the ships; he bought drinks for sad, talkative strangers in dim bars. He learned of other farms forsaken, old hopes abandoned; the land, after all, had already washed thousands of driftwood lives, wave on wave, into the asphalt wastes of New Zealand's sprawling cities. He was in no way unique. And if he was in any particular different, it was simply because unlike them—the wistful old men and the sad strangers—he had no desire to return to the land.

He saw Susan again, and to his surprise, on the stage, in an amateur performance of *Hamlet*. The play was poorly produced, and Susan's Ophelia no more than a brave attempt, but the evening, for Mark, was transfigured by his discovery of Susan in so startling a guise. He waited for her at the stage door afterwards. That was, perhaps, where their affair really began. She sparkled on seeing him. 'I'm glad,' she announced, 'that I've found someone, at last, who takes me seriously.' But the truth was that Mark felt sorry rather than serious, intrigued rather than concerned.

Their engagement came suddenly. Susan was offered a small role with a touring company; her parents were unhappy about the proposition, and Susan called in Mark to help. To convince her puritan parents that she could not lose her good name she wished, first of all, to become respectably engaged. Mark failed to see the point of this elaborate subterfuge; there was, as he observed, no reason why an engagement ring should specially protect a girl from the ravaging immorality of the theatre. Much later Mark understood that Susan really wanted the engagement for another reason altogether. He was to act as a kind of insurance policy against her failure in the theatre. If she could not make something of the theatre, she would make something of Mark; and Mark, at that time, did not even have enough money for an engagement ring. Susan bought the ring, Mark placed it on her finger, and Susan's father, a bluff prosperous city lawyer, talked to Mark man to man over a bottle of Johnnie Walker.

'You'll have to be careful with our girl, you know,' he told Mark. 'In her time she's picked up a lot of ideas.'

'Ideas?' Mark said, perplexed.

'Yes,' he said flatly. 'Ideas.' He cleared his throat and added confidently, 'But I shouldn't worry. They grow out of them, you know.'

Susan's mother, on the other hand, still regarded Mark with some suspicion, even though he discarded his worn corduroys and dressed well for his visits to Susan's home. 'Your father's a farmer?' she said.

'That's right,' Mark answered casually.

'And what do you plan to be? A farmer too?'

'Not exactly,' Mark said evasively.

'Mark is already something,' Susan interjected.

'Oh?'

'Yes,' said Susan sweetly. 'Mark is a poet.'

'Well,' said her mother, even more sweetly, 'his father will need to be a very rich farmer, won't he?'

Mark listened with detachment. They might have been talking about a stranger. He felt he had brought it all off rather well. Never in his life had he felt less involved. Never in his life had he been committed to anything so casually.

Then Susan went off on tour.

Mark, the morning of her unexpected return, had already been awake some time, though it was too early to rise; there was the soft beat of a sea breeze on his windows, the rattle of tramcars in the street outside. In peaceful mood, he considered the prospect of an actress wife; and found it congenial. She would, involved with her own career, make no great demands; the more so if she were to spend long periods of time away from home. It appeared that he had, by accident, come across the means for a perfect truce with the world.

Then the door crashed open and Susan blazed in. 'Why didn't you write to me?' she cried. 'Is that any way to keep a fiancée?' She paused for breath while he dragged himself from bed, she looked about his untidy room with disgust. 'How can you go on like this? You live like a pig in this slum. I'm taking you out for something to eat. You look as if you need it. Then we're going to have a really serious talk, you and me.'

They breakfasted in a small truck-drivers' cafe on the waterfront. Mark learned about Susan's disastrous tour. It appeared that Susan had fallen ill for a few days; another actress, in an even smaller role, had taken her place and done very well indeed. Also this actress had slept with the producer. After illness Susan found herself relegated to the smaller role; she decided she was finished with the theatre. Through the plate-glass window of the cafe, as Susan talked, Mark wistfully studied the glittering sea, the busy white ferries travelling the harbour; his view was blocked now and then by unloaded crowds of neat accountants and leggy typists scurrying to their nine o'clock jobs. They and Susan together produced in him a thickening despair. 'What do you think they'd say?' Susan demanded.

'Who?' he said, distracted.

'My parents,' she said.

He felt baffled, but he felt also that he should retain some grip on the conversation. 'I've never noticed you worrying much about what they say,' he observed generally and amicably.

'Of course I worry,' Susan said firmly. 'They've been very kind and very patient. And in return I've only been unfair—I see it all now. And it's all finished.'

'Finished?'

'Finished. I've made up my mind. I've tried their patience long enough and far enough. But what do you think they'd say?'

'About what?' he said, still puzzled.

'About you, of course. And the kind of life you live.'

'I don't know,' he said frankly, and applied himself diligently to his ham and eggs.

'I don't think you've listened to a word I've been saying. I think you've just been staring out that window.'

It was useless to deny it.

'And what's more,' she added huskily. 'I don't think you really care.'

He was about to reply that he didn't, particularly, when he looked up, seeking the cause of the sudden strangeness in her voice, and saw her lower lip tremble. For a moment he seemed suspended motionless, powerless, in a curious vacuum. Why, he thought, she's about to weep. She's about to weep because of me; what have I done, or what haven't I?

Then she did weep. He thought of her calamitous stage career, of her absurd engagement; and pity, without warning, overwhelmed him. 'Of course I do,' he submitted finally. 'Of course I care.'

'Then behave as if you do.'

'I expect I could try,' he conceded, feeling suddenly tired.

'I know you'll see it my way, Mark,' she declared, drying her eyes. 'After all, we've both had our little fling, haven't we? You've had your poetry and I've had my acting. Now it's time to grow up.'

Growing up meant looking for a job, improving his dress, finding a better room. The job was the most difficult thing. 'It's just that you've been too confused to find anything,' Susan said briskly. 'Finish your degree, and we'll decide on something together.'

She decided he could be a schoolteacher. He felt trapped by his one foolish moment of pity; doors seemed to be slamming shut behind him. He enrolled to train as a teacher and began to drink heavily. One Sunday afternoon, arriving drunk on a visit to Susan's parents, he staggered against a frail table and sent a precious china tea-set smashing to the floor.

'You see?' Susan said afterwards. 'They took it rather well, all things considered. The main thing now is to pull yourself together.'

After that he tried not to drink before visiting Susan's home. This resulted in his drinking becoming more concentrated, and damaging, in other parts of the week. On the whole Susan was so very calm, so very reasonable, that the more he drank the more sorry for her he became. When he discovered this, he stopped drinking, sat his examinations and got his degree; and then felt obscurely that he had done it all under false pretences. For Susan's satisfaction was altogether alarming; she took him out to prickly parties where he was displayed sleek in a dark suit, like a prize unwrapped.

The game, he decided, had gone far enough. He'd only wanted, after all, to give Susan back some confidence in herself. Surely he'd done that. But where, to call a stop? So when she discussed marriage, he tried to phrase his objections in the abstract. He said marriage corrupted character; in fact he didn't believe in marriage.

'Don't split hairs,' she replied.

Susan, carrying about their future like so much weighty baggage, had no time for unimportant side-issues. Yet there was no excuse for leading her along. Guilt-stricken, he began to drink again; and out of pure desperation one night picked a trivial argument with her. This led, presently, to Susan announcing, 'It's just that you want to go to bed with me, isn't it? Why don't you come right out with it?'

Until then it hadn't struck him that Susan might have some guilt of her own.

'Don't be silly,' he answered. Then, despite himself, he added impulsively, 'But seeing you've raised the subject, I must say you haven't been very encouraging in that direction anyway.'

'I see it all very clearly now,' she said curtly. 'That's all you want. I see it all very clearly indeed.'

'For God's sake,' he cried. This is ridiculous.'

'Exactly. I don't really see any point in talking to you. You're just deliberately working yourself up into a mood. Look at yourself. Look at the way you're dressed. Those frightful corduroys again. And you might at least have combed your hair.'

It was about that time he began to think about the farm. He saw he'd been too preoccupied with city problems to consider the farm as a refuge. With Susan he gently tested the subject. 'You know,' he said, 'Dad's getting old now, and I thought—'

'Yes,' she replied swiftly. 'We'll see about making a visit sometime, I expect. When we're a little less busy. That's what you mean, isn't it? Just a short visit. You don't surely mean—'

'No,' he agreed. 'Of course not.' He found her reaction entirely satisfactory.

Then, when his father died, the farm became an issue. His mother had already been dead six years; his civil servant brother, the only other member of the family, announced after they returned to the city from the funeral that he wanted the farm sold. Susan also wanted the farm sold. Mark devised intricate excuses for delaying his own decision. Susan became anxious.

The crisis came one night when he returned to his room late and found Susan draped invitingly upon his bed. The situation did not even have the virtue of ambiguity. It was as if, in disposing herself so carelessly, she had tripped some warning signal; alarms sang all around him. He blundered about the room, ransacking drawers, packing suitcases. Susan sat up on the bed, distraught and dismayed. 'What are you doing?'

'Going back,' he announced. He squeezed some books into a suitcase and thumped down the lid. 'To the farm.'

'But you can't,' she said sensibly.

'You know something?' he said. 'I think I'll make up my own mind.'

The next day he came to a hard-driven financial arrangement with his brother, and discovered himself sole owner of the farm. Afterwards he said good-bye to Susan, ———————

'You won't last two weeks,' she said. 'But don't expect to find me here when you come back.'

'No?' He managed to sound disappointed.

'No. I'm going back to the theatre. And I'm going to England to study.'

'To England?' he said with mild dismay.

'Naturally. I'm told people are a little more civilized there. You hear that? Civilized.' She paused before she stamped defiantly out of his life. 'You think you can escape everything, don't you? Well, I wouldn't be too sure about that. You can't escape so easily.'

He considered this pronouncement, dismissed it as vague and obscure, and went back to the farm, shorn of problems, with a tremendous feeling of relief. Already, in the last months in the city, he had discovered a sentimental regard for the farm; something compounded from boyhood memories of crystal mornings, smoky sunsets, brown salty flesh, fishing trips, bush and sea and sky. As a child he had, of course, also trudged beside his stolid pipe-smoking countryman father and heard how his ancestors had hewn farm and homestead from the virgin forest; they all, those hard-working and god-fearing folk, seemed to have elected as their permanent representative in the homestead Mark's gaunt, bearded great-grandfather. His portrait glared down from the wall in the library. After a month or two back on the farm, Mark turned the portrait to the wall.

The homestead, largest and oldest pioneer building surviving in the district, was a rambling white place with sagging doors and squealing hinges, draughty in winter, cool in summer. Apart from the homestead he also owned a broken-down launch, which he thought pointless to repair, and an antique Ford, in which he often jolted along through the patchy, desolate landscape. He took an interest again in photography, a hobby forgotten since adolescence, and clicked his camera at tumbling buildings and garrulous old men. He listened to their stories of past wild times on gumfields now ransacked, in timber mills now forsaken. He even played, for a while, with the idea of becoming local historian. He was well placed for it. From the homestead he could look down on beaches where some of the country's first settlers, hesitant among swarms of brown men, had found the substance of a new country, and perhaps new hope, at last beneath their feet. There they were stranded with their forlorn possessions when the ships crowded with white sail vanished with a flutter of farewell across the sandbar and behind the discoloured headlands at the entrance of the harbour. There they might have been given pause, with a moment of pure wonder, before they launched themselves like assassins upon the forest. Afterwards, for a time, the district had thrived, and the harbour was busy with shipping. But now the last of the forest was tumbled, the last of the precious gum filched from the earth; energy went south, like the ships and the sound of the axe, and only farms lingered among the stripped hills.

Mark had never seen his new life in terms of cream cheques. He found it possible to leave most of the practical things to Rangi, the amiable old Maori sharemilker, who was already quite happily milking the dwindled herd anyway; and to give himself entirely to the business of living at peace with the world. He meditated, sprawled on the veranda on sunlit mornings, on sea and shore and sky; recalled, with incredulity, the life he had lately lived in the city; recollected, with astonishment, the ambitions he had once had for Europe, for wilder seas and wider shores. They all seemed positively unreal now.

He received, like a thin cry from the past, a note from Susan. It was brief, and expressed the unlikely hope that he was happy. She enclosed a photograph of herself in Paris, sitting on the steps of the Sacre Coeur. Her face was slightly blurred, but it was evident she was smilng. He put the photograph away carefully, so that he might find it again, but later, when he went looking, he could not find it. He was not greatly disturbed. It was certainly around the homestead, some place or other. He fetched a book and a bottle of beer and went out on the veranda to study the morning.

He soon ceased to care about what the thin-blooded pakehas said about him down in the village. He was, they said, a disgrace to his father and family, the way he let the farm go to seed, did nothing while the homestead fell to pieces around him, and ran wild with Maoris.

Sometimes old friends from the city called. They complimented him on his choice of life, said he looked happy, and fled back to the city.

These encounters tended to irritate him. After one in particular he began writing a projected three-volume work titled *The Anatomy of Tranquillity*. It was left unfinished, after ten untidily written pages, when Tommy Patu took him out on a shooting trip up harbour. Later, more modestly, he converted it into a short essay, re-titled it *Several Good Reasons for being a Polynesian,* and sent it away for publication. When he had gathered sufficient rejection slips, he read it aloud sometimes, to amuse visitors from the city, and finally mislaid the manuscript somewhere about the house.

With wife and infant son, his brother came up on holiday from the city. His brother, who had acquired a toothbrush moustache and a crisp military tone in the civil service, complained about the the small mountain of beer-bottles outside the back door; his sister-in-law, who didn't know how Mark managed without washing-machine or refrigerator, complained that there was a smell somewhere. Only their toddler son, who was not yet of an age to complain, appeared happy and was delighted to wander hand in hand with his Uncle Mark. After three days they shifted to a resort down the coast. 'Jesus, boy,' his brother said, before departing, 'I just wish you could see yourself, that's all. I just wish you could see yourself.'

He shook his head in pity, crammed family and luggage into his sleek shiny car, and drove away. Mark, watching the dust clear, shook his own head in bewilderment, and went fishing.

Huia, Rangi's daughter, found him on the rocks after sunset. Huia was a tall, fiercely upright girl with quick bright eyes and a sharp, disconcerting intelligence. She and Mark had known each other as children. But after her tubercular mother died, and Rangi made a vain and fumbling attempt to bring her up, she went off to a convent for education. For some years she nursed in a city hospital. Lately she had been back at the farm on prolonged holiday. Rangi sometimes sent her up to the homestead to cook for Mark. Barefoot, a flax kit of shellfish on her shoulder, she came upon him softly. 'What you doing?' she asked, startling him from thought.

'Fishing. What does it look like?'

'But the tide's out,' she observed. 'It's no use fishing now.'

His line, made silver in the last light, trailed away across puddled sand and lank seaweed into shallow water. 'I don't suppose it is,' he agreed finally. It occurred to him that he had not even baited the line for several hours. He began to wind it in.

'Where are they?' Huia said.

'Who?'

'Your visitors. Where are they?'

'Them? They've gone.' He wound in the last of the line and, rising, hitched his trousers. 'The party's over.'

Huia did not seem greatly surprised. 'Nice little boy they had,' she said conversationally.

'Yes. Lovely little kid. Followed me everywhere. I got on very well with him. More than I can say of his parents.'

'I saw you with him. You'd make a good father.'

'I doubt it. Not me.'

Huia grinned. 'Anyway,' she said, 'I bet you've had nothing to eat all day.'

'No. Not really.'

'I'll come up and fix you something.'

'Funny thing,' Mark said. 'I'll miss that kid.'

They walked up to the farm together. Huia, her legs dark against the pale grass, ran into the sharemilker's cottage to drop her kit of shellfish. Mark continued up to the belt of pines near the homestead and waited for her there. The dusk was perfect, with a thin melting light on the water, and the ocean only a murmur out on the sand-bar. In the west pastel cloud survived the sunset; in the east there was already a scatter of stars. The pines were drenched with the thick smell of summer. He heard the door of the cottage bang, and then Huia's feet travelling lightly across the dry grass. She seemed to rise as a swimmer might, surfacing strangely from the liquid blue evening. 'So you're all alone again,' she laughed.

She went about the kitchen brisk and efficient, slicing steaks, preparing a meal. He sat at the table, uncapped a bottle of beer, and watched her with curiosity. 'Huia,' he asked presently, 'why did you leave the city?'

'I don't know,' she said. 'Too much noise, maybe.'

'But you had a good job, didn't you? Why did you leave it?'

'I don't know.' She tossed her head. 'Too many bosses, maybe.'

'Why did you come back here, then?'

'You ask a terrible lot of questions.' She tossed her head again and her hair flashed black and bright.

'Don't you miss things?'

'I'm all right,' she said.

'But wouldn't you,' he persisted, 'like to get around and see things, see some more of the world?'

'I got enough of the world here, thanks very much. I don't want any more.'

'Wouldn't you like to see Europe? Wouldn't you like to go to England?'

'But what for?' she said, astonished. 'I belong here.'

'They're very civilized there. So I'm told.'

'Hell,' said Huia. 'The way you talk.'

'But wouldn't you like,' he continued, ignoring her and conducting a private and obscure argument with himself, 'to go to Paris, for example? And,' he added presently, 'have your photograph taken on the steps of the Sacre Coeur?'

'My word,' Huia said, busy over the stove, 'you do ask a terrible lot of questions.'

That night, after walking Huia home through the pines, he sat troubled in the library. The weather was changing. A wind risen from the sea came clashing through the pines, creaking through the homestead. He closed the windows against the summer storm and looked along the bookshelves for something to read. He found a book, buried and grown dusty since the depression years, on the theory of Social Credit.

He blew off the dust and flicked through the pages, regarding the book with amusement until a disquieting thought overtook him. Then he flung the book across the room into the fireplace where it settled under an explosion of dust and last winter's ash. If he were living on credit, and social credit at that, just how much more did he have?

His brother would probably know. That bastard knew everything. Susan would probably know too. She was another one who knew everything.

He went outside, looked at the seething night, and retreated to bed.

The morning of the second day after the storm, rising early, he saw Huia plodding in gumboots down to the cowsheds. In tight jeans, the sleeves of Rangi's old patched shirt rolled above her elbows, she looked very businesslike. He called her name and she waited, smiling and patient, until he caught up with her. 'Rangi's not so good this morning,' she explained. 'So I'm doing the milking.'

'In that case I might as well give you a hand.'

'You're up early,' she observed. 'After being up so late.'

'How did you know? Was there much noise?'

'Not much. Guitars and singing, mostly. It sounded like a good party.'

'Sorry if it kept you awake,' he said. 'I tried to keep it quiet. It was Tommy Patu's fault, really. He arrived round with a lot of people just when I was going off to bed. Everything just sort of—' He broke off, seeing her smile.

'No need to apologize. Just ask me along next time.'

'All right,' he promised. 'I will.'

In the cowshed he made a vain attempt to start the milking machine. Hands on hips, Huia watched him with amusement. 'Tell me just one thing,' she said. 'You ever done that before?'

'Not really.'

'Then maybe you better let me do it.' She shifted him aside, slid expertly round the machine, and started the engine. Then she went quickly about the business of milking the cows. He followed her about the shed, marvelling politely at her energy. 'You make it look so damn easy,' he said.

'It is,' she insisted. 'Look, do you really want to help with the milking? Or is it just me you want to help?'

'I imagine it's you.'

'Well if you're just helping because of me, maybe you'd be better down the rocks. The tide's in and there ought to be good fishing. I'll see you there later. If you stay here, you only distract me.'

Disconsolate, he wandered away from the cowshed and down to the sea. Finally, waiting for Huia, he fell asleep on the warm rocks. When he woke the sun was high in the sky and Huia's shadow cool across his face. She was barefoot again, the kit over her shoulder, her loose hair tied with a blue ribbon, the jeans rolled above her bare brown knees. 'Ready?' she said.

'What's in the kit?'

'Lunch, and swimming togs.'

'Mine too?'

'Yours too.'

'Well,' he said.'You think of everything, don't you?'

'I try,' she smiled.

They tramped out to the heads. Away from the inland part of the harbour, a mild breeze cooled them. Near the heads there was a small white beach, overhung with fern and pohutukawa, where giant rocks cast sharp patterns of shade. They rested and then went separate behind the rocks to change.

Stripped for the water, Huia was brown and sturdy. She swam with precision. They raced out to a rock which rose, some distance from the beach, in a choppy tidal rip. They stroked together evenly and steadily and together fell breathless upon the rock. 'You mightn't be able to milk cows,' Huia gasped, 'but you can certainly swim.' Mark felt dizzy from the effort: the horizon see-sawed and settled. For a while they lay face down, surrendering to the sun while the water slapped at their feet. When Mark stirred, Huia shifted.

'No funny business,' she instructed.

'I wasn't thinking of any, exactly,' he said. He sat up on the rock, hugging his knees, while Huia drowsed again. There was a steady booming of sea across the sand-bar, and gulls drifted high above the falling spray. Now and then, wandering like a spotlight through the wild white spray, the sun lit vanishing rainbows.

'A lot of people died out there,' Mark said suddenly.

'What's that?' Huia sat up, startled.

'Sorry,' he said. 'Just thinking aloud. Didn't mean to give you a fright. I was thinking how a lot of people died out there. Trying to get across the sand-bar in the old days. It just struck me that now nobody wants to get across the bar, one way or the other, any more. I wonder how long since anyone's done it? A long time, probably. That must have been how quite a few people first saw this country, the wind and spray in their faces as they came riding in over the bar.'

Huia looked at him with open curiosity, then spread herself on the rock again. 'I remember Rangi telling me stories when I was a little girl,' she murmured.

'They say if you go out there on a calm day, you can see the masts of some wrecked ship sticking out above the water.'

'I've heard that too,' she said. 'But I've never seen it.'

'That doesn't prove it isn't there, though,' Mark persisted. 'There must be a few ships, and people buried down there somewhere.'

'Well?' said Huia. 'So what? You can't bring them back again.'

'No. That's the one thing you can't do.'

Huia began humming a tune softly to herself.

'There's one story,' Mark continued, 'about an immigrant ship sinking out there. They were on their way south to settle. All the land here had gone by then.'

'I know,' Huia said. Pinched off us. We looked up to heaven while you stole the land.'

'Not my family,' Mark said defensively. 'We've supposed to have bought ours honestly.'

'For a few guns, a couple of blankets and a bit of jewellery. Maybe a Bible too. Go on. It doesn't matter. Tell me about the ship.'

'Nothing much to tell, really. Perhaps it was trying to get in here to shelter from a storm, make a few repairs or something. Nobody really knew. There was nobody alive to tell. It just sank out there. That's all the story.' Mark paused and looked out over the water. Huia closed her eyes and began to breathe evenly. She seemed asleep.

Well, he thought, it wasn't quite all the story. How could it have been? Were they out on deck, those thin sun-starved English faces lining the rail, the men in suits and the women in bonnets, while the sight and smell of their new country grew around them? Probably not; probably the weather was rough, the waves high, and they were fastened sick in cabins and steerage as the ship lurched and slipped beneath a misty sea. Already coffined, denied sight of their promised land, they would not even have had, at that last moment, the wind and the spray in their faces. So, however else it might have been, it had been cruel: too cruel.

'I wonder what they wanted,' he said.

'What's that?' Huia asked sleepily.

'I wonder what they wanted. All those people. The ones who died out there and the ones who didn't—the ones who made it over the bar.'

'Like your folks, you mean?'

'If you like. Yes. Like my folks.'

'Don't ask me. I only belong here.'

'I mean it must have been something more than just escape. Don't you think so? It must have been something more than just that they were failures back there where they came from. A country deserves something better than being a refuge for failure, wouldn't you say?'

'The way you talk,' she said.

'They must have wanted something very special. To come all that way, to take all those chances. Don't you think so?'

'I don't know. You tell me.'

'Well, I don't know what they wanted, exactly. Except that this was just about the last place left in the world to take a new chance, to begin all over again. Perhaps they didn't know what they wanted exactly either; perhaps that was their trouble. I can only tell you the one thing they didn't want.'

'What's that?'

'The same damn thing all over again.' He sprang to his feet.

'Hey,' Huia cried, 'what are you getting so angry about? What's eating you?'

'Nothing,' he said. 'Nothing at all. Let's swim back to the beach.'

After lunch they went around the heads, climbing over rocks, and gathered shellfish. It was dusk by the time they returned to the farm. Huia cooked mussels in a batter and afterwards, as they drank tea and talked across the kitchen table, Mark felt tired and content. They talked about the homestead.

'But I still don't see why,' Huia insisted. 'Why you should let it fall down. Why you don't keep it up. What is it?'

'Let's just say I don't want anyone else to have it. I don't want anyone else to inherit it.'

'But *why?*'

His answer presented no difficulty; he had formulated it a long time before, addressing the empty kitchen, the library with the turned portrait, the broken veranda, the sea-invaded rocks. He'd walked with the why of it so long now, these last months, that he knew the answer better than he knew anything else in the world. 'Why? So that after I die, as the beams fall, the walls tumble, the bush will grow through it again. So that one day perhaps some kids, out shooting and fishing, will find it collapsed and tangled with green. Kids of your colour. Tommy Patu's kids maybe. So they'll find it and wonder at the foolishness of it. And kids of my colour, who might find it too, will wonder at the shame of it. Or perhaps, and even better, kids of no colour—no colour because they'll be the same—will find it, and play about the ruin. Yes; I like that even better.'

'You mean you want this place like a monument?'

'No. Like a memory. A monument stays. A memory fades.'

'All very poetic,' Huia said. 'You ever wrote poems?'

'Once. Before I started trying to live one.'

'I see,' she said, puzzled.

Huia was uneasy. After sunset the homestead filled with small strange noises as the old warped timber and corrugated roof, creaking and cracking, contracted in the cool of night.

'I better go,' she said finally, rinsing her cup. 'I think Rangi'll be expecting me down at the cottage.'

'So soon?'

'Besides,' she added quickly, 'I don't like this place at night. It's creepy. I just don't like being here.'

'All right. I'll walk you home.'

Outside they found the sky brilliant with stars. They walked in silence and in the sudden gloom of the pines he took her arm to guide her along the path; she seemed, for a moment, to flinch at his touch. He already guessed that some profound unhappiness or discontent had driven her back to the farm; the rumours he'd heard of her shattered affairs, her broken engagements, appeared only to confirm it. There was a sadness in her jaunty body. It seemed a very long time since Huia and himself, as children, had played innocently about the beaches. When she stumbled as if by accident, he caught and steadied her, and she did not pull away. She was strong in his arms. 'I thought you said no funny business,' he observed presently.

'That was this morning. I like my loving in the evening.' They emerged from the pines and found the stars again. The harbour shone faint silver and the hills were vague silhouettes. 'Besides,' she added, as if it were irrelevant, 'I like you.'

'I don't expect there's any law against that.'

'And I'll be back if you wait.' Her feet hit away and he heard voices as she entered the cottage.

He waited perhaps an hour. The lights in the cottage went out, there was no longer sound of voices, and he was alone with the rattle of insects in the night. The pines were warm and musty from the heat of day. The tide was rising, and out on the bar the waves crashed like distant guns. He heard a slight noise, perhaps a window lifting. Then the slow feet rustling across grass and crackling over pine-needles. After she had fallen near him, neither moved or spoke for a while; as if already exhausted, already depleted, they simply lay watching the brilliant sky.

A day or two later Tommy Patu called in, to tell Mark about a party. 'Sorry,' Mark said. 'I'm pretty busy about the farm these days, Tommy.'

'Jesus, boy,' Tommy said. 'What's eating you?' He looked at Mark closely. 'What you drinking these days, boy? Milk? Because it's the first time I ever seen a milk-stain on your gumboots.'

'I'm on the wagon for a bit,' Mark said. 'Taking things quietly. If you like, tell the boys it's doctor's orders.'

Together they watched Huia wander out of the pines, flickering through shadow and sunlight. She walked long-legged in tight shorts and flapping shirt; her bright hair fell about her shoulders.

'I'd say,' Tommy murmured, 'that it was nurse's orders, myself.' He climbed back on his horse and regarded Mark sadly. 'I guess I'll be seeing you sometime.'

'Sure,' Mark agreed. 'Be seeing you, Tommy.'

Huia's approach to life was straightforward. 'Take things where you find them,' she said, 'and you have fun. Start getting dragged down like everyone else and you have no fun. I'm free and I stay that way. Know why I like you? Because you're free too. You're not like everyone else. You don't want to own me.'

But towards the end of summer Mark began to suffer a strange unease; at last he collected words for the question. 'You're not,' he said, 'going back to the city?'

'I might. I don't know.'

'You mean you're thinking of it seriously?'

'I'm not thinking of anything seriously.'

'Then you are thinking of going back.'

'It's your fault,' Huia said. 'You started it. You shouldn't ask questions.'

'I thought you might like to stay on. After all, everything's gone so well and I thought—'

'You're getting like everyone else now. You want to own me.'

'That's silly. Putting it like that.'

'I thought I was safe with you. Now I know better.'

'I only meant—'

'You know why I still creep out of the window to meet you here at night?'

'Of course. Because you don't want Rangi to know.'

'And you know why I don't want Rangi to know? Because he'd be glad, not angry, if he knew. He'd like to keep me here too.'

'Naturally. Rangi's your father. And he's lonely.' Mark stopped, baffled. 'But I don't see what this has to do with him, not really.'

'It's got a lot to do with him. just like it's got a lot to do with you. Because I'm going to do what I want to do.'

'And you wouldn't marry me?' He hadn't meant to say it, at least not so soon, so suddenly.

'You haven't asked,' she said. 'Ask me properly.' He couldn't see her face in the dark, but he heard the smile in her voice.

'Won't you marry me?'

'That's nice,' she sighed. 'I like people to ask properly.'

'Well?'

'There you are,' she said. 'I was right. That proves it.'

'Proves what?'

'That you're getting like everyone else.'

Autumn became winter, and winter became spring, before Huia departed abruptly. 'I might be back,' she said. But he didn't believe it.

He began drinking heavily again that desolate summer. There were parties in the homestead, girls and guitars; a new mountain of bottles rose in the backyard.

Few people drifted up from the city now. His brother wrote to say he and his family were taking their holiday in the south.

Then Susan's letter came from Panama.

2

Of course, she wrote, *I have never really regarded our engagement as broken off. This may sound strange to you—*

He slapped at a mosquito and refilled his glass. Then he watched Rangi walking up from the cowshed to the cottage. It was still very early in the day.

—but just the same I want you to know that this is how I have always felt. Why, I've even still got your engagement ring. I tried it on my finger the other day. It still fits.

He stopped reading and wondered if he should tear up the letter, burn it, anything to stop him reading more. But she anticipated him.

You can do what you like with this letter. Tear it up or burn it, if you like.

He discovered a fuzz of sweat grown on his upper lip. He wiped it away and wondered if he should shave. He stroked his chin and found a three-day growth.

England of course was a farce. Once I was out of drama school I soon saw it was hopeless trying to get work in the theatre. I did actually get a job for three weeks in a Midlands repertory, but it seemed to make no difference when I arrived back in London. After months of tramping the streets and a bit part in a television play (oh yes, I got something) I saw it was just as hopeless. I decided I couldn't stand another English winter.

At this point he decided definitely on a shave. He was some time boiling water and finding a razor blade before actually shaving and returning, fidgety, to the letter.

You seem, in memory, such a solid, stable personality. After so many pale English faces, I remember your face as glowing honestly as the sun; after hearing clipped English voices so long, I even remember your drawl with affection. Really, you're someone I can depend on, lean on, at a time like this. It's no good expecting my friends or my parents to understand. They'll only say they told me so.

Perplexed, he read these lines again. They didn't, somehow, make entire sense. He read on down the page.

I imagine you must be really settled on the farm now. It's the best thing you could have done, really. I mean it's a healthy, active life and all that sort of thing. If I can escape up on to the farm with you after I arrive, believe me it will make a world of difference. I'm not, you understand, asking anything of you. If you can just understand my situation it will help a lot.

He lifted his eyes again and became conscious of a number of things. Of the strip of rusted guttering fallen from the roof; the broken boards of the veranda; the smashed window patched with sacking. Finally he studied a stack of sawn timber, overgrown with weeds; his father had bought the timber, years before, with the idea of repairing the homestead.

It still didn't make sense. Then he saw why. He had managed to get the pages out of order. The page he should have read earlier began:

Besides, I should tell you this—I'm in some trouble.

He decided, finally, on a bath.

As he'd once surmised, Susan knew all about social credit: certainly she appeared to know when he had exhausted his credit. Even the condition of the homestead seemed not to dismay her. They were married at the beginning of autumn, three weeks after she arrived. She had, as soon as she landed back in the country, arranged a convenient and explosive argument with her parents, so that she might have excuse for not communicating with them for some months. She didn't even write to say she had married Mark. 'It will come,' she explained, 'as a complete surprise to them—marriage, baby, everything.' Mark didn't doubt it.

At the end of autumn Susan thought she had the greater part of the homestead in reasonable condition. She became irritable, and firm about Rangi. 'But how do you know,' she said, 'that he has been looking after everything well?'

'I'd trust Rangi with anything.'

'But how do you know?'

'I don't know. I just trust him, that's all.'

'It's time you took some responsibility,' she declared.

'It seems to me I've enough responsibilities.'

'Good God,' she said. 'It's your farm, isn't it?'

Sometimes, still, he went out to look at the stars. At least they appeared unchanged.

'Another thing,' she said. 'I don't particularly like these people, these Maoris, who keep turning up here at all hours. What do they come here for, anyway?'

'They come here,' he explained, 'to pass the time of day. They come, you might say to talk about old times.'

'Old times?' She paused. 'Sometimes, honestly, I can't understand you. If you mean that these people are friends of yours, then I'm astonished and alarmed. You'd better just tell them to keep away, that's all. Why, you can't even be sure that they're honest.'

Once, escaping the homestead on the pretext of discussing business with Rangi, he went down on the rocks and shot his fishing line out into a bleak and swollen sea. He should, he thought, have seen it before. Huia had been his last chance; he'd spent the last of his credit on her. And she only left him weak, softened up for Susan. Susan happened to choose her moment well; that was all. But then the Susans of this world always seemed to choose their moments well.

He caught a small fish and compassionately threw it back into the sea. Silly, he thought: leaking blood like that, the poor little bastard is sure to be swallowed by some hungry kingfish. Shrugging, he wound in the line and walked heavily back up to the homestead.

He steered conversation, at last, to the subject which currently most interested him. 'Who was the father?' he asked.

Susan was large now, and went about the homestead with a white, strained face. She was a stranger comfortably settled in his imagination. He could not imagine a Susan any different. A Susan who did not worry about diet, dirt and draughts.

'No,' she said, after considering the question. 'No, there's no reason why I shouldn't tell you. He was an Englishman.' She paused.

'Is that all?' he said.

'What do you mean—is that all?' Susan asked, her face haggard. 'Isn't it enough?'

'I suppose it is enough. Enough for me, anyway. But I mean—is that all you've got to tell me? Was he very civilized?'

'If you must know,' she said, 'he was about forty, and married. And a television producer.'

'I see. Very civilized, probably.' He studied the surface of the kitchen table with some intensity. Then he added quietly, 'And that, I suppose, accounts for your bit part in the television play.'

There was a silence. Then he looked up and saw she was near tears.

'I don't see there's any need to be nasty,' she cried.

'Sorry. I just wondered as a matter of interest. Sorry if it sounded—'

She fled the room. Her feet struck down the passage and the door of her bedroom crashed. Presently there was the sound of prolonged, wrenching sobs. Mark seldom saw the inside of that room anyway; and it seemed inappropriate to follow her there now. Instead he sat at the table, his head in his hands, wishing he hadn't asked. He'd meant only to clear away some debris, not expecting to find pity, like a lost talisman, beneath it all.

Over the past eighteen months, long before Susan's arrival, he had begun to absorb himself in the detail of the farm. It probably dated from the day he found himself unable to start the milking-machine. If he left the handling of money, and most crucial decisions, to Rangi, it was only because Rangi had more experience. But now he began to take most decisions upon himself. He culled and improved the herd, bought new milkers, and cleared space for new pasture.

Anyway, at the moment, problems crowded him out of the homestead and he found a physical pleasure in working alongside Rangi about the farm. There was, for one thing, the problem of Susan's delivery. The nearest district nurse was sixteen miles away, over rough road; the nearest hospital thirty. He was not looking forward to a midnight dash, in the old and capricious Ford, over muddy winter road; he seemed always to see it as a midnight dash, and not as something which might happen in the light of day. He mentioned the problem casually to Rangi. A week later, one blustery day when they were out together, Rangi told him Huia was on her way back to the farm.

'But why?' Mark cried.

'I wrote to her,' Rangi said. 'I tell her.'

'But my God—what did you tell her?'

'I tell her everything. Now she coming back.'

'But what for?'

'She got a midwife certificate,' Rangi said proudly. 'Everything fix now. No trouble about going to hospital.'

Mark sat on a pine stump and groaned. 'You mean to say that she's giving up her job to come back here?'

'She didn't have no job,' Rangi said. 'She looking for another one. Then I write. I tell her. I think she really want to come back anyhow. I think she really want to come back and see her old man. She like it up on the farm here, I reckon.'

Mark rose. A heavy pain pressed down between his shoulder-blades. A sudden fierce slant of rain needled into his face, dribbled under his oilskin. 'It's not too late?' he said, as they walked for shelter. 'You couldn't tell her not to come?'

Rangi was hurt. 'She be here the day after tomorrow,' he said. 'I reckon it's too late now, boy, too late.'

Mark spent some time wondering how he might explain Huia's coming arrival to Susan. In the end he found he need not have worried. 'But it's marvellous,' Susan said. 'The whole idea. It's wonderful of you to think of it, dear. I mean I shan't have to go to hospital now.'

'No. I don't expect so.'

'Besides, it'll mean company for me.' Susan paused and frowned. 'She's a nice girl, is she? I mean clean and everything?'

'Yes,' Mark said. 'A nice girl. Clean and everything.'

3

His fear afterwards seemed absurd.

The day Huia arrived he deliberately placed himself a great distance from the homestead. With blistering hands and swinging slasher, he repelled an invasion of gorse and weed from a derelict neighbouring farm. He also repaired three fences and turned the cows into winter pasture. Then he sat smoking in a hay-barn.

Rangi, who observed with alarm some smoke issuing from a fissure in the wall of the barn, found Mark there among a litter of butts. Rangi brought the first progress report. Huia had arrived. She was up at the homestead now, talking to Susan. The two had been in conference some time already. They appeared to get on very well together. 'I think they good friends soon,' Rangi said with innocent pleasure. 'You know that?'

Mark rose and walked out of the barn.

'Where you going? You not going up to see them?'

'No,' Mark said. 'I'm going to find work.'

'Work?' said Rangi. 'By God, I think you going crazy on the work lately, boy. Work, work, work. You never stop.'

Mark stopped and considered this pronouncement. It had a certain truth.

'I think you really love this farm after all,' Rangi said. 'Like your old man, eh?'

An hour later Mark found himself wandering the farm blindly; the time between seemed to have vanished. An uprooted tree, torn down by a winter gale, lay directly across his path. In falling, the branches had raked the earth wildly, leaving great open scars in the land. Absently he stooped and gathered a handful of loose earth. He contemplated his father, his grandfather, all his line, and wondered at the separate pains they might each have sunk in the soil. He felt, for the first time, at one with them. And at peace with them. He couldn't be angry at them, or anyone, any more. They'd built the only way they knew, lived the only way they knew. And what had they escaped? Everything, in the end, except themselves.

Yes, he thought, silently addressing the fallen tree, the broken soil, he could even see himself rebuilding the homestead soon. It was, after all, only a matter of time.

His search for work, suddenly remembered and renewed, took him finally to the corner of the farm most remote from the homestead. There he found the launch. He'd almost forgotten it: it had lain idle in a tidal creek, tied to a flimsy jetty among mud and mangroves, ever since Mark arrived back on the farm. Though his father once used it a good deal, travelling about the harbour, Mark hadn't found it necessary. If he travelled at all, it was always in the car, or in a launch belonging to someone else.

The launch lurched in the water as it took his weight. He trod the length of it carefully, thoughtfully, like a captain new to his command. Birds had nested in the cabin and the engine was white with droppings. It was some time before he left the launch and began to walk back to the homestead.

Near the cottage he met Rangi, who had a second progress report. 'They still talking up there,' Rangi said. 'What you reckon they talk about, eh?'

'God knows,' Mark said.

There was no doubt about it: Huia had changed. Her face was hardened, her hair was cut short, she held herself more erect; her body seemed stiffer, tighter, than Mark remembered. It seemed incredible to Mark that she should have changed so much in so short a time; it was as if some final shock of unhappiness had overtaken her in the city, and now she held herself void of promise. An austerity of figure and feature would, it appeared, be her new protection against the world. The more he meditated on the mystery, the more he felt memory a cheat. She could not really have changed so quickly; she could not really have been so different before.

Still, enough mystery remained to disturb him. He would have liked to have tracked it down, or at least to have drawn a line about the mystery, isolated the inexplicable in Huia. But the fact was that he could seldom talk to Huia; and then only in Susan's presence. After that first day Huia and Susan were so often in conference that Mark began to feel himself merely an empty chair at table or a picture on the wall.

These conferences, though unpredictable in frequency, occupied the best part of a great number of days and caused mealtimes to vary a good deal from day to day. Usually they were held behind a closed door in Susan's bedroom; but on fine days Huia walked Susan through the pale winter sunshine. Very soon Huia's face became that of an expressionless stranger across the meal-table. Mark did his best to escape from the homestead in the evenings. Often he found refuge down in the cottage with Rangi, who had begun to smuggle beer on to the farm for Mark. While he pondered the world slowly with Rangi, he found it easier not to think about Huia.

'Why,' Susan said to Mark in a rare and brief burst of confidence, 'Huia's a wonderful creature. So calm and so understanding. As if she'd been through it all herself. Why didn't you tell me about her before?'

That night Mark brooded over his beer. Rangi threw more wood on the fire, turned and said, 'Something worrying you, boy?'

'Tell me,' Mark began, 'did Huia ever have a job in the city after she went back?'

'No,' Rangi said. 'That something I don't know.'

'You mean she didn't write?'

Rangi puzzled a while. 'That what I mean, all right. She never write. Funny thing, that. She always write. What you think, eh?'

'I don't know what to think,' Mark confessed. 'I don't know what to think at all.'

During the day, now that there was little work about the wintry farm, he spent time on the launch. He studied the engine and called in Rangi for advice. Together they cleaned out flaking rust and crusted salt. After three days, and one or two small repairs, they had the engine turning over. On the fourth day Mark and Rangi ran the launch down the creek, across the harbour and back again. The engine performed well, but the hull sprang several leaks. After that Mark no longer needed Rangi, and worked alone on the launch. He made small journeys up and down the harbour, and presently even the business of steering up the shallow creek gave him no great difficulty. He liked going out on rough days, when the waves battled up the rocks, to see just how expert he was becoming.

At Susan's insistence Huia moved from the cottage up to the homestead. She prepared a small room for herself at the back of the place. Mark, sitting in the library with the door ajar, heard her talking to Susan in the kitchen. 'I think Mark must have used that room for sleeping,' Huia said.

'Quite probably,' Susan replied. 'He seems to have slept in every room, at some time or other. And moved out whenever one became cluttered.'

'I found some of his clothes,' Huia said. 'A pair of old corduroy trousers—'

'My God. Has he still got those? Any poems in the pockets? There ought to be.'

'—and a torn shirt and a couple of pairs of old socks,' Huia continued. 'They were stuffed in a cupboard by the bed.'

'You might as well burn the lot.'

'And I found this. It was in an envelope with a French stamp, tucked under the mattress at the head of the bed. Looks like somebody sitting outside a church.'

'A photograph?' Susan said with curiosity. 'But that's me, dear. That's me in my heyday. Silly, isn't it? You can't even see my face properly. I'd forgotten I sent that to Mark. What on earth did he keep it for?' Some thought must have struck Susan; she laughed. 'Poor Mark,' she said. 'Didn't you feel sorry for him?'

'Sorry for him?' said Huia. She paused and added, 'I suppose I might have. I don't know.'

4

Susan's first pains came in the morning. About noon the district nurse visited the homestead, saw Susan, talked to Huia, and promised to return with the doctor later in the day. It looked as though everything might be over by evening.

Mark tried to read through part of the afternoon. But he was distracted by Huia's feet thudding up and down the passage outside the library. He lifted his eyes and met a stare of reproof from his great-grandfather: Susan had set the portrait straight, facing into the room again. 'He's a quaint old darling,' she said. 'Really something out of the history-book, isn't he?'

Mark rose and studied the gaunt features, the straggling beard, the fierce eyes. He felt the need to apologize. 'I'm sorry,' he said. 'But sometimes there can be too much.'

He went to the kitchen and made tea. After a while Huia came from the bedroom, where Susan now rested quietly, and joined him. They sat in a vast silence, the old pendulum clock on the mantelpiece ticking like gunshot. It seemed to Mark his fault that there was so great and strange a distance between them. He should, now they were at last alone, be the first to speak. He cleared his throat and, with an effort, began.

'Well,' he said tentatively, 'what do you think of it all?'

'It should be all right.' Huia's answer was crisp and professional. 'She's very relaxed.'

'It wasn't that I meant, exactly.'

Huia slowly stirred sugar in her tea. 'Well if you mean about the other thing,' she said, 'I think you've got a very nice wife. And you don't need to worry. Because I told her.'

'You what?'

'I told her everything, silly. It's stupid to have something like that hanging about the house, isn't it? Susan said she understood. She said you were lonely on the farm, and everything.'

'That's damn generous. And what else did she say?'

'That it was natural that anyone should—' Huia broke off, shaking her head.

'Feel sorry for me?' Mark said. 'That it?'

'Yes,' Huia said. 'I suppose it is. You see? You've been worrying about nothing.'

'Yes. I see.'

'Susan's not worried either. Besides I told her I was finished with everything now, finished with men.'

'And what did she say?'

'She said it was perfectly understandable in any woman.'

'Yes. That's Susan, all right. Go on.'

'I think Susan understands you very well. She says the farm's your trouble. It'll be better when you get back to the city.'

'Who's going back to the city?'

'Why, you are, of course.'

'That's interesting,' he observed. He rose from the table, went out to the back door, and pulled on his gumboots. Huia followed him.

'You're angry,' she said.

'Of course not.'

'You are angry,' she said. 'I can tell. You're different.'

'Really?' he said. 'Perhaps everyone's different.'

Huia was dressed neatly in grey slacks and blue sweater. He remembered her shoulders, bare and brown, with a faint twinge. But when he reached out, she arched away. An expression of pain was distinct upon her face.

'It's all right,' he said. 'Don't panic.' He took his oilskin down off a hook. 'I just wanted to prove something, that's all.'

'Prove what?'

'That everyone's different.' He held to the doorway a moment to keep himself steady, his voice in check. 'There's just one other thing I'd like to know. This baby—'

'Baby?' Huia said in dismay.

'This baby you had in the city. It was mine, was it?'

There was a silence.

'Yes,' she agreed finally. 'Yours. Probably.'

'That's all I wanted to know, really. Thanks. It took me a while to add everything up.' He turned for the door.

'And that's all you want to know?' she asked tersely. 'Don't you want to know if it was adopted or anything? Because it was.'

He turned back. 'I had that worked out too. That it was still around somewhere, most likely. Thanks for telling me, though. It really makes my day.'

He dragged his oilskin over his shoulder, swung open the door, and stalked out into the bleak light.

It was not raining. But among the pines, along the muddy track between the trees, water still dripped down on sodden needles. Everything had the sour smell of winter.

He could, he supposed, have gone down to the cottage; but he was in no mood to be good company for anyone, least of all cheerful Rangi. He stopped at the edge of the pines and looked out on the grey harbour.

Then he spread his oilskin on the pine-needles and sat down.

He thought he heard a car pull into the homestead. Probably the district nurse, or the doctor.

The afternoon was darkening early. He lit a cigarette and waited.

When he realized that he had, without thinking, chosen to sit in the place where he once waited for Huia in the summer, he rose quickly and stiffly. Then he imagined he heard a faint, thin cry from the homestead. It was probably Susan.

But then again, it might have been someone else. Someone he'd never really considered until now.

A faint drizzle began as he walked down to the creek. The launch rose rolling beside the creaking jetty: the tide was coming in. He slipped the moorings, coaxed the engine and persuaded the launch gently down the creek.

Out in the harbour, bouncing on the waves, he took the launch about in a full, wide circle. Then, making another half-circle, he steered it down harbour. The farm, the old white homestead above the pines, slipped into the mist. The waves, as the water grew wilder, came smashing across the bow. The windows of the cabin swam. Mark lifted himself through the trapdoor in the roof, fastening his feet on the spokes of the bucking wheel, and felt the wind and the spray sharp and exhilarating on his face.

Long before he actually saw the tall rising feathers of water, he heard the surf cannoning over the sand-bar. The air very soon became so dense with fine spray that he could not see his direction. Presently the launch crashed down into the trough of the first roller.

Jesus, he thought, those waves are big.

Homecoming

When Eve returned to New Zealand, she expected she might be irritated at finding everything much the same. This could have happened in the way she expected if she had remained longer in Auckland, her port of arrival, but the morning she left the ship she tried to telephone an old friend and found the telephone number changed. Eve, an efficient girl who sometimes liked to consider herself a creature of impulse, decided to leave immediately for the farm: she was in fact irritated, but not in the way she expected. The different telephone number, with its attendant frustration, symbolized the other changes. Trams no longer banged along the ugly streets; instead, trolley-buses slid almost soundless round corners. Spanning the harbour, the sleek new bridge carried a glittering stream of traffic. The tiny cafe opposite her hotel was transformed into a busy espresso coffee-bar. It did not seem at all the city she had once known well. It flashed with chrome and prosperity. Absurdly oversized television sets crammed shop windows; newspapers were fat with advertising. Everything seemed to have grown gross and sprawling.

Still on the telephone, she located not the friend to whom she most desired to speak, but another. It did not alter her decision to leave, as soon as possible, for the farm. She talked to Iris, a friend with whom she had once worked in a newspaper office; her original intention was to ask about the prospects of a job. But Iris was little help. 'Everyone's in advertising these days,' she said. 'Or in public relations. Everyone we knew.'

'Oh,' Eve said. 'I see.'

'That's where the money is,' Iris observed.

'Of course.'

'You might as well be in while the going's good.'

'Yes,' Eve replied. 'Why not?'

'If there's a rat race, you might as well get your teeth sharp. That's what Jim says. He says there'll be a big bust in a year or two. This country's living beyond its means.'

'Jim? Who's Jim?'

'My husband, darling. Jim Campbell. I married him, or didn't I tell you? Perhaps I didn't. I always meant to write, but I kept losing your address.'

'No need to apologize.'

'But I really did mean to write.'

'Of course you did.'

'And, Eve, there's just one thing I ought to tell you—' The voice at the other end of the line grew strange.

'Yes? What's that?'

'Well,' the awkward voice began, 'I just want you to know, Eve, that I haven't been one of those people who've been saying things about you.'

Eve had a hollow feeling in her chest. But her voice remained cool. 'What things?' she asked. 'Who's been saying them? Whatever for?'

'Oh you know, Eve, the usual kind of things. And you can guess the kind of people too. This country's still a village, darling, with an unusually high percentage of village idiots.'

'I'm sorry,' Eve said. 'But—'

'You've probably forgotten what it's like. Being away so long.'

'I don't think so. But you might tell me—'

'Jim says the literary scene is the same. Loaded with catty freaks and frustrates. If anyone has success anywhere else they're down on him like a ton of hot bricks. Jim's literary, you know.'

'Yes,' Eve said. 'I remember.'

'He's finishing off a novel. He says he's really going to pull this place apart.'

Eve, with a mildly desperate feeling, found she was being dragged farther from the point. 'What has been said about me?' she got out at last.

'I told you. What you might expect. Since you've been such a success in London, they talk about the way you must have slept round Fleet Street to get what you wanted.'

'Oh,' Eve said. 'I see.' It was like a slosh of dirty water in the face for a welcome.

'Are you going to be in the city long?' Iris said. 'We'd love to have you round if you'll excuse the mess. We're off on holidays tomorrow.

We're just doing our packing.'

'No,' said Eve, with renewed determination. 'I'm just passing through. I'm going straight back to the farm.'

'Anyway, you'll be back here soon.'

Eve sighed. 'Yes,' she agreed. 'I suppose I will be.'

On the train, travelling north, she relaxed for the first time. The dirty little carriage had survived change: so had the bleached, ragged countryside racing past her window. She allowed herself no excitement: she hardened herself against twinges of memory.

At the river town, where launches rocked at anchor in a mangroved tidal estuary, she waited an hour before finding someone who would take her up the creek to the farm. She could have arranged for her father to be there to meet her, as he had once done when she returned from the city for holidays. But Eve had written her parents from Panama, telling them not to expect her back until about three or four days after her arrival in Auckland; she also insisted that they should not go down to Auckland to meet her. She had hoped, in those free days, to meet old friends, renew contacts, investigate jobs offering. With all the panic of rediscovery, plus Iris, she no longer wished to do these things. And she was about to take her parents by surprise.

Though she passed familiar faces, no one recognised her in the dusty little township; she felt a wry satisfaction. And then, contrarily, when she realized she had hardly met a friendly smile since she arrived in the country, she felt impossibly lonely.

Eventually she rode home in the afternoon launch, which dropped empty cream cans and mail on to the farm jetties up the creek. The driver of the launch, with whom Eve travelled alone for most of the journey, was an agile and handsome young Maori boy clad only in a pair of torn shorts. In casual conversation he revealed he was a stranger to the district. He liked working on the launches: that was why he had come to the township. He hoped one day to own a launch for himself.

Eve, spread comfortably on the sunlit bow of the boat, watched as he steered expertly up the creek, and listened to him singing. With careless energy, he swung the launch against jetties and leapt off to deposit his empty cans and bags of mail. Then, his hands stroking the wheel again, he ran the launch between steep banks strung with bush, through forests of mangrove, and around islands of raupo, where startled shags flapped into the air.

Eve could not remember a homecoming so pleasant: as they dawdled up the creek, from jetty to jetty, she found herself glad that her father, whose welcome would have been staid, had not been at the township to meet her. This stranger made her feel at home again.

'You live here once?' he asked with a smile.

'Once,' Eve said. 'A long time ago.'

'When the timber-mill was here?' he said. 'When they used to float the logs down?'

'Not that long ago,' Eve laughed. It must have been thirty years since milling along the creek ended, and the last logs floated. Now the noisy mills were gone, and only quiet farms remained. Her father was one of those who, after destruction of the forest, stayed to farm on indifferent soil. 'I'm not that old, you know.'

'Sorry,' he grinned cheekily. 'But you said you was here a long time ago, eh?'

'My mistake,' she agreed. 'I exaggerated.'

Finally he dropped Eve on the jetty of her father's farm. 'The name's Sonny,' he said. 'Be seeing you sometime.' He waved good-bye and continued up the creek.

He left Eve in cheerful mood. Carrying only a light bag, and leaving her suitcases on the jetty for her father to pick up on his sledge, she began the walk up to the homestead. She had forgotten how naturally the place, small and white among trees, set itself in the landscape. She had forgotten too how the late afternoon light hit sharp ridges; how the rising tide shimmered among the mangroves; how the vivid bush, tangling in the gullies, spilled down like small green streams from the ragged flung-back forest on the hill-tops. She felt a prickling excitement, as if some long-promised holiday were only now beginning, and when she heard the cry from the homestead, the cry which signalled her parents' recognition and approach, she broke into a girlish jog-trot, her light bag swinging against her thigh. But within moments she remembered herself, and walked sedately, briskly, up the path to meet them.

Her parents were no great surprise. Her father was quieter and slower of speech than she remembered; he went through the shy motions of greeting his daughter and making her feel at home again. Her mother was no less fussy, no less demanding in her eager questions. Together they appeared slightly faded, like a photograph from the past, two people grown effortlessly old. But the interior of the homestead, background to the picture, was not at all faded. It had, like the green top-dressed acres of the farm, the colour of prosperity—new thick carpets and furnishings, a huge white refrigerator and pale-varnished radiogram, a remodelled kitchen impressive with gadgets.

On the other hand Eve, slender and well-groomed at twenty-nine, had no doubt that she was a surprise to her parents. She had after all said good-bye to them, still rather plump and awkward and inarticulate at twenty-three, a raw young journalist about to seek the world. Now she was, at least in their eyes, a success: hadn't they seen her by-line in bold type above articles in London newspapers? Only her brother Eric remained profoundly unimpressed. Eric, a short square boy with fair hair and jutting jaw, alone seemed to present nothing in common with the person she remembered. The timid, diffident student was displaced by a scowling young man with sunburned legs who took pleasure in flinging himself on a horse, escaping his parents' farm to spend unpredictable periods of time with Maori friends. He helped little about the farm and was plainly a trial to her parents. Eve had been told, in letters, about Eric's abortive marriage to an Auckland girl: after the break-up the girl went to England and Eve met her there, by accident, at a party. At the time Eve wondered how Eric could possibly have become involved with the girl. Vague almost to the point of anonymity, she talked to Eve about her impending invitation to a Palace garden party; if she irritated Eve, it was not merely because of Eric, but also because she recognized in the girl the kind of witless colonial she might once herself have appeared. So she had anticipated change in Eric, if not change so great. She had not really expected a sullen stranger. Nor did she expect open hostility. Each time, at her parents' insistence, she began to talk of Europe, Eric made a point of leaving the room. 'For God's sake,' he cried finally. 'There are other subjects for conversation, you know.'

'You're mean and unfair, Eric,' Eve's mother said. 'Eve has a perfect right to tell us about her adventures.'

'But not for breakfast, dinner and tea,' Eric said. 'And, anyway, haven't we been hearing about them for years already? She did write letters, you know.'

'Letters aren't the same thing at all. You could be nicer to your sister.'

Eve pleaded for her brother. 'Of course Eric doesn't have to listen,' she said, very fairly.

'And I'm not,' Eric agreed, leaving the room.

Eve's mother paused. 'You mustn't mind Eric she said. 'He hasn't been right ever since he came back from the city. He's jealous of you, and you must make allowances for him. You've been a success, you see, and he hasn't.' She folded her hands comfortably and hurried on, anxious to conceal the silence fallen in the room. 'There are a lot of things you still haven't told us,' she observed. 'You were all that time in Spain.'

Eve, that night, excused herself with a headache: she did not want to talk about Spain. 'Another time,' she offered. 'I think I'll just walk for a bit, before I go to bed.'

'You're well?' her mother asked anxiously.

'Of course,' Eve said. 'I'm perfectly well.'

She went out into the dry-scented evening, and descended from the homestead along a narrow track edged with small brushing fern and upright punga. It was still warm, and she walked tall and white through the shadows. She left the track, emerged from the punga, and at length stood motionless on a ridge in the peaceful evening, the paddocks of the farm strewn in clumsy pattern below her. A rim of moon lifted beyond the hills. A morepork cried faintly.

Tension slowly left her.

She could easily have invented some story for her mother; but she still lacked the heart for it. To scissor Philip from those Spanish landscapes was too immense a task. Philip, so neat and English and precise, was possibly still unaware of what he meant to her. He was younger than herself, as fair as Eric: sitting on a gently rocking houseboat in the calm of early morning, he made London seem a wonderland with his urchin smile; he conjured a city strange and new from the old grey buildings heaped beside the Thames. In return she nursed him through those months in Spain, and helped his novel into print back in London.

She seemed for a while, as his confidante, something more than a simple silly girl, a cheap ambitious journalist. But then Philip never needed a woman: in London again, his book published and praised, he slid away from her, back among his smart little men friends: he had grown up, it seemed, away from mother. When Eve, in a quiet moment, suggested a return to Spain, Philip made excuses: there were parties, people to see, his next book to finish. Perhaps all she needed to say to Philip was: 'Safety. I only want safety. No more.'

Safety? By then she didn't even have a job.

She sat on the ridge, hugging her knees. A figure came noiseless out of the evening: Eric sat beside her. They were silent for some time.

'You might have fooled them,' Eric finally said. 'But you don't fool me, much.'

He rose swiftly and walked away.

Eve raced down from the ridge, in another direction, the earth quick beneath her feet; she stumbled, fell face down in grass. She stayed in that position for some time, her shoulders heaving.

She levered herself up from the ground, and discovered she was on a cliff which jutted out above the creek. Dizzily she realized that if she had run much farther, she would have plunged over into the creek. Only her stumble had saved her.

The evening, here, was alive. The creek was emptying, the water running out to the sea, sucking and hissing faintly among the mangroves. There was a rattle of insects and leaves, and strange anonymous splashings. The world was flooded with moonlight and sharp shadow.

If there were promise in the evening, hope still left in this country or anywhere, she was powerless to confront it. It was as elusive as the moon's silver on water.

She was friendless. Once, of course, she had a great many friends of her own age in the district; she'd gone through school with them. But most moved away, to town or city, at the same time as herself; Sarah Arapata, perhaps her best friend, went to teacher's training college at the same time as Eve left for a city newspaper. She was no longer sure she would have much in common with those who might remain in the district. So she did not inquire after them; she had no wish to fumble in an already depleted purse for the small change of domestic conversation.

But she did ride about the farm with her father, and keep him company on visits to neighbours. English friends had marvelled politely at her ability as a horsewoman; Eve, in fact, had never considered it an accomplishment at all until she went to England. Now she enjoyed days thudding along beside her father; on the whole she preferred his quiet company. Her mother was still talkative, still questioning.

'I know it's none of my business,' her mother said, 'but what are you planning to do?'

'I don't know, really,' Eve said. 'I expect I'll make up my mind soon.'

'There's nothing to stop you staying here, of course,' her mother said warmly.

'Like Eric?' Eve said, amused.

'Of course not. Eric's different altogether.'

'I've never really understood about Eric. I've always felt there's a lot you haven't told me.'

'Really? I can't imagine how you got that impression.'

'I don't see why a bad marriage should cause him to throw up a career, or to leave the city for a life of idleness.'

'Well, perhaps it was a little more than that.'

'Oh?'

'Perhaps,' her mother observed, moulding dough with her stubby hands, 'it was fortunate, all things considered, that it didn't end in court—or gaol.'

'What was it then?'

'I think you should understand, first, that the marriage wasn't all it appeared. Eric married his employer's daughter, you know.'

'No. I didn't know.'

'Oh yes. Quite suddenly. We didn't understand, really, at the time.'

'Nor did I. When I met the girl.'

'Eric ran around with some fast crowd. If we'd known he was in trouble with money, of course your father and I would have helped him. But we didn't know. They were very pleased with him in the office, they trusted him with a lot. And before they discovered how he was abusing their trust, he married his boss's daughter. And when they discovered money missing from an estate, it was all kept quiet. Eric's boss didn't want to prosecute his son-in-law. He made good the loss himself.'

'Well,' Eve said, 'Eric seems to have fended for himself quite well. He certainly solved his problem.'

'How can you say that?' her mother cried. 'You ought to be ashamed of him.'

'Ashamed?'

'Of course. Can't you see? He's wrecked his life.'

'I don't see,' Eve said, 'that that is so very unusual.'

'And look at him now,' her mother went on. 'No decent girl would look at him, the way he runs round with Maoris all the time. Of course they don't care about him, or what he's done. It doesn't worry them at all. They've no moral code.'

'What is it that you're really frightened of?' Eve said. 'That he might take up with some Maori girl?'

'It's too late to worry about that. He's taken up with plenty already, as anyone in the neighbourhood can tell you. And that's not all, either.'

'No?'

'No. It's not. Some of them have been married women. Like that Sarah—' Her mother paused. 'You know, I'd forgotten—that she was a friend of yours, I mean.'

'Sarah Arapata? But she—'

'Oh yes, Sarah's back here all right. Different name now, of course. It just shows you, doesn't it? Education doesn't do a Maori a bit of good.'

'I think you must be confusing her with someone else, mother. Sarah was a very talented girl. She'd hardly be the same—'

'No, I'm not mistaken, dear. It's the same Sarah. She came back here from the city some time ago. She carried on with quite a few apart from Eric. The last I heard, she was living with someone down the creek. Not,' her mother concluded, 'her husband.'

'Well,' said Eve. 'There we are.' She hoped her mother would leave off the subject; sooner or later she would find out about Sarah for herself.

'She married a European boy too. Someone from down south. A very pleasant boy, I heard, a schoolteacher. Clean living and—'

'Yes, mother,' Eve said.

'What's wrong? You don't sound very interested.'

'But I am,' Eve sighed.

'Well, then. Don't you want to listen to what I'm saying? Don't you want to hear the worst about your friends? Is that it?'

'No. It's not that. It's just,' she invented, 'that I think I've had enough for one day. After hearing about Eric.'

'Of course. I'd forgotten. It must be a great shock for you, hearing the truth about your brother.'

'It has been,' Eve agreed.

She felt at times, as she galloped away from the farm towards the hills, or swam solitary in freshwater creeks, that she could easily give herself up to this landscape, and remain here at home. Like Eric, perhaps, she was capable of giving up entirely. What would she leave behind? Very little. Philip? That was a joke. Here, measured against these hills, her life became of little substance, almost transparent. She could not find much use for it.

She made no decision on the future. She simply remained, like a victim of some accident, where she had fallen.

It was a hot day. She tethered her horse near a patch of scruffy grass and approached the farmhouse. An old stripped Ford, rusting in the weather, lay to one side of the place. The weatherboards were unpainted, and broken windows were nailed up with boxwood. It was a square, decaying place set in thick manuka. It looked as if it might once have belonged to the land now sunken beneath the dry grey scrub.

She knocked on the door. There was a shuffle of bare feet somewhere towards the back of the place. They sorted themselves out into one pair of feet advancing up the passage. Then the door opened. A Maori filled the doorway. He was perhaps thirty, with immense shoulders and strong arms; his face had a flattened, aggressive look. His nose appeared as though it might once or twice have been broken, and his eyes were narrow and vivid. He wore jeans and a soiled singlet.

'Hullo,' he said. 'You want something?'

He stared at her, his expression somewhere between insolence and suspicion. She felt naked for a moment.

'I'm looking for Sarah,' she said finally, asserting herself.

'Well, then, you come to the right place.'

But he just stood there, leaning against the door. He studied her, and seemed amused.

'She's home?' Eve asked.

'Sure,' he said. 'Sure she's home.' He didn't move.

'Then I wonder if I might see her?'

'Sure thing. Soon as you tell me who the hell you are, and what you want.' His eyes flickered, and his expression was no longer one of amusement; he was in earnest. 'This is my place, and I'm fussy about visitors. Before I let them in.'

'Obviously,' she said.

'You're smart,' he said. 'You catch on. Not much of a place I got here, but I'm fussy like. Terribly particular. You get me?'

'I think I understood the first time,' she replied coolly.

'Know something? I don't know if I like you. I don't know if I will invite you in.'

'Who is it, Muru?' came a woman's voice from inside the place. But the question went without reply.

'Now that's interesting,' he said. 'Something I'd like to know. Who are you?'

'An old friend of Sarah's.'

'How long you know her?'

'Most of my life. I haven't seen her for years.'

He studied her again. 'Well, what do you know?' He began slowly to roll a cigarette. His eyes roved the length of her body. 'I guess you'll pass,' he said at length. 'Come in.' He stood aside for her to enter the house. She could smell his sweaty body as she brushed past.

Eve went down the long dim passage and came upon Sarah in the kitchen. She was brushing her hair before a shard of mirror. Dressed only in her slip, she looked up, startled, her hair dark and loose about her shoulders. She was not as slim as she had once been, but filling out. Her face had lost its open look.

'Hello, Sarah,' Eve said quietly.

Sarah was perplexed. 'Who—' she began. Then a smile trembled. 'It's Eve,' she said.

Eve nodded. There was the sound of feet behind her: the Maori had followed her into the kitchen. Sarah now looked over Eve's shoulder at him.

'This is Eve, Muru,' Sarah said. 'My old friend. Eric's sister.'

'Eric's sister, eh?' Muru said. 'Why didn't you say?'

'You didn't ask,' Eve answered. 'And, anyway, I didn't know you knew my brother.'

Muru crossed the room and sat down at the table. He remained silent, watching the two women. In his presence, they felt constraint: they simply looked at each other, smiling, and did not embrace.

'How long you been home?' Sarah asked.

'A few days.'

'We haven't seen Eric lately. He'd have told us you were back.' Sarah smiled. 'We like Eric. He often comes round. You here for long?'

'I don't know.'

'I expect you'll be going back to England.'

Eve shook her head. 'I doubt it.'

'Well,' said Sarah cheerfully, 'it's nice seeing you back.'

Muru sat silent at the table. His gaze wandered between the two women. Presently he rose and left them.

'You have to excuse Muru,' Sarah then announced. 'He's a bit funny about things. He keep you waiting out there long?'

'A while. He wanted to find out who I was.'

'He's suspicious of people coming to see me. He thinks they might start trying to drag me back.'

'Drag you back where?'

Sarah shrugged with nonchalance. 'Oh, you know. Back to everything. Back to my husband.'

'Oh,' Eve said.

'He gets funny about that. Last time a pakeha girl called here, it was my husband's sister. Perhaps Muru thought you were another sister come to fetch me back.'

'I see.'

'I suppose you've heard all about me. You don't look surprised.'

'I've heard a little.'

'What do you think of Muru?' Sarah said, switching from the subject.

'I've hardly had time to form , an impression.'

'He's a good man.' Sarah spoke firmly. 'Better than the one I married. He doesn't ask me to be anything.'

'And your husband did?'

'That's right. He did.' She grew quiet at the mention of her husband and added, 'Muru's not like that. He loves me like I am. He doesn't ask me to be anything. Except myself. And I like him the way he is. I wouldn't like him any different. So we get along·all right.' She looked defiant, as though Eve might dare to contradict her.

'What does Muru do? How do you live here?'

'Sometimes he goes south for a while, and makes big money in the freezing works. Enough to live for a while back here. And if we ever get short here he cuts scrub or works on the roads. Anything that's going.'

'Not much future in that.'

'He's very strong, Muru, he doesn't care what work he does. So long as there's money at the end. That's all that worries him. And even money doesn't really worry him much. The only thing he ever really worried about was football.'

'I see.'

'He was very good. He might have gone places. Until he decided people in this country only had use for an intelligent Maori on the football field. Off the field, they didn't want to know. A Maori was useful on the roads. Or out of sight. At the end of one season, after he'd been picked to play in Britain, and while he was still having problems getting a decent job, he drove a car over a bank. Drunk. He was months in hospital. That was the end of football. And the end of looking for a good job.'

'Why?'

Sarah shrugged. 'Sometimes when he gets mad, or drunk, he shouts that this is his country, and maybe one day the Africans and Chinese might come and help the Maoris throw you pakehas back where you belong.'

'Well,' Eve said. 'And he means it?'

'Well,' said Sarah, 'I suppose he does.' She paused. 'But he says all kinds of things. He went through high school, Muru, he used to read a lot. He doesn't read much now. He's not interested. He says it's more comfortable for a Maori to be ignorant.'

'And what about you? You haven't said much about yourself.'

'Me?' Sarah became reticent. 'I'm all right.'

'You like being back here?'

'I like being the way I am.' Again there was a flash of stubbornness, but this time Eve thought she detected a faint uneasiness beneath, as if the cloth of defiance were not cut quite to her figure. 'I'm all right.'

So don't try to shift me, she seemed to add, don't try to change my mind: because I won't move from this house, even if it is old and falling, and I won't shift from this kitchen, even if it does look terrible with empty tins and scraps and bottles. This is the way I want to be. Why? Don't ask me that, either.

Eve was quiet for a moment.

'I'll make you a cup of tea,' Sarah said, suddenly domestic. 'Or would you like a glass of beer?'

'I think beer,' Eve said. 'It's less trouble.'

'You never used to drink beer,' Sarah said. 'I remember now, at parties you'd turn your nose up. You start in England? They say English beer is good.' Sarah expertly uncapped a bottle.

'It was just beer to me. I never noticed much difference.'

'We'll take the bottle out on the veranda. It's a wonder Muru hasn't come back—he can smell a bottle opening a mile off. I thought you would've brought a husband home from England. Didn't you get around to that?'

'No,' Eve said. 'I didn't, exactly.'

She must have tried to sound casual, and perhaps almost succeeded, but something must have given her away; for then Sarah crossed the room and laid her hand on Eve's arm in an odd, gentle gesture of comfort, as if she knew everything that was to be known.

'Sorry,' Sarah said. 'I'm sorry.'

'For what?' Eve flushed.

'For, you know—a silly question.'

'Not so silly.'

'Let's go out on the veranda,' Sarah said.

They sat in shade, on two decrepit chairs. The scrub-laden land descended, before them, to the tidal creek; and lifted again, on the other side, to patchy pyramid hills. Beyond were taller hills blue with heat-haze and distance.

'Muru's sense of smell is certainly bad today,' Sarah said as she tasted the beer. 'You're puzzled about me. I know, I can tell.'

'A little,' Eve agreed. 'Perhaps I can guess some of it.'

'I don't think you can. I mean, I don't think you could guess.'

'No?'

'No. Because you're a pakeha. You're all right, you're comfortable. You couldn't see it my way.'

'I don't know. If it's true, then I'm sorry. But how can I know if you don't—'

'Drink your beer,' Sarah said. 'You haven't touched it yet. Look, there's Muru down there. He must have decided to go fishing.'

They saw Muru row a dinghy out into the middle of the creek. He had stripped off his singlet, and his brown bulk was bent over the oars. He looked, to Eve, tremendously powerful as he sent the dinghy swiftly down the creek towards the harbour. Soon—too soon, she felt—he was lost to sight beyond mangroves; she had only a perplexing glimpse of a man wonderfully intent upon his own strength.

'You must come and see us often,' Sarah was saying. 'While you're here.'

'They tell me,' said Eric, 'that you've been down to see your old mate Sarah.'

'Well?' Eve said. 'What about it?'

'Leave her alone. That's all. Don't interfere.'

'I don't know what you're talking about.'

'Just stop trying to upset her.'

'I told you, I don't know—'

'She's all right, you hear? So don't start making her unhappy.'

'Look,' Eve said. 'What is all this? Be reasonable.'

'Reasonable?' Eric laughed. 'That's lovely, coming from you. You walk into someone else's place and start trying to put their lives in order. You'd do a damn sight better to put your own life in order. Before you start playing round with other people. But I see through you, all right. I read you like a book.'

It was evening. Eric had come upon Eve, after the meal, walking near the homestead, in the dusk.

'I haven't the vaguest idea what you're talking about.'

'I just happened to bump into Muru down in the township. How's everything, I asked him. And he told me about your going round to his place. And he said that after you'd gone, Sarah was very upset. He came home and found her crying on the bed. She wouldn't tell him what was wrong. She wouldn't tell him what you'd said to her.'

'But I didn't say anything. Well, hardly anything.'

'You don't fool me. Not on your sweet life.'

'Sarah was perfectly happy while I was there. I just can't understand.'

'I can. By God, I can.'

'How very fortunate—for you.'

'What did you say to Sarah, anyway?'

'I told you. Nothing.'

'You make me sick,' he said finally. He strode away. 'All your kind,' he called over his shoulder.

And Eve was left alone with her wonder in the thickening dark. She was powerless to find an answer; she couldn't even find the question.

So she saw Sarah again.

Eve's attitude to Maoris, if in fact she had one, was equivocal; it veered this way and that with individuals. Brought up among them, she neither knew nor particularly desired to know what lay behind the things she regarded as odd quirks. They sometimes said things in a certain way, or did things in a certain way, which marked them out as different. They behaved strangely at times; that was all it amounted to, really. But, then, so did most people at times. She treated a difficult Maori, then, much as she might treat an eccentric European friend. She felt, with an instinctive liberalism, that to do otherwise might be an act of discrimination.

It was easy, considering Muru's influence, to see why Sarah should discriminate. 'You're a pakeha,' she had said. 'You're all right, you're comfortable. You couldn't see it my way.' How did she know, how could Sarah be sure? There had never been anything like this in their friendship before. Eve—even in the city, before she left for England— was always close to Sarah. It was she who helped Sarah manage the European world. It might have been different had she not been out of the country these past years, if Sarah had a European friend to whom she might turn in crisis. But Eve wasn't to have known; she had her own life. Who was to blame? Muru, perhaps. It wasn't difficult to find him detestable.

When she visited the farmhouse in the scrub for the second time.

Muru slouched away, leaving her alone again with Sarah. His face was without expression.

'I don't think Muru likes me much,' she observed to Sarah when he had gone. They sat together on the veranda.

'Sometimes Muru doesn't like anyone much,' Sarah said. 'You get used to him.'

Sarah looked quite composed. Eve began to wonder if Eric had invented the story of Sarah being found distraught after her last visit. The more she considered it, with Sarah sitting serenely beside her, the more it seemed unlikely. Yet how could she find out, for her own satisfaction?

'How did you get to know him?' Eve said suddenly.

'Who? Muru? Oh, he was around the place. I just got to know him.'

'When you came back here? Or before?'

'When I came back. I came back with my husband, on a holiday. We had a cottage on a beach down the harbour. That was how it all started. People heard I was down there and came down to see me. And I came up to see them. And then, afterwards, Peter went back to the city and I didn't.'

'Peter?'

'My husband. I suppose you think I wasn't fair to him,' Sarah said.

'I don't think anything. How can I? I don't even know him.'

'No; but I can tell. That's what you really think.'

She seemed determined to be unreasonable. 'No,' Eve said. 'I don't make any judgement. How can I?'

'People do,' Sarah replied. 'It's so easy.'

'Of course. But I don't,' Eve insisted.

'You want to know what he was like, then,' Sarah said. 'He was a nice boy. Good-looking, always well dressed. He's very keen on Maori culture. He's studied it for years. He speaks Maori better than I do. He even used to talk Maori round the house all the time. just for practice, he said, and to make me feel comfortable. I never told him that my people mostly spoke English at home. I didn't have the heart. He made me feel uncomfortable because I spoke so badly. I tell you, he was dead keen on everything Maori. I think that might have been why he married one, in the finish.'

'Well,' said Eve, 'I don't quite see—'

'No,' Sarah went on, 'I'm sorry. I shouldn't really have said that, about him marrying me just because I was Maori. I think he loved me, all right. But it might have had something to do with his loving me, if you know what I mean. If it all didn't work out, it was my fault, you see, not his. The marriage, I mean.'

Now Eve was too confused.

'He wanted me to be a credit to my race,' Sarah explained. 'He liked showing me off. He liked people to think we had a perfect marriage. I did my best to help along. He worried in case I might have a drop too much to drink at a party. If he thought that might happen, he'd rush me off home early. He didn't want people to say his Maori wife liked her liquor. He worried in case housework got too much for me. He bought everything to help me along. And before visitors came, he'd go snooping round the house quietly to make sure everything was in place and tidy. He didn't want people to say things about his Maori wife being careless and sloppy. I couldn't relax. I had to be a credit all the time. Did anyone ever ask you to be a credit to your race?'

'No,' Eve said. 'Not that I remember.'

'That's what I mean. Then why should I have to be? It wasn't fair. It just got me, in the end. You can only go on being a credit to your race just so long. Because, you know, I do like my liquor, and I am a bit careless and sloppy. And I liked my liquor more, and got more careless and sloppy, the longer I was married to him. So the first chance I got to be myself again, I grabbed. When we came up here for a holiday. I went off one night to see a friend. Just by accident I landed in on a party. Muru was there, and Eric. It was the first chance I'd had in a long time to let my hair down. And I did. Peter found out about it, afterwards, and we had a row. You know something? That was the first real row we'd had in about three years of married life. We'd been so careful of each other, you see, that we didn't have arguments. Then it all boiled over. Anyway, it finished up with me staying here, and him going back.'

'Didn't he put up a fight?'

'Oh, yes. He put up a fight, all right. Only he didn't have much chance.' Sarah paused. 'Like I said, he even sent his sister up here to try and fetch me back. He's still got hopes.'

'He knows about Muru?'

'I expect he does,' Sarah said. 'Yes.'

'And he still wants you back.'

'It looks like it.' Sarah appeared under some sudden strain. 'You're disappointed in me, Eve,' she added quietly. 'Aren't you? I can tell. I could tell the other day.'

'You jump to too many conclusions,' Eve replied. Yet she felt queerly moved. She had no need, now, to inquire into the reason for Sarah's tears after her previous visit. Sarah apparently, astonishingly, had wept because she felt she had failed Eve. It was all quite plain. Eve felt a disconcerting sense of power. She would have to be very careful in what she said to Sarah. 'I was surprised,' she went on, 'finding you here. That's all. Finding you living like this. Surprised and puzzled. I simply didn't understand the other day. I'm sorry if I showed it.'

'You showed it,' Sarah said. 'You showed it, all right. It was all over your face.'

'Look,' Eve said. 'There's Muru.' She felt foolish, suddenly: she realized that she had unconsciously been watching for him all the time they sat on the veranda. And there he was, at last, pulling the dinghy out into the creek and down towards the harbour, just as he had on her last visit. He didn't once look up in the direction of the two women on the veranda.

'Fishing again,' Sarah said. 'He likes getting off on his own, sometimes.'

He began to row strongly away.

'Are you sure you're doing the right thing, though?' Eve said carefully. 'That's what I wonder.'

'The right thing?'

'Yes.' Muru was still within sight. 'By yourself. And by your husband. And by Muru, if it comes to that.'

'You make it sound terribly complicated.'

'Do you really think you're doing yourself justice, living here, living like this?' Eve asked. 'Do you, really?'

Sarah looked disturbed. Eve wondered if she might have gone too far. Muru was out of sight. Somehow she had lost the impetus of what she wanted to say to Sarah. Perhaps she had best leave the subject alone.

'I don't understand,' Sarah said. 'What do you mean I should do?'

'I don't know,' Eve said weakly. 'That's up to you.'

'You think this is all wrong?'

'Wrong?' Eve replied. 'I didn't say anything like that.'

Eve returned home troubled at herself. She hadn't meant to say anything at all. Least of all had she intended to give Eric, for one, reason to accuse her of interference. She meant to live and let live. But she hadn't. Why? Perhaps because Sarah's collapse into squalor was just too much, in the end, to stomach. There was no logic in it. Sarah deserved better than she had. The words had just escaped her. Once she knew she still commanded Sarah's respect and attention—with that brief, rather frightening sensation of power—she spoke out, astonishing herself. But why? What right had she to say anything, and why should she? She was no great success, to be lecturing others. But, then, she wasn't lecturing or proposing solutions to Sarah. She was simply asking the very ordinary questions Sarah should have asked herself. And if she hadn't, then it was time someone asked them; Eve, in that case, was simply filling a need. If those questions disturbed Sarah, then Sarah deserved to be disturbed. That was all. All told, Eve thought, it was a very plausible piece of rationalization: she surprised herself.

That evening her mother chose to start asking questions again. Eric, fortunately, was absent—away seeing some of his mysterious friends. Eve had never seen him with any of his friends. But that of course, didn't disprove their existence.

'Well,' her mother said, 'have you come to any decision yet?'

'Decision?' Eve said absently.

'You know—about what you intend doing.'

Eve felt at once inexplicably irritated. 'Yes,' she said. 'As a matter of fact, I've thought lately I might go back to England.'

It might have been thunder out of a clear sky. In the silence afterwards her mother groped blindly, foolishly, across the table for bread and butter. Eve finally passed both. She felt pity for her parents. They didn't deserve their children.

'You don't mean it, surely,' her mother said. 'Surely—'

And then Eve thought, why not? Why shouldn't she mean it? But it was, of course, impossible. The gate had closed; Philip's was the hand on the gate. What use to force it open again, only to wander the ruined garden, with the yellow weeds sprouting from the rubble?

'It's just—' Eve began to explain, 'just that I don't feel very settled. Everything's changed. I had that feeling when I was in the city—that I mightn't fit in anywhere any more.'

'But up here?' her mother said. 'Surely you feel—'

'I feel at home. But things change here too. Though I expect,' she added, in a fit of compassion, 'that I'll stay for quite a while yet.'

Her mother looked relieved. 'I think something's upset you,' she said shrewdly. 'That's it. Isn't it? Is it Eric? Or is it,' she added, 'your friend Sarah? Perhaps you've seen enough of her now. You didn't look very happy when you got back today.'

'Yes, mother.' The next thing, if she weren't careful, her mother would be suggesting some healthy interest. 'You might be right.' She rose from the table. 'Excuse me. I've some letters I should have written before now. I'll do them tonight.'

She went to her room. She had no letters to write. She had no one to whom she might write, not to any real purpose; no one about whom she felt deeply enough to share her experience. She still floated in a void, between worlds. To put pen to paper would, in a sense, be a committal; she would have to organize her thought, profess an attitude.

Exhausted, she lay on her bed, still fully clothed, and slept. After a while she was trying to fight her way up to break the surface of sleep, to split the skin of a dream. She walked a wasteland littered with broken stumps and dead trees tangled and white with intricate shadow; hills rose ulcered and bleeding. The light and dark rippled inexplicably, as though in some fantastic dance or battle, and she walked alone. She came to the farmhouse she had lately visited in the scrub. No scrub surrounded it now: it stood apart, alone in the wasteland. Muru stood in the doorway, as he had before. He had the same sardonic smile.

'So this,' Eve laughed maliciously, 'is your country. Take it, and welcome.'

He didn't move from the doorway. His smile didn't shift, or change. Then they were facing each other, the house dissolved or vanished, and the darkness was growing all around. She was under the impression he hadn't heard what she said.

'So this,' she repeated, 'is your country.'

He leaned forward, his teeth showing in the smile, and his face seemed suspended in the dark. 'I am,' he said.

'Take it—' she began, before she realized the words no longer applied, and she choked and woke to the light burning beside her bed and the rapping on the door. She had no idea of the time. 'Come in,' she said.

Eric entered. For the first time since she had arrived home, he looked mildly amiable.

'Wondered if you might still be up,' he said. 'Saw your light.' He sat on the end of her bed, gingerly, as though at any moment she might chase him away. Then, seeing he was not unwelcome, he crossed his legs comfortably and lit a cigarette. She wondered if he had come to make his peace at last. It seemed possible.

'I've been reading,' she said, nodding towards a book which lay face down on her table.

'It must have been exciting. You look very tousled.'

'Do I? I suppose I must have dozed off.'

'How you feeling? You like being home?'

'It's all right for the moment.'

'Think you'll stay long?'

'I said tonight I would be. It's hard to say.'

'You seen Sarah again?'

'Yes. This afternoon.'

'You might do her some good. She probably gets lonely at times, down there. Most of the time she's only got Muru for company. She doesn't even see much of her own people. They don't understand her at all.'

It was surprising: he seemed to have forgiven her, entirely. Perhaps he now regretted his foolish flare of anger about her first visit to Sarah. He talked agreeably for some time while she lay on the bed.

'Tell you what,' he said finally. 'Why don't you come along with me tomorrow night? There's a party, sort of barbecue affair, down on the harbour. You might like it, meet a few people. It might do you good. Think you might come?'

'Well,' Eve said. 'I'll see.' But she could not have rejected this attempt at reconciliation.

They took an old clay road which ran across abandoned gumland, between darkened hills. The jogging horses brushed through scrub.

Then the scrub fell away and they saw the fires burning on the shore, above the water.

They were greeted warmly when they arrived. The party was already under way, with bottles of beer passing from hand to hand and sausages skewered on sticks toasting above the fires. There were about fifty people, mostly Maori, with a few pakehas from the township and neighbouring farms.

Guitars strummed, and voices rode off into the night.

Eve, dubious about Eric's invitation at first, now thought she might enjoy herself after all. It was all so attractive: the fires, the singing, the leaping reflections on the water; she could lose herself easily here. She had, she realized, been wanting to be part of something, to belong somewhere, and now she had a chance; she felt grateful to Eric for having given her the chance.

She wandered in and out of groups of people with Eric, shaking hands, drinking and eating, sharing jokes, joining in the songs.

She was quickly accepted. 'Why didn't you bring your sister along before, Eric?' a Maori boy asked.

'She wasn't around,' Eric explained. 'She's been away.'

'Sit down,' said the boy to Eve. 'Sit down here beside me and tell me where you been all my life.'

Eve laughed and sat beside him.

'Have a sausage,' he urged. 'And some beer to wash it down. Jesus, I've had enough. My guts are in a turmoil. Say, you didn't tell me. Where you been all my life?'

'Oh,' said Eve. 'Around.'

Then she saw Muru.

He sat the other side of the fire, about five yards away from her. 'Excuse me,' she said to the friendly boy. And she went over to Muru. He looked at her with surprise.

'Is Sarah here?' she asked.

'No,' he said, unsmiling. 'She's not feeling so good. She didn't come.'

For the first time Eve noticed the girl sitting beside Muru. She looked up at Eve, giggling. She was a half-caste with a spotty complexion, and drunk. 'Who's this, Muru?' she said. 'Who's your frien'? Won't you 'troduce me to your frien'?'

'Shut up,' Muru said. He looked up at Eve again: 'No. Sarah's not here. She's home. Anything else you want to know?'

'No,' Eve replied. 'Not particularly.'

She turned, and walked back to where she had been. The friendly boy, perhaps hurt by her abrupt departure, had vanished from his place by the fire. Eric, too, was not to be seen. Perplexed, she looked about for them.

She was just in time to see Muru guiding his drunken partner out of the firelight into the darkness. He helped her along with one arm about her waist. There seemed no doubt about their intention. Once, when he stopped to help her over a log, she began frantically trying to cover his mouth with her own. They became indistinct, and were lost, in shadows.

Upset, and wondering why she should be, Eve turned away. She joined up with a noisy group she had met earlier. They were dancing, whirling round the fires to guitars and clapping hands. Potatoes were thrown into the ashes to cook, fossicked out again, and thrown hot from hand to hand. Eve's head tingled—whether from noise, music or simply drink, she did not know. Heaps of scrub were flung energetically on to the fires and, in the new violent leap of flame, faces spun and swarmed, sweating and laughing; some of the bolder boys made spectacular leaps through the flame to bounce, unsinged, on the warm sand. People appeared, vanished, re-appeared. Eric was sometimes there; sometimes not. At one stage Muru lurched out of the dark with his friend.

At length Eve had enough. She walked away from the fires, the noise, into the quiet of the evening. She seated herself on a rock and looked on from a distance. She was deceiving herself, she thought, when she imagined she might have been part of it; the trouble was that she could not define, for her own satisfaction, just where she parted company, the exact point.

She might, on that rock, have contrived a thought to explain. But she did not.

She was tired, and tomorrow she would see Sarah again. She would have an argument of some substance now. But what argument? Her head reeled: what on earth was she thinking about? She'd had far too much to drink. That was the trouble.

Unsteadily, she began to make her way along the shore. She would find Eric and go home. Her feet sank into deep, sliding sand. The fires were still some distance away: she saw brief silhouetted figures, and the noise came closer. Her feet were oddly heavy and she fought to retain her balance on the sand as she made her way, as if in some oppressive dream, towards the light.

Something, or someone, sprang at her from out of the dark: she fell heavily, and was pressed to the sand. She could scarcely breathe for the sudden, immense weight. But she felt no weakness. On the contrary, her limbs came alive and, sobered, she fought. Despairingly she caught her attacker a sidelong blow to the head.

'Jesus,' a voice said. 'Enough.'

He rolled off her. Suddenly she thought: Eric. Eric had planned this; that this should happen. It would be his way of humiliating her, of bringing her down to his level. She saw it all too clearly.

'Who are you?' she said. 'Leave me alone.'

'Jesus, Dulcie,' said the voice. 'I thought it was you. But it's not you, eh? That's not your voice.'

'No,' Eve agreed with relief. 'I'm not Dulcie.'

'Jesus, I thought you was Dulcie. I'm bloody sorry.'

Eve recognized the voice of the young and friendly Maori to whom she had spoken earlier, before she saw Muru.

'Who are you, then?' he said.

'Eve. Eric's sister.'

'Jesus, I didn't know you was Eric's sister. Honest. I thought you was Dulcie.'

'And who, I wonder, is Dulcie?'

'Oh, Dulcie's a good friend of mine, eh.'

'She seems a very good friend,' Eve observed.

'Dulcie? Oh she's a pretty good friend, all right. Don't you know Dulcie?'

'No,' Eve said. 'And what's more I don't think you do either. In fact I'm inclined to think Dulcie doesn't exist.'

There was a silence.

Presently the boy got to his feet. 'Sorry,' he said.

'Just for interest's sake,' Eve went on, 'who sent you after me? Someone did—am I right?'

The boy didn't answer.

'Eric?' Eve suggested.

'I'm a bit drunk,' the boy said. 'Sorry. He told me you was easy.'

'Who did?'

'Muru,' the boy replied.

Eve stood in the kitchen, facing Sarah.

She had found Sarah alone. And in the course of her argument she had told Sarah most of what there was to tell about the night before. Sarah said very little. She simply looked miserable. Eve made good use of her advantage.

The kitchen was in much the same condition as when Eve first saw it. There might have been some vain recent attempt to tidy things; the floor at least had been swept. But there was the same greasy stack of dishes, the same line of empty bottles and unwashed glasses by the sink.

'I've never understood it,' Eve said. 'I haven't understood it from the first day I came here. You don't belong here. You don't belong with Muru. You've only been fooling yourself that you do.'

'Yes,' Sarah conceded weakly. 'I've been fooling myself.'

'He's as casual as any animal,' Eve went on. 'I saw that for myself last night. That girl—'

'Yes,' Sarah said. 'You told me.'

'Perhaps your marriage was difficult. But this is no alternative. Surely you see that. This is just surrender, the way you live here. And don't think you mean anything to Muru. Because you don't. He'll find someone else sooner or later. I don't imagine he'll have any difficulty at all.'

Sarah flinched. 'No,' she agreed.

'And someone more suited to him. Someone he's not going to drag down. That's all he's done for you. Drag you down.'

Sarah was silent, stricken.

'You can make a decent life for yourself if you want,' Eve said. 'If not with your husband, then without. You'll find someone else. You'll love someone else.'

'But I love Muru,' Sarah said abruptly. 'I love him.'

Eve, for some reason, had not taken that possibility into account. She felt shocked, as though at an obscenity. 'Even if—' she began.

'Yes,' Sarah declared. 'Even if. No matter what.'

'You're insane.' The words flew out before Eve could trap them.

Sarah slumped to a table. 'Yes,' she said finally. 'Perhaps I am. But it's been a nice kind of insanity, all the same.'

Eve was irritated beyond measure now. There was plainly nothing more she could do or say.

'I'm sorry then,' she said. 'And I'm glad I won't be here to see how it all finishes. Perhaps you deserve Muru.'

Sarah looked up, alarmed. 'You're going away?'

'As a matter of fact, I might be,' Eve said. 'I had a letter this morning from—well, from a friend of mine in England. I think I'll be going back.'

'You're going to get married?'

'I didn't say that,' Eve said.

'But you want to, you hope—'

'Well yes, perhaps.'

Eve turned and went towards the door. 'I'm sorry,' she said. 'Sorry I haven't been able to help you.'

Then Sarah's voice rose softly behind her. 'What do you think I should do?' she pleaded.

Eve stepped back into the kitchen to claim her victory.

Little more than an hour later she saw Sarah, with her bag packed, off on the afternoon launch down the creek. The launch connected with a bus in the township which in turn connected with a slow train to the city. Sarah had been doubtful about so sudden a move. But Eve urged her to go at once, if she were to go at all. It was better to go while Muru was out of the way. This afternoon was her chance. She could leave a note of explanation for Muru. The note was written, placed in an envelope, and tacked to the front door so that he would see it as soon as he arrived back at the house. Eve, after helping Sarah pack, could not relax until she saw Sarah actually aboard the launch. She looked, there, slightly shrunken and still bewildered. She waved farewell forlornly and insisted that Eve visit her in the city.

'Come soon,' Sarah cried finally, above the throbbing launch, as it turned into the creek and moved away.

Eve watched until launch and Sarah were out of sight. Then, with an agreeable sense of duty done, she walked back up the hill to where her horse was tethered. Only one thing marred the afternoon for her. That was the stupid lie about the letter from Philip. It was so unnecessary, and she couldn't understand why she should have blurted it out. The letter, in fact, was merely a Christmas card with an abstract design. At the foot of the card were a few words in Philip's characteristically neat hand: 'Surprised to hear you'd gone. You'll miss my New Year party. When are you coming back? Love, P.' And that was all. There was no reason, there, for hope. And yet she allowed herself the fantasy that there might be, yet; that beneath the tight little cluster of words Philip was trying to convey more than he said. And that now, at last, she had an excuse to return.

It was absurd.

She felt emptied, after the effort of the afternoon. If she were incapable of salvaging herself, she had at least saved Sarah. She was allowed that much satisfaction.

Of course Eric, now, would make life uncomfortable for a while. But she wouldn't permit herself to go under.

She reached her tethered horse. Finding the day still too bright for her eyes, she felt in her pocket for sun-glasses, and realized she must have left them in the farmhouse, probably in the kitchen. She went to fetch them.

She found the cool gloom of the house pleasant as she went down the long passage. She emerged into the sudden brightness of the untidy kitchen. She and Sarah, in their haste, had not even cleared up for Muru. They might at least have done that. It would have needed no great effort to leave the place partially presentable. Neither of them had thought of it.

Well, it was too late now. There wasn't the time. Muru could quite well arrive back at any moment. She would pick up her sun-glasses and leave.

She searched the kitchen. She could have placed them down anywhere among the clutter. She couldn't imagine why she hadn't simply dropped them into her pocket. She could faintly remember placing the sun-glasses down somewhere, thinking that she would pick them up later. Why should she have done that?

The moment she caught sight of them at last, and reached out towards them, she heard the chop of hooves on the grass outside. For a moment she thought she might have left her horse untethered and something had frightened it away. But then she remembered she hadn't got so far as untethering it before she discovered the loss of her sunglasses.

She hesitated. It could only be Muru.

She had an impulse to flee out of the back door, and go round the house, while he came through the front; that way she could avoid him. But she decided against the act. There was something sneaky about it. And she had her dignity, after all. She could face him with the contempt he deserved.

In any case he would already have seen her tethered horse.

There was a silence, then the sound of booted feet on the boards of the veranda. Then a ripping sound. He had discovered the envelope tacked to the front door. He could scarcely have missed it.

There was another, longer silence. Eve froze. Flesh seemed thin above her racing heart.

It would still, she thought, be so easy to move quietly out the back door, before he came. Now he would be reading the note, perhaps reading it for a second time, or simply turning it over in his hand, trying to make sense of it all; she had no idea how long the silence was lasting.

She had no idea how long it was before, finally, the feet began to tramp down the passage. She was still poised as if in mid-flight, the sunglasses an idiotic appendage in her hand. She seemed not to know what to do with them, or with her hands. She seemed not to know, in that last moment before he arrived, what she was doing there at all.

He only came as far as the door. Then he saw her. Sarah's note was still in his hand. His face was expressionless. If he felt shock at Sarah's note, surprise at seeing Eve, he did not show it.

Eve did not speak. It was up to him to say something, after all. But he said nothing. He simply looked at her, looked impassively through her and somewhere beyond. Perhaps, long before this day, he had refused to allow himself hurt. Perhaps, also, he refused to allow Eve her triumph.

Only his fingers, at length, moved. They began to shred Sarah's note. The pieces fluttered to his feet. He did not even look down.

For the first time he seemed actually to see Eve. His eyes fastened slowly on her. His face changed slightly. His familiar smile grew. Yet he still did not speak, or move.

'I came back,' Eve said at last, for some reason. 'I thought I might clear up for you.' She wondered why she said it, and for a moment stared intensely down at the sun-glasses in her hand. 'It's the least I can do,' she added. Her voice was shaky, but inwardly she was as calm as windless water. She went without hesitation to the sink and drew an apron about her waist. She deposited dishes in the sink and ran the tap. After a while she looked up, guiltily, with a faint shiver of apprehension.

Muru had not moved. He still, apparently, saw no need to speak. He just stood there smiling, filling the doorway.

The Room

The family kept the room. After all, there was no point point in letting it go; Margaret might be dead, but life persisted no matter how inscrutably, traffic ran on the highway and seasons changed, and Sonny would be going up to university, like Margaret before him, at the end of summer. It would have been foolish indeed to let so convenient a room—a short distance from the Gothic-spired university—escape simply for the sake of a couple of months' rent. With the room in mind Mr Hamilton travelled up to the city after the funeral; at the time everyone was still too preoccupied with grief to question the point of his journey. For he brought almost none of Margaret's possessions back with him. All he had done, apparently, was instruct the landlady to keep the room aside for Sonny, pay the rent for the intervening two months, and close the door—nothing, in fact, that could not have been done by letter; except of course that final thing, which someone else might have just as easily done, the closing of the door.

Mr Hamilton's earlier journey to the city, when the news first came, had not been so pointless: for then he travelled, with the undertaker, to bring back Margaret's body, that cold and shrunken thing which Sonny had recognized, with difficulty, as his sister. It was right on Christmas, and they had been expecting Margaret's return at that time anyway; they buried her on Boxing Day, near the sharp out-flung shadow of the steep-roofed wooden church on the hill above the tidal lagoon and mangrove forest. It was a cloudless and perfect summer day, scarcely flawed by the sad dark group among the tangled crosses in the graveyard. Margaret was buried in the last of the Hamilton plots; they occupied a small corner of the graveyard. Now the family would have to take plots in the ugly new cemetery growing near the town. For the graveyard was filled; most of the graves, many overgrown and anonymous, went back fifty years at least—some even a hundred or more, to the time when the first settlers in the district, one with the name of Hamilton, walked the pale beaches and forested valleys of a new country. Sonny had often idly wondered who might claim that last plot. He supposed his parents might one day share it. Now Margaret, unlikeliest of all, had taken it first.

At the end of the service he turned with conscious maturity away from the grave, his eyes travelling quickly over his father's sagging face, his mother's swollen features; he saw them as old at the same time as he felt himself older. It seemed, now, they were all castaways on the same shore. He faced the day; the sun was dazzling on the lagoon beyond the glinting mangroves. It did not pain him to see a day so brilliant; he had no wish to project his grief upon it. On such a day it was easier to fix his best memories of Margaret—in tight shorts and light shirt, with clean sunburned limbs—more sharply. Margaret had been a summer girl.

Later, after his father's second visit to the city, he began to wonder about the room. What was it had caused his father to flee the room so suddenly, so inexplicably? And, more to the point, what was it, precisely, that waited for Sonny there? He felt it unfair, suddenly, that it should be left to him to unriddle whatever secret remained; whatever lay behind that quickly-shut door. The burden of discovery might at least have been shared; why should it all fall to him? Then he understood slowly that after the grief and the burial, the shock and shame of the coroner's report, his parents wanted no part of such discovery. They wanted the past buried as simply as Margaret. They escaped quickly, greedily, into the trivia of their lives again; Margaret had already been gone too long a time—there was no discernible vacuum in their lives, no empty place at table. There were simply no longer those rare, cryptic letters from the city; no longer the evenings when his mother, with huge effort, arranged pen and ink and paper on the scrubbed kitchen table and began those long letters, filled with vague warnings, to Margaret. It was quite enough for them to know that Margaret had haemorrhaged to death, in hospital sheets, among strangers, and in circumstances so appalling; the worst had come to pass, after all. And, having come to pass, it was best now forgotten. But there was one thing for which Sonny was grateful: despite all that had happened, they at least did not try to dissuade him from university, from the city. They seemed still to accept, in their stoic way, that he, like Margaret, should flee the nest and take his chance. Perhaps they considered that his sex was more often on the side of safety; that, when all was said and done, there was less risk for Sonny. He didn't know for sure, though; they didn't talk about it with him.

He watched them, with an aching lump of misery in his mind, as they went about their day; his father, with a face as eroded as the upper hills, plodding in gumboots about his dry brown acres; his mother, with pain lightly shadowing her cheerful eyes, busy in the kitchen or gossiping with callers on the back porch. He should have liked, as a gesture, to be able to say he would stay on with them, after all: they would have been relieved, astonished, grateful. But the pull away was still too strong. And they accepted that he should leave just as they had always accepted him as a strange, bookish child. He would go, at the end of summer, as Margaret had gone three years before.

He wandered often into the library which lay to the front of the homestead. Its long windows overlooked the harbour the first Hamilton had travelled on his way to site his shelter in this lonely and perhaps menacing place, to plant his life and learning down where he cleared the kauri forest. The library served, while he battled with the land, as a receptacle for his knowledge and his philosophy of happiness which he had brought to the new country bundled as tightly as the blankets he carried for barter with the brown men. And when his dream of happiness dissolved like smoke upon ravaged hills it became a place of refuge, a place in which to shut himself off from his rebellious sons, intolerant and landhungry, and where he could assuage his bitterness in his diaries now, ninety years later, crinkling with age. The library had survived like a curiosity through three generations of the family; it was something of wonder to Sonny that the large room was never cleared and put to other use, the books emptied from the shelves, the diaries consigned to the fire. Probably, once past the temptations of the first generation, the library had won its reprieve. No one appeared to have much use for it in the past; there was little time, on a struggling farm, for books. And the interest he and Margaret showed in the library, as children and adolescents, was regarded as something unhealthy by parents and relatives. Perhaps that only drove them more upon themselves, even more hungrily upon the books; looking back, he didn't know, couldn't remember. All he could remember was that so much of their lives had been spent not only on the hills and beaches, but here among dusty shelves. If ever there had been a time to put an end to the library, it should have been then. He and Margaret might have been salvaged, saved from the city, preserved for the less introspective life of their easy-going country cousins. Instead, the inevitable happened and Margaret had shaken free, as easily as a leaf from an autumn tree; first Margaret, now himself.

The day Sonny began packing for the city—he had left it late, and it was the day before he was due to leave—he went into the library for the last time; he intended selecting a few useful books to take along in his suitcases. Here and there, among the ranks of old leather-bound books with gold-lettered spines, stood new bright-covered books; the library had changed and grown since he and Margaret first invaded it. But he found the task of selection too painful; it was like wading upstream, against the current of a dark river lately travelled, seeking something of value lost beneath the opaque, swirling surface; or sorting through a scatter of rock, searching out true gold among fool's gold. After a while he gave up. He had thought he might find something there to help chart his way across new and strange terrain. But there was nothing; nothing, after all, that seemed immediately relevant. He felt naked and vulnerable. He would, depending on his own meagre knowledge, and without even quick-witted Margaret's help, have to chart his way alone. Disquieted, he wandered slowly across the library to the long windows. The more he considered it, the more he felt the direction of these windows marvellously chosen; he was lifted from his bleak mood—he might have been looking out upon some last shimmering vision of the country, preserved intact and framed by the first Hamilton, for it was still almost as it must once all have been, the bush and sea and sky delivered up to the onlooker in a bewildering sweep of beauty. The land, the farm itself, was absent from the picture: the stripped, sunburned acres which had drained all wonder, hope and memory. The land lay behind, on the other side of the homestead, a world away. On one side, the vision; on the other, the truth. Why should he and Margaret have inhabited this divide? What had brought them into the library in the first place? Perhaps boredom, a rainy day; perhaps something waiting to be fed within them. He didn't know; perhaps he would never know. Anyway, whatever it was, it had sent Margaret off to destruction; and now was sending him off—where? He turned from the windows with a gently helpless feeling; he crossed the library and closed the door softly. This act of shutting away the past, made so deliberately, reminded him—if he really needed to be reminded—that in a short time he would be opening a new door.

So it happened that he trod the worn carpet of a gloomy stairway on a late February day in a vague terror of apprehension; his feet struck dully up the stairs, and his suitcases bumped heavily and awkwardly against his legs. He had left, with regret, the warm golden sunshine which poured out of a clear sky upon the pale city and bright harbour. The street in which his new home stood was one of ugly old colonial homes with façades gently peeling, wandering verandas, elaborately frilled cornices. It was a quiet street, a stale backwater among large white modern buildings; a street neglected, or just forgotten. He found the right place—the number was marked clearly on the gate and, besides, he had called there once before, when on a brief visit to the city, to see Margaret. She wasn't in; and he left disappointed. But he found her by accident, shortly after, wandering with a bearded young man through the park beside the university. This young man pumped Sonny's hand—or so Sonny felt at the time—with a good deal of insincerity. He wore suede shoes, corduroys and a grey roll-neck sweater; he would have looked odd enough, anyway, even without the beard.

Margaret was at once delighted and apologetic. 'But why didn't you say you were coming?' she cried. 'You should have written and told me.' And, turning to the young man, she added, 'Sonny's really such an innocent in the city. I haven't the faintest idea how he'd get on if he hadn't found me.'

It was all so like Margaret: her eyes flashed back and forward from Sonny to the young man, as if she were simultaneously apologizing to the young man for Sonny's presence, and to Sonny for the young man's presence. Margaret always apologized for no reason at all. It seemed her fear of hurting anyone made her apologetic to the world simply for being herself. Taken by surprise that day, she appeared remarkably different, possessed of some new and extraordinary beauty. It wasn't at all the wild outdoor beauty she had at home, when she cantered long-legged beside Sonny about the farm. It was something more suited to the chill of a sunny late-winter day in a city park, with the first thin green leaves sprouting on the bare limbs of deciduous trees above their heads, a beauty of pale skin, dark hair, blue eyes; she wore her hair long and loose, had a bright scarf wound carelessly about her neck, and her hands were thrust deep in the pockets of her warm duffle-jacket; her legs were hidden in slender slacks. After they talked a while, uneasily, they went, the three of them, to a coffee-cellar. There, on even more unfamiliar ground—the cellar was a dimly-lit place, with Parisian murals—he felt dismayed; he distrusted Margaret's odd, bearded companion and, in a strange way, distrusted Margaret too. They talked across him about the theatre, the cinema, subjects on which he could express no opinion. And Sonny sat sullenly like someone who had discovered himself, against his will, in a foreign country, who did not understand the language and had no wish to learn it for they seemed, on the whole, to be talking in an elaborate code. He resisted Margaret's attempts to draw him into the conversation; or into comment on the farm and their parents and his study. His stupid silence, his surliness, must have at last become apparent to the others; for they fell silent too. He wished the young man, whom he now actively disliked, would go away and leave him with Margaret. But the young man didn't go away. He sat idly playing with lumps of sugar, looking up now and then at Margaret, the flicker of a smile on his lips, and his eyes signalling in an even more mysterious code. It was then that Sonny felt altogether an intruder. He was irritated, angry at himself for having hoped for anything from Margaret, appalled by the fiasco of his first trip alone to the city.

Now the landlady shuffled ahead of him up the stairs, across a landing, down a dark passage. He followed her with his suitcases. Halfway along the passage she stopped. In the gloom, her gross face enormous and pale, she clinked two keys from her apron pocket. 'The room,' she said. 'And the keys. Two keys—upstairs and downstairs, your door and the front door.' She seemed, for the moment, more than ever like a gaoler. Then the keys fell into his hand. 'I don't know exactly what happened to that sister of yours,' she said. 'And I don't want to know neither. It's your business. And my business is keeping a decent place here. That's why I usually only let my rooms to girls. They're safer. I'm making an exception for you on account of your father being such a nice man. After all that trouble, and him looking so miserable, I didn't have the heart to say no. It's a wonder I didn't say no. It's the first time

I ever had the police call here making inquiries in twenty years, mind you, in twenty years. Still, apart from that, I didn't have no trouble. That's why I made an exception for your father. I hope you appreciate it, that's all.'

'I do,' Sonny insisted. 'I do appreciate it.'

'You clean out your own room,' she continued. 'You do your own cooking in that long kitchen down the end of the passage. You share it with all the other people on this floor. The toilet's up the other end, and the bathroom's next to it. There's hot water, but you pay for the gas—pennies in the meter. And no visitors after eleven. And no parties and no nonsense. And a fortnight's notice either side.'

'Yes,' said Sonny. 'I understand.'

'Good,' she said. 'Then I won't keep you. There's your room.' She clumped off abruptly, along the passage, down the stairs. He was alone; quite alone. He tried to force a key into the lock: it was the wrong one. He had a dry urgent feeling in his throat. He took a deep breath and tried the second key. It fitted with difficulty, as if grown unfamiliar with the stiff lock. He twisted the key sharply and the door fell open. Then he took up his suitcases and, shouldering the door wide, banged into the room. He stopped as suddenly as he entered, overcome by the stillness of the room; he set down his suitcases quietly, turned, and shut the door. Then, with his back to the door, he let himself slowly observe the place.

At first it was neither more nor less than he expected. Everything already, had a faintly preserved quality. The bed with its faded check cover; the rug with the strange design—it might have been Persian or Indian, a gift from someone—fastened to the wall; the swimming championship pennant tacked near it; the photographs on the bookshelf by the bed, together with the little carved wooden Chinaman, with coolie hat and opium pipe, who gazed deeply into the silence; the neat rows of books—Sonny recognized some of the gold-lettered titles; the sheepskin rug on the varnished floor and, across the room, the compact desk with tidied heaps of paper, pens and a paua-shell ashtray. On the desk stood a lamp with red rattan, shade tilted jauntily on an odd-shaped raffia-worked bottle on which the word *Ruffino* stood out plainly and, in smaller letters, *vino chianti*; there was also a clock with the hands stopped at five past twelve. Above the desk, suspended on a triangle of cord, hung an old greenstone tiki. Everything was precise, uncluttered; the simple formality of the room told him little he did not already know. For a moment, though, it seemed odd to him that in three years his sister should have impressed her personality so lightly upon the room. Then he saw that lightness of touch as unmistakably Margaret's. The room was actually small; it could have appeared poky and miserable. Instead she gave it something of her own open, fresh quality. Someone else might have conducted a vain assault upon the cramped, shabby room; she went about it more subtly. Yes, the room was Margaret: he could not have thought otherwise.

Sunlight slanted through the lace of the closed window; stale air was trapped with the lengthening shadows. He went across the room in five, exact paces and lifted the window; there was a rumbling sound of old, worn window-cord as he did so. In the moment the sound died, he was looking at some athritic fruit-trees in the meagre backyard. Trapped and sunless beneath new-risen office buildings, they were like survivors of some more mellow, spacious time. Nothing, they seemed to say, was ever quite the same. A mild breeze, off the sea, cooled his face. Through a gap in the new buildings he was given a narrow view of the city crowding down to the harbour, ships and warehouses and great crane-beaks packed along the waterfront, a pale ferry-boat gliding like a seabird, homes sprinkled thickly on a green distant shore.

He half-turned back into the room, pausing as if on the edge of some dizzying height. He would, he supposed, have a long time to get used to the room; certainly he would need a long time to make any impression of his own upon it. At the moment it was altogether alien and forbidding. His eyes fell to the top of the bookshelf, and he was looking at himself: at a photograph of himself, taken years before, when slight and brown in swimshorts. He grinned shyly at Margaret's box-camera; the beach showed between fronds of fern in the background. He remembered, now, when it was taken: the last summer before Margaret left for university. Together they filled warm lengths of time easily, on lonely lagoons and gleaming beaches strewn with bleached driftwood. It was a summer when, for some reason, the unexpected became normal: they ceased being surprised by their own discoveries. They found the spars of some old wrecked sailing ship, uncovered by shifting sand, out near the harbour heads where the sand-bar had taken some of the old voyagers; they dug with sticks and turned up not only an old rusting ship's bell, but some long-buried Maori artifacts. And they found the entrance to an ancient Maori burial-cave, overhung with toi toi, where heaped bones and skulls lay on rock ledges; the sea rang about the cave, but inside there was a queer vibrant silence. They did not touch anything: they peered within and went quietly away, without breaking *tapu*. Only at the end, in the last days of thick February heat, did time grow heavy with Margaret's coming departure: she went about like a last-minute tourist desperate for souvenirs, gathering stones and shells and twisted sticks of seaworn pohutukawa; that was when she took the picture of Sonny. Finding the photograph in some way reassured him; he was not, after all, entirely a stranger here.

Only the clock, the clock silent on the desk at five minutes past twelve, now disturbed him. He went across to the desk, conscious of his footsteps, of his own slight rustling sound, in the silence. He wound the clock, set it aside, and sat at the desk: the ticking sounded sharply beside him, keeping him company as his hand hovered indecisively over the papers on the desk. He was some time making up his mind. Then he drew all the papers on the desk towards him.

He felt a thin pang of disappointment; there was very little there. A circular from the university literary society. Another circular for a film programme. The titles of the films were in French. Some hasty notes for an essay on the modern novel. Nothing rewarding or revealing. He looked at the notes, at Margaret's large oblique handwriting, seeking something—a clue perhaps, leading to other clues—obscure to himself there. But he was not to find anything so deliberately. As he shuffled the notes together, a scrap of paper, hidden till then, glided to the floor. He picked it up; on it was written a few lines of poetry. The handwriting trailed off in the middle of a stanza. He thought for a moment that the poem, like the notes, had simply been copied from some prescribed book; he might have placed it aside, with the other papers, if the first two lines had not told him something of the lumpy texture of the imagery. He was halted, then surprised: with a lurch of the stomach he saw, in the third line, his own name. He saw also, vividly, the poem as Margaret's own; written, perhaps, in the silence of the university library, when boredom or disquiet had taken her mind from textbooks to sunlight upon a window, and then to a more distant place. Until now he had no suspicion that his sister might have written poetry; his only confirmation of the fact lay lightly in his hand. The poem was not directly relevant to him, or to his experience; his name just seemed to sit uneasily among other words. The lines appeared to be written out of some agony of mind. But the subject of the poem, if a poem so wandering could be said to have a subject, was their discovery of the Maori burial cave. She was using their discovery, and their creeping away, as a parallel for some other thing, investing some other experience with the same unique, magical significance: it baffled him for a while until he saw it, at last, as a love poem.

The chair-legs gave a quick cry as he pushed himself out from the desk, let the poem fall with the other papers. The soft explosion of shock within him, fading as he crossed the room, seemed suddenly and entirely unreasonable. He stood staring blankly out into the declining afternoon, his hands fastened on the windowsill. Why should he feel so betrayed? He sought to unravel the separate strands of grief and anger within himself: they had, after all, made no pact, no secret, about the cave; it had simply not occurred to him that Margaret might, looking back, have seen the discovery in relation to someone other than himself. And might have used the experience as if she alone had right to it; as if it had never been shared. It had simply not occurred to him, in fact, that Margaret might have loved so tangibly as to make all other love, all other loves, transparent. And he, apparently, belonged to that transparent order of things; his was only a name dropped casually, perhaps just for metre's sake, in an unfinished poem. He was, above all, a convenient disguise for that other, that faceless and nameless person whose presence grew behind the scrambled images. And whose absence, possibly, had dictated the poem in the first place. He could not have named his feeling, at least not yet: he could not have named it jealousy.

He forced himself back into the room: he had been standing at the window in some frozen attitude of escape. But there was, he knew now more surely than he had ever known, to be no escape. The sun had slid down behind the buildings; the room had darkened. But it seemed, for one hallucinatory second as he turned back, that it was his own inner oppression which dimmed his eyes. Yet it was, after all, only the change in light, the movement of the world towards evening; it had, until now, escaped him. He crossed to the desk again and sat slumped, with his head in his hands, for some time. When he lifted his eyes finally, it was still darker; outside, above the buildings, light drained from the sky. Strips of cloud held flecks of sunset like a sediment. He felt heavy and tired; the effort of the long day's journey had overtaken him. Yet he had to go on; there was no question of his not continuing with the search until, perhaps, he had nothing left. He had hardly even begun; there was still the inside of the desk to be ransacked. And papers, perhaps letters, to be scavenged through, sorted into heaps of probabilities and possibilities; somewhere there would be one clue, and another. Now he knew a little, he felt impelled to know all. He had to see himself as naked as he felt; he had to shed the last ragged garment of illusion, and see the colour of his loneliness. He needed light; above all, light. He groped in the gloom for the switch of the rattan-shaded desk lamp. Then he was caught, with the desk, in a patch of red light; the rest of the room shaded off into thickening darkness. He raised his eyes to the tiki, swinging gently on the ultimate tip of its triangle of cord: his movement, his clumsy feeling for the lamp-switch, had set it in motion. He did not know how his family had come by the tiki: no one knew, no one remembered; no more than most of the family remembered how or why they came to be in this country. The tiki had lain unwanted, among family trinkets and trivia, for a long time before Margaret claimed it for herself. It was old, probably three hundred years or more; old enough anyway for generations of brown flesh to have worn down the clean lines of the carving. The tiki, he thought: the first man, creation of the devious and incestuous god Tane: or the human embryo crushed in the womb, head twisted, tongue lolling: a vision, tantalizing and terrible, of an older, darker, god-begun world. It settled presently, hung still in the pale red glow of the lamp; it settled steadily in his sight as his hands hesitated on the top drawers of the desk. There seemed, before he went farther, something he had to say, admit to himself.

He had loved his sister.

But there seemed, after all, nothing terrible in the words. They sounded, in fact, ordinary and usual. Yet that was all there was to say; the words were simply not enough. He was powerless to find others. There was, within himself, a vast void uncovered; he had to beat down the darkness as he might beat down fire, beat it down into the remotest depths of his feverish flesh.

He was still paused in the act of opening the desk. He had a bitter taste in his mouth; and the red of the lamplight burned irritatingly at the corners of his tired eyes. The dark grew enormously around him. It was not all right; it would not be all right for a long time. But it was better, having said it; not much better, but a little.

There was a scraping sound as the first drawer opened. A half-smoked pack of cigarettes lay in it; some paper-clips, hairpins. And the strange harvest of talismans he had half-expected to find somewhere, the stones and shells she had apparently been unable to discard. He tried another drawer. More notes; and a tidy heap of typewritten essays. Bundles of letters fastened with rubber-bands. He took out the letters and placed them on top of the desk. Then he began to go systematically through all the drawers. There were more letters, here and there. And a long letter of Margaret's own, unfinished.

Dear Geoff,

I have all your letters now. What should I say—that I'm pleased and happy for you? But you know that wouldn't be true. I know you think I'm an obstinate creature, but perhaps my obstinacy is an honesty. Too often the obstinate person is seen as an oddity and placed in the category of perverse troublemaker. As if he or she doesn't already suffer enough from the affliction—sickness, even—of honesty. But probably there is a justice, somewhere, in the quarantine imposed upon them, such people are, after all, a menace. Given the chance they might infect others with their disease. And where would we be without our daily lies, daily hypocrisy? In the abyss, probably; in the abyss which I seem, at present, to inhabit. So please don't call me dishonest again. Call me obstinate if you like—but concede me honesty for the moment.

You say you feel

It was typically, painfully Margaret: long-winded, oblique, in an effort to avoid abrupt hurt. She had written Sonny a letter with just such a rambling preliminary after his disastrous visit to the city. *I have all your letters now.* What letters? It was the excuse he needed, just then, to escape Margaret's own voice.

Some of the letters on the desk were his; most of those he had written Margaret from the farm had been kept. He could not have read them again; they would, with their innocence, have been embarrassing. There were one or two letters surviving from his mother: he saw her again labouring to produce the letters on the kitchen table. He, in turn, would soon be receiving the same letters, suffering the same reproaches. They, for different reasons, would also have been painful to read; he eliminated them along with his own, dropping them back into a drawer. Other letters were less easy to eliminate. Letters from girl friends, vague and ambiguous. He scanned a number of these opaque letters before casting them aside. The pile of letters on the desk diminished quickly. Soon he was aware of something which linked the few letters remaining. There was a pattern in the stamps and postmarks. Sydney, Jakarta, Colombo, Aden, Naples: the pattern, and story, of voyage. The handwriting on the envelopes was precise and masculine. Yet there was something missing, like an inexplicably silent note in a phrase of music. Then he found the letter which had slid out from among the others and fallen, unobserved, to the floor. He picked it up and the picture was complete: the envelope was postmarked London; there was the same precise, masculine hand.

Looking at the letters in sequence, Sonny felt they told him just about as much as he was ever likely to know. He didn't need to read them. In a way he didn't even need to know any more about Geoff. To know more might spoil the picture. But Margaret?

You say you feel at home again. Well you are, aren't you? At home, I mean. You came out here to get away from something. I often wonder if I really know all the story. You only ever gave me bits and pieces. A grey childhood, some mean smoky city, a brilliant scholastic career—a break with everything you knew, Oxford, London, an unhappy marriage. (What was she really like, I wonder? I always felt she was more important than you'd allow me to know. You only ever let me see a snobbish girl with rather a sulky face.) And then a nervous breakdown, a chance for escape, a chance perhaps for happiness—a job in a country twelve thousand miles away, so remote from everything you'd known. You weren't the first to imagine that simply by exchanging one patch of earth for another you might find happiness. It's an old story, and mostly a sad one.

No: it was no use. He had been foolish to imagine he might learn anything about Margaret from a letter anyway. They all seemed so irrelevant, these words which confused him. He was likely to lose Margaret altogether in their thickets and by-ways.

The knock on the door jolted him in his seat, set his body clamouring. He had been locked away with shadows so long now, the least sound would have sparked fright in his body. Then there was the landlady's voice.

'Telephone,' she said. 'Telephone.'

He rose and went bewildered to the door. Who was there, in the city, who might call him by telephone? Perhaps it was a toll call from the country, from his parents. He opened the door. The landlady was dressed in Saturday night finery, in a black dress with silvery trimmings. She smelt of wine and had a cigarette burning in one hand. 'Downstairs,' she said. 'On the right, under the stairs. You'll find it easily.' She tramped down the passage ahead of him.

'For me?' he said, still perplexed.

'No,' she said. 'Not exactly. For your sister. She still gets calls, though they've been dropping off a bit lately. People have been away on holidays and things—I expect they're slow hearing. Anyway I'm tired of explaining. Now it's your turn.'

They were half-way down the stairs now. The landlady stopped, turned off to the door of her apartment.

'You mean—' he began. 'You mean you didn't say.'

'That's right,' she replied. 'I didn't say. Like I told you, I'm tired of explaining. Down that way—on the right, under the stairs. It might be someone you know.'

He doubted that. He knew none of Margaret's friends. The landlady looked at him curiously, almost sympathetically; but only for a moment. She went into her apartment, closing the door. He heard muffled voices beyond the door.

'What happened?' said a man's voice. 'What's the trouble?'

'Nothing,' the landlady said. 'Just the new kid upstairs, the one I was telling you about. The one whose sister died. Nice kid, brown as a berry. Straight from the country, it's written all over him. There was a call for his sister, that's all. I went up to get him.'

'Christ,' said the man. 'Is that all? You looked worried. How's your glass?'

'Empty,' she said. 'Thanks.' Sonny heard a rattle of springs as she fell into a chair. 'Isn't the world a bloody awful place?'

'Cheers,' said the man. 'How do you mean?'

'Christ, don't ask me,' she said. 'Don't ask me. I don't know. It's just I can't sleep nights, sometimes, thinking about it. The world, I mean, and everything.'

No; it was no use delaying; no place to learn anything new. Sonny went on down. There was a feeble light under the stairs, above the place where the telephone receiver dangled from its cradle. He took the receiver and held it to his ear, but remained silent as though paralysed. The sounds of a party, music and voices, pressed violently against his brain.

'Hello,' said someone irritated. 'Are you there? Is that you, Marg?'

He spoke at last. 'Hello?' he said tentatively.

'For Christ's sake,' said the voice. 'Who is it? Where's Marg?'

'She's not here,' he began. 'She's—'

'For crying out loud,' said the drunken voice. 'Who is it? Where's Marg? Who's talking? Is that you, Geoff? I thought you'd gone home to England. Come on, where are you hiding her?'

'It's not Geoff,' Sonny said. 'I'm—'

But it was no use. Whoever it was, at the other end, wasn't listening. Against the background of party noise, he heard the voice explaining to someone else, 'Some bastard at the other end won't tell me where she is. Says he isn't Geoff. God knows.' The voice came back full into the receiver again. 'Look here, who the hell is it talking?'

'Margaret's brother,' Sonny said.

'Well, for God's sake. What do you know about that? I didn't even know she had one. I'm not even sure about it now—I mean are you sure you're Marg's brother? I mean I've heard this story before. Brothers, cousins—I know the line. You sure about it? You sure you're Marg's brother?'

'Perfectly sure,' Sonny said.

'Well, I'll believe you,' said the voice. 'Thousands wouldn't. Do me a favour, will you? Will you root round and dig Marg out, wherever she is, and tell her Ken's back in town and having a bloody marvellous party. You get the name? Ken. Just tell her Ken—Ken's having a party. Gallons of grog and dozens of people. Tell her, won't you? She's sure to come. Come along too, if you like.'

'Thanks,' Sonny said. 'But Margaret's dead.'

'You're kidding,' the voice said. 'You're—'

'She's dead,' Sonny said quietly.

'Christ,' the voice exploded. 'You're not serious. You mean—?'

'Yes,' Sonny said. 'I mean she's dead.' He cried it out this time as if to convince himself. At the other end there was a baffled pause, a confusion of voices against the music, and then he was left with the humming receiver. He dropped it back into its cradle and walked away. Near the foot of the stairs, in the darkness, a nausea overcame him; he trembled, swayed, and held to the bottom stair-post.

Somewhere outside there was a rush of high, clicking heels over pavement; then over the wooden boards of the veranda. The front door banged open. In the brief invasion of streetlight Sonny saw a girl silhouetted for a moment. There was a glitter of hair, and the flash of a silver brooch; he did not have time to see more. Her face remained in shadow. She was small, slight-figured, and had one arm across her front, half-bent as though in pain. The door slammed behind her. She did not see him in the dark, at the foot of the stairs; she fled past him, up the stairs, leaving behind a faint smell of perfume.

The girl was sobbing.

She was gone quickly. Somewhere upstairs, in a remote part of the building, a door opened and closed. Then the place grew silent again. Wonder at the girl, wonder at her tears, for the moment eased his own pain. Slowly he made his way up the stairs, holding to the banister as if old and tired. There was still a faint trail of scent. Who was she, and what was her grief? What caused her to flee a summer evening? He crossed the landing and went down the passage and back to his room. In the room he stood in shadow, before the desk in its patch of red light; he heard, through the slender wall, the fall of a body upon a mattress and renewed sobbing. So the girl, whoever she was, lived in the next room, so close to him. Yet it made no difference: there was nothing, really, he could do; she was trapped as securely in her privacy as he was in his own; she might as well have wept a hundred miles away. He wondered if he might have this helpless feeling often in the city. For this, it seemed, was the condition on which life here was to be lived.

He went to the desk and sat down again. His eyes found Margaret's letter. For some reason he no longer wished to read it. He turned the pages slowly, but they might have been blank for all he saw. Until he came to the last paragraph. The handwriting, with haste, became more and more shapeless, broken up by deletions; Sonny had to read back and forward to decipher the words, follow their meaning.

Nice of you to say you want to rescue me from the healthy squalor of this place. I suppose I should be pleading for rescue. But what if I'm too deep in this squalor, too deep to get out? Of course you wouldn't understand; you wouldn't wish to understand. Anyhow I've seen you get to work like a surgeon on too much I've said. I'm sure you can always reduce everything to the absurd. You see, I'm about to join my family on the farm for Xmas. You really ought

Sonny shifted his eyes. Through the window, between the dark buildings, he saw lights glittering on the harbour. In the next room the sobbing had died to a faint whimper. He waited until he was calm again.

to have met my family. My parents, for example—I used to despise them. Then, imagining myself more tolerant, I thought I had the right to pity them. Then I saw that pity was only arrogance in a new disguise. So I've had to try making sense of it all over again. Then there's my brother. I never told you about him. He's due here next year. In fact I've been hunting for a room for him all this past week. I feel I have to help him. If I don't, no one else will. I've a lot I want to tell him. I'm responsible. I suppose that's what I'm saying. In an odd way you've made me aware of this responsibility. You probably wouldn't understand that either. You say I sound a little distraught, as if there's something wrong. Well, perhaps I am a little distraught. Perhaps there is something wrong. I guess it was too good to be true—that it should end so cleanly, I mean. I knew three weeks after you left, but you were more than half-way to London by then. I didn't want to tell you until I made up my mind, and this letter has been making up my mind. (I wonder if I shall ever post it.) I haven't decided quite what to do yet. I've only a few days before I go off to join the family on the farm for Xmas. Yes, I know someone who knows someone who helps, at a price, with these things. Though I don't know if I'm strong enough—cold blooded enough?—to go through with that. On the other hand I worry about the alternative—getting through next year, when I'll be needed, with all this complication. I hope you're not too shocked. After all you always said it was the wildness in me you liked, and wildness has its consequence. So please don't worry. Because

Because what? Because she knew someone who knew someone? Anyway that was where the letter ended. Perhaps he had learned all he would ever learn. He folded the pages and, after some hesitation, put them together with the other letters, those of the voyager. Between them there might be an answer; he didn't know what or why. But it seemed the least he could do.

It might have been an hour or year later: he sat at the window and the room was in darkness; the lamp on the desk had been turned out long before. In the next room the girl had lately begun to stir. He heard her slippered feet across the floor, the snip of a radio-switch, soft music. She must have been sitting at her window, too, with a cigarette, for he could smell the drift of smoke. He wondered where she came from; had she a family escaped, a farm forsaken? And why should she sprinkle tears upon a city pavement? He might never know; just as he might never know, finally, about Margaret. It was now frightening to believe that he might, after all, have been important to Margaret.

He had suffered this sensation before, once when listening to music he imagined he knew well; everything had been as familiar as ever, as beautiful as ever, but suddenly strange and terrible too. It was like contemplating the dark spaces beyond the stars from the porch steps on the farm at night. He felt the weight of new questions in his mind. He had been silent too long. He rose and whispered into the room.

'What is it, Margaret? What is it we never knew, never counted on? Weren't you strong enough, or were you too strong? Whatever it is, I should know. It's important to me. I only want one good reason why I should be alive tonight, and not you. What was it you were going to tell me? How were you going to help me? Why is it? What is it?' He whispered his last question into the room, and there was silence.

* * *

In a world where uncertainty was the rule, perhaps one thing was certain: he would have some kind of answer very soon. He was hungry. And he was tired. He had not eaten; he had not even unpacked. He crossed the room and switched on the desk-lamp. He had not touched anything in the room yet, but it was as if in the darkness everything had shifted imperceptibly. Certainly the room no longer looked so alien. The clock, as he turned back to the desk again, swung into his vision. He looked at it, baffled. It said five o'clock; it was surely near eleven, or midnight. Then he remembered that he hadn't, when winding the clock, shifted the hands to the correct time. His wrist-watch said fifteen minutes past eleven. He put the clock right with a feeling of satisfaction.

He went to his suitcases. There was no urgency about unpacking. It was just that he wanted to deposit a few things of his own around the room, as if to reinforce his own claim to possession. Afterwards he would go out into the night and find, perhaps down near the waterfront, an all-night eating place. There were such places in the city. There were a great many places, a great many places to which he might walk, in the city. He unfastened the straps of his suitcases and began to unpack.

Neither Profit nor Salvation

Of course it was crazy. Everyone said so.

But then Diana had a certain reputation for craziness. Everyone might have said that too, for all Diana knew; she did not hear everything that was said of her. It seemed fantastic to them that she should give up her good job, her fine flat with its splendid sea view, her marvellous parties. Perhaps that was what rankled in their minds most of all, the loss of her parties. Saturday nights would be duller. So selfishly they wished her failure. Optimistically they declared she'd be back soon.

And, of course, it was in a way incredible that Diana, so much a woman of the city, should hope to succeed in the country. And hope to succeed in bringing back to life a rundown orchard in the middle of nowhere. Or at least it seemed in the middle of nowhere. People who visited her during that first year were able to report more precisely on the location of the place. It was a hundred and fifty odd miles from the city, and near the sea. There was no town close at hand, only fitful transport, and there was difficulty getting fruit to the market. There was no denying the place had a grisly attraction, they agreed; the sea, the rocks, the burnt-off headlands. There were only one or two European neighbours, farmers. And a ramshackle Maori village not far away along the shore. But the soil was poor, mostly tough gumland, and no site for an orchard. Whoever planted it there, in that battered landscape, had no sense. Diana was simply expending herself on someone else's eccentricity.

And, of course, with that girl: that silly Simpson girl. She had been the real surprise. No one expected Diana to drag her along too. It was one thing to shelter the girl a while, in her flat. Another to take her off, into the country, and expect her to be of any help.

But then, that was Diana for you.

* * *

People became fewer that second year. Diana felt obscurely that she should be sorry. Plainly she was missed in fewer lives now. Perhaps others filled the gap, gave the parties she once gave. She had no way of knowing. Her old friends might simply have sunk into the lethargy of the suburbs.

But she wasn't sorry that fewer people came. In a way, this was a surprise to her. She had always imagined herself as gregarious, imagined she needed people. Now she found herself more and more content without them. She had the orchard, her books and records; and Merlyn was sufficient company. She wasn't altogether lonely, a total hermit. So her departure from the city turned out, after all, to be painless. She had discovered her real nature, and not too late. And she missed very little of her old life.

Her reason for leaving was—like so much else in her life—a simple thing which grew complex: like a seed, dropped casually to earth, destined to take deep root, push a thick trunk in the air, throw out sturdy branches and green clusters of leaf. It began with the vague and wistful, apparently irrational desire to return to the land; she supposed such a feeling common enough. Later Diana grew sure that, on the land, she might better be able to find a cure for the apathy of the spirit, the atrophy of the moral sense, which afflicted her as well as so many of her friends. She might be able to make much more sense of her life. Within her environment, she seemed powerless. And nothing, after all, could be more natural than a return to the land since Diana had been born, the best part of forty years before, on a farm. In this she had something in common with many of her friends. And she suffered at the hands of these same friends when, once or twice, she expressed her early, wistful desire to escape the city and go back to the land. They, apparently, had found some way to suffocate or destroy the desire in themselves—if it ever existed. Certainly they were able to call her desire sentimental. 'Sentimentality, Di,' they said. 'All of it. You can't go back again.'

And perhaps, for them, it was true: they couldn't go back again. They couldn't allow themselves to dream of it. This, though she didn't know it at the time, was her first step free of friends, like an infant's first tottering fight with gravity; she stumbled forward, but did not fall, along the track which would make her separate. She was different. And perhaps different because, finally, she had not been a great success in the city. She had only two collapsed marriages, and no children, to show for her life. So she was free, and they were not. She was free to allow herself the dream; to wander, if she liked, back along the grassy paths of her country girlhood. Outwardly Diana looked successful. First in journalism, then in advertising, she climbed quickly to the top. Now an executive, she commanded an impressive salary. She had her flat, her books and records, her clothes. She had no apparent reason to worry at her life with questions. Yet she did. And the only answers to her questions were flimsy. Inwardly she was not only dissatisfied, but a failure: if failure could be taken to mean unexplored potential, lack of fulfilment. Diana lacked not only fulfilment, but also content. Something, sooner or later, was bound to happen.

And when it did, she was astonished that it should occasion so much vehemence. There were those who attacked her—as if she were affronting them personally—and those who were simply dismayed. And those who were merely cynical.

'You'll be back,' they said. 'Within six months, probably. You won't be able to stand it. The isolation, Di. You're just not built that way.'

They all, in their different ways, tended to upset her. So, in those last weeks in the city, she avoided friends and threw herself back upon Merlyn. She had taken Merlyn Simpson into her flat not long before. Diana wasn't, at the time, particularly happy about it. But the poor girl had nowhere else to go. She virtually lived in coffee-bars, sleeping wherever she could find a bed—which meant she seldom slept alone. A victim of an unfortunate marriage—with one of Diana's more remote men friends—she seemed incapable, since her divorce, of making her way alone in the world. Which wasn't surprising, since she was only twenty-two; and had been married at seventeen. She'd never had much chance of learning to make her own way. She'd made, since her marriage, almost every blunder she could. Finally the police heaved her, along with two other girls, out of a squalid flat which they shared with a couple of marijuana-smoking layabouts. Merlyn was lucky to escape court, and probation. She drifted a while, circling the coffee-bars like some rouged ghost; and then spent the night at Diana's after a particularly hectic party. The next morning Diana woke to find her kitchen occupied by a perky, clear-eyed creature still in party garb—

long black stockings, black sweater, and mock-suede jerkin.

'I'm cooking your breakfast,' Merlyn announced. 'It's the least I can do.'

Diana, who had lived alone the past five years, was rather touched. Actually she seldom ate breakfast. But she didn't want to disappoint the girl. Also she observed that the flat had been scrupulously tidied, all the glasses and dishes cleared and washed. The girl must have been up for hours.

'Well,' Diana said. 'That's nice.'

'Only an omelet,' the girl said. 'That's just about all I can cook. I love your flat, and the view.'

'I rather like it myself,' Diana confessed.

Beyond the wide windows, the city sprawled down to the water and the harbour shimmered in the morning sun. After breakfast Merlyn declared that it was probably time for her to leave. Diana inquired if she had far to go. Merlyn made a brave face of it, avoided the question. So Diana repeated it.

'I haven't anywhere to go,' the girl said. Her face trembled as if the confession were some last humiliation forced upon her. 'I've nowhere.'

And that was the beginning. In retrospect, Diana felt she didn't have much choice. And, like many tricks of chance, it all turned out for the best. The way things were, in those last weeks before she left the city, Diana needed Merlyn for support. It was odd that their positions should so soon have been reversed, that Diana should so soon lean on Merlyn. She might have come to doubt herself altogether if she hadn't had Merlyn.

Merlyn's approach to life was simple. 'I think people should do whatever they want most to do,' she declared bravely, with an angry toss of the head. 'And it's no one else's business. There are,' she added characteristically, 'a lot of small, mean-minded people in this world. You know that?'

Diana knew. Oh yes, Diana knew only too well.

'And I think,' Merlyn continued, 'that if you want to get out of here, and go back to the country, it's your business. I think a lot of your friends are only jealous because they can't. That's all. They're envious because you're free and brave enough to do it, and they're not. I feel sorry for them, really I do.'

Diana thought this extremely sensitive, coming as it did from a girl apparently so simple and uncomplicated. Moreover, it was remarkable how exactly Merlyn confirmed her own opinion of her friends. For the first time she began to wonder if Merlyn might keep her company. But she didn't till some time later ask Merlyn how she might like the country. The girl was, in a sense, still on trial. She had settled comfortably into the flat, and seldom went out. She seemed to entertain herself successfully while Diana was at work. And she was certainly no drain on Diana's purse—she was a skimpy eater. Nor were new clothes a problem; she politely rejected Diana's offer to help, but did accept cast-offs. Around the flat, anyway, she was seldom out of a pair of old jeans and an absurdly oversize baggy man's sweater she had picked up from one of her past residences. She showed no desire to return to her old ways.

Then Diana saw, with mingled pleasure and dismay, that she was again presented with no choice. For if she were to depart the city, and leave Merlyn behind, she would simply be turning the girl loose on the streets again. Obviously all the girl had lacked was a home. Now, when she had one, it was about to be wrenched away from her again. Diana discovered that responsibility, easily accepted, was not so easy to abdicate. She couldn't turn Merlyn out. Her conscience wouldn't allow her, for one thing.

So it was settled; or almost settled. She would have to take Merlyn with her. Providing, of course, that she wanted to come.

And Merlyn, as it turned out, did want to come. She even performed a jubilant little dance to show her feelings when Diana asked her.

There was the place, the location for their new life.

Months before they left the city—even before Diana had met Merlyn—Diana had chosen a place; or a place had chosen her.

From the time she first decided on an orchard, she was in difficulty. Her savings couldn't accommodate a really prosperous orchard: in any case most of these places, in rather dull inland districts, had no appeal for her. Some of these solidly-packed orchards reminded her of nothing less than a row of factories. They didn't offer the kind of life she envisaged. She travelled farther and farther up the island in her station wagon, seeking without success. Her real aim was a modest orchard, with enough free land for a decent garden; somewhere, in fact, where she could win at the least a subsistence living from the earth. Also it should be near the sea. Apart from its summer attractions, the sea would also offer a secondary supply of food—one could fish, gather shellfish from rocks and beach.

But, for a long time, she found no place to suit. She drove on, through quite impossible districts, in despair. Finally—in a place which was almost literally a sandy desert wasteland, and the end of the road— she turned back towards the city and tried a new tactic. She kept off the main highways, hunted down side roads, and clung to the coast. The place arrived finally, like a mirage. It was too good to be true: there was even a FOR SALE notice tacked to the gate.

The orchard lay near the sea, in the folds of old gumland. It had been begun by a Dalmatian, a survivor of the gum-digging days, who had stayed on after his companions moved away. As an ageing bachelor, he'd apparently tried before his death to bring relatives out from Yugoslavia to keep the place going; but without success. After his death the property passed to a nephew in the city, a cafe-owner who had no interest in land, and who wished to dispose of it as quickly as he could. He'd already waited three years for a buyer.

It wasn't ideal by any means. But it was the best she could hope to find. It would also be easy there to keep people at a distance, or so she thought: there would be no inquisitive neighbours. The Maori settlement was a mile away. It was a mixed tribal settlement, not a traditional one: many of the people had come there to be employed, years before, in a timber mill. But after fire destroyed the kauri forest, the mill was abandoned. The people in the settlement lived the best way they could, fishing, growing vegetables, dispatching crayfish to the city; the young people usually went to find work in the towns. The Europeans were at a greater distance. Dull, pleasant farming people, they were unlikely to intrude.

Looking back to their uncertain beginning, across a score of months, Diana had every reason for satisfaction. The unexpected was often a joy to her. When they climbed wearily from the dusty station wagon, late that hot summer afternoon, they found on the porch a string of three fresh snapper, and two flax baskets—one of shellfish, the other of kumara. It was a welcome gift from the people in the Maori settlement; and Diana understood, at last, why they had insisted she write ahead and tell them exactly when she was coming. The cynic in her might have said the gift was part repayment for the use the settlement had made of the orchard these past three years; but Diana usually rejected the cynic in herself. The optimist in her saw an omen, more promising than any other, that their life here despite all fears and prophecies— would not be too difficult. After all, the point surely was that they asked so little of this place. They asked only a refuge, these two refugees from the city. They asked neither profit nor salvation. That, anyhow, was the way Diana liked to think about it.

Of course there were difficulties. There was the house. Diana had virtually to teach herself carpentry—simply to seal the cracks, make sure the place held together. There was the orchard. And the projected garden. And there, if anywhere, Merlyn was her delight. She made herself, at once, so much at home outdoors. Who would have dreamt it? Diana wouldn't. She, like most of her friends, had seen Merlyn pessimistically, as a probable drag. But this creature of the coffee-bars— she of the rouge and eye-shadow—gave herself with enthusiasm to the breaking up of the heavy clotted soil. In tattered shorts, with shirt-sleeves rolled, she shone with sun and perspiration. Her arms and legs browned quickly. A child of the suburbs, the country had always been, for her, a place for holiday. And in holiday mood she went, for months, about her work. Planting new trees, pruning the old, weeding the garden, hoeing among the vines, gathering mussels from the rocks—it was all pure holiday for Merlyn.

Diana expected it not to last. Sooner or later the girl would grow restless.

But Merlyn remained a daily miracle. Even through their first long and comfortless winter she continued cheerful. She was still so much a child, Diana concluded; perhaps even discomfort could still be an adventure. And with summer, Merlyn bloomed again. She was browner, sturdier.

'Do you feel sometimes you'd like to go back?' Diana asked.

'Go back?' Merlyn said, astonished. 'But what for?'

Indeed, Diana wondered, what for? 'I thought you might miss people,' she said. 'People, and things.'

'I've never had much use for people,' Merlyn replied. She paused thoughtfully, and smiled. 'For most people, anyway.' It seemed, then, that there were exceptions. 'And as for things—well, I don't have much use for them either. Things are all right, I suppose, if you've got the knack of acquiring them. But then, I've never had the knack.'

'It wasn't that I meant, exactly. But it doesn't matter.' Diana hesitated before she added quietly. 'Neither profit nor salvation.'

'What's that?' Merlyn said, perplexed.

'Nothing. Or, rather, just a thought I have now and again. When I think about us—and this place.'

'I think I like it. Say it again.'

'Neither profit nor salvation.'

'Yes,' Merlyn said. 'I like it.'

They were swimming in a fresh-water creek at the back of the orchard. About the creek, within a steep gully, native bush had found a refuge from fire and axe. Diana thought the place marvellously pleasant when she first discovered it—water jetting between boulders into wide brimming pools, drooping fern and erect karaka, sunlight and shadow. They usually only swam there at certain times of day, when the tide was sucked out from shore. Then their favourite beach presented a rather bleak appearance, with grey mudbanks, mangrove swamp, and black rock. They always swam in the creek when the tide was out.

Merlyn climbed from the water and spread herself to sunbathe on warm rock. She didn't have a very spectacular figure, if Diana were any judge. It was rather too slim, too slight about the hips. And her breasts were far too small. Her limbs possessed a sprightly, nervous quality. Whatever others might think of it, Diana thought it attractive. Everything about Merlyn was at one with her character. Diana felt her own powerful figure lumpy by contrast; her own character craggy, with unexpected deeps. She supposed, though, that she and Merlyn had one thing at least in common: they had both been ill-used by men. She often wondered about the girl's marriage, of which Merlyn spoke little. She felt that if she knew more she might find in Merlyn's story a remarkable parallel to her own. But Diana disliked being inquisitive, disliked fossicking too much over the past. It didn't matter now. Here they were exiles not only from the city, but also from the small, grubby hells men created. This thought took Diana by surprise; she examined it as she might some unusual stone. And she toyed with it for days until it was lost, somewhere, in the routine of the orchard.

Often her wonder about Merlyn seemed an elaborate mental subterfuge for wonder about herself: every time she went seeking Merlyn in her imagination, she found only herself. At Merlyn's age—give or take a year or two—she had been a smart, rather capricious junior reporter. Unlike Merlyn, though, she had her mind set rather firmly on people, and things. She was also on the brink of her first, disastrous marriage. Her husband judged her as an acquisition; she herself, paradoxically enough, became a thing—a fashionable and rather versatile domestic appliance. Well, she'd fought her way out of that soon enough. What she did win from it, however, was confidence in dealing with men. In some ways it was an advantage; in others a disadvantage. It was an advantage in terms of profit, in terms of money or simple social profit. But it was a disadvantage in that it allowed her little illusion. Some might count this as gain; Diana didn't. Loss of illusion, loss of mystery, only left her, in a way, the more naked. And the more vulnerable to loneliness and unhappiness. Some illusion, after all, was necessary for happiness. She was farther away from it than ever. She might free her body of its appetites, but at her centre was still a thin core of discontent. The front she turned to the world, impressive, commanding, a little eccentric, was simply convenient; but allowed little flexibility for manoeuvre. Secretly she sought instruction in the Catholic Church, but turned back when she became aware of the surrender of logic, of ordinary common sense, involved. It was the surrender to mystery she most desired, not the mental tyranny, the preposterous dogma. She had less trouble than most with some of the minor points of doctrine—on birth control, for example. She had no patience with those who wished to strip sex of its crude power and dark dignity; who wished to make of it a hygienic, inconsequential frolic. The more devious the ritual, the more taboos, the more sex was buried darkly in life, the better; and the better to pay it adequate tribute. But even the accumulation of small agreements did not, in the end, give her enough strength for decision. She still, when she thought she might enter a church unobserved, found comfort inside. But because she had not been able to make surrender total, her discontent increased. She was reaching out for something she could never really have. And she grew to despise the yearning adolescent in herself.

She married again. She did not do so for convenience. Nor, on the other hand, was she swept away. She married, experimentally, someone who had lived with her on and off over a period of years; she was, she supposed, in dabbling mood. George Francis had been most things at some time or other—it was difficult to pin him down. Though large and heavily athletic, he was mercurial of temperament, at times dreamy. He'd travelled—once lived, painting and writing, three years in Spain— and returned with traveller's tales. Since his return, he'd wandered from place to place—fire-watching in the forests, deer-stalking in the south, sheep-mustering in the high country. He seldom spoke, any more, of endeavour in the arts. He had made an uneasy peace with that side of himself, and gave himself vigorously to the business of living. Diana, who felt herself slowly solidifying in her advertising work, thought he might be the leaven to her lump. Physically she found him attractive; as company he was often stimulating. Marriage gave him a home, in a sense, a base to work from. And, of course, he never lasted long in the city. She didn't really expect him to last long. He went away, more and more frequently. He wrote sometimes. Then he virtually vanished altogether. They hadn't divorced: there was no point. Unless one or other of them wanted another marriage, which was unlikely. It wouldn't be fair to say George had ill-used her, like her first husband: he simply never thought of her. It was surprising, really, that he'd ever paused long enough to marry her. She'd asked little of George, and received little. It was all so perfectly reasonable, and perfectly pointless. She sometimes imagined George growing older, and wanting to settle; but without much success.

She trembled on the point of action for years. Then she fell out of her old life as easily as she fell into the new. Her friends were probably right when they called her desire to return to the country sentimental: the dream of the garden, the retreat to innocence—it was all so absurd, almost high comedy, in relation to Diana. Sentimentality, she often thought when working in orchard or garden; so be it. She was, in fact, almost happy.

2

Their second winter was milder. The orchard blossomed early, in August, and there were few winds to scatter the flowers from the trees. They were not idle; there was always work, particularly in spring. Diana still, after twenty months, looked for signs of restlessness in Merlyn, but detected none. They seldom grew impatient with each other's company. If they sought other company they usually went down to the Maori settlement—they were always welcome visitors at huis, weddings or feast days; and they paid respect to the dead at tangis. Often Diana or Merlyn ran people from the settlement into the nearest town, some twenty miles away, in the station wagon. It was, after all, the least they could do; the people down there were always too generous. Diana and Merlyn seldom had to go fishing for themselves—there were always, from that first day, those gifts on the porch. Their relationship with other neighbours, the Europeans, was friendly but distant. They were, naturally, a butt for neighbouring wits, these two women living alone. And there were—perhaps in response—the shabby young men with hot, furtive eyes who studied them when they walked together in the town.

Where once Diana feared restlessness in Merlyn, now she became perversely and increasingly disturbed by the girl's lack of restlessness. It was incredible that she should be so content. She was too tame for her own good, too submissive. She fell in too easily with Diana's ideas. Diana would have been delighted had the girl raised some objection, provoked some argument. Had she no ideas of her own, no ambition for her own future? Was she to be so utterly dependent? Not that Diana minded her dependence. Nor did she wish Merlyn to leave. She simply felt her own personality might be too dominating, her own character impinging too greatly on Merlyn's. She might only be building a prison out of which Merlyn could one day break, a parental tower which Merlyn might one day topple. Diana was in quest of incipient rebellion; and, in a way, in quest of herself.

So it was with a feeling of relief that she came upon Merlyn, one afternoon, toying with some clay. She had found the clay in a gully, not far away from the orchard. It looked ideal for pottery.

'Well, why don't you?' Diana said. 'Do some pottery, I mean.'

'I'd like to,' Merlyn confessed, wistfully. 'I used to do quite a bit, once. You know, before I—' Again there was that painful hesitation when speaking of her past; it was this obvious sensitivity which caused Diana to draw back from asking Merlyn the questions she most desired to ask '—well, before I married. Yes, I did quite a bit. You know, not seriously, But they said I was good at it. They said I had the right feeling.'

'You'd like to do some more,' Diana said. 'Isn't that it?' She had to be careful, she reminded herself: she didn't want to push the girl too fast.

'Well, yes,' Merlyn answered. 'I think I would. I don't know. I hadn't really thought about it. I mean I probably wasn't very good at it, really. People used to say things to me just to be kind.'

'But you would like to do some more,' Diana persisted.

'Yes,' Merlyn agreed finally. 'I think I would.'

So in the end, as with most things, she had to be talked into something she desired to do; or apparently desired to do. Diana could never be quite sure of Merlyn.

'But there's so much work here,' Merlyn objected. 'We're so busy. There wouldn't be the time.'

'We can always make the time,' Diana insisted. 'There's no difficulty about that. You see,' she added, to make the issue plain, 'I want you to be happy here.'

For one moment, then, Merlyn gave Diana one of her curious little lopsided stares: it was an odd wrinkling of the face, not quite a smile, and a half-squint of one eye. It usually meant she had fastened on something which pleased her. Then that strangely characteristic tilt of her face and expression was gone.

'You do?' she said, almost primly. 'That's nice. But I don't think—'

'We'll see about it,' Diana promised briskly.

'There are so many things. You know, a potters' wheel and everything. And a kiln. I don't know where I could find a kiln to fire my pottery. There probably isn't one between here and the city.'

'We can build our own.'

'But it would all mean so much money,' Merlyn pleaded.

It was true; it would all mean money. Though they lived modestly, there wasn't much to spare. And the station wagon was due for a rebore. Diana had lately begun to wonder if she might have to sell the station wagon altogether.

'We'll find the money, like the time,' Diana said. 'Don't worry.'

'But I'm not worried,' Merlyn replied. 'Really I'm not.'

But Diana was worried. She didn't feel safe until everything was finished. Within two months, taking time off from the orchard and garden, they had built an outdoor kiln, under a rough shelter, and installed a potters' wheel in a back room of the house. This room was set aside for Merlyn's special use—there were shelves for her pottery, a large box for raw clay.

'You make me feel guilty,' Merlyn said. 'All this just for me.'

'For us,' Diana said. 'You never know. I might make use of it too, one day. And it's not for you to feel guilty about. I'd sooner you felt happy.'

'But I am. I am happy.'

Diana wished she could wholly believe it. At the beginning she wouldn't have grieved, particularly, if Merlyn had left. After all Diana was seeking herself here—much in the same way as, in the city, she had sought herself in gloomy churches—and no one else. She had wanted to place herself physically apart, as well as spiritually. But Merlyn, who could so easily have been a distraction, moved into the centre of her search, no longer excrescent at all; against Merlyn she more and more defined herself—as a traveller in a desert might, more or less, find reassurance and definition in his own shifting shadow. Now she was terrified that Merlyn might one day leave. That was why the expense involved in getting Merlyn what she wanted—or might want—seemed so unimportant. Diana, scraping and running her bank account thin, managed to get the money without selling the station wagon. But she would have sold the station wagon if necessary.

Anyway there would be some saving. They no longer had to buy crockery. And perhaps the time might come when Merlyn would sell some of her pottery. Diana parcelled everything neatly in her mind; there was no excuse to herself that she had neglected.

They all seemed flimsy, anyway, beside Merlyn's serene joy in her new work. Not that she avoided her other work in the orchard. On the contrary—she went at it harder, to justify the time she spent in the back room with the potters' wheel. The shelves filled quickly with interestingly-shaped pots, plates, mugs. Plainly the girl had a talent.

But even then Diana did not feel altogether easy in mind. Perhaps there was something she had forgotten in her haste to please Merlyn.

It was late spring, then the beginning of summer, and warm enough to swim again.

Working more often alone now, Diana managed sometimes to indulge in contentment. Often she surveyed herself, the newly-painted house, the orchard to which she had given new life. She remembered the phrases of friends in half-lost snatches. 'You aren't built that way, Di,' they'd said. She wished some of them—just some of them—could see her now. They would never have dreamt she was built for anything else. Her face was roughened with sun and rain. Her hands had a new, tough skin. She seldom worried about clothes. Clothing had become very elementary—jeans and sweater in winter, shorts and light shirt in summer; sometimes only a swimming costume, since she and Merlyn were always in and out of the water, often three or four times a day either at the beach or in the fresh-water creek.

She supposed that this contentment was something of what she sought, when she left the city; but she wasn't entirely sure, any longer, of just what she had sought at that time.

After all it wasn't a return to the kind of land from which she'd come. Her girlhood was spent on a flat dairy farm, at the centre of a dreary grass-grown valley, far away from the sea. She recaptured few of the sensations of girlhood, of country innocence, in this place. It was all too different—the orchard, the sea. She wasn't certain that she really wanted to recapture those sensations anyway; many, in retrospect, seemed coloured with pain. Well, then, had she been deceiving herself when she talked of returning to the land? Perhaps. Certainly it had all turned out rather differently. She hadn't, for example, counted on companionship; she hadn't counted on Merlyn. But she couldn't be other than glad that Merlyn had come along at the right time.

She would never be able to take the city again: that was certain. Not after the quiet satisfactions, those rare moments of total content, she had known here. These moments came upon her unexpectedly, like pale birds shimmering out of a clear sky. And, almost always, with Merlyn. Sometimes in the house at night, before a winter fire, with storm booming outside. Sometimes on the beach, in the shade of their favourite pohutukawa, with the sea dazzling before them. Sometimes— most often—in their secluded sun-trap, in the bush beside the creek. She liked, at these times, to confide in Merlyn and talk of the future.

'You know,' she'd say, 'in two or three years we'll have the beginnings of a fine new orchard here. This place was almost a total loss when we took it over. And we've made something of it. We've every reason to be proud of ourselves.'

'Yes,' Merlyn said. 'We have, haven't we? I hadn't thought of it like that.'

'Of course you haven't. I don't often think of it like that, either. When you're busy, as we are, you never have time to see things in perspective. But look at what we've done in two years. Why, we even have a pottery now, as a sideline.'

'Yes,' said Merlyn. 'We have.'

They became silent. They were in their usual place by the creek, naked to the sun on moss and grass. Fern and tangled creeper shadowed the edge of the clearing. Everything was very quiet. Only cicadas crackled in the heat.

Merlyn stirred lazily. 'Diana,' she said.

'What is it?'

'Are you sure you want me here? Really sure?'

Diana at once was gripped by panic. What caused the question? She had never been asked it before. There must, she thought, be a reason for it. Yet there had been no mail from the city lately, no visitors.

'Of course I'm sure. Don't be silly.'

'Sometimes I wonder if I might be a nuisance.'

Diana laughed with relief. 'But you've been wonderful. I couldn't have managed without you.'

'I sometimes have the feeling you could—manage without me, I mean. Sometimes I feel people are unnecessary for you—other people.'

'I thought it was you who said that, a long time ago. Of yourself. That you hadn't much use for people.'

'Did I say that? Well, that's what I mean then. We're both alike. That's what I mean.'

It might have been perfectly clear to Merlyn, but Diana was baffled. The conversation seemed to have spiralled into some place where she could not follow. Lazily, as curiously as Merlyn had spoken them, the words circled in her mind. Diana faltered, grappling in her confusion for the other words she desired to speak.

'As a matter of fact,' she began, 'there's something I've been wanting to talk about. And I might as well do it now.'

'Yes?' Merlyn said.

'Well—it's to do with you, and this place. I don't want to make you feel uncomfortable. But you've worked so hard, given so much of yourself, here. And all I've given you, after all, is your keep.'

'It's all I've wanted,' Merlyn replied. 'Really. Just my keep. Somewhere to live. It's enough, really.'

'It's not enough. Not for my conscience, anyway. You see, I think you should have a share in this place.'

'A share?'

'Say a third or half. We could work it out with a lawyer.'

'But what would I want that for? I've got a share in this place already. That's something more precious than any bit of paper you get from a lawyer. It's something that can't be bought and sold.'

'Perhaps not.'

'Anyway there's the pottery. If you want me to have an official share, then that's mine. That's all I need.'

'Well, then, there's another alternative. I've been thinking lately of making my will.'

'Your will? But you're not going to die.' The words came almost as a cry from Merlyn's perplexed face. Diana had noticed this before: the girl's reaction to death; she was always overwhelmed by a nausea. Down in the Maori settlement, at tangis, she always left it to Diana to pay respects to the actual corpse; she could accept the peripheral mourning, with relative equanimity, but not the cold dead flesh at the centre.

'Of course I'm going to die,' Diana said. 'At some time or other. After all, I'm forty. Past the halfway mark. I have to think about it. And now's as good a time as any. I've no close relatives, you see. True, I've a husband somewhere, but he doesn't count anymore. I thought I might draw up a will which gives this place to you, entirely.'

'But why should you worry about me?'

'Oh, you needn't worry—the reason's purely selfish. I'd like to be able to think of this place as having a future. It's as simple and selfish as that. Here I've been talking about the future—but what is it really? A space of time until I die; that's all. A rather insignificant space of time at that. No, there's not much satisfaction in it for me. There couldn't have been much satisfaction in it for that old Dalmatian either, living here and dying alone, knowing that there would be no one to keep the place going. I think of him, sometimes.'

'I still don't understand,' Merlyn declared.

'I'm doing my best to explain, if you'll give me time. There must be something in the land that makes us, when we've taken it, desire to bless it with continuity. What is it, I wonder? This spark, I mean, given off between us and the land; this desire for continuity. Well, here we are then. I'm unlikely to have children now. But you're young, of a different generation altogether. You'll probably marry again, sooner or later. Have a husband, children. Can't you see what I mean?'

'I think so.' Merlyn appeared disturbed by something, or afflicted by some odd embarrassment. She sat up suddenly, and then rolled over on her flank, looking away from Diana. It occurred to Diana that the girl might not be seeing it her way at all. She might only regard land as a life-bleeding trap, as Diana certainly had when young. On the other hand she'd given every sign of sharing Diana's present sympathies. Diana could never be absolutely sure of what Merlyn thought or felt.

'Well,' Diana said, 'we'll leave it for now, anyway. Perhaps we can talk about it all again some other time. But I'd be very happy if you thought it was a good idea.'

'It is a good idea,' Merlyn said slowly. 'But I mean—it does put so much on to me, doesn't it? So much responsibility.'

'I don't see that at all. Your life is still your own. You can come or go—well, as you please. Sometime or other you might meet someone you like. Well, you can bring him here too. I won't feel crowded out. This place will support quite a few people, eventually. There'll be more than a modest living. And it'd be nice to have a man around the place— for the heavy work. You might even have more time for your pottery, if you don't have too many children in the way. But then, children could run wild in this place. That's the glory of it, really.' Diana found a sharp pleasure in her sudden vision of the future: children were what this place needed, among the newly growing things, the fruitful trees.

She had never really seen that before; and never before had she felt so acutely her own sterility. She should have had children. She had never wanted them, in her first farce of a marriage. And they were out of the question in the second. A child needed a father; and George Francis would never have been much of a parent. Or would he? Perhaps a child would have been the anchor he needed. It was said the unlikeliest of men made the best fathers. 'So anyway,' she finished, 'I thought I'd better make that perfectly clear to you now. just in case you do meet someone you like.'

'But I have,' Merlyn replied quickly.

'You have what?'

'Met someone I like. Quite a while back.' She still wasn't looking at Diana. She rolled over swiftly, to the edge of the creek, and dangled her legs into the water. She sat spritely, with a grave smile, among the lichened stone and the small fern sprouting above the creek. The picture she made at that moment remained distinctly in Diana's mind for some time afterwards. She was so very brown. She had never really lost the last summer's tan, and now it was reinforced with the new. Her colouring was perfect against the green of foliage and fern.

'Oh?'

'Yes,' said Merlyn. 'Quite a while back.'

'Who?'

'Oh,' Merlyn laughed, 'I don't think you'd know.' And she flung herself into the creek, with an eruption of sparkling spray, and stroked strongly upstream to the first waterfall.

Afterwards, on the way back to the house, Diana wondered about young men in the Maori settlement. But of course it was absurd. Merlyn would scarcely have been able to conceal such an affair from Diana. It was quite baffling. Diana began to wonder if she really knew Merlyn at all.

3

It was mid-afternoon. Diana and Merlyn had been up since five in the morning. They tried, in summer, to do the bulk of their work in the cool of morning or evening, leaving the warm middle stretch of the day for leisure. After lunch Diana rested on her bed, and Merlyn went off to

her pottery. Diana fell asleep in the heat and woke with a heavy head.
A swim would cure it, she thought, looking from her bedroom window
across the glinting ranks of fruit-trees to the sea. The tide was in. The
rocky, scrubby hills about their bay were hazy. The vast day lay like a
dead weight on the silent land. There was no wind; not a whisper or
ripple in the sharply chiselled leaves of the orchard.

She pulled on her swimming costume, draped a towel on her
shoulders, and went seeking Merlyn. She had never swum alone—nor
had Merlyn—in all the time they'd been there. To steal solitary delight
in the water was unthinkable.

She came upon Merlyn in the pottery. The girl sat rapt, concentrated,
as though shaped and fired in clay herself, before her wheel. On the
wheel lay a twisted lump of clay. It was clear that it had at least once
found some form, beneath Merlyn's quick hands, only to be rejected:
given back to original chaos, it lay damp and forlorn. Merlyn shook her
head finally, and muttered something to herself: she still had not
noticed Diana standing at the door. Her hair swung long and loose with
the abrupt motion of her head. In the city Merlyn's hair had been short,
elfin-style; in the country she had simply let it grow long—and longer
and longer. Diana felt that Merlyn should really do something about
her hair; it was becoming quite impossible. But the girl wouldn't even
plait it for convenience. In the sea, or the creek, it swarmed around her
on the surface of the water.

'No,' Merlyn said fiercely, to herself. 'No, no, no.' She still gazed with
intensity at the shapeless clay on the wheel. Diana wondered what
forms travelled through the girl's mind; what caused her to reject them
with such vehemence. What was she searching for? Diana struggled to
set right, in her own mind, this new picture of Merlyn. A different
Merlyn; a Merlyn wilful enough to be angered or even tormented by
frustration. Someone no longer amiably apathetic, riding on the whims
and wills of others, but distinct, sharp in herself. And at her centre not
stillness or transparent calm, but strife and unease. It was all there,
somehow, in the girl before the wheel. It seemed that Diana had never
quite seen Merlyn before; it was something of wonder and revelation.
And, for some reason, painful; as if blinkers had been rugged cruelly
from her eyes, leaving bitter light to pour in upon her smarting pupils.
She had arranged the pottery for Merlyn with the idea that the girl

might amuse, entertain herself; she had never suspected this concentration, this struggle. It just wasn't what Diana expected at all.

Then Merlyn turned and saw Diana: her eyes widened. 'Oh,' was all she said. Her eyes seemed to soften. Then she added, 'Yes, it is time for a swim, isn't it?'

In the confusion of the moment Diana almost forgot she was standing there in swimming costume, the towel round her shoulders. 'I came to see—' she began, and faltered, as if she had been caught out in some dishonesty.

'Yes?' Merlyn said, smiling. She looked perfectly calm.

'Well—if you were ready. That's all. But you looked so busy.'

'I'm not busy, not really. I've just been having a bit of a fight, ever since lunch. Something I've been trying to get right. But I can't. Who cares? I don't. It'll be nicer in the water.'

Merlyn changed and they walked a dusty path through the orchard, across scrubland, to the sea. The tide brimmed up the thinning white lip of beach. Merlyn danced along the edge of the water, scattering bright spray with her feet. 'It's almost lukewarm,' she declared.

But Diana, after the walk, chose to rest a while in shade before entering the sea. She watched Merlyn grow smaller with distance along the margin of the long beach. She stopped now and then, apparently examining the debris of the sea. Clearly Merlyn was on holiday again. She might have been walking this beach for the first, and not the two hundredth time; Diana wished she possessed the same capacity for delight. The girl was inexhaustible.

Their beach lay cupped between two long, scarred headlands, blackened here and there by scrub fire, and dappled with erosion. Between the headlands and out to sea lay a slender green island, its thick vegetation undisturbed by fire, its slopes packed solid, earth as close to rock as flesh to bone. At times, in Diana's mind, the famished and abused land seemed to be reaching out towards this virgin island with two vainly questing fingers—the headlands—which never quite reached their goal. The deep, dangerously narrow channels each side of the island were seldom travelled now, not since the days of the timber boats. The island acted as breakwater for their beach, holding back the swells of the Pacific.

Diana and Merlyn had once travelled out there, in a boat with boys from the settlement. The dense bush rang with birds; they might have been the first people on the island. Only the smallness of the island had saved it from the axe of man; only its isolation from fire. Diana often thought she and Merlyn might visit it again, but they possessed no boat, and it was too far to swim. Still, she promised herself the trip again. The island's tiny beaches, craggy old trees and looping creeper, held the charm of another, lost time: it was still possible to walk the world there in innocence, as a stranger. But no sound of the island's birdsong reached her across the water here: it was too far away. The island lay, green and silent, against the horizon and between the headlands, the questing fingers. One day some fool from the city was bound to put a match to it: there would be one more summer blaze, one more blackening memory for the land. She flinched from the thought. She sensed the impermanence of all things—soil with water, sea with sand, light with sea, cloud with sky. And, above all, human with land. Then the scattered pieces did not shift with the earth's dance, the patterns did not multiply; there was no delicate balance of impermanence— only destruction. The human element was the destructive element. And human with human? Did, she wondered, the same apply? Perhaps the human element was still the destructive element.

Merlyn returned along the beach with a handful of shells. She dropped them at Diana's feet. Merlyn harvested the beach, month after month, and hoarded the best shells. She had never quite lost the novelty of having her own beach.

'Well, now,' Diana said. 'I supppose it's time.'

They wandered down to the sea, together, paddling and then wading into the water. Diana was about to launch herself out into the sea when Merlyn's cry came as a check. 'Look,' she cried. 'Look there.'

Diana stopped and, following the direction of Merlyn's panicky gaze, saw the cruising shadow beneath the sunlit sea. It swam a leisurely curve before them, its dark wide wings barely thrusting, gliding with current or tide, basking in the warm shallow water—a solitary stingray. Diana felt no extreme fear, as apparently did Merlyn; she knew stingrays were harmless enough as long as one didn't get in their way or interfere with them. So long as they stayed still they were safe. She felt only a repugnance at the thought that she might have launched herself forward against that pointed snout, been lashed in panic by that spiky and poisonous tail.

'Don't move,' Diana said. 'Just stay quiet and still. Otherwise it might get curious.'

No, it was not danger, exactly, Diana saw in that slow winged creature: rather it was evil, or the presence of evil, within placid everyday depths. She and Merlyn had swum here for nearly two years without thought of menace. Merlyn, plainly terrified, would never find the sea the same again. And as Diana stared, fascinated, at the cruising shadow she accepted the word evil—irrationally, she afterwards supposed. She had never been quite able to stomach the word before; certainly not from the dry lips of a celibate priest.

'Look,' Merlyn said, distraught. 'There are more.'

Two, three shadows followed the first; there seemed to be a regular school. She'd never heard of a school of stingrays before; she always imagined them solitary. There they were, anyway. So this was the shape, the pattern, the word become flesh—and wing, and poisonous tail; the meaningless become meaningful.

And because this sea would never be the same again for Merlyn, it would never be the same again for her. This came to her as if with a stirring of shadows within her own depths.

'No,' Merlyn cried. 'I can't, can't.'

She dashed herself at Diana, across the small space of water between them. The shadows veered abruptly away, out to sea. Diana was left holding the trembling girl.

'I couldn't,' she said. 'I couldn't just stand still and watch them. Not like that.' She paused and, when the clamour in her body quietened, added, 'I'm not like you, you see. I'm not like you at all.'

For a moment it seemed she was trying to tell Diana a great deal more.

'You just stood there, so cool,' Merlyn continued lamely, by way of explanation. 'I couldn't. I just had to give way. And they didn't, did they? They didn't come after us, I mean. Not when I moved.'

'No,' Diana agreed. 'They didn't. You scared them off. They scare easily, I'm told.'

'So do I. Scare easily, I mean.'

The sea was peaceful, harmless again with the shadows fled. Yet neither of them had desire for it now. One of Merlyn's hands had curled into Diana's hair. She seemed, again, as powerless as she had always been; the picture she had made in the pottery, an hour before, was forgotten. Gently Diana lifted the hand away.

'It's all right,' she said. 'It's all right now.'

Yet it seemed that timid flesh still needed support, reassurance. She helped Merlyn back to shore and they lay on the sand. Perhaps they would swim, later, in the creek behind the orchard. Merlyn grew quiet and strange.

'I sometimes wonder,' she said, lying on her back and looking up at the sky, 'why you put up with me.'

'That's an odd thing to say,' Diana replied briskly.

'Because I'm not much use,' she explained. 'You don't really need me.'

'That's ridiculous. You've been a lot of use, a lot of help. And you know it. And as for needing you, well I've explained that too—or at least I thought I'd explained it well enough.'

'But it's not the same way.'

'Not the same way as what?'

Diana glanced at Merlyn, and caught again that shrewd tilting expression of her face: they had stolen glances at each other simultaneously, and their eyes met briefly before travelling apart again.

'Not the same way as what?' Diana repeated.

'As I need you,' Merlyn answered lightly. She stood up suddenly. 'But perhaps it doesn't matter. Perhaps it doesn't matter at all.'

'What doesn't matter?' Diana felt a queer quickening of her pulse.

'Us. How could it matter, anyway?'

Diana lay awake till late that night, the words scraping in her mind, scraping back and forward as if in rhythm with her shifting body. Merlyn did not go to sleep till late, either. Diana could hear the clumping of the potters' wheel at the back of the house.

4

There had been a hui down at the settlement. Diana and Merlyn made their way home late in the day, sated and dizzy with sun and food and drink. The sun flared beyond the western hills. Ragged cloud flashed with the colour of the guttering day. It was still very warm. After the noise and good burnout of the hui, constraint fell between them again; they walked home in silence.

In the growing dark they arrived at the house and found George Francis sitting in the kitchen, as cool as a mountain creek, his feet comfortably on the table, the coffee percolator bubbling on the stove beside him. He looked as if he had always belonged there.

'Nice place you've got here,' he observed. 'Took me a long while finding it. You've certainly cut yourself off. But I rather like it. Mind if I stay?'

'You look at home already,' Diana said curtly, smothering her surprise. 'Anyway we can always use an extra body in the orchard. We'll be picking and packing soon.' It was better, Diana thought, to put things on a proper basis as soon as possible; it always paid, with George. 'You can earn your keep while you're here—that's what I mean. You think you might stay long?'

'Oh,' said George with a large grin, 'it depends.'

'You mean your rambling might have finished?'

'It might,' George answered. 'It might not. But I've had the idea lately that I might reclaim my conjugal rights.'

There was a silence. Then Merlyn giggled. Diana, with the shock of George's appearance, had forgotten her. Really, Diana thought, the girl sounded as though she'd had far too much to drink.

'I have rights, haven't I?' he said.

'I suppose you have.' Diana held herself tightly. 'Legally. I'm not sure about morally.'

'Don't panic,' George said. 'I only intend to reclaim them one by one. Like living here. That'll do for a start. Why don't you two sit down? I'm real, you know. Not a ghost.' He rose from the table. 'Have some coffee. Make yourself at home. Nice place I've got here, don't you think? And, by the way, you might introduce me to your friend.'

'This is Merlyn. Merlyn, George.'

'And very nice too. Now, where was I? Ah, yes—coffee. You both look as if you need a strong brew.'

While George fetched and filled some mugs, Diana sat and tried to recover herself. In a corner lay George's immense hiker's pack and his Spanish guitar. So he still carried both, wherever he went, like a wandering minstrel. And what happened to minstrels when they grew old? For that was the real shock. George had never shown his age before. Now something seemed to have gone slack in his rugged face: he was almost a caricature of himself. There were streaks of grey in his hair. Yet he still hadn't grown up, not really. His cheeky manner—had it once charmed her?—seemed much the same; but now it appeared intolerable, vaguely indecent, in a man who showed his age so plainly. Whatever it was that had gone loose in him—perhaps some inner tension which had at last snapped—left him as pathetic as a middle-aged Peter Pan. Once she had forgiven much—probably too much— because he seemed representative, to an extreme, of his time and his country. Now she no longer cared particularly what he was representative of. It didn't matter. In the city he had brought her something, she supposed; perhaps some message of freedom, of different lives and different places. That might well have been his mild magic. But he had nothing to bring her here. Paradoxically he even seemed to bring with him, now, the smell of the city. The city was there in his manner, his speech. And what would George have been, anyway, without the cities to kick against and despise? He would have been nothing without that mock rebellion; she might never have noticed him, never have been interested in him. He was even talking about the city now.

'Oh yes,' he said. 'When I found you were gone—that was a surprise, I don't mind telling you—I kicked around town a while. Couldn't stand it long, as usual. The people get worse than ever. You should see some of your old friends now, Di. They reek of money. One or two of them didn't even want to know me. Remember Ben Chalmers—your great Marxist friend of the working man? Well, he's doing public relations for some big company now. He says he's interested in making capitalism work efficiently for the benefit of the workers. But come the revolution, and he'll be on the right side of the barricades. No doubt, no doubt. And remember Tom Dwyer, that grubby little poet, the bitter enemy of the academy—well, he's lecturing
… '

And so it went on; there was little Diana didn't already know, or couldn't guess. 'Then why was it,' she asked finally, 'that you stayed around?'

'Oh, I got along all right. Sang some nights in a coffee-bar. I even got a five-minute spot on television one night. Some fellow in a recording company said he was interested in doing something for me. So I stuck it out a while, a few months in the finish. But it didn't come to anything.'

Diana, suddenly, felt uncomfortable: he was too naked. So everything had dwindled to this, with the novels unwritten, the paintings unpainted, the free life abandoned: George Francis loitered about a studio door with fading hope of fame, waiting on someone else's pleasure for the chance to use someone else's words to put his own voice on record.

'I got my usual gutsful,' he went on. 'They don't fool me, none of them. No, I couldn't stick it for long. I started thinking about places I might head out for. The funny thing was, I couldn't think of too many. I'm not as good for a lot of jobs as I used to be. I don't mind telling you there's a creak in the old bones after a night out in the open now. So I finally thought of you.'

'How nice,' Diana said. 'For me.'

'No, that's what I thought to myself. What's better than marriage for old age?'

Once, this honesty might have disarmed her. Now it only chilled her. Was he really serious? Not even his confession of age mitigated his faded, worn appearance: if anything, it amplified it, made it the more shameless and shocking.

'And what more cosy place than this?' he added mercilessly. 'My God, Di, I've got to hand it to you. You've done things well. It's a lovely set-up.'

'We've worked hard for it,' Diana said coldly.

'We? You mean you both—' His gaze flickered for a moment, across the table, towards Merlyn.

'We've both worked hard for it. Merlyn and I.'

'I see.' He nodded towards Merlyn in apology. 'Sorry,' he said to her. 'I just had a bit of trouble fitting you into the picture. I didn't know you belonged here too. I don't know why I thought Di had done it all herself. I thought you might have been like me. A guest here, so to speak.'

'Well,' said Merlyn, speaking for the first time. 'I suppose I might be, in a way.'

It was quite enough for Diana: quite enough for one evening. She rose. 'We go to bed early here,' she announced. 'We get up at five, in summer.'

'A good thing too,' George said amiably. 'Early to bed and early to rise—how does the rhyme go?'

'I'll show you to your room,' Diana said with finality.

In her room that night she lay sleepless and rigid listening to George, in a neighbouring room, strum lightly a strain of flamenco from his guitar as he rested on his bed. Probably he was still fully clothed, his boots on the bedcover—she could picture it. And she wondered why the sound should so curiously colour her despair, like chinks of silver moonlight through a curtained window. She waited for a rattle at her locked door, but did not really expect it.

How did that foolish rhyme go? Early to bed, early to rise—healthy, wealthy and wise. Well, she had health in good measure; wealth, of a kind; but wisdom?

Yet George could still surprise her—as she discovered, next morning, when he helped Merlyn and herself with the work about the place. Stripped to the sun, he looked almost as handsome a brown animal as ever he had been; his body was still firm and muscular. None of the slackness she had seen in his face showed in his figure. The importance of the grey hairs diminished in the sunlight. And down at the beach, as he lolled between herself and Merlyn on the the sand, be showed flashes of his old jovial self. Perhaps it was because he was not talking of the city now, but of the last winter he'd spent shepherding in the mountains. He told the kind of stories—some, admittedly, a little frayed with time and frequent telling—she'd once delighted in hearing from him. Perhaps it was the presence of Merlyn, an apparent innocent and a stranger, which caused the stories to unreel so freely. There was something mischievous in the wide-eyed way Merlyn played up to him. Often she traded glances of sly amusement with Diana. The girl appeared to know instinctively the right way to handle George. Curiously, George seemed to bring them closer; he dissolved the constraint of the last week or two. He was like a guest appearing too late at a party, perversely unaware of intimacy cemented long before his arrival, and in spite of his attempts to ingratiate himself, a figure of fun. No, it was no use—for all his effort, George no longer cut an impressive figure. Last night she had even been a little afraid of him. This morning as he walked through the orchard, the light splintering on his body, she had seen him again as she once saw him: that too was reason for a twinge of fear. Now, as she and Merlyn were entertained by George, she found a deep and genuine pity. Nothing could have told her more plainly that she was herself again, no longer afraid.

Presently George stood up. 'Well,' he said. 'How about a swim?'

He was puzzled by the silence in reply. Eventually Diana said, 'Merlyn's not very keen on swimming here any more. She had a shock a week or two ago.'

'Don't tell me there's sharks,' George said. 'I don't believe it.'

'Not sharks. Stingrays. We almost walked on top of them.'

'But they're harmless,' George protested. 'They scare away as soon as you make a splash. You don't want to let those things worry you.'

'I don't,' Diana said. 'But Merlyn's not very keen, just the same. Are you?'

She looked at Merlyn. Merlyn shook her head silently. She seemed ashamed of herself, her weakness.

'It'll be all right again in a week or two,' Diana continued. 'When she's got used to the idea that they're harmless. We still come down here to sunbathe out of habit. And because it's so pleasant when the tide's in.'

'I still don't get it. Does that mean neither of you go swimming here? Just because one is afraid?'

'We both go swimming afterwards,' Diana replied, avoiding a direct answer. 'In a creek, up the back.'

'I still don't get it. Damned if I do. Well, you know your own business best. I hope you both enjoy staying up here as much as I'm going to enjoy the sea.'

He gave them both a scornful look, and raced down the beach to the water. He waded and then dived. He vanished entirely, travelling underwater, and then emerged a surprising distance out, his head tossing and bobbing on the vivid sea. He looked back and waved. Then he began to swim.

Unlike Diana, who had won championships when young, George was not really a good swimmer. She had discovered that in the days when she and George visited beaches near the city. He put everything he had into the effort of keeping afloat; he had no idea of developing a style to conserve his energy. He bludgeoned, he flailed the water. It might make an impression, but it was all vigour and no technique. That seemed the flaw in everything he did: it accounted for his failure in the arts, his paintings, his writing, and possibly now his singing—all vigour, no technique. He'd never had the patience for technique, even in lovemaking. It was probably too late for him to acquire such patience now. And what would happen when the raw vigour failed, as it was already failing? He lacked even a technique for living. He'd always just blundered along somehow. But surely he couldn't do that for ever.

There he was anyway, out in the sea, making his usual great show of strength. He swam away in a wide curve, the water churning around him, and headed in a straight line back to shore. He knew his limits: he didn't go out too far. He had the knack of making it appear he had swum farther than he had. Or having done more than he really had. She could grant him that small success in technique. It was plainly a knack he'd developed instinctively over the last few years.

'Why did you marry him?' Merlyn asked suddenly.

The question disconcerted her. For a moment she looked blankly at the sea, the sky. 'There were probably reasons,' she said, 'I don't really remember now.' She groped for some image of George, at the time of their marriage, but he seemed to escape her altogether. 'Yes,' she added limply, 'there must have been reasons.'

George loped up the sand. Water sparkled on his body. 'I don't suppose it's any use telling you the water's fine,' he said. He towelled himself briskly, and looked across the sea. 'That island out there,' he added. 'It looks pretty good to me. Ever been there?'

'Once,' Diana answered. 'About a year ago. We went over with some people from the settlement. They were collecting shellfish. It's very pleasant—not much of it, but what's there is pleasant, I mean. Merlyn and I wandered over the place together—it's full of tiny beaches and bays, almost like a miniature country. The bush has never been touched, and you can hardly hear yourself speak for the sound of the birds.' Diana found she was enthusing despite her inward desire not to share too much of the experience with George. 'We've often thought—or I've often thought—of going back again. But we haven't, yet.'

'I've been looking for an island all my life,' George said. 'Sounds like it might suit me. Anyone own it?'

'I shouldn't think so. Unless it's Maori land.'

'Yes,' George said presently. 'I might have a shot at it one day.'

'It's a long way to swim. And the only boats round here are down at the settlement. They'd take you over, all right. But you'd still have no way of getting back again. That's if you wanted to stay.'

'Why should I want to come back again?'

'Well, I shouldn't bother them, all the same. They need their boats for fishing. We make it a rule not to bother them with things like that. They're good enough to us, as it is. So I'd rather you didn't ask them.'

'Well, that's plain enough. Never mind. I'll find some way.'

'Please yourself,' Diana said. 'You'll probably be very disappointed.'

'What makes you so sure?'

'I'm not sure. I didn't say I was.' She hesitated and added, 'You know I'm seldom sure about anything.'

She was simply saying what she knew he liked, and expected her to say. He smiled. 'Di, old girl,' he said. 'You don't change much.'

But she had changed. If he couldn't see it then, he should surely have seen it in the busy days that followed, when they began picking and packing. And if he didn't see it at all, it was because he didn't want to see it: he wanted Diana to remain the woman of the city, on whom he made some impression; he couldn't accept a sturdy countrywoman on whom he made none. Apart from George, she also had hired helpers from the settlement. She managed everyone efficiently, and briskly. It was a good crop, better than that of the first meagre year. Some of the pruned, carefully-tended younger trees gave magnificently. George sometimes avoided work, but not often enough to annoy her. On the whole he more than earned his keep. When he did slink away, it was usually down to the settlement, where he and his guitar became quickly popular; sometimes he went off drinking in the town with some of the Maori boys. But he was really no nuisance to them, or to Diana. She had no reason for complaint.

Possibly he was only a nuisance to Merlyn. And even then Diana could not be sure, since Merlyn was far too polite. George frequently invaded the pottery while Merlyn was working there—either sitting in a corner with his guitar, or fiddling clay into little pieces of sculpture which he later fired in the kiln with Merlyn's pots. Merlyn appeared able to tolerate his presence. Certainly it was very convenient for Diana, having George out of the way; she could take her rest properly, and relax, when work in the orchard finished for the day. Often she watched the two go off swimming together with a feeling of relief. And sometimes a little guiltily. It was really unfair, she supposed, the way she left Merlyn to cope with George. Merlyn's was really a valiant effort of politeness and patience. Diana had every reason to be grateful to the girl.

But for how much longer? Even when the last case of fruit had been packed and dispatched from the orchard, George showed no sign of restlessness. Or of intention to leave soon. Perhaps Diana had allowed him too comfortable a life. Perhaps he had actually been serious about reclaiming his marriage. If so, she would have done better to order him away from the place the moment he arrived. It was too late now. If she weren't careful, she might have trouble with Merlyn. That might even be George's aim, to drive Merlyn away so that he could have the place, and Diana, to himself. For now, at times, there was something like despair in Merlyn's face as she sat listening to George at the meal-table. The girl must have had just about enough of him. It was time for Diana to step in.

'What are your plans?' Diana asked George one evening.

'Plans?' he said. 'I never make them, Di. You know that.'

'I thought you might have some ideas about the future.'

'What are you getting at?'

'Nothing. I just wondered.'

'You want me to go? Is that it?'

'I didn't say so.'

Merlyn sat silent, curled in a corner of the room with a book, while their words flashed.

'Come on, Di. Out with it. Say what you want to say.'

'I didn't say I wanted you to go. I just thought you might be going. That's all. You've always gone before.'

The atmosphere in the room was oddly heightened; Diana sensed some alien element which she could not identify. She hadn't imagined George would be so put out, or look so flustered.

'And say I don't want to go this time?' George said. 'Say I've struck gold at last—after a lot of prospecting. I'd be a fool to move, wouldn't I?'

Merlyn sat staring into her book. Diana knew she was not reading at all. There was a tension in the way she sat now.

'Would you, George? I don't know. You know your own business best.'

'If you want me to go, just say so. I'll go, all right. But I'm just warning you—'

At that moment Merlyn closed her book firmly, rose, and left the room without a word. George looked after her, baffled.

'Yes, George. You were saying? Or warning me, rather.'

'I'm just warning you. I mightn't be the only one to go.'

'How interesting,' was all Diana said. It was odd how calm she found herself. And she reflected on how typical such a bluff was of George. He always overplayed his poor cards. And he had no sense of timing. None at all. Once Merlyn had left the room, without reaction, his dash was done. Merlyn hadn't stayed to support him, and Diana felt no fear at all. The girl, by leaving, made it only too plain how she felt.

Now she twisted the knife. 'If you think you're upsetting me, George, you're quite mistaken. Fall in love with Merlyn if you like. If she'll let you, and you want to, go ahead and make love to her. I don't mind.'

'Do you think I've waited for your permission?' George scratched back. He was trying for a weak spot, and finding it at last. Yet he looked wretched. And Diana, even taken aback, still had the advantage.

'I don't think I want the details,' she said finally. 'Stay as long as you like. You know you're welcome here.'

It was Merlyn who released the real panic in Diana. They were sitting together at breakfast; George had already gone out into the morning. He had bought some timber in the town and was building a flat-bottomed dinghy. Some boys had been up from the settlement to advise and help him; they were entertained by George's crude efforts. Already he'd had to throw away half his timber. As they sat together, at the table, they heard the hammering begin in the orchard. Merlyn took nothing for breakfast except coffee. Diana was disturbed by her appearance.

'You should eat something,' Diana protested. 'You don't look well.'

Merlyn seemed to suffer discomfort. 'Perhaps I'm not,' she said at last.

'Then eat. It's the best thing.' Diana paused. 'Or perhaps you should see a doctor.'

'I think I'll have to go soon,' Merlyn said quietly.

'Of course,' Diana replied. 'If you feel you need a doctor, of course you should go.'

'It wasn't that I meant. I meant going away, leaving here.'

Diana was silent, shocked.

'You're not serious. It's just your mood. You've been happy here, haven't you?'

'I have been. Yes.'

'Then why—?'

'Oh,' Merlyn cried. 'Do I have to spell it all out? You know as well as I do. George told you, didn't he? He told me he did. And he told me you just sat there and said nothing. I didn't want to believe him. I knew then, if it was true, that I'd have to think about going away— that it wouldn't be any use for me to stay here any more. I'd only be wasting my time. Now I can see it is true. You just sat there and said nothing, didn't you? Just like he said.'

'And what was I supposed to do? Make a scene? How was I to know what you wanted?'

'I only want everything like it was before. If it's not going to be like that again, I'll have to leave. He's your husband, after all.'

'Yes,' Diana agreed. 'He is. But I shouldn't let that worry you. I'm surprised if it does. If you want him, you have him.' She hesitated, then added with unusual bitterness, 'He's no gift for anyone.'

'Then why, why?' Merlyn cried. 'It doesn't make sense.'

'What doesn't?'

'Any of it. I thought I was only doing what you really wanted. I thought I might just be doing you a good turn. If he didn't pester me, he'd only pester you. Only I didn't mean it to go so far. Then he started to blackmail me. By saying he'd tell you if I didn't do what he wanted. So I grew afraid of the way you'd react. And when you didn't react at all—'

'How does he know, how do you know, what I felt?'

'I'll have to leave,' Merlyn insisted. 'It's the only way now. I can't go on like this. Not any more.'

'No,' Diana agreed. 'I don't suppose any of us can. Have a good long rest this morning. And see the doctor this afternoon. Take the station wagon and go into town.'

'You think that'll make things better?'

'It might help.'

'Oh, it'll help, all right,' Merlyn said bitterly. 'Help finish everything. I'll be leaving soon, just the same.'

And this time Diana was afraid she meant it.

That afternoon, when Merlyn had gone in the station wagon, Diana went into the orchard and found George. The dinghy appeared almost finished. He was tarring the boards.

'I wouldn't like to risk a trip in that,' Diana observed.

'No one's asking you to.'

He didn't look up from his work. His brush slapped back and forward. 'It'll float,' he said. 'That's all I want. Where did Merlyn go?'

'Out for a while,' Diana said. 'Into town for the afternoon.'

'Nothing wrong?'

'Nothing. Should anything be?'

But he still didn't look up. She sat on the grass and studied the dinghy. It looked solid, anyway. There were no obvious defects.

'I think you know perfectly well she's gone to the doctor,' Diana added. 'Don't you?'

'So what? I've been to a doctor myself, once or twice.'

'I think we should go swimming,' Diana said. 'It's a nice afternoon.'

'Is that all you came to say?'

'Almost all.'

'What if I told you to leave me alone?'

'I could say the same thing to you.'

'Yes.' George sighed. 'Fair enough. I suppose you could.' He hesitated before he added, 'First you make it clear you don't want me round. Then you want to go swimming with me. It doesn't add up. You just being polite?'

'No. I don't think so.'

'Well, I would go swimming, only I've promised the boys in the settlement that I'd be down there this afternoon. After I've finished with this.' He kicked at the dinghy. 'I might give it a try on the water tomorrow or the next day. Sorry about the swimming this afternoon.'

'Yes. I see. I'm sorry too.' Diana stood up, paused indecisively for a moment, then walked through the orchard, away from her husband.

George did not arrive back from the settlement at all that evening. Merlyn returned pale from town, and went to bed early. Diana heard her weeping in her room. It was a quiet, listless sound. Diana went into the room. She sat on the edge of Merlyn's bed.

'I won't ask the trouble,' she said presently.

'There's no need, is there?' Merlyn said. 'You know already. You knew this morning.'

'I guessed. That's different from knowing. Is it certain?'

'The doctor said he'd be definite, one way or the other, in a couple of days. He's taken a test.' Merlyn had stopped weeping.

'Well,' Diana said, almost with relief. 'That's that, then.'

'It's all right,' Merlyn murmured. 'I'm going away. I told you I was. I went to the bus depot and booked a seat down to the city.'

'Only one seat?'

'Yes. One.'

'I thought so. Well, I'll ring up and cancel it. That's easy enough. What do you want to go back for, anyway?'

'I thought I might have something done, if it's certain. It's easier there.'

'Of course. So many things are.'

'I'm going. You won't stop me.'

'I told you once we needed children. Didn't I? Well, perhaps one child would be enough.'

'You mean you're happy about it?'

'Very happy. You'll stay here. And I'll look after you. Everything will be all right. So don't worry. George won't stay the pace. Not now. Not once I start putting pressure on him to divorce me and marry you.'

'But what if he wants to?'

'I doubt it. But then, of course, there's just the chance he may want to marry you. In that case he'll have to discover that you don't want

him. Because you don't, do you? You'll just have to make it clear—
humiliatingly clear—that you don't need him.'

'I don't suppose we do, neither of us. Not now,' Merlyn agreed. 'Not
any more.'

5

Two days later Diana took George aside and asked what he intended
to do about Merlyn. At first he bluffed and blustered, as she might have
expected. He was trapped, and knew it.

'How do I know who she sleeps with?' he said. 'How do I know it's
mine?'

'She knows, George. And I know.'

He quietened after a while. 'A kid, eh?' he said, as if the news were
registering for the first time. 'Well, what do you know about that? Tell
you what, Di. We could adopt it, you and I. How's that? What about
it?'

'You're not serious.'

'But I am, Di. Perfectly. We should have had a kid, you and I. That's
probably been our trouble. It might have been the making of us.'

'Yes, George,' she said quietly. 'It might have been. I had that
thought myself, once.' She felt a small moment of weakness, but
hardened again. 'You can't settle this so easily, George. Your
responsibility's towards Merlyn now. Not towards me. You'll have to
settle this with her, the best way you can. Would you marry her, for
example?'

'Don't be so bloody Victorian.'

'I'm not being Victorian. Just human.'

'God, Di. She's only a silly kid.'

'That didn't seem to worry you.'

'Look,' I'm not a block of wood. You might as well get that straight.
I saw how you felt about me. As soon as I arrived.'

'Yes?'

'You made it plain. Too bloody plain. A man's only human.'

'Yes. That's always the trouble, isn't it?'

'I don't get you. What about laying off? Have a heart, Di.'

'I have one. That's my trouble. I rescued Merlyn from one mess in the city. I don't like having to pull her out of another.'

'There's no mess, so far as I can see. Only a kid. That's easily fixed, if she doesn't want it.'

'But there is, George, there is a mess. Our lives, for one thing. We, you and I and a lot of others like us, just muddle through. Without a single ideal, without God, without pride in the past or faith in the future, without anything. We've no right to involve her in our squalor.'

'Who's involving her?' he said. 'Me? That's a joke. Who brought her here in the first place? I didn't.'

'I only brought her here to help her to find her own way. To make her own way. You've seen her in the pottery.' Diana hesitated. 'The land's been my way. And the pottery's become hers.'

'You're kidding yourself, Di. You're fooling yourself all along the line. And you know something? I think you're kidding about having a heart too. I don't think you've got a heart left any more. Because I have a feeling you're glad all this has happened. I have a feeling you even wanted this to happen all along. It's all starting to add up.'

'You're wrong,' Diana said. 'So wrong.'

'I might be,' George said. 'But I doubt it.'

They parted with suppressed anger. Nevertheless, some part of her appeal must have touched him. Because later in the morning she saw George talking earnestly to Merlyn in the orchard. She also saw Merlyn shaking her head vigorously. It was, really, all she needed to see.

Merlyn was due to visit the doctor again that afternoon. Diana saw her off in the station wagon. The girl sat small and expressionless behind the wheel, the engine idling. 'Come back quickly,' Diana said. 'Everything's going to be all right again. I know it will.' The station wagon roared away, dust swirling out from under its wheels.

As Diana turned away, and drew nearer the house, she heard an abrupt, disconcerting noise from within. For a moment, confused, she thought of a thief: a thief in bright daylight. Then she thought that something, carelessly placed, might have tumbled from a shelf in the kitchen. At the kitchen window she stopped, and looked inside.

George was there, ransacking the place for food. He pushed tin after tin into the huge mouth of his pack. He moved hastily, guiltily, about the kitchen, opening cupboards and drawing back curtains.

She thought that she might as well give him time to get clear of the place.

She walked away through the orchard, quickly, in case he saw her; and then across a space of gumland grown sparsely with manuka. She took a line of stepping-stones over the creek where she and Merlyn bathed, and climbed a thin track through bush and finally scrub country again. As she ascended, the scrub thinned out, and only sickly patches of grass grew from the dusty earth. Sheep grazed here and there, on the steep slopes; there were frozen explosions of grey rock along wind-shaped ridges. High up, she could look down on the orchard, the house; farther away was their long half-moon of beach, the sea, the headlands, the island. The Maori settlement was a distant patch of crazy roof-tops.

She wondered why she seldom came up here for this view. It was probably only because she'd been too busy. There bad been too many claims on her. In time, perhaps, she would win the leisure to stand off and look a while. She would have time for pride, for most things.

There was a movement on the beach, down towards the water. The sight—George and his dinghy—took her by surprise. She had imagined him already clear of the house, walking a new road. She had entirely forgotten the dinghy. He'd loaded his pack into it, his guitar, and now he was dragging it down to the water. She saw the craft, tiny with distance, rock on the sea; and George, stripped, climbing into it, fastening oars and rowlocks. She knew that he had tested the dinghy the day before, and apparently found it seaworthy—she hadn't really troubled to inquire.

Now he was rowing out from shore. The flashing thrust of his oars left a faintly silver wake behind. The boat lurched a little, as he adjusted his direction and balance. It was only then, as he began to glide out from land, that Diana wondered at the purpose of his journey. Until then the fact of the journey seemed enough for her to grasp, the fact of his leaving; now she remembered the island. Of course, the island. He was pointed straight for it. She felt pain, and dismay. Was he fool enough to imagine he could live there? Perhaps, when his food went, he could live on fish and fern-root, grow kumara. It would be a last stand. Except that he wouldn't, and couldn't, be independent. Inevitably people down in the settlement would hear he was over there, sympathize, and take across gifts of their own hard-won food. George would scarcely discourage them: unlike Diana, he didn't set too high a price on his independence. He could even depend wholly on others, if necessary. Well, he was welcome to that kind of freedom, so long as it lasted. It wouldn't last, she was sure. He would have to return, if only to find someone to crow over. Experience should have shown him that neither she nor Merlyn were likely to be sympathetic listeners. Almost certainly be would go straight back to the city from the island.

And Merlyn—the thought sprang up quickly—Merlyn need not know he was over there at all. Diana would make a point of asking people in the settlement not to say anything to Merlyn about George being on the island; they would probably understand. In the meantime she could remain secure in the knowledge that he had gone. By this time, surely, Merlyn would be in town; she might even know for certain.

At once, with the thought of the child, Diana was invaded by a strange calm, and content. Everything had worked out for the best, in the end. Soon they would have to make preparations for the child.

The dinghy was way out in the sea, perhaps halfway to the island. George appeared to be flagging. As usual, he had probably set himself too hard a pace.

They would have the winter to prepare. There would have to be clothes, a cot. And of course both she and Merlyn would have to learn a great deal about children, if they hoped to rear it properly. They were probably both very ignorant. Merlyn had some excuse, the ignorance of youth. She had none. Yet she was confident that, together, they would make a good job of it. But would she—or Merlyn for that matter, if the girl were to find out—have any real happiness with the child when the father was still so near, across a strip of sea?

The dinghy—was it only her imagination?—seemed to have stopped altogether. It wasn't far from the island, though the distance of course appeared foreshortened from where she sat. No, she wasn't deceived: there was no longer a flash of oars. It was perfectly still. She thought she discerned George rocking in the boat. Perhaps he was resting and bailing. That looked the most likely explanation. Then she remembered what once had been pointed out to her, when she and Merlyn visited the island—a periphery of rock, hidden by full tide.

Whatever had happened out there, anyway, the dinghy was sinking. She saw George in the water, hanging on to the side. Perhaps the dinghy had struck a rock; or perhaps it wasn't, after all, seaworthy and had sprung some leak. It could have been any one of a number of things. Just as Diana could have done any one of a number of things when she saw the dinghy sinking.

She could, perhaps, have swum out herself to help him. She might have made it, but she would have been too exhausted to be of much assistance when she reached him. She could have raced to the settlement for help. He might keep himself afloat some time out there. Long enough for the settlement boats to reach him.

She was slow to realize he might drown.

She sat frozen. The seconds passed, and the minutes.

Of course it was absurd. She couldn't just sit there and watch. In a moment she would rise, race for help. She couldn't just sit there.

But she could. It astonished her. She was powerless, in a way; quite powerless. Because George wouldn't thank her for rescue. It would be a final cruelty which she was incapable, now, of inflicting.

Besides, as she watched, he made the decision his own. He apparently decided to take his chance: he released the dinghy and, plainly despairing, began to swim. Oddly, he still seemed to have energy enough to push on towards the island; she half-expected him, for some reason, to make back to land again. She imagined him flailing away at the water in his usual style. Yet he appeared to be closing a good deal of the gap between himself and the island. He might even still make it.

Then she could no longer look. She watched the sky, lonely gulls, and desolate hills.

When she looked again, the sea was empty. There was not even sign of the dinghy.

The island still looked vacant, and green. There was no longer any way of telling whether or not he had arrived there. It was perfectly isolated. People from the settlement seldom went over there—once or twice a year at most, for shellfish. Their usual fishing grounds were not far from shore. Without line or knife, without clothes in all weathers, it might still be possible to survive there indefinitely. And it might not. A return from the island was not impossible, either: the deep channels each side of the island were only forty or fifty yards wide. It would be a tricky swim, through tidal currents, across to the headlands. Yet not impossible, on a calm day with the tide at turn. All things were possible. There was no way, at this distance, of telling.

He might never have made it. She might never know. In her paralysis the day began to recede from her, as slowly as a dream of fulfilment, but she fought to retain her grip.

She could always mention to someone in the settlement that it was possible, just possible, that George had taken up residence on the island. Yes, of course; she could always do that, if it would make her feel any better. She could present it only as a casual surmise. For she had, of course, seen nothing this afternoon. Nothing at all.

Released, she rose stiffly to her feet. The cool nip of late afternoon promised early winter. She wondered if Merlyn might have arrived back from the doctor with good news. She shuddered or shivered—she was not sure which—and, after one terrifying moment of total emptiness within, she began the walk home. Think of anything, she told herself; and after a while she contemplated the preparations they would have to make, that winter. Without reason she started to hurry to Merlyn. In her blind haste she tripped on sticks and jutting rocks.

The People Before

1

My father took on that farm not long after he came back from the first war. It was pretty well the last farm up the river. Behind our farm, and up the river, there was all kind of wild country. Scrub and jagged black stumps on the hills, bush in gullies where fire hadn't reached; hills and more hills, deep valleys with caves and twisting rivers, and mountains white with winter in the distance. We had the last piece of really flat land up the river. It wasn't the first farm my father'd taken on—and it certainly wasn't to be the last—but it was the most remote. He always said that was why he'd got the place for a song. This puzzled me as a child. For I'd heard, of course, of having to sing for your supper. I wondered what words, to what tune, he was obliged to sing for the farm; and where, and why? Had he travelled up the river, singing a strange song, charming his way into possession of the land? It always perplexed me.

And it perplexed me because there wasn't much room for singing in my father's life. I can't remember ever having heard him sing. There was room for plodding his paddocks in all weathers, milking cows and sending cream down river to the dairy factory, and cursing the bloody government; there was room in his life for all these things and more, but not for singing.

In time, of course, I understood that he only meant he'd bought the place cheaply. Cheaply meant for a song. I couldn't, even then, quite make the connexion. It remained for a long while one of those adult mysteries. And it was no use puzzling over it, no use asking my father for a more coherent explanation.

'Don't be difficult,' he'd say. 'Don't ask so many damn questions. Life's difficult enough, boy, without all your damn questions. '

He didn't mean to be unkind; it was just his way. His life was committed to winning order from wilderness. Questions were a disorderly intrusion, like gorse or weed springing up on good pasture.

The best way was to hack them down, grub out the roots, before they could spread. And in the same way as he checked anarchy on his land he hoped, perhaps, to check it in his son.

By that time I was old enough to understand a good many of the things that were to be understood. One of them, for example, was that we weren't the first people on that particular stretch of land. Thirty or forty years before, when white men first came into our part of the country, it was mostly forest. Those first people fired the forest, right back into the hills, and ran sheep. The sheep grazed not only the flat, but the hills which rose sharply behind our farm; the hills which, in our time, had become stubbly with manuka and fern. The flatland had been pretty much scrub too, the day my father first saw it; and the original people had been gone twenty years—they'd given up, or been ruined by the land; we never quite knew the story. The farmhouse stood derelict among the returning wilderness.

Well, my father saw right away that the land—the flat land—was a reasonable proposition for a dairy farm. There was a new launch service down to the nearest dairy factory, in the township a few miles away; only in the event of flood, or a launch breakdown, would he have to dispose of his cream by carrying it on a sledge across country to the nearest road.

So he moved in, cleared the scrub, sowed new grass, and brought in cows. Strictly speaking, the hills at the back of the farm were his too, but he had no use for them. They made good shelter from the westerlies. Otherwise he never gave the hills a thought, since he had all the land he could safely manage; he roamed across them after wild pig, and that was about all. There were bones up there, scattered skeletons of lost sheep, in and about the scrub and burnt stumps.

Everything went well; he had the place almost paid off by the time of the depression. 'I never looked back, those years,' he said long afterwards. It was characteristic of him not to look back. He was not interested in who had the farm before him. He had never troubled to inquire. So far as he was concerned, history only began the day he first set foot on the land. It was his, by sweat and legal title; that was all that mattered. That was all that could matter.

He had two boys; I was the eldest son. 'You and Jim will take this place over one day,' he often told me. 'You'll run it when I get tired.'

But he didn't look like getting tired. He wasn't a big man, but he was wiry and thin with a lean face and cool blue eyes; he was one of those people who can't keep still. When neighbours called he couldn't ever keep comfortable in a chair, just sitting and sipping tea, but had to start walking them round the farm—or at least the male neighbours—pointing out things here and there. Usually work he'd done, improvements he'd made: the new milking-shed, the new water-pump on the river. He didn't strut or boast, though; he just pointed them out quietly, these jobs well done. He wanted others to share his satisfaction. There was talk of electricity coming through to the farm, the telephone; a road up the river was scheduled. It would all put the value of the property up. The risk he'd taken on the remote and abandoned land seemed justified in every way.

He didn't ever look like getting tired. It was as if he'd been wound up years before, like something clockwork, and set going: first fighting in the war, then fighting with the land; now most of the fighting was done, he sometimes found it quite an effort to keep busy. He never took a holiday. There was talk of taking a holiday, one winter when the cows dried off; talk of us all going down to the sea, and leaving a neighbour to look after the place. But I don't think he could have trusted anyone to look after his land, not even for a week or two in winter when the cows were dried off. Perhaps, when Jim and I were grown, it would be different. But not until. He always found some reason for us not to get away. Like our schooling.

'I don't want to interfere with their schooling,' he said once. 'They only get it once in their lives. And they might as well get it while they can. I didn't get much. And, by God, I regret it now. I don't know much, and I might have got along all right, but I might have got along a damn sight better if I'd had more schooling. And I'm not going to interfere with theirs by carting them off for a holiday in the middle of the year.'

Yet even then I wondered if he meant a word of it, if he really wasn't just saying that for something to say. He was wrangling at the time with my mother, who held opinions on a dwindling number of subjects. She never surrendered any of these opinions, exactly; she just kept them more and more to herself until, presumably, they lapsed quietly and died. As she herself, much later, was to lapse quietly from life, without much complaint.

For if he'd really been concerned about our schooling, he might have been more concerned about the way we fell asleep in afternoon classes. Not that we were the only ones. Others started getting pretty ragged in the afternoons too. A lot of us had been up helping our fathers since early in the morning. Jim and I were up at half-past four most mornings to help with the milking and working the separators. My father increased his herd year after year, right up to the depression. After school we rode home just in time for the evening milking. And by the time we finished it was getting dark; in winter it was dark by the time we were half-way through the herd.

I sometimes worried about Jim looking worn in the evenings, and I often chased him off inside before milking was finished. I thought Jim needed looking after; he wasn't anywhere near as big as me. I'd hear him scamper off to the house, and then I'd set about stripping the cows he had left. Father sometimes complained.

'You'll make that brother of yours a softy,' he said. 'The boy's got to learn what work means.'

'Jim's all right,' I answered. 'He's not a softy. He's just not very big. That's all.'

He detested softies, even the accomplices of softies. My mother, in a way, was such an accomplice. She'd never been keen about first me, then Jim, helping with work on the farm. But my father said he couldn't afford to hire a man to help with the herd. And he certainly couldn't manage by himself, without Jim and me.

'Besides,' he said, 'my Dad and me used to milk two hundred cows'—sometimes, when he became heated, the number rose to three hundred—'when I was eight years old. And thin as a rake too, I was. Eight years old and thin as a rake. It didn't do me no harm. You boys don't know what work is, let me tell you.'

So there all argument finished. My mother kept one more opinion to herself.

And I suppose that, when I chased Jim off inside, I was only taking my mother's side in the argument, and was only another accomplice of softies. Anyway, it would give me a good feeling afterwards—despite anything my father would have to say—when we tramped back to the house, through the night smelling of frost or rain, to find Jim sitting up at the table beside my mother while she ladled out soup under the warm yellow lamplight. He looked as if he belonged there, beside her; and she always looked, at those times, a little triumphant. Her look seemed to say that one child of hers, at least, was going to be saved from the muck of the cowshed. And I suppose that was how Jim became his mother's boy.

I remained my father's. I wouldn't have exchanged him for another father. I liked seeing him with people, a man among men. This happened on winter Saturdays when we rode to the township for the football. We usually left Jim behind to look after my mother. We tethered our horses near the football field and went off to join the crowd. Football was one of the few things which interested my father outside the farm. He'd been a fine rugby forward in his day and people respected what he had to say about the game. He could out-argue most people; probably out-fight them too, if it ever came to that. He often talked about the fights he'd had when young. For he'd done a bit of boxing too, only he couldn't spare the time from his father's farm to train properly. He knocked me down once, with his bare fists, in the cowshed; and I was careful never to let it happen again. I just kept my head down for days afterwards, so that he wouldn't see the bruises on my face or the swelling round my eye.

At the football he barracked with the best of them in the thick of the crowd. Sometimes he called out when the rest of the crowd was silent and tense; he could be very sarcastic about poor players, softies who were afraid to tackle properly.

After the game he often called in, on the way home, to have a few beers with friends in the township pub while I looked after the horses outside. Usually he'd find time, while he gossiped with friends, to bring me out a glass of lemonade. At times it could be very cold out there, holding the horses while the winter wind swept round, but it would be nice to know that I was remembered. When he finished we rode home together for a late milking. He would grow talkative, as we cantered towards dark, and even give me the impression he was glad of my company. He told me about the time he was young, what the world looked like when he was my age. His father was a sharemilker, travelling from place to place; that is, he owned no land of his own and did other people's work.

'So I made up my mind, boy,' he told me as we rode along together, 'I made up my mind I'd never be like that. I'd bend my head to no man. And you know what the secret of that is, boy? Land. Land of your own. You're independent, boy. You can say no to the world. That's if you got your own little kingdom. I reckon it was what kept me alive, down there on the beach at Gallipoli, knowing I'd have some land I could call my own.' This final declaration seemed to dismay him for some reason or other, perhaps because he feared he'd given too much of himself away. So he added half-apologetically, 'I had to think of something, you know, while all that shooting was going on. They say it's best to fix your mind on something if you don't want to be afraid. That's what I fixed my mind on, anyhow. Maybe it did keep me alive.'

In late winter or spring we sometimes arrived back, on Saturdays, to see the last trembling light of sunset fade from the hills and land. We'd canter along a straight stretch, coast up a rise, rein in the horses, and there it was—his green kingdom, his tight tamed acres beneath the hills and beside the river, a thick spread of fenced grass from the dark fringe of hill-scrub down to the ragged willows above the water. And at the centre was his castle, the farmhouse, with the sheds scattered round, and the pine trees.

Reining in on that rise, I knew, gave him a good feeling. It would also be the time when he remembered all the jobs he'd neglected, all the work he should have done instead of going to the football. His conscience would keep him busy all day Sunday.

At times he wondered—it was a conversation out loud with himself—why he didn't sell up and buy another place. There were, after all, more comfortable farms, in more convenient locations nearer towns or cities. 'I've built this place up from nothing,' he said. 'I've made it pay, and pay well. I've made this land worth something. I could sell out for a packet. Why don't I?'

He never really—in my presence anyway—offered himself a convincing explanation. Why didn't he? He'd hardly have said he loved the land: love, in any case, would have been an extravagance. Part of whatever it was, I suppose, was the knowledge that he'd built where someone else had failed; part was that he'd given too much of himself there, to be really free anywhere else. It wouldn't be the same, walking on to another successful farm, a going concern, everything in order. No, this place—this land from the river back up to the hills—was his. In a sense it had only ever been his. That was why he felt so secure.

If Sunday was often the day when he worked hardest, it was also the best day for Jim and me, our free day. After morning milking, and breakfast, we did more or less what we liked. In summer we swam down under the river-willows; we also had a canoe tied there and sometimes we paddled up-river, under great limestone bluffs shaggy with toi toi, into country which grew wilder and wilder. There were huge bearded caves in the bush above the water which we explored from time to time. There were also big eels to be fished from the pools of the river.

As he grew older Jim turned more into himself, and became still quieter. You could never guess exactly what he was thinking. It wasn't that he didn't enjoy life; he just had his own way of enjoying it. He didn't like being with his father, as I did; I don't even know that he always enjoyed being with me. He just tagged along with me: we were, after all, brothers. When I was old enough, my father presented me with a .22 rifle; Jim never showed great enthusiasm for shooting. He came along with me, all right, but he never seemed interested in the rabbits or wild goat I shot, or just missed. He wandered around the hills, way behind me, entertaining himself and collecting things. He gathered leaves, and tried to identify the plants from which the leaves came. He also collected stones, those of some interesting shape or texture; he had a big collection of stones. He tramped along, in his slow, quiet way, poking into everything, adding to his collections. He wasn't too slow and quiet at school, though; he was faster than most of us with an answer. He borrowed books from the teacher, and took them home. So in time he became even smarter with his answers. I grew to accept his difference from most people. It didn't disturb me particularly: on the farm he was still quiet, small Jim. He was never too busy with his books to come along with me on Sundays.

There was a night when Jim was going through some new stones he'd gathered. Usually, in the house, my father didn't take much notice of Jim, his reading or his hobbies. He'd fought a losing battle for Jim, through the years, and now accepted his defeat. Jim still helped us with the herd, night and morning, but in the house he was ignored. But this night my father went across to the table and picked up a couple of the new stones. They were greenish, both the same triangular shape.

'Where'd you get these?' he asked.

Jim thought for a moment he seemed pleased by the interest taken in him. 'One was back in the hills,' he said. 'The other was in a cave up the river. I just picked them up.'

'You mean you didn't find them together?'

'No,' Jim said.

'Funny,' my father said. 'They look like greenstone. I seen some greenstone once. A joker found it, picked it up in the bush. Jade, it is; same thing. This joker sold it in the city for a packet. Maori stuff. Some people'll buy anything.'

We all crossed to the table and looked down at the greenish stones. Jim's eyes were bright with excitement.

'You mean these used to belong to the Maoris?' he said. 'These stones?'

'Must have,' my father said. 'Greenstone doesn't come natural round here. You look it up in your books and you'll see. Comes from way down south, near the mountains and glaciers. Had to come up here all the way by canoe. They used to fight about greenstone, once.' He paused and looked at the stones again. 'Yes,' he added. 'I reckon that's greenstone, all right. You never know, might be some money in that stuff.'

Money was a very important subject in our house at that time. It was in a lot of households, since that time was the depression. In the cities they were marching in the streets and breaking shop windows. Here on the farm it wasn't anywhere near so dramatic. The grass looked much the same as it had always looked; so did the hills and river. All that had happened, really, was that the farm had lost its value. Prices had fallen; my father sometimes wondered if it was worth while sending cream to the factory. Some of the people on poorer land, down the river, had walked off their properties. Everything was tighter. We had to do without new clothes, and there wasn't much variety in our eating. We ran a bigger garden, and my father went out more frequently shooting wild pig for meat. He had nothing but contempt for the noisy people in the city, the idlers and wasters who preferred to go shouting in the streets rather than fetch a square meal for their families, as he did with his rifle. He thought they, in some way, were to blame for the failure of things. Even so, he became gripped by the idea that he might have failed himself, somehow; he tried to talk himself out of this idea— in my presence—but without much success. Now he had the land solid beneath his feet, owned it entirely, it wasn't much help at all. If it wasn't for our garden and the wild pig, we might starve. The land didn't bring him any money; he might even have to leave it. He had failed, perhaps much as the land's former owners had failed; why? He might have answered the question for himself satisfactorily, while he grubbed away at the scrub encroaching on our pasture; but I doubt it.

'Yes,' he said. 'Might be some money in that stuff.'

But Jim didn't seem to hear, or understand. His eyes were still bright. 'That means there must have been Maoris here in the old days,' he said.

'I suppose there must have,' my father agreed. He didn't seem much interested. Maoris were Maoris. There weren't many around our part of the river; they were mainly along the coast. 'They were most places, weren't they?' he added.

'Yes,' Jim said. 'But I mean they must have been here. On our place.'

'Well, yes. They could of been. Like I said, they were most places.' It didn't seem to register as important. He picked up the greenstone again. 'We ought to find out about this,' he continued. 'There might be a bit of money in it.'

Later Jim took the stones to school and had them identified as Maori adzes. My father said once again that perhaps there was money in them. But the thing was, where to find a buyer? It mightn't be as easy as it used to be. So somehow it was all forgotten. Jim kept the adzes.

Jim and I did try to find again that cave in which he had picked up an adze. We found a lot of caves, but none of them seemed the right one. Anyway we didn't pick up another adze. We did wander down one long dripping cave, striking matches, and in the dark I tripped on something. I struck another match and saw some brownish-looking bones. 'A sheep,' I said. 'It must have come in here and got lost.'

Jim was silent; I wondered why. Then I saw he wasn't looking at the bones, but at a human skull propped on a ledge of the cave, shadows dancing in its sockets.

We got out of that cave quickly. We didn't even talk about it when we reached home. On the whole I preferred going out with my .22 after rabbits.

2

It was near the end of the depression. But we didn't know that then, of course. It might have been just the beginning, for all we knew. My father didn't have as much interest in finishing jobs as he used to have. He tired easily. He'd given his best to the land, and yet his best still wasn't good enough. There wasn't much sense in anything, and his dash was done. He kept going out of habit.

I'd been pulled out of school to help with the farm. Jim still more or less went to school. I say more or less because he went irreglarly. This was because of sickness. Once he was away in hospital two months. And of course it cost money; my father said we were to blame, we who allowed Jim to become soft and sickly. But the doctor thought otherwise; he thought Jim had been worked hard enough already. And when Jim returned to the farm he no longer helped with the herd. And this was why I had to leave school: if he couldn't have both of us working with him part-time, my father wanted one full-time. Jim was entirely surrendered at last, to the house and his books, to school and my mother. I didn't mind working on the farm all day, with my father; it was, after all, what I'd always wanted. All the same, I would have been happier if he had been: his doubts about himself, more and more frequently expressed, disturbed me. It wasn't like my father at all. He was convinced now he'd done the wrong thing, somewhere. He went back through the years, levering each year up like a stone, to see what lay beneath; he never seemed to find anything. It was worst of all in winter, when the land looked bleak, the hills were grey with low cloud, and the rain swirled out of the sky. All life vanished from his face and I knew he detested everything: the land which had promised him independence was now only a muddy snare; he was bogged here, between hills and river, and couldn't escape. He had no pride left in him for the place. If he could have got a price for the farm he would have gone. But there was no longer any question of a price. He could walk off if he liked. Only the bush would claim it back.

It was my mother who told us there were people coming. She had taken the telephone message while we were out of the house, and Jim was at school.

'Who are they?' my father said.

'I couldn't understand very well. It was a bad connexion. I think they said they were the people who were here before.'

'The people who were here before? What the hell do they want here?' His eyes became suspicious under his frown.

'I think they said they just wanted to have a look around.'

'What the hell do they want here?' my father repeated, baffled. 'Nothing for them to see. This farm's not like it was when they were here. Everything's different. I've made a lot of changes. They wouldn't know the place. What do they want to come back for?'

'Well,' my mother sighed, 'I'm sure I don't know.'

'Perhaps they want to buy it,' he said abruptly; the words seemed simultaneous with his thought, and he stiffened with astonishment. 'By God, yes. They might want to buy the place back again. I hadn't thought of that. Wouldn't that be a joke? I'd sell, all right—for just about as much as I paid for the place. I tell you, I'd let it go for a song, for a bloody song. They're welcome.'

'But where would we go?' she said, alarmed.

'Somewhere,' he said. 'Somewhere new. Anywhere.'

'But there's nowhere,' she protested. 'Nowhere any better. You know that.'

'And there's nowhere any worse,' he answered. 'I'd start again somewhere. Make a better go of things.'

'You're too old to start again,' my mother observed softly.

There was a silence. And in the silence I knew that what my mother said was true. We all knew it was true.

'So we just stay here,' he said. 'And rot. Is that it?' But he really wished to change the subject. 'When are these people coming?'

'Tomorrow, I think. They're staying the night down in the township. Then they're coming up on the launch.'

'They didn't say why they were interested in the place?'

'No. And they certainly didn't say they wanted to buy it. They said they just wanted to look around.'

'I don't get it. I just don't get it. If I walked off this place I wouldn't ever want to see it again.'

'Perhaps they're different,' my mother said. 'Perhaps they've got happy memories of this place.'

'Perhaps they have. God knows.'

It was early summer, with warm lengthening days. That sunny Saturday morning I loitered about the house with Jim, waiting for the people to arrive. Eventually, as the sun climbed higher in the sky, I grew impatient and went across the paddocks to help my father. We were working together when we heard the sound of the launch coming up the river.

'That's them,' he said briefly. He dropped his slasher for a moment, and spat on his hands. Then he took up the slasher again and chopped into a new patch of unruly gorse.

I was perplexed. 'Well,' I said, 'aren't you going down to meet them?'

'I'll see them soon enough. Don't worry.' He seemed to be conducting an argument with himself as he hacked into the gorse. 'I'm in no hurry. No, I'm in no hurry to see them.'

I just kept silent beside him.

'Who are they, anyway?' he went on. 'What do they want to come traipsing round my property for? They've got a bloody cheek.'

The sound of the launch grew. It was probably travelling round the last bend in the river now, past the swamp of raupo, and banks prickly with flax and toi toi. They were almost at the farm. Still chopping jerkily, my father tried to conceal his unease.

'What do they want?' he asked for the last time. 'By God, if they've come to gloat, they've got another think coming. I've made something decent out of this place, and I don't care who knows it.'

He had tried everything in his mind and it was no use: he was empty of explanation. Now we could see the launch white on the gleaming river. It was coasting up to the bank. We could also see people clustered on board.

'Looks like a few of them,' I observed. If I could have done so without upsetting my father, I would have run down to meet the launch, eager with curiosity. But I kept my distance until he finished arguing with himself.

'Well,' he said, as if he'd never suggested otherwise, 'we'd better go down to meet them, now they're here.' He dug his slasher into the earth and began to stalk off down to the river. I followed him. His quick strides soon took him well ahead of me; I had to run to keep up.

* * *

Then we had our surprise. My father's step faltered; I blundered up alongside him. We saw the people climbing off the launch. And we saw who they were, at last. My father stopped perfectly still and silent. They were Maoris. We were still a hundred yards or more away, but there was no mistaking their clothing and colour. They were Maoris, all right.

'There's something wrong somewhere,' he said at last. 'It doesn't make sense. No Maori ever owned this place. I'd have known. Who the hell do they think they are, coming here?'

I couldn't answer him. He strode on down to the river. There were young men, and two old women with black head-scarves. And last of all there was something the young men carried. As we drew nearer we saw it was an old man in a rough litter. The whole party of them fussed over making the old man comfortable. The old women, particularly; they had tattoos on their chins and wore shark-tooth necklaces. They straightened the old man's blankets and fixed the pillow behind his head. He had a sunken, withered face and he didn't look so much sick, as tired. His eyes were only half-open as everyone fussed around. It looked as if it were a great effort to keep them that much open. His hair was mostly grey, and his dry flesh sagged in thin folds about his ancient neck. I reckoned that he must have been near enough to a hundred years old. The young men talked quickly among themselves as they saw my father approaching. One came forward, apparently as spokesman. He looked about the oldest of them, perhaps thirty. He had a fat, shiny face.

'Here,' said my father. 'What's all this about?' I knew his opinion of Maoris: they were lazy, drank too much, and caused trouble. They just rode on the backs of the men on the land, like the loafers in the cities. He always said we were lucky there were so few in our district. 'What do you people think you're doing here?' he demanded.

'We rang up yesterday,' the spokesman said. 'We told your missus we might be coming today.'

'I don't know about that. She said someone else was coming. The people who were here before.'

'Well,' said the young man, smiling. 'We were the people before.'

'I don't get you. You trying to tell me you owned this place?'

'That's right. We owned all the land round this end of the river. Our tribe.'

'That must have been a hell of a long time ago.'

'Yes,' agreed the stranger. 'A long time.' He was pleasantly spoken and patient. His round face, which I could imagine looking jolly, was very solemn just then.

I looked around and saw my mother and Jim coming slowly down from the house.

'I still don't get it,' my father said. 'What do you want?'

'We just want to go across your land, if that's all right. Look, we better introduce ourselves. My name's Tom Taikaka. And this is—'

My father was lost in a confusion of introductions. But he still didn't shake anyone's hand. He just stood his ground, aloof and faintly hostile. Finally there was the old man. He looked as though he had gone to sleep again.

'You see he's old,' Tom explained. 'And has not so long to live. He is the last great man of our tribe, the oldest. He wishes to see again where he was born. The land over which his father was chief. He wishes to see this before his spirit departs for Rerengawairua.'

By this time my mother and Jim had joined us. They were as confused as we were.

'You mean you've come just to—' my father began.

'We've come a long way,' Tom said. 'From up the coast. That's where we live now.'

'All this way. Just so—'

'Yes,' Tom said. 'That's right.'

'Well,' said my father. 'What do you know? What do you know about that?' Baffled, he looked at me, at my mother, and even finally at Jim. None of us had anything to say.

'I hope we're not troubling you,' Tom said politely. 'We don't want to be any trouble. We just want to go across your land, if that's all right. We got our own tucker and everything.'

We saw this was true. The two old women had large flax kits of food.

'No liquor?' my father said suspiciously. 'I don't want any drinking round my place.'

'No,' Tom replied. His face was still patient. 'No liquor. We don't plan on any drinking.'

The other young men shyly agreed in the background. It was not, they seemed to say, an occasion for drinking.

'Well,' said my father stiffly, 'I suppose it's all right. Where are you going to take him?' He nodded towards the old sleeping man.

'Just across your land. And up to the old *pa*.'

'I didn't know there used to be any *pa* round here.'

'Well,' said Tom. 'It used to be up there.' He pointed out the largest hill behind our farm, one that stood well apart and above the others. We called it Craggy Hill, because of limestone outcrops. Its flanks and summit were patchy with tall scrub. We seldom went near it, except perhaps when out shooting; then we circled its steep slopes rather than climbed it. 'You'd see the terraces,' Tom said, 'if it wasn't for the scrub. It's all hidden now.'

Now my father looked strangely at Tom. 'Hey,' he said, 'you sure you aren't having me on? How come you know that hill straight off? You ever been here before?'

'No,' Tom said. His face shone as he sweated with the effort of trying to explain everything. 'I never been here before. I never been in this part of the country before.'

'Then how do you know that's the hill, eh?'

'Because,' Tom said simply, 'the old men told me. They described it so well I could find the place blindfold. All the stories of our tribe are connected with that hill. That's where we lived, up there, for hundreds of years.'

'Well, I'll be damned. What do you know about that?' My father blinked, and looked up at the hill again. 'Just up there, eh? And for hundreds of years.'

'That's right.'

'And I never knew. Well, I'll be damned.'

'There's lots of stories about that hill,' Tom said. 'And a lot of battles fought round here. Over your place.'

'Right over my land?'

'That's right. Up and down here along the river.'

My father was so astonished he forgot to be aloof. He was trying to fit everything into his mind at once—the hill where they'd lived hundreds of years, the battles fought across his land—and it was too much.

'The war canoes would come up here,' Tom went on. 'I reckon they'd drag them up somewhere here'—he indicated the grassy bank on which we were standing—'in the night, and go on up to attack the *pa* before sunrise. That's if we hadn't sprung a trap for them down here. There'd be a lot of blood soaked into this soil.' He kicked at the earth beneath our feet. 'We had to fight a long while to keep this land here, a lot of battles. Until there was a day when it was no use fighting any more. That was when we left.'

We knew, without him having to say it, what he meant. He meant the day when the European took the land. So we all stood quietly for a moment. Then my mother spoke.

'You'd better come up to the house,' she said. 'I'll make you all a cup of tea.'

A cup of tea was her solution to most problems.

We went up to the house slowly. The young men followed behind, carrying the litter. They put the old man in the shade of a tree, outside the house. Since it seemed the best thing to do, we all sat around him; there wouldn't have been room for everyone in our small kitchen anyway. We waited for my mother to bring, out the tea.

Then the old man awoke. He seemed to shiver, his eyes opened wide, and he said something in Maori. 'He wonders where he is,' Tom explained. He turned back to the old man and spoke in Maori.

He gestured, he pointed. Then the old man knew. We all saw it the moment the old man knew. It was as if we were all willing him towards that moment of knowledge. He quivered and tried to lift himself weakly; the old women rushed forward to help him. His eyes had a faint glitter as he looked up to the place we called Craggy Hill. He did not see us, the house, or anything else. Some more Maori words escaped him in a long, sighing rush. '*Te Wahiokoahoki*,' he said.

'It is the name,' Tom said, repeating it. 'The name of the place.'

The old man lay back against the women, but his eyes were still bright and trembling. They seemed to have a life independent of his wrinkled flesh. Then the lids came down, and they were gone again. We could all relax.

'*Te Wahiokoahoki*,' Tom said. 'It means the place of happy return. It got the name when we returned there after our victories against other tribes.'

My father nodded. 'Well, I'll be damned,' he said. 'That place there. And I never knew.' He appeared quite affable now.

My mother brought out tea. The hot cups passed from hand to hand, steaming and sweet.

'But not so happy now, eh?' Tom said. 'Not for us.'

'No. I don't suppose so.'

Tom nodded towards the old man. 'I reckon he was just about the last child born here. Before we had to leave. Soon there'll be nobody left who lived there. That's why they wanted young men to come back. So we'd remember too.'

Jim went into the house and soon returned. I saw he carried the greenstone adzes he'd found. He approached Tom shyly.

'I think these are really yours,' he said, the words an effort.

Tom turned the adzes over in his hand. Jim had polished them until they were a vivid green. 'Where'd you get these, eh?' he asked.

Jim explained how and where he'd found them. 'I think they're really yours,' he repeated.

There was a brief silence. Jim stood with his eyes downcast, his treasure surrendered. My father watched anxiously; he plainly thought Jim a fool.

'You see,' Jim added apologetically, 'I didn't think they really belonged to anyone. That's why I kept them.'

'Well,' Tom said, embarrassed. 'That's real nice of you. Real nice of you, son. But you better keep them, eh? They're yours now. You find, you keep. We got no claims here any more. This is your father's land now.'

Then it was my father who seemed embarrassed. 'Leave me out of this,' he said sharply. 'You two settle it between you. It's none of my business.'

'I think you better keep them all the same,' Tom said to Jim.

Jim was, glad to keep the greenstone, yet a little hurt by rejection of his gift. He received the adzes back silently.

'I tell you what,' Tom went on cheerfully, 'you ever find another one, you send it to me, eh? Like a present. But you keep those two.'

'All right,' Jim answered, clutching the adzes. He seemed much happier. 'I promise if I find any more, I'll send them to you.'

'Fair enough,' Tom smiled, his face jolly. Yet I could see that he too really wanted the greenstone.

After a while they got up to leave. They made the old man comfortable again and lifted him. 'We'll see you again,' Tom said. 'When we catch the launch home.'

'Tomorrow?' my father said. He began to understand that they were proposing to camp on his land.

'When we're ready to go home,' Tom said. 'Maybe in two or three days if that's all right by you.'

'Well, I suppose it's all right.' My father didn't know quite what to say. 'Nothing you want?'

'No,' Tom said. 'We got all we want, thanks. We'll be all right. We got ourselves. That's the important thing, eh?'

We watched them move away, the women followed by the young men with the litter. Tom went last, Jim trotting along beside him. They seemed, since the business of the greenstone, to have made friends quickly. Tom appeared to be telling Jim a story.

I thought for a moment that my father might call Jim back. But he didn't. He let him go.

The old women were chanting or singing. Their figures grew smaller with distance. Soon they were clear of the paddocks and beginning to climb Craggy Hill.

My father thumbed back his hat and rubbed a handkerchief across his brow. 'Well, I'll be damned,' he said.

* * *

We sat together on the porch that evening, as we often did in summer after milking and our meal. Yet that evening was very different from any other. The sun had set, and in the dusk we saw faint smoke rising from their campfire on Craggy Hill, the place of happy return. Sometimes I thought I heard the wailing sound of the women again, but I couldn't quite be sure.

What were they doing up there, what did they hope to find? We both wondered and puzzled, yet didn't speak to each other.

Jim had returned long before, with stories. It seemed he had learned, one way and another, just about all there was to be learned about the tribe that had once lived on Craggy Hill. At the dinner table he told the stories breathlessly. My father affected to be not much interested; and so, my father's son, did I. Yet we listened, all the same.

'Then there was the first musket,' Jim said. 'The first musket in this part of the country. Someone bought it from a trader down south and carried it back to the *pa*. Another tribe, one of their old enemies, came seeking *utu*—*utu* means revenge—for something that had been done to them the year before. And when they started climbing up the hill they were knocked off, one by one, with the musket. They'd never seen anything like it before. So the chief of the tribe on Craggy Hill made a sign of peace and called up his enemies. It wasn't a fair fight, he said, only one tribe with a musket. So he'd let his enemies have the musket for a while. They would have turns with the musket, each tribe. He taught the other tribe how to fire and point the musket. Then they separated and started the battle again. And the next man to be killed by the musket was the chief's eldest son. That was the old man's uncle—the old man who was here today.'

'Well, I don't know,' said my father. 'Sounds bloody queer to me. That's no way to fight a battle.'

'That's the way they fought,' Jim maintained.

So we left Jim, still telling stories to my mother, and went out on the porch.

The evening thickened. Soon the smoke of the campfire was lost. The hills grew dark against the pale sky. And at last my father, looking up at the largest hill of all, spoke softly.

'I suppose a man's a fool,' he said. 'I should never have let that land go. Shouldn't ever have let it go back to scrub. I could of run a few sheep up there. But I just let it go. Perhaps I'll burn it off one day, run a few sheep. Sheep might pay better too, the way things are now.'

But it wasn't, somehow, quite what I expected him to say. I suppose he was just trying to make sense of things in his own fashion.

3

They came down off Craggy Hill three days later, in time to catch the cream launch.

When we saw the cluster of tiny figures, moving at a fair pace down the hills, we sensed there was something wrong. Then, as they drew nearer, approaching us across the paddocks, we saw that was wrong. There was no litter, no old man. They all walked freely, separately. They were no longer burdened.

Astonished, my father strode up to Tom. 'Where is he?' he demanded.

'We left him back up there,' Tom said. He smiled sadly and I had a queer feeling that I knew exactly what he would say.

'Left him up there?'

'He died. When we went to wake him he was cold. So we left him up there. That's where he asked to be.'

'You can't do that,' my father protested. 'You can't just leave a dead man like that. Leave him anywhere. And, besides, it's my land you're leaving him on.'

'Yes,' Tom said. 'Your land.'

'Don't you understand? You can't just leave dead people around. Not like that.'

'But we didn't just leave him around. We didn't just leave him anywhere. We made him all safe and comfortable. He's all right. You needn't worry.'

'Christ, man,' my father said. 'Don't you see?'

But he might have been asking a blind man to see. Tom just smiled patiently and said not to worry. Also he said they'd better be catching the launch. They had a long way to go home, a tiring journey ahead.

And as he walked off, my father still arguing beside him, the old women clashed their dry greenery, wailing, and their shark-tooth necklaces danced under their heaving throats.

In a little while the launch went noisily off down the river. My father stood on the bank, still yelling after them. When he returned to the house, his voice was hoarse.

He had a police party out, a health officer too. They scoured the hills, and most of the caves they could find. They discovered no trace of a burial, nor did they find anything in the caves. At one stage someone foolishly suggested we might have imagined it all. So my father produced the launchman and people from the township as witnesses to the fact that an old Maori, dying, had actually been brought to our farm.

That convinced them. But it didn't take them anywhere near finding the body. They traced the remnants of the tribe, living up the coast, and found that indeed an old man of the tribe was missing. No one denied that there had been a visit to our farm. But they maintained that they knew nothing about a body. The old man, they said, had just wandered off into the bush; they hadn't found him again.

He might, they added, even still be alive. Just to be on the safe side, in case there was any truth in their story, the police put the old man on the missing persons register, for all the good that might have done.

But we knew. We knew every night we looked up at the hills that he was there, somewhere.

So he was still alive, in a way. Certainly it was a long time before he let us alone.

And by then my father had lost all taste for the farm. It seemed the land itself had made a fool of him. He never talked again, anyway, about running sheep on the hills.

When butter prices rose and land values improved, a year or two afterwards, he had no hesitation in selling out. We shifted into another part of the country entirely, for a year or two, and then into another. Finally we found ourselves milking a small herd for town supply, not far from the city. We're still on that farm, though there's talk of the place being purchased soon for a city subdivision. We think we might sell, but we'll face the issue when it arises.

Now and then Jim comes to see us, smart in a city suit, a lecturer at the university. My father always found it difficult to talk to Jim, and very often now he goes off to bed and leaves us to it. One thing I must say about Jim: he has no objection to helping with the milking. He insists that he enjoys it; perhaps he does. It's all flatland round our present farm, with one farm much like another, green grass and square farmhouses and pine shelter belts, and it's not exactly the place to sit out on a summer evening and watch shadows gathering on the hills. Because there aren't hills within sight; or shadows either, for that matter. It's all very tame and quiet, apart from cars speeding on the highway.

I get on reasonably well with Jim. We read much the same books, have much the same opinions on a great many subjects. The city hasn't made a great deal of difference to him. We're both married, with young families. We also have something else in common: we were both in the war, fighting in the desert. One evening after milking, when we stood smoking and yarning in the cool, I remembered something.

'You know,' I began, 'they say it's best, when you're under fire in the war, to fix your mind on something remote. So you won't be afraid. I remember Dad telling me that. I used to try. But it never seemed any good. I couldn't think of anything. I was still as scared as hell.'

'I was too. Who wasn't?'

'But, I mean, did you ever think of anything?'

'Funny thing,' he said. 'Now I come to think of it, I did. I thought of the old place—you know, the old place by the river. Where,' he added, and his face puckered into a grin, 'where they buried that old Maori. And where I found those greenstone adzes. I've still got them at home, you know, up on the mantelpiece. I seem to remember trying to give them away once, to those Maoris. Now I'm glad I didn't. It's my only souvenir from there, the only thing that makes that place still live for me.' He paused. 'Well, anyway, that's what I thought about. That old place of ours.'

I had a sharp pain. I felt the dismay of a long-distance runner who, coasting confidently to victory, imagining himself well ahead of the field, finds himself overtaken and the tape snapped at the very moment he leans forward to breast it. For one black moment it seemed I had been robbed of something which was rightfully mine.

I don't think I'll ever forgive him.

The Voyagers

1

'What's going to happen to me?' she said. She paused thoughtfully, then looked at me. Swiftly she corrected herself. 'To us?' she asked.

'Nothing,' I said.

'Nothing?' The dismay on her face was quite intimidating. I wished I had told a lie. But for once I began to speak the truth, for my own sake too, I had to finish.

'Nothing much ever happens to people like us,' I said brutally. 'We've just got to make the best of it.'

'And what does that mean?' she said.

'I don't know,' I confessed.

* * *

In dark moments I still remember that conversation. I should have seen it coming. But with all the tumult of Mike's departure I didn't have time to think about Betty. It was absurd that she should have been forgotten: I suppose I was just as much at fault as Mike.

Her telephone call came like conscience when I was upstairs, in our room, helping Mike pack. He was shovelling clothes, shoes and books helter-skelter into a large suitcase. He'd already packed his best paintings carefully. The rest he burned. Except, that is, for one or two which I salvaged to keep on the walls of the room we had shared.

Mike and I lived together three years or more. But we'd known each other much longer. We grew up together, in fact, in a King Country town. We ran wild on the hills and hunted through bush with a shared .22 and fought side by side in schoolboy gang battles on the riverbank. We both almost drowned, in our capricious river, when our home-made canoe came unstuck in rapids. Mike claimed to have rescued me; I claimed to have rescued him. We were like that as children. No one had the upper hand, though Mike tried his hardest.

I was the only son of one of the town's two lawyers, Mike the fourth son of a railway engine-driver. Mike's family was more or less itinerant, mine long established in the district. Socially our fathers were a mile apart; politically too. My father was austerely right-wing, president of the local National Party; Mike's was an old Labour Party militant. I don't recall any of this making much difference to us. I'm not saying it mightn't have, in later years; but Mike and his family moved out of town before those years came.

Then there was a gap of about five years. I went through high school, dawdled away a year in my father's office, then went on to university. To study law, of course. I was a normal enough young man from the King Country. I liked my rugby, and had some talent as a full-back and goal-kicker. I liked my liquor, most often sampled outside dry dance halls. I'd had one girl in the back of a van, a first fumbled tumble among muddied football gear, and another much more revelatory on the riverbank one summer. Our town would have been short on revelation without a riverbank.

So I was quite unprepared for what Mike had become. I met him through a restless, sporty university crowd with which I trailed along. It was my first or second year in Auckland. I don't wish to leave the impression I wasn't working hard. Because I was; my father emphasised, and I agreed, that I wasn't at university to fool around. Rugby was still my major diversion; I turned out for a university team. I knew I had at least five years in the city before I got my degree. That was why I worked hard; I didn't see much future in being round the university ten years. I wanted to get home again, where I knew my way about. And where I was distinct enough as an individual to be selected by the crowd at Rugby Park for applause, or even hooting, on Saturday afternoons. I was still uneasy in the city. I knew where I was, back there, and who I was. So I worked.

But work was one thing, Saturday nights another. It was a bad week when I had to surrender Saturday night to my books. Put it down to background. I suppose Saturday nights are what they are in the King Country, a kind of weekly fever, because of the impending tedium of Sunday; a quick, wild hunt for hedonism before the Sabbath suffocates. You would have to experience the life of an inland New Zealand town to appreciate what I mean. Anyway I didn't lose the fever when I reached Auckland. My temperature rose on schedule every Saturday afternoon. I soon learned that the thing was to have contacts. By contacts I mean people who knew what was doing, where the parties were. Hence my tagging round with this restless, sporty crowd I've mentioned. A couple of that crowd I'd met through turning out for a university team.

We crashed parties quite often. I soon became as expert as the others. For there was a technique in successful crashing. We scattered as soon as we arrived at a party we never clustered guiltily at a door. We latched on to all the people we knew, and quite a few we didn't. It was a matter of establishing ourselves before the host, if any, objected to our presence. Certain parties were of course walkovers for crashers; or walk-ins. These were the arty parties, those thrown on the university's corduroy fringe. There no one ever knew who invited who anyway. So long as we brought along a bottle or two we were all right.

At one such party I met Mike again. It was held on the gloomy ground floor of a damp old house just above the cemetery in Grafton gully. There were candles dripping grease on Vat 69 bottles and mattresses flung on the floor. All the furniture was shattered and a couple of windows broken. A group of Samoans strummed guitars. People danced in a wild erotic way. It was before the days of the twist; before even rock and roll. That dates me, I suppose, but the point I am trying to make is that these dancers anticipated both twist and rock and roll with some gusto. After a while I danced too. For some reason I pursued a rather tubercular-looking little girl with tight slacks, loose sweater and crabby face. Finally she said that frankly I wasn't her type. I collapsed on to some free floor space with a brimming glass of beer for consolation. I finished the glass in one quick gulp—I had quite a reputation for my performance in the university drinking-horn championships—and looked up and saw Mike.

He might have been another party-crasher, but he didn't look it. With his jeans and soiled tartan shirt, he looked as though he belonged if anyone did. Again, to make myself clear at the risk of seeming dated I should point out that Mike and a lot of his friends anticipated the beats, or the beatniks, whatever these noisy imitation San Franciscans are called; they were Pacific originals, almost as indigenous as the Polynesian. We called them hobohemian. A way of saying they were different.

I recognised Mike without difficulty. His face hadn't changed much. What was there in the child had just developed. I suppose some might have called it a strong face. It never struck me as strong, though it was solid enough. This was before his beard, of course; that beard which hid most of his face in the newspaper photographs published here after his European success five years ago, along with the local-boy-makes-good caption. Mike had no weak chin to hide: I can say that much for his face. But what did I see that night? I think I was most aware of his eyes. They were quick, and over-bright. If anything, his expression was surly. For defence probably. But his eyes, reddened rifts, flawed that fortress.

I forget what I said in my surprise, but anyway it startled him. Particularly when I stammered out my name. Possibly he suffered shock similar to my own. After all, I was part—perhaps an important part—of his King Country childhood sprung to life once more. There might even have been a moment when he was floundering about in those rapids again; or stalking through thick bush with a rifle. I say this because I'm making an effort now to put myself in Mike's place. I never was very good at that. But the effort is still occasionally necessary, even if I make it less and less as the years go by.

I believe we said all the predictable things at that reunion. He asked, 'What the hell are you doing here, anyway?'

'I'm at university,' I explained.

'Law, naturally. Like your old man.'

'That's right. Like my old man.'

'And you'll take over his practice.'

'That's the general idea,' I agreed.

'Quite a future you've got already,' he observed. 'All tied up. Neat, safe, secure.'

'Well, yes.' I said. 'Security's a big thing, you know. Half the battle, as they say.'

If he was throwing darts, they didn't hurt me; they simply landed where my hide was thickest.

'What battle?' he said with sarcasm. 'What battle have you ever had? Tell me about it. I'm interested. I really am.'

'Any old battle,' I replied. I was impervious to sarcasm, and anyway seldom heard what I didn't like to hear. 'The sex war, if you like.'

He grunted. 'Oh Christ,' was all he said. He seemed about to turn away in disgust. But he didn't. He simply looked away for a while. The past held him, however tenuously: he was prepared to be patient.

'Tell me one thing,' he went on. 'I'm interested. Why don't you please yourself what you do?'

'Oh,' I said, 'I've got that worked out. It's like this. First I please my old man. Then, the rest of my life, I please myself. Get the idea?'

He just grunted again. Naturally I could have expanded on my theme; but it wasn't the time or place. I could have pointed out, for example, that my father was a lonely old widower in a dusty office and had no one but me. If I failed him, he wouldn't have much in life to which he might hang on. This was one of the disadvantages of being an only child; I was late-born in a marriage which was never much more than satisfactory. I believe my parents both tried to make the best of their marriage, but the only result was me, and my mother's long illness afterwards. I've always been aware that I came along too late, really.

Perhaps none of this would have interested Mike anyway. In some perverse way it might only have proved his point. For Mike the important thing was preserving himself intact; and that meant thrusting aside other lives, with their direct or implied imperatives. As applied to his own situation. I could see his point of view very well. He had to scramble out of a large family in the first place. And the way he chose for himself afterwards meant he had to toughen himself against the pressures, cajolings, demands and even mockery of other people. I failed to see that his point of view had relevance to me; indeed he was as blind to my situation as others were to his own.

That night Mike and I talked a while longer. We grew more relaxed, and began to recall shared adventures from the past as the bottles emptied between us. People milled around in the candlelight, but we grew less aware of them. More of our friendship had survived than I at first thought possible. This might have been because I was prepared to listen to what he said. I don't know. There are other possibilities.

But certainly I was careful. To ask pertinent questions of Mike was to run full tilt against a barbed-wire fence. And to face the problem of getting free of the barbs afterwards. I don't remember much else, to be honest—I was drinking after a bruising game of football, and on an empty stomach. I remember how the conversation ended, though.

Mike began peering at the other people round.

'I've just remembered,' he said. 'I brought a woman along tonight. I wonder where she's got to?'

Finally, with some reluctance, he rose and searched for her. At some later stage, when I was hazier than ever, he turned up with a girl on his arm. It wasn't Betty; this was before the days of Betty. She was a Philippa or a Miranda, one of those unusually named girls it always seemed Mike's fancy to acquire; these girls jell into a type in my memory. They were well-groomed and tall with flawless complexions. Not that he looked happy with any of them. Why Mike attracted them I can't say; perhaps it was a kind of sexual slumming. What I mean, of course, is that the worse Mike treated them, the more they appeared to like it. That kind of thing was, and still is, beyond my understanding. I have to make my own limitations clear.

Anyway they were leaving the party. Mike and I exchanged addresses and telephone numbers and agreed to meet at some unspecified time in the future. In point of fact I promptly lost both his address and telephone number when I blundered out of the party and vomited in long grass by the edge of the cemetery. In the moonlight those pale pioneer headstones seemed vaguely to accuse me. I attempted to hold myself erect as befitted a grandson of the frontier; and lurched homewards. Next morning, with church bells banging into my room, I saw soberly that my meeting with Mike was an interesting experience, no more. I doubted that I would see him again. We had little in common apart from our childhood. I couldn't contact him, and it was most unlikely that he would trouble himself to get in touch with me.

But I was wrong. There was a space of months, then he rang me. I don't flatter myself and pretend it was because we had something in common. It was because I had something he hadn't. A room. This soon became clear after he'd made an inquiry about my health.

'Look,' he said. 'I've just been thrown out of my digs. I never got along with that landlady anyway. I wonder could you put me up a day or two?'

I said it wouldn't be any trouble, which was true. I had a large room at an absurdly low rent. My landlady was an old dear, a gentlewoman of a vanished school; she just didn't belong in the Auckland of the 1950s. She let rooms on the upper floor of her old family home, and the rents would have been modest enough in the 1920s. Some early colonial governor, perhaps Sir George Grey, had once stayed in my room as a guest of her grandfather; I've forgotten the story. The place stood on the higher slopes of Parnell, overlooking the Waitemata harbour, among a half-dozen tall Norfolk Island pines; my room had a good view.

Mike turned up, with baggage, less than an hour after the telephone call. He had to borrow from me to pay off the taxi.

'Well,' he said, inspecting the room, 'nice place you've got here. Kitchenette too. You've done well for yourself. Very airy, very bright. How did you strike it? I've been after something like this for years.'

'Make yourself at home,' I said. 'I won't be away long. I've just got to dodge off to a lecture.'

I was away perhaps two hours. By the time I returned he'd made himself at home, all right. His suitcases were emptied. He'd taken over the table and buried it beneath brushes, paints, paper and a large sheet of hardboard. A series of preliminary drawings—some bush scene, as I recall—had been pinned to the wall nearby. A few finished paintings were propped against the wall. Gaps in my bookshelf were plugged with new books of Mike's. Some of his clothes already hung askew on my hangers. The spare bed, which had only been used before when my father came to visit, was in disarray; it looked as though Mike had flung himself solidly upon it a couple of times to test the comfort of the mattress. An antique ashtray, which went with the room, was half filled with butts and ash. And yet another cigarette hung limply from the corner of Mike's mouth as he brooded over the table.

I stood astonished at the door.

'Don't let me disturb you,' Mike said generously. 'Just go on with whatever you were going to do. I'm thinking.'

So was I. I was quite dizzy with thinking. Mike wasn't just settled in; he was entrenched. Coffee, strong and black, seemed logical. I saw that I would have to deal with him firmly. I went through to the kitchenette.

I returned to the room with two steaming mugs of coffee and handed one to Mike. He muttered something in acknowledgement; he might even have thanked me. But clearly I was an unfortunate distraction. Apparently I had walked in at a critical moment, puncturing his thought.

I took my own coffee to my desk. And sat quiet.

Actually his paintings surprised me. I knew he painted; he'd made his preoccupation with art clear when I met him at the party. But I wasn't able to take him seriously, perhaps because he'd shown no special talent, except for talking his way out of trouble, as a child. And according to the books I'd read, artists were born and not made; their true talent was on show from the cradle. Clearly I'd been misled and didn't know much; or didn't know Mike. His paintings shocked with their vigour. At first they didn't seem more than grand flourishes in colour. Yet there was something real there all the same, something that held the eye. Like everyone else, it seems, I don't know much about modern art. But unlike the people who declare that they know what they like, I don't know what I like, not until the moment I discover I've already been liking it for some time. I didn't like Mike's paintings, though they impressed me. As Mike probably meant me to be impressed.

'Well,' he said. 'That's that.' Grimacing, he moved from the table and made a mock gesture of dusting his hands. He sipped his coffee and lit still another cigarette. 'Where were we?'

Before I could move to the attack he added, 'By the way, in case I forget to tell you, there's a party Saturday night. At Gerry Morgan's.'

I didn't know Gerry Morgan, but that hardly mattered. What mattered was that I could relax for the rest of the week without the worry of a bleak Saturday night. I'd spent months developing contacts who often proved unreliable. I saw Mike in a new light. For he went on, 'I think there's something, the Saturday after, at Beryl Ferguson's. I'm not sure, but I'll find out about that.'

I'd never heard of Beryl Ferguson either, but by then I was glowing with good fellowship.

'Can I top your coffee up?' I said quickly.

'Thanks,' he said. 'It has got a bit cool.'

'Are you comfortable? Got all you want?'

'Sure. Everything's fine, thanks.'

'And enough space?' I asked. 'For all your gear?'

'Plenty. Thanks.'

'If you have any trouble,' I said, 'let me know. We could always change the room round somehow.'

'Now you mention it,' he said, 'things could be improved. To get the best from the view. And the light.'

He explained. Within an hour everything was arranged to his satisfaction. I wondered why I hadn't thought of shifting furniture about before; was it just preoccupation with work? For the change seemed miraculous. I never dreamed my room could have so much space. But by then, of course, it was no longer my room: it was a joint affair.

And any resentment I'd felt about his total invasion had evaporated entirely; he'd won without a word fired in anger. The room could contain both our lives. Neither of us need encroach on the other. There was my desk, his table. (We could always, I supposed, clear a space to eat.) I would have been selfish to refuse him a share of the room. I'd always had a greater share of the world's wealth than Mike. Though we'd never been much aware of this as children, I was certainly conscious of it now.

Gerry Morgan's party wasn't very exciting. I seem to remember that some girl fell screaming out of a window and that there were eyes blacked and teeth broken in a fight; but that hardly made a party either rewarding or unusual. Gerry was an intense black-bearded little man with glittering eyes. He made odd creations of stray materials like knitting-needles and burnt-out electric toasters. The party was to celebrate his latest confection: something made of wire, wheels and car batteries.

I gazed at it perplexed. 'What's it all about?' I whispered to Mike.

'Can't you see?' he said loudly. 'The individual, prophetic voice speaking out of chaos. Isn't that right, Gerry?'

'That's right, Mike,' Gerry said in his cautious voice. 'You understand, as always.'

Yet it seemed the sculpture, whatever it was, amused Mike. For when Gerry left the room at one stage, Mike grinned, shook his head and muttered, 'Poor old Gerry. Won't he ever learn?'

Gerry was almost humble when he spoke to Mike. This surprised me because he was, after all, so much older.

And Mike always replied in a tolerant tone, 'Of course, Gerry. Of course.'

'But don't you *see*, Mike?' Gerry pleaded desperately. 'Don't you *see?*'

And his hands worked feverishly at invisible things in the air, as if he were drowning.

Perhaps he was. The last I heard of Gerry Morgan he was serving time for an immensely complicated confidence trick which involved three married women and not a few single ones.

Beryl Ferguson's party celebrated nothing in particular except possibly her second husband's admission into a mental hospital. An attractive and myopic mystic, always talking about the soul, she blinked gravely and sat nervously still whenever Mike spoke. Again I was surprised at the respect he commanded. At first I presumed she was idiotically in love with him. But I soon realised that this, even if true, was irrelevant. The point was that she, and a lot of people besides, took Mike very seriously, as if their lives depended on it. I didn't know what to make of this at all.

Any more than I knew what to say when Mike told me, 'Go on. Say something intelligent, for Christ's sake.' This while I stood in a circle of his acquaintances who looked at me expectantly. They had just been talking about how insensitive and unintelligent their fellow-countrymen were; presumably Mike selected me, while I swayed tipsily on my feet, to prove their point. To them I was all but anonymous: simply 'Mike's friend'. I imagine people sometimes speculated on why Mike should have so unlikely a friend; and came to some equally unlikely conclusions.

'Something intelligent?' I said beerily.

'I mean,' Mike added, 'just to prove that you're *there*.'

'But I am,' I said, 'otherwise what would you people have to growl about?'

'He's right, you know,' someone agreed. Surprisingly, the laugh turned on Mike.

After that Mike didn't bother me again, at least not publicly; I didn't understand till later that I'd won some sort of victory. Anyway from then on Mike appeared to allow that I had a viewpoint.

'You were quite bright as a kid,' he once said. 'That's why I hate seeing you go this way.'

'What way?'

'The way you're going. Towards having your mind buttoned up tight. Against anything new or strange.'

So that was it. Mike lectured me with missionary fervour on art and other subjects near his heart. In time he even said he preferred my judgment of his work to that of most other people. 'You haven't an axe to grind,' he insisted. 'Your mind's still fresh.'

I suppose he meant I didn't flatter him.

And there actually came a day when he turned to me, in the middle of a conversation, and asked quite seriously, 'Well, come on. Tell us what you think.' It was an advance all right; he at last conceded that I thought.

This was at Les Palmerston's place.

Les was a thin sad man, a vehement vegetarian and angry anarchist, who lived on the reputation of an unpublished novel. It had actually been accepted by an English publisher who later broke his contract to print, with the outbreak of war, because of the anti-militarist tone of the manuscript. Les hadn't forgiven the publisher or the world. Above all he couldn't forgive success.

What made him estimable in our eyes, along with Gerry Morgan and Beryl Ferguson, was that from time to time he threw parties. You could say our sense of values was corrupt, and probably you'd be right. But I don't see that you'd prove anything one way or the other.

'The big trouble with Les,' Mike told me, 'is that he wants disciples. I suppose he counted on me, for a while. I have to admit he did open my eyes to a lot of things. But then he discovered I had an opinion of my own. Formed without his help. He's never forgiven me.'

Les liked to needle Mike, and did at this particular party. 'You're drying up,' he argued. 'Your paintings are empty. You've nothing to say.' The subject obsessed him: possibly it inspired those rather hysterical articles and reviews he sometimes published. It seemed everyone was drying up, no one had anything to say.

'Really?' Mike said, amused.

'You don't even know the rules of the game,' Les maintained.

'What rules?' Mike said. 'What game?'

'There you are,' said Les smugly. 'That's what I mean.'

'I don't play any games,' Mike replied. 'And as for rules they're for people who play games.'

'That's you all over,' Les sighed. 'Well, ignorance is certainly bliss.'

Beryl Ferguson, out of her true element as a guest, edged and groped into the conversation and placed a protective and reassuring hand on Mike's arm. 'Please, Les,' she said, 'I do think you're unfair. Sometimes you're downright absurd.'

But she was rather late in her intervention; Les was already picking himself up off the floor. Mike's fist had flicked out so quickly I seemed to have imagined the blow. Mike looked more astonished than anyone. I thought he'd been holding Les off very well without using his knuckles. But there was still another surprise for me. Les just seemed to take it. As if he'd expected or wanted something of the sort. Mike's apology appeared to swim past him and, mumbling something, he wandered out of the room. Mike and Beryl resumed the conversation where it had been left off. Then Mike nudged me. 'Well, come on. Tell us what you think.' He was perfectly serious.

'There are always rules,' I said. Something painful lurched beneath my ribs. I felt sick for no reason at all. 'At least I've always thought so.'

'Yes,' he said. He seemed disappointed in me. 'Well, you're honest anyway. And you're not laying down the law.'

But he'd missed the point. I was, in my fashion. The smoky room was closing in on me; I needed clean air. I staggered between Mike and Beryl—who looked as if they might couple routinely some time that night—and crashed out on to a veranda. But there was to be no escape. For there Les sat, collapsed in an old wicker chair. He didn't notice me. He was weeping.

Not long afterwards, apparently recovered, Les had occasion for another of his acid reviews. It was Mike's first one-man exhibition. Three people paid a total of nineteen guineas for four of his paintings. Mike seemed to have arrived, at last, and he gave me two guineas towards the room. This eased his conscience, he said, and he borrowed the money back from me a week later. Perhaps his reviews were slightly better than his sales.

From time to time there are echoes of those people I met through Mike. Beryl Ferguson, for example. Not long ago a popular weekly described how she ran a coffee-house in London, somewhere in Hampstead, a 'home away from home' for young, stray, homesick Commonwealth musicians, artists, and writers. It sounded sad and soulful, like one of her old parties. And only the other day I came across Les Palmerston's name again. It wasn't a by-line on an article. It was in the report of an inquest, and the coroner's verdict was suicide. His flat darkened in my memory. Les himself grew pale and pathetic in retrospect. It seemed to me that, even at his most vindictive, he had always been crying for help.

The party-goers were, on the whole, more pleasant than the party-givers; at least more various. There were poets destined for advertising agencies. There was a red-bearded, wild-eyed young communist who has since become Asian correspondent for an American news agency, and now writes tough sexy spy fiction on the side. There were some painters and sculptors who may have been as talented as Mike. And a fat, dazed-looking youth with unruly hair, crooked smile, and high-pitched giggle; I thought him dull-witted but he has lately, from some perch in Europe, published some melancholy stories which quite staggered me with their insight. Not least because I appeared to figure in one of them as a kind of hearty and insensitive philistine fall guy; the central character was a malicious portrait of Mike. I must admit, though, that this particular story was marred for me by some unpleasant sexual overtones. Anyway he—that youth—seems typical. For, looking back, I can see the unlikeliest among them succeeded. That thin pimply architect, for example, who always slithered sly-faced round the periphery of conversation. I see he's helped design one of London's new skyscrapers. While his friends who remain here do their best to create epics in wood and glass for thriving suburbia. I'm not suggesting they're less talented, though they may have been less ambitious. It's just his success, and the nature of it, which surprises. Skyscrapers have so much more prestige; like English success. He's unlikely to go short of employment if ever he decides to return home.

Mike could become savage about this. 'If Christ himself was born here,' he once said sourly, 'he'd have to go overseas first to get okayed. Otherwise we wouldn't know whether we had the genuine article.' He paused. 'On the other hand though, he'd never go short on a congregation once he got back. It really wouldn't matter whether he was the genuine article or not. So long as someone said so over there.' And he sank into a heavy silence.

We had meeting places. One where we drank coffee. This was

before the espresso bars began to breed; to find reasonable coffee in Auckland then was a feat. We drank it in a place which, from the front, seemed just another chromed milk-bar. Coffee was to be found at the rear, where we sat in dingy wooden cubicles. But it was good coffee. The owner of the place, irritated by our presence, the voices loud in argument, could easily have got rid of us by changing his coffee. But that idea never struck him. We also met in a dim and poky pub just off Queen Street. On visits to the city I've gone, out of curiosity, to the old meeting places. The place where we drank coffee—the espresso bars would have killed it anyway—has vanished beneath fifteen or twenty storeys of bright glass and concrete. I found the pub modern and expansive, filled with slick and sleek young men from offices around.

I wasn't pained, especially; just bewildered. I stood on the pavement, in the heat and glare and noise of a summery Queen Street, bumped by pounding pedestrians. I wondered where everyone had gone, all their argument and excitement. Yet I wasn't certain that I wanted to meet old faces again. Any more than they would want to meet me: a lacklustre country lawyer up for a day in the city. But where were they? Surely they couldn't all, like Mike, have sailed away? Was I the only one left behind? I was stricken for a moment by the thought that I was: I stood appalled and lonely between banging feet and booming traffic. Then I dismissed the thought. Some, I knew, had followed Mike: the natural expatriates. The others were probably now as tight in their personal worlds as I was in my own. And as content? Well, perhaps; I had no way of knowing. I could hardly generalise from myself. I had pretty much what I wanted. Whereas they, once, seemed to want the world.

Again I'm way ahead.

Mike wasn't able to change my mind about pleasing my father first. What else could I do? He didn't seem clear about that. He offered me no real alternative.

'You'll grow up,' he'd say vaguely. 'It's only a matter of time.'

'But growing up isn't going to earn me a living,' I observed. 'I mean, it's not a profession.'

'What I mean is,' he said, slightly irritated, 'you can't inhabit your father's mental slum.'

I suppose I might have replied that he should, in all fairness, remember that he was living off my father. My father supported me; I supported Mike. Not that my father ever knew: when he visited me in Auckland Mike always shifted out for a couple of days. My father did, of course, express more than mild surprise at the number of paintings I seemed to have acquired.

'I hope you don't spend good money on that stuff,' he said.

'Not really.'

'What do you mean—not really?'

'I mean I don't really spend very much.'

He considered this. 'Well,' he said, 'I suppose it's better than spending all your money on beer. Though I'm not so sure.'

Something was still worrying him, however: it was plain on his face.

'These pictures,' he said finally, 'you sure you didn't paint them yourself?'

I laughed. 'Do you really think I could?'

'I hope to God not.'

'Well, I didn't anyway.'

His relief was spectacular. 'Well,' he confessed, 'I wasn't sure. Anything can happen to a young man in the city. I know I had some wild ideas myself once.'

'Yes?' I said hopefully.

But he wasn't inclined either to remember or to tell me. 'Anyway,' he'd always say before he left for home, 'you're all right for money?'

'Well, now you mention it...'

I never asked Mike to share expenses; I knew how he was placed. And he had enough on his mind.

'It's no use,' he said despairingly. 'You can try as hard as you like here. And it doesn't matter. How could it matter? Nobody cares enough here. Nobody really cares at all. Even the people you might expect to care, the people you know.'

We were sitting in our room, on a quiet Sunday night, when this outburst came. I understood his general drift. I'd heard most of it before.

'Even you,' he added bitterly.

Why he selected me, that night, I can't imagine. Perhaps he thought I might be feeling left out.

'I do my best,' I replied. 'I'm sorry.'

And appeared preoccupied with filling and lighting my pipe. I didn't want to provoke him. I was sitting at my desk with an unfinished essay before me, due the next morning.

'There's something missing here,' he complained. 'Something missing altogether. Something that wasn't plugged in properly.'

'Perhaps we don't need to plug in,' I suggested.

'There you are,' he said angrily. 'That's what I mean. You don't take me seriously.'

I was quite safe. The only thing he could have done to show his contempt adequately would have been to collect his belongings and walk out on me. When all I'd done was try to amplify or at least elucidate his image. But he wouldn't go. I knew that. I could have been even more rampantly parochial and philistine, and he still wouldn't have gone. For a very good reason. He couldn't do without me; and in more ways than one. Without me, he wouldn't have understood himself entirely. I was a kind of touchstone. He tested himself on me time and again. That night was such an occasion. For one thing, I didn't share his compulsion to escape the country.

And when Mike finally escaped, I think he was also escaping me. Or trying to. But I don't think he ever did, not really. Because I was that part of himself which he rejected or tried to. For I'm certain that at times he would willingly have changed places with me, even if just to find out why I should be content. But that, of course, would have meant downright capitulation.

That night he paced about the room for a while.

'You must admit this is a safe little country,' I urged. 'It must be the safest little country in the world. You couldn't starve to death here even if you wanted to.'

'Exactly,' he said. 'That's just the trouble.'

Sometimes he was beyond me, entirely.

He continued pacing about the room. 'There'll come a time,' he went on. 'It's not far off. I'll have to make the break sooner or later.'

'Yes,' I agreed. 'I can see that.' There seemed to be nothing else for it. At least he might stop wearing out my floor.

'What the hell do you know about it?' he challenged.

'Less every day,' I answered.

When I decided it was safe, I went back to my essay. Shortly afterwards Mike went out in aggrieved silence. Possibly to meet Betty.

I forget just when she became involved with us. Certainly it must have been when Mike's supply of willowy, flawless Philippas and Mirandas was temporarily exhausted; they had come, by and large, from the art school which he attended for just one term. Betty was different. She wasn't tall. She was in fact rather dumpy. Her dress was functional: slacks and oversize sweaters, thick tartan skirts and flat-heeled shoes. She may have had a very feminine frock somewhere, but I never saw it in those days. Her legs were a shade too thick. One possible reason why she seldom smoked was that her hands were busy pushing her long listless fair hair back from her face. It didn't seem to have been cut since she left the farm where she grew up. Her eyes, when not hidden by hair, were pleasant and frank.

She had been around quite a while, one way and another. Her most characteristic pose was in the coffee shop, black-spectacled and hunched up in a loose and wrinkled mock-suede jacket, with a caffeine-stained volume of verse open in front of her. But she was always ready to remove her reading glasses, close up the book, and engage fiercely in some intricate conversation. She'd tried both acting and writing without startling success. On the side, though, she was quite a brilliant scholar. She'd acquired a good half-dozen languages, including Latin, Greek, and Maori. She was coasting through her B.A. on to an M.A. with first-class honours. She never made anything seem an effort. Certainly she gave herself all the time she wanted for random talk or parties. While I—just to take an example—sweated till late at night over textbooks to get, among other things, the solitary Latin unit essential for my law degree.

Her father was a classical scholar who took Homer and Virgil to a sheep farm in a remote district; later in life he became a student of Maori language and lore and evolved elaborate theories connecting Polynesia with ancient Greece. The background accounted for most of her languages. She was, like me, an only child.

The general verdict on Betty was that she was an odd little girl, far too intense. 'She could drive a man crazy,' Mike declared. 'Talk, talk, talk. Never met anyone like her.'

He implied that he gagged her somehow.

Betty wasn't as promiscuous as she seemed. She gave the impression that she tired of a lot of men quickly. This was quite misleading. The fact was that a lot of men tired of her quickly. She had few illusions about herself or her attractions, and refused to be made use of as a sexual stopover. I speak with some authority. Long before she became entangled with Mike, I made a drunken but concentrated attempt upon her body in a room adjoining a noisy party.

'What do you think you're doing?' she inquired gravely.

'At the moment,' I replied thickly, 'unzipping this zip.'

'And where do you think that's going to get you?'

'Who knows?' I murmured into the deepening haze. 'Perhaps even to the gates of paradise.'

'Then you might at least consult the keeper of the keys.'

She ditched me coolly, no-nonsense style, and left me floundering among discarded overcoats and scarves. Later I assuaged my male pride by telling myself she already had her eye on Mike.

Which was possibly the truth. Enough people, of both sexes, already trailed after him. I might fairly count myself an exception. If I happened to be round a lot of the time, it was because he lived with me; not because I trailed after him. I often failed to share his enthusiasms, though I was naturally involved in them. There was the time, for example, when Mike took up the cause of world peace. I arrived home one night to find the room in uproar. It seemed everyone from the pub and coffee shop was jammed into the place. They were all painting or snipping busily away at sheets of paper.

'What the hell's all this?' I demanded angrily.

'The peace congress,' someone muttered. 'Joe Stalin and our boy Mike are going to settle the world between them.'

'Take a look at this,' said one of the snappers, holding up a strange-shaped silhouette of white paper. 'Mike's Picasso peace doves. Of his slightly improved design, of course.'

It appeared Mike was in charge of decorating the congress hall. Naturally, ankle-deep in flawed doves, I had to clean out the room alone next morning. It seems, one way and another, I did a lot of tidying up for Mike afterwards.

But I went along with everyone else to hear the speeches. The congress hall swarmed with Mike's dangling doves, blazed with his dramatic posters. He had every reason to feel pleased with himself, but the setting deserved something better than the speeches. There was a procession of clergymen and trade union leaders across the platform. I saw Mike becoming restless; the seats were hard too.

At the end of one speech he rose in visible disgust. We filed out behind him. On the steps of the hall, in windy Queen Street, we stood shuffling. No one seemed prepared to say anything. Until Mike spoke.

'And there isn't even a damn party tonight,' he said.

Someone contradicted him: there was one near, just outside town. But the location was vague. We were soon prowling one of these rambling Auckland suburbs beneath an extinct volcanic cone. We had no definite street number, and saw no sign of a party. Almost every house was shut up tight, with blinds drawn, as though plague-stricken. Mike's dismay seemed to increase.

'It's about time someone woke up this country,' he muttered. He paused. 'Let's do some climbing.'

There were grumbles, but we followed him out of the empty, dimly lit streets and up the dark scrubby slopes above the suburb. I heard Betty's voice rattling on intensely as she tried to explain something to Mike about a novel she had lent him, and about which they disagreed.

'You see,' she said, 'he clears off in the end, seeks a new context. But everything remains unchanged, intact. Is flight the only answer? Or is it an answer? When you come right down to it, it's no answer at all.'

Mike's reply was indistinct. I'd noticed lately that he was showing a tremendous amount of patience with Betty. An unusual amount.

At length we stood atop the old cone. 'Right,' he said briskly. 'Who's game for a bonfire?'

Again there were grumbles.

'I mean,' he went on, 'the fire died out of this place a long time ago. It's time someone started it off again.'

We got the idea and collected wood and scrub and pine cones. Scavenging all over the hillside we collided with each other, and with terrified sheep, in the dark. In no time at all a huge fire blazed. Mike was delighted. 'There it is,' he cried, in tall silhouette against the flames. 'Let's wake up this whole bloody country.'

It was quite impressive. I've no doubt that, from a distance, it did appear that the volcano had begun erupting again.

House lights multiplied in the streets below: the city certainly seemed to be coming to life. (Monday morning's newspaper told us some households actually began to prepare for evacuation. There was also a ponderous editorial on hooliganism, the outrages of teddy-boys and their like. This was followed by a lengthy correspondence, contributed by anonymous writers like 'Worried Mother', 'Stop Them Now' and 'B. Tough' who all urged the return of flogging for delinquents.)

Then some citizen had the idea that the eruption might be ended by calling police and fire brigade. Sirens seemed to be converging from everywhere. We scattered.

I plunged into a patch of scrub. Headlights were flashing, car doors slamming, feet crashing. The fire gave great guttering sighs and everything grew large and mysterious in the violent orange glow.

I held my breath, as if that would help me evade the thundering constabulary, and pressed deeper into the dry-smelling fern and scrub. I thought of my future as a lawyer and wondered how I'd ever become involved with Mike.

Near by someone else was hiding. I heard rapid whispers. A couple of lovers, apparently; we'd probably given them a fright. After the whispers I heard movement and quickened breathing. They seemed determined not to let fire or police disturb their lovemaking. All in all, I found that rather admirable; I envied them their ability to dismiss the world.

Then, with strange dismay, I recognised Betty's voice. Obviously she was with Mike. I had fallen somewhere near their hiding place. I wished they had chosen a better moment, or at least a different place, to become lovers. With the law literally breathing down our necks, it indicated a rather appalling lack of responsibility on their part. That orange glow palpitated on the fern before my eyes, danced on the thick foliage above my head. I had to stay there until the fire was extinguished, until the last policeman tramped off down the hill. And of course until Mike and Betty left; I wouldn't have liked them to think I was spying.

Later Mike explained his difficulties with Betty. 'The trouble is she's so sincere,' he told me. 'So damn earnest. I don't know what in hell I'm supposed to do with her.'

That was typical. He couldn't coast along and rest content with anything, not even Betty's virginity, without making an issue of it.

'How did I ever get caught up with her?' he appealed.

I might have attempted an explanation. But the way I saw it, any explanation would only create new issues.

'What can I do?' he asked, rather pathetically. 'She'll trap me. I know it.'

Betty did nothing of the sort. And after his initial panic, Mike grew to accept that she wouldn't. He had to hunt-out other reasons for unease.

Actually I found Betty the least objectionable of all his women. The others so exasperated me, one way and another, that I usually forbade Mike to bring them near our room. It was one of the few things on which I took a stand. It wasn't exactly that I made an exception of Betty; she seemed to make an exception of herself. Anyway she often came up to cook meals and brew coffee for us. Her cooking was terrible, the coffee marginal, but I always managed to allow for the thought behind it. If I was at my desk, and Mike at work, I'd often forget that Betty was around. But she was there somewhere, reading deep in a chair or washing up out in the kitchenette. She mightn't have found our lack of attention flattering, but she accepted it. When she did talk, she made it clear she could reminisce about country childhood too. This helped harmony. The fact that she was female didn't much matter. We gathered she'd always been a tomboy, shooting and fishing with her father, helping in the shearing shed like a son.

All this must have lasted a year or eighteen months, though it seemed years. Mike and I were balanced very neatly by Betty. She often saved us from open conflict; and possibly kept us together longer than we might otherwise have been. I should perhaps make it clear that it wasn't a triangular situation, though the fact was that Betty generally criticised my girlfriends.

'That one's got no brains,' she would insist. 'What do you find to talk to her about?'

'We don't talk,' I answered, grimly defensive. 'Much.'

Or:

'If that girl at least had a good figure,' she would complain, 'it might be some compensation for downright ignorance. But she's all out of proportion, almost grotesque.'

'That,' I replied, 'is a matter of opinion.'

Or, more bluntly:

'I think she's frigid,' she would declare. 'Or a lesbian. Still, she's probably got some intelligence, though I can't imagine where she hides it.'

Which, as might be observed, were variations on a theme.

So there was seldom a comfortable foursome. The most unsatisfactory thing, from my point of view, was that sooner or later I saw all my girlfriends through Betty's eyes. Few lasted more than a month or two.

In other ways, though, Betty was more tactful and sympathetic. 'A lot of things baffle you, don't they?' she said quietly one day. She had turned up at the room to find Mike was out. Waiting on his return she peered with subdued melancholy out of the window at the thin yachts and faintly smoking ships on the bright harbour.

'Well, yes,' I agreed. 'If you mean Mike and his friends. And what they rage on about.'

'And yet you keep listening,' she observed.

'I don't know why,' I said. 'Perhaps because I'd like to understand.' It sounded weak. Sober, I always felt at a distinct disadvantage with Betty. I thrust my hands rather too casually in my pockets and wandered across the room to stand beside her at the window. The city shimmered. It was the first really hot day of spring. I was preoccupied with the knowledge that Mike was out that afternoon with another girl; I was almost equally preoccupied with the idea that Betty knew this, and also knew I knew. I felt growing guilt, and a perplexing pain, and prayed she wouldn't say anything.

'I suppose your trouble is that you can't pretend,' she said.

'Really?' I said shakily.

'Really,' she affirmed. 'You're just hopeless at it.'

'All right,' I said abruptly. 'So you know. I—'

'All I know,' she went on, 'is that you don't even pretend to know what everything's about, or what everyone else is talking about. As all the others do. It irritates them, of course.'

To my relief I realised she wasn't being specific after all: she was speaking generally.

'Perhaps it makes them feel guilty somehow,' she added. 'Uncomfortable, at least. Couldn't you pretend now and then?'

'I've never been much good at it. But I'll try, if you like.'

'To tell the truth,' she began, and hesitated. She looked flustered, on the brink of confession. She tried again: 'To tell the truth, I'm not much good at it either.'

It wasn't any news to me.

'We're alike in that respect,' she murmured. 'Sometimes I wonder if—'

'Yes?' I said. Now, I thought, the real confession.

But she seemed to change her mind and go off in another direction. 'Well, sometimes I wonder about what's going to happen to us. To Mike. To you. To me.'

'Well, I've a fair idea what's going to happen to me.' I hesitated. 'I can't answer for Mike. Or you.'

'Why does Mike need us?' she sighed. 'Because he does need us both. You know that, don't you?'

At the time I just shrugged. Not until much later did I really think about what Betty said. Then it seemed to me that personalities like ours, Betty's and mine, were some necessary humus out of which Mike's talent flowered. This thought wasn't flattering, not least because it implied that we were, in our different ways, interchangeable with other people and thus, despite what Betty said, quite dispensable as individuals. But it was the nearest I ever got to an explanation.

After all, I settled most of Mike's material problems. And among other things Betty gave him—well, gave him greater stability, if you like.

Yet he still had his outbursts, to which we listened in silence. We both learned it wasn't wise to interject. After one of these—about the time he was turned down for an art scholarship overseas—he stalked down into Queen Street, one bracing spring morning, and gave his name and telephone number to a shipping company. This was on the off-chance of working his passage to England in place of a deserting seaman. In the event he would have to take the job and leave with less than twenty-four hours' notice.

Betty and I accepted this, as we accepted his more dramatic gestures, without comment; we just exchanged knowing glances. We were confident nothing would come of it. Rather like people who refuse to accept that the world will end simply because it hasn't ended before.

Summer came. I went back to the King Country for a while, and Betty spent some of her vacation on her father's farm. While I was away Mike looked after the room; he kept his promise not to hold noisy parties and upset my landlady. Later in summer, with my latest girlfriend along to make a foursome, we tramped around the Coromandel Peninsula and camped on an isolated beach beneath bulky hills bearded with bush. I recall a day when my girlfriend, who wasn't to last out the vacation, retired to the tent to sleep off some sunburn. Mike was away painting at the end of the beach. Betty and I had picked oysters before the tide reached full, and then gone swimming now we were sunbathing on the rocks, and the sea smacked occasional cool spray across our warm bodies. In emulation of Mike, perhaps to win his approval, Betty had lately taken up painting rather muddy water-colours. With another of these in mind she had gathered some sprigs of late-blooming pohutukawa and strewn them on a rock. It was an attractive subject, but proved too much for her.

'It's no good,' she declared in despair. 'I can't get the right shades.' She thrust aside her sketchbook and colours.

We began to talk of our visits home. Idly I tossed the blooms upon the lazily turning tide. They drifted, slowly spinning, small patches of crimson on the blue water. I spoke of an argument I'd had with my father; an entirely pointless argument I now deeply regretted.

'It was all so trivial,' I tried to explain. 'And I hurt his feelings badly, more than I ever have before. About so little. I can't bring myself to argue with him about anything really important, I don't know why. Perhaps that's why I get so violent about small things.'

The patches of crimson were now riding a quickening ebb tide out to sea. Some were sinking.

'I know,' Betty said. 'I mean I think I know. I'm rather like that too. Though at one stage I started trying to tell my parents about Mike. It was hopeless. My father's understanding up to a point, but only up to a point. Mike, and a lot of things, are well beyond that point. When I look at my father, really look at him, I see he's not so very different from anyone else. Yet he must have been different once. He must have been.'

'I suppose I've had the same feeling about my father,' I said.

Now the crimson had floated out of sight altogether. Mike came drifting back along the beach. He nodded vaguely when we explained we were talking about our visits home. And he listened, only half attentive. Then I saw what made Betty and me alike. For us the past was still alive, very much of the present; something we could dip into speculatively, with an eye to the future. For Mike the past was the past, a vanishing sunlit island; a place which he could recall with affection at times, but which really had no relevance. Or so it must have seemed to him; perhaps he was wrong.

We returned brown and fit to the city in time for the university year. Two or three weeks afterwards, the phone rang downstairs early one morning. Mike was still sleeping heavily after a late night; I took the call.

It was the shipping company. A cargo boat bound for England had suffered some desertions. There was a vacancy for Mike to work his way, if he liked. Did he still want the job? The boat was sailing in a few hours, at three in the afternoon. I explained that Mike would ring them back, and went upstairs to wake him.

At first he didn't understand what I was talking about. Then his eyes gleamed. He fell out of bed in excitement.

'My God,' he said. 'This is what I've always been waiting for. Isn't it? And now it's come. Right out of an empty sky. It's a sign. Isn't it?'

I didn't know what I was expected to say. I hadn't imagined for a moment he'd take the job. The idea of his careering off into the unknown without a penny appalled me. I'd never have done such a thing. And I never thought, when it came to a point, that Mike would either. I thought he knew where he was safe. But I was wrong.

He couldn't get dressed and downstairs to the phone quickly enough. He returned upstairs at speed.

'Well,' he said, bursting in with face alight. 'At least you'll be glad to get rid of me. Can you give me a hand to pack?'

I forgot my morning lecture and helped him. We kept the fireplace busy. The heat became unbearable. His part of the room was like a rats' nest. Old paper and unwanted paintings went up in a swoosh of flame.

'A new start,' he insisted. 'That's what it's going to be. Where people really care.'

I wanted to tell him there were people, at least a few, who cared about him here. But he was in no mood to listen.

'Yes,' he repeated. 'Where people really care. Europe's the place for me.'

As the packing and burning went on I grew more and more depressed. In some way, true, I would be glad to see the last of Mike; the last of his black moods and random rages. I was generally the only victim, though he claimed society was his target.

But already my room—it was clearly my room again—was beginning to look impossibly empty. I wondered what sort of thin colourless life I would lead for the rest of my time in the city or back home in the country, for that matter.

I thought wildly of shifting to another room, where I might be less lost in space. I began to comprehend that Mike had given my life a distinctive flavour. I've said Mike used me as a touchstone. Well, Mike had been a touchstone for me too. He'd helped me define myself. I saw that for the first time. Without him, I might never have been sure of what I really wanted.

Then the phone went downstairs again. It sounded even more urgent. I sensed that the call was ours and moved to the door.

'Probably the shipping company,' Mike said. 'Checking on something. Tell them I'm on my way. Or perhaps their wandering boys have been picked up by the police. God, I hope not.'

But as I hurried down the stairs to pick up the receiver I knew it wouldn't be the shipping company. It was bound to be Betty; she usually rang at some time in the morning. I'd forgotten all about her. So had Mike.

I couldn't bring myself to tell her anything. I muttered something and went upstairs to tell Mike. When he went down to talk to her, I closed the door after him. I couldn't bear to overhear the conversation. It would have been too painful.

He was out of the room some time. I could see Betty's face, quite vividly, in my imagination. I could also imagine Mike talking jubilantly at his end of the line. While she perhaps pleaded pathetically at her end. It was all too much for one morning. I sat with my head in my hands.

When he returned to the room finally—he must have been gone a good half-hour—he was much quieter, though not at all crestfallen.

There wasn't much packing left. He still had to race into the city to obtain a tax clearance and arrange for a passport to be forwarded.

'She'll be round later,' he informed me. 'We'll have a last drink together before I go down to the ship.'

The last drink turned out a sombre affair. Betty looked with flushed face into her gin and orange and hardly spoke. I felt giddy on the strength of four or five double whiskies. Mike drank sparingly and kept looking at the clock; he seemed already beyond us.

On the wharf Betty and I both looked vainly for a Black Maria, carrying deserters, which would end Mike's journey. It never came. After being given some small job immediately he was on board, Mike scrambled out on to an upper deck of the boat to wave us goodbye. It was a quiet departure: no crowds, no streamers, no music. Just one or two bored watersiders, a couple of dishevelled girls. Engines throbbed, the gangway was removed abruptly, moorings were cast off; with a hoot or two the ship moved away. It edged out into the stream and Mike's figure grew smaller. Then he appeared to vanish altogether. Perhaps he had been called below decks.

After a while Betty and I were the only people left on the wharf. Already I felt the emptiness between us. Still, she was remarkably brave about the whole thing. She only once needed her handkerchief

The ship turned round North Head and disappeared into Rangitoto channel. I felt we'd seen Mike for the last time. He wouldn't be back. A determined Columbus, he'd find his New World, even if he had to invent it for himself. I tried to imagine it: I couldn't. Who were they, these mysterious and shadowy people who cared? I couldn't imagine them either. Yet the idea of them haunted Mike. Perhaps like Columbus he had evidence: a green branch, a bird. No, plainly my imagination was at fault; Mike always said I was unimaginative.

Betty and I turned at the same moment and walked silently away. We went along the waterfront, past the gulls and the old men sunning themselves by the ferry buildings, past the export wharves and the fishing boats, the nets hanging to dry, the catches unloading. We didn't stop. I didn't know where we were going; nor did she. We still didn't talk.

Eventually we came to the boat harbour, a forest of yachts and pleasure craft. It seemed we could go no further. We went out along a jetty and sat, our legs dangling, above the gentle water.

'I'm not going to cry,' she announced. 'There's not much point.'

'No,' I agreed.

'Crying didn't stop him going,' she observed. 'It certainly won't bring him back.'

'No,' I said. 'It won't.'

She cried for about twenty minutes.

'I was in love with him, you know,' she said at length.

'Yes,' I said. 'I know.'

She wept again.

'He'll never be back,' she said finally.

'I wouldn't say that,' I said, though I would have.

'I wonder what'll happen to him over there.'

'Anything. Anything could happen to Mike. He's that kind of person, I suppose. Things just seem to happen round him all the time. At least life's never dull for him.'

'Or with him,' she added. This time she didn't weep.

'Well,' I said, 'there it is. He had to go. We just didn't want to face it.'

'No I suppose not.' She pushed back her hair. I thought she'd recovered very well, all things considered. 'I'd just like to clear out somewhere,' she went on. 'Anywhere. Where I won't be reminded.'

'We could always take a boat,' I said, gesturing expansively. 'There are plenty here.'

It was a joke, of course. At first.

'There's one over there,' I said pointing. I still spoke half in jest, but with the help of the whisky the wild idea to clear out became more real every second. 'About our size too. All ready to go.'

It was a fourteen-footer, with sails loosely furled. It looked as if it had just been out on the harbour. Perhaps the owner had gone off to the pub, for a quick drink before closing time, and meant to return to it later. Anyway it just rocked there, waiting. There were few people round.

'We could clear off across the Gulf to Coromandel,' I said. 'No one would ever know. The owners would get their insurance.'

The whole thing sounded utterly reasonable. I didn't realise, even then, just how serious I'd become. Or how seriously she was taking what I said. In her astonished eyes there seemed to be admiration. Or at least something I hadn't seen before. I guessed she might have looked at Mike that way; I felt a rising exhilaration.

'To Coromandel?' Her face brightened with the memory of our holiday. 'You mean it?'

'Of course,' I said recklessly. By now I really did mean it. Or thought I did. 'I'll sail it. I've done a bit of sailing.'

Looking back, I can see I was temporarily unbalanced. But then so was she. It was a madness Mike must have left in his wake; nothing else will account for it. For we were scrambling into the yacht. I struggled to hoist the main sail as we cast off, starting to drift and bump and scrape other boats. Betty paddled to get us moving. We got around the breakwater, all right. And ran straight into the heaving Waitemata. As we lurched in the choppy water, I gave my attention to the sails again. I had a fair amount of trouble.

There was quite a breeze out there on the harbour, much stronger than I thought. And the water was much rougher than it had looked from a distance. I saw whitecaps bobbing over towards North Head. It was a tricky afternoon for a yacht. There were few other small craft on the harbour.

I was chilled, but not only by the breeze. I seemed to have just recovered consciousness. Certainly those last drinks with Mike had ceased to warm me; the lightness in my head vanished, and my body grew heavily round me again. What were we doing out there? Where were we going?

I looked down at Betty. She sat miserably by the tiller. The brightness or madness had gone from her eyes too. But she wasn't going to admit it.

It must have become obvious that I really knew little about sailing; most of my yachting had been done inside pubs in rainy weather. Canoes on gentle inland water were more my style. Yet there'd been rapids too. I remembered our craft breaking up on black rocks, Mike and I struggling in the white water. Who had rescued whom? It no longer mattered. For that had led directly to this.

Theft; there was no other word for it. Hopeless to explain in a courtroom why we stole the yacht: facing a grey magistrate to whom delinquent students were probably anathema anyway. A fine end to my career in law.

As urgent was the thought that we were about to drown, either in the harbour or out in the Gulf. It would be dark in a couple of hours.

'Look,' I said abruptly. 'This is crazy.'

'Yes,' she sighed. 'I know.'

'What are we doing, for God's sake?'

'I don't know,' she said wearily. 'I've just been wondering the same thing.'

'I don't even know how it happened,' I declared.

The breeze was getting sharper. I wore only a light shirt under my jacket. In my pockets I had perhaps a pound in loose change. Even if we reached Coromandel, how would we manage without warm clothes, without money?

'We'd better go back,' she said.

Someone had to say it first.

'Yes,' I agreed gratefully.

The yacht almost capsized as we made a clumsy attempt to turn about. But we managed in the end. It was only a short run back to the boat harbour, not more than two or three hundred yards. Yet it took us a good half-hour against changing wind and outgoing tide.

Then bliss. We drifted lightly into the boat harbour. The owner or owners of the yacht hadn't returned. There was no one to witness our arrival.

As we tapped gently and safely against the jetty, back in the yacht's mooring place, I felt an enormous relief, an explosion of warmth in the pit of my stomach. I relaxed for the first time. Never had land, the ordinariness of everything I knew, my predictable future, offered so much comfort. I didn't dare think about what might have been.

We tied the yacht up and walked quickly back along the jetty. When we were at a safe distance, our pace slackened off. Then Betty stopped and took a deep breath. I stopped too. She seemed recovered.

'What's going to happen to me?' she said. She paused thoughtfully, then looked at me. Swiftly she corrected herself. 'To us?' she asked.

'Nothing,' I said.

'Nothing?' The dismay on her face was quite intimidating. I wished I had told a lie. But once I began to speak the truth, for my own sake too, I had to finish.

'Nothing much ever happens to people like us,' I said brutally. 'We've just got to make the best of it.'

'And what does that mean?' she said.

'I don't know,' I confessed.

2

I was wrong, of course. Something did happen to us. We married about two years later, a month after I finished my degree. And we've had children: Eric aged six, Janet aged four, and Karen who is just six months. The important things have happened to us. That's what I often tell Betty. She smiles when I say this, smiles rather mysteriously, and I never quite know whether she's taking me seriously or not.

So, lest she misunderstand, I usually add that we've made the real voyage, the true discovery. Others circle the world endlessly without ever finding the important things.

Again she smiles. And I am more perplexed than ever.

We came back to the King Country to be married in the same month as I went into partnership with my father. He gave up regular practice about three years after I returned. For a while he made short visits to the office every day to see how I was managing. He was pleased to see I managed very well. In his quiet way he was delighted with Betty as a daughter-in-law, and he became very fond of his grandchildren before he died. I think I can say I made his last years happier than most of his life had been. I felt a surprising glow of pleasure when I realised this, and his death was I easier to take when it came. I was able to stand at the graveside without regrets.

We heard very little from Mike after he left. We had one brief letter each, and two or three postcards. The last of these said he was living on a small Spanish island called Formentera. 'Wonderful place,' he scrawled, 'ruled by witches and priests.' I located the place eventually on a large-scale map of Europe, and Betty managed to excavate a few facts. We learned that the island is bare and rocky, that the peasants are poor and living is cheap. We tried to imagine Mike there, among witches and priests and poor peasants, without great success.

About five years ago, long after we'd last heard from him, there was that newspaper report on his success. Betty clipped out the report and the photograph which showed his new beard. We supposed he must have grown it on Formentera. Betty soon lost the clipping, somewhere about the house, but from memory I believe the point of the report was that Mike had an exhibition, first in Paris and then in London, which made quite an impression on some discerning critics. Their opinions were quoted at some length.

It seemed that Mike had made landfall too; the people who cared were not a myth after all. We presumed he would go from strength to strength. We were both pleased for him. We would have written to offer our congratulations, but we had no address. For a while we watched for more news of him in the papers, but there was no more. And presently, in the way these things happen, we even got out of the way of talking about Mike. To tell the truth I've thought every little about him in the last year or two.

Until this morning, that is.

I walked down to the office this morning. Betty seldom drives me unless it is raining. I enjoy the walk. And I enjoy it especially in autumn. I often think our town is at its best in autumn. Poplar and maple, sycamore and willow bring vivid and exotic colour to hillside and riverbank. Beyond their ephemeral blaze is the dark and durable green of native bush. The days are usually fine and crisp and bright, the sunsets are spectacular, and the nights bring the first frosts of the year. On Rugby Park the serious games of the season have begun; there is a certain amount of excited anticipation in the air. Our town mightn't have much in the way of population, but in the last four years we've produced three All Blacks, three sturdy young men who have hammered down all opposition on the rugby fields of the world, and we don't let strangers forget it. I no longer play, of course; I coach. This gives me rather more standing in the town than my legal practice, though naturally my practice benefits in the end.

I suppose there is now good reason for my proprietary pleasure in the town. Last year I took a vacant seat on the borough council and there is talk of my name being put forward as a candidate when our present mayor retires. It's said that the town, which is fast growing and progressive, needs a young mayor. There is a seat in Parliament in prospect beyond that too; I inherited my father's politics along with his practice, for simple convenience. I've no wish to upset or offend anyone. There was that painting of Mike's which hung for a short time in my office. I liked it, but I soon saw that it made some of my older clients uneasy. Naturally I took it down. What else could I do? Betty insisted on hanging it at home, where it certainly makes conversational opening for new visitors. Most of her women friends regard her as pleasantly eccentric anyway.

On my way to work I paused for a while on the war memorial bridge and, looking downstream, saw the trembling gold reflections the shedding poplars cast on the dark water. Leaves like little rusty boats spun and raced in the current. Something flashed in my mind, like a signal, and I remembered it was the third anniversary of my father's death. Disturbed that I should have forgotten, I stood for a dizzy moment at his graveside again. True, I'd had no regrets; I had found pleasure in pleasing him. But what was it I often said? 'First I please him. Then, the rest of my life, I please myself.' Was I now pleasing myself, or was I still pleasing him? It seemed odd that I'd once been able to separate the two things. What had I meant? Well, there wasn't much point in puzzling over it now. Still watching the leaves skid unnavigated down the river, I recalled, for no particular reason, that it was time to take the children for another visit to Betty's parents. I felt lighter in mind at the thought of the children.

And at the thought of Betty; the early sunlight filled the thinning foliage with a gently quivering orange glow, as if slow flames were playing somewhere behind. In her face there is a new quietness, a purity of expression which is often a surprise to me. I believe we have a good marriage. I still thrill to the sight of her hair on the pillow beside me in the mornings, when I wake to find our limbs lightly linked. She is a wonderful mother. I have a secret delight in watching her with the children. She functions without effort on their separate levels of awareness, and really kindles their imagination with the stories she invents.

I walked on to the office. As usual, I first unfolded the morning paper, just arrived from Auckland. Most mornings I read it through before I do anything else, and take it home to Betty at lunchtime.

The world news was at its most depressing. Nor did the local news afford much comfort: rising road deaths, falling export prices. Nevertheless, I read through the paper slowly. And I came eventually to the short heading, 'Artist Returns'.

The item was brief. Rather too brief, I thought, as if Mike had been hostile towards the reporter. It recorded that Mike had returned to the country on a passenger boat from England. There were one or two biographical details which were accurate enough. The item also recalled Mike's European success of five years before, the one we'd already learned about. Something about this puzzled me for a while, and I sat staring at the words with a growing numbness.

I must confess to an utterly unreasonable moment of panic. I could see Betty dashing up to Auckland to greet Mike. I could see everything starting again, and our marriage collapsing. I would have to keep the news of his arrival from her; I would have to make the pretence of having forgotten to take the paper home at lunchtime. At all costs, I felt, I must keep her from knowing. At all costs I must save our marriage.

But it soon passed, that panic. I saw how foolish it had been. The Betty who would dash to Mike was ten years gone. I often find it difficult to remember her as she was then, that scruffy little creature in mock-suede jacket sipping coffee with a book of poetry beside her. She has changed astonishingly; but then she's no longer a girl. She seems taller and perhaps she is, perhaps she did have a late growth. Her figure is more slender anyway and she moves unflustered, with slow dreamy grace, about the house. Little troubles her. And I realised, for the first time, how few words of anger have ever been spoken in the time of our marriage. I thought of her with the children again, and wondered if others ever sensed the warmth in our marriage; I felt sure they must. I know now, more certainly than I have ever known, that she would not give it away.

While panic came and went I must have sat there and read that heading, and the report along with it, a dozen times. Then I saw what was puzzling and troubling me. I couldn't understand why the reporter needed to go back five years to recall that earlier success, which must after all have just been a beginning.

And then I knew why; and knew everything, I felt, about Mike. It was simply because there were no other successes to record. There was nothing else at all to recall as notable in his past ten years. The report did not even say he was married; at least there was no mention of a wife accompanying him. He'd been beaten, over there, and he'd come back. He'd found another wall to butt against, and he'd tired of it in the end. And so he'd come back, lonely, to where he was safe. But what about the people who cared? Had they suddenly ceased to care, or had they never really cared at all? It was all a mystery to me.

I wondered what he would be like now. Would he be more bitter than ever? Possibly. Would he be less pleasant to know? That seemed possible too. Would I really care to see him again, or would Betty? I couldn't make up my mind about that. And I still can't. I'm sure we will see him again, sooner or later. I might know the answer then. I know, in advance, that he will despise me simply for becoming what I am. Yet what else could I have become? And he is unlikely to forgive me for apparently having made so conventional a housewife out of Betty. But this, of course, is nonsense. I don't believe that people really change. They just become what they really are; they shed the frills too often mistaken for the fabric. There was always a good housewife and mother in Betty. Someone would have revealed that sooner or later. Am I to blame?

I asked myself a lot of questions this morning. It was troubling to be in possession of so few answers.

Presently I looked up from the newspaper. At an oblique angle, through my office window, I saw again the seasonal flashes of brightness on the hills, the sober green beyond. It struck me for the first time that my father had really put his desk in the wrong place to get the best from the view and the light. Well, it was too late to tell him now; I might get around to shifting it myself one weekend soon.

I made a final effort to balance what I did know against what I didn't. The effort was worth making. I understood, for one thing, that Mike would probably have little to worry about now he was back. He was safe, really safe. I recalled his bitter words about those who came back to the country to trade on some remote applause; they rang sadly in my memory. He'd once said he knew neither game nor rules, but it seemed to me the rules were clear at last. I supposed people who once ignored his work would buy it now. Not because it was any different or any better, though it could be either or both, but because it had once been quite respectably approved, somewhere else. I think I know my fellow countrymen well enough to say that; for at the very least I know something of myself. So he would, after so many years of vain search, find people who cared, in a way. Did it matter that they cared mainly for reassurance, about not being wrong? That is, after all, something we all care about, and not just some of the time. I remember feeling reassured myself by news of his success; I was, in fact, half-tempted to repeat that indiscretion of hanging his painting in my office. If he is accepted here, as I suspect he might be, I may be able to do just that. Perhaps he will no longer be an outsider here, no matter how hard he tries. At first, of course, he might despise those who accept him. But this is difficult to do for long without erosion of self-respect. Given time he will surely change; given time. There is comfort in the thought.

I wondered how he felt when he stepped off the ship. Then it seemed, oddly enough, that I already knew. I remembered the afternoon Betty and I took the yacht. I recalled my enormous feeling of relief when I realised we wouldn't have to go through with it. When the yacht bumped gently back into its mooring place, and I knew I was safe again, the relief leapt through me, warm and tingling from the pit of my stomach. I'm sure Mike must have felt something the same when he stepped off that ship yesterday. I'm positive he must have. Though, all things considered, he did try rather a larger sea.

Figures in Light

For Pat Hanly

I do not see my sister often. Strange, for we were intimate as children. Or perhaps not so strange, perhaps that is the reason. We didn't grow apart, we fell apart. I had little use for her friends, when we were students, and she had little use for mine. I started university only a year behind her, but the gap was sufficient: she was already established among friends of her own temperament and inclination, and the gap soon widened. Since then, I've seen less and less of her.

Once I marvelled that children of the same parents could be so different. Nowadays, of course, we live in cities some four hundred miles apart. It is true that there is seldom a year in which we do not see each other, but in this case 'see' is the critical word. I cannot honestly say that we converse. She asks after my children, I ask after her life: there is no real exchange. I no longer, for example, ask why she has no husband, no children. No more than I would pose such a question to a total stranger. On the other hand, I am not suggesting that my sister is a total stranger to me. I think I understand her rather better than she will ever allow. Perhaps I deceive myself, but I do not think so. That tall, sullen, untidy woman is not really so remote from the elder sister I worshipped, to put it mildly, through childhood into adolescence.

The failure, then, is not one of understanding, at least not on my side. Yet when I try to define some other point of failure, I know beforehand that I cannot do it. And if I cannot define failure in myself, I can scarcely impute it to her; it surely cannot all be hers. And if we do not share the failure, where then must we look? Where? Questions like that ring in my head on sleepless nights; I slide soundless from beneath the bedcovers, careful not to disturb my sleeping wife, and brew black coffee in the kitchen until the multiplying questions, at first churning wildly, collapse exhausted in my brain. Unhappiness is not uppermost of my emotions when I return to bed beside my wife, or when I wake heavily in the morning. It is more perplexity—if one can call perplexity an emotion, as I certainly do. For I am sure that my sister is unhappy, but why? And I know that I should help her, or should be able to help her, but how?

If I feel baffled and helpless, it is at least in part because I have gone through the usual motions. We once, my wife and I, invited Ruth—my sister—to stay with us. I imagine my idea was to help Ruth feel part of a family again; aside from our father, who has since died, I have been her only close relative. But her visit was not a success. My wife, Helen, usually so understanding in so many things, was troubled by Ruth's presence in the house. That was clear from the beginning; and, since I could exact nothing by way of confession from Helen, and perhaps offer some explanation to clear the air, there was very little I could do about it.

There was no real unpleasantness. It was all a matter of discomfort. Ruth was uncomfortable in our house; Helen was uncomfortable with Ruth. Caught between, I was uncomfortable for them both; uncomfortable, and for a while unreasonably though quietly angered. For our house, of all houses, warm and carpeted and cushioned, and sheltered by a remnant of native bush high above the city, seemed designed to contain every possible situation with some degree of comfort; my actual physical security seemed threatened, along with my peace of mind, as if the solid scenic windows in the living room had split, allowing frosty winds off the mountains entrance to our lives. The mountains are literal; on clear days it is possible to see them from our windows, across the rough water of the Cook Strait. In the steeply descending foreground there are treeferns which toss their fronds in the wind against the tall trunks of spiky cabbage trees; in the middle distance, the oval harbour busy with shipping and the city of Wellington tight-packed beneath bleak hills and eroded gullies which freak with shadow in the late sunlight; beyond are the peaks of the South Island, blue and remote in summer, often white and close in winter.

Ruth spent a great deal of her time flopped in a basket chair before the wide windows. As quiet and sleepy as a cat, her eyes dreamy with distance, her long loose body apparently empty of all tension, she seems in my memory of her visit to have spent all her time there. Her half-brushed hair fell untidily over the hand which propped her head; she seldom changed out of her check woollen shirt and jeans during her stay, and rarely left the house at all though the fact that she had business in Wellington, some plan for a future exhibition in the city, was part of my excuse for inviting her to stay. Apparently it was all quickly settled, in a single afternoon, and the city as such had no further attraction for her,

I imagined that she missed some excitement or vivid interest which was part of her daily life in the north; though I had never known that life well, this appeared a reasonable supposition. On the other hand she seemed content—or as content as she could be—with our remarkable view. Common sense tells me, though, that she couldn't have been all the time in that chair with the city and harbour, hills and mountains for company. For the one small success of her visit was the pleasure she took in the children. I was about to say surprising pleasure, but in retrospect I see there was nothing surprising about it at all. With our children Ruth established a satisfying relationship, one which was impossible with the adults of the family, Helen and myself. She told them stories; she walked them up the patchily pine-clad hill behind the house on fine days, and romped with them on the needles among the trees. There was no doubt of Aunt Ruth's popularity. The children asked about her for a long time afterwards. I saw clearly that Helen did not like it, It was as if Ruth had left infection in the house, as in a way she had.

Certainly things took time to settle after she left, and comfort was slow to return. Nothing was said. Helen has never once raised the subject of Ruth with me and, though I've tried fitfully, I've never yet persuaded her to talk about my sister, so I have been unable to get to the bottom of her dislike or distaste, whatever it is.

'Your sister,' she once said, 'is an exceptional girl.'

Which is the nearest she has ever come to passing judgement. Well, perhaps not quite. Judgement of a kind was passed a month or two after Ruth's visit. I came home from the office one evening to find a decisive change in the living room. The paintings were rearranged, and one had vanished altogether, to find a new place on the wall of the small spare bedroom (Ruth's, when she stayed) which I use, when the children are at large in the house, as a study; with the idea of escaping my job in market research for something more stable in the university or civil service I am taking a second, part-time degree, which means I need a certain minimum of peace and quiet at home.

Anyway the painting was the one Ruth had given us when we married. Surprised, for things like this seldom happen in our house without prolonged consultation, I made some comment.

'You need to change paintings round now and again,' was all Helen said. 'Otherwise you stop seeing them. Everyone knows that.'

This was, of course, perfectly true. The subject was dropped. The infection Ruth had left behind her was still at work. As I took my glass of sherry behind the evening paper I wondered what it was that so much troubled Helen. Perhaps there had been some argument with Ruth, when I was out of the house, and about which I was still ignorant? Hardly likely. There would have been some echo. No: the whole thing seemed impossible, beyond explanation. The two did not get along, and that was that. It was odd, even so, because I should have thought them extremely compatible. Helen herself was by no means a conventional girl and that, I admit, was part—a large part—of her appeal at the time I married her. If Ruth had been with me at the time I was first involved with Helen, I am sure she would have approved. Even to the extent of nudging me and urging, 'Yes, her. Don't hesitate, you idiot. She's the one for you.' Now that I have said this it seems to me, quite uncannily, that Ruth *was* at my side at the time, and did nudge me and say those words. But it is absurd. Ruth was never near me in those days, no more than she has been since; she came to the wedding, a rather sullen stranger among Helen's friends and mine, and departed in the middle of the wedding breakfast—without a word, and while I was on my feet fumbling with a speech. My words crumbled, my voice faltered; there was one prolonged, horribly blank moment— or minute—while I stood there foolishly, my mouth open, staring at the empty seat at the long, festive table. I seemed to be struggling up out of some slippery pit to find myself, and my voice, again. Which, after a time, I did. Was that Helen's grievance, then, that incident at the wedding breakfast? We never talked of that, either; as I recall the incident was lost, forgotten, in all the change and commotion of the time. Could it be, though, that Helen has never forgotten or forgiven that ungraceful and unexplained departure? We should have talked of it, we should have talked freely of Ruth from the beginning. The fault is mine. I see that now. I should never have allowed Ruth, or some notion of Ruth, to become an irritant in our lives.

I think it is safe to say that ours is a comfortable marriage. With Helen I have felt a degree of security which I once thought impossible in my life; it pleases me to think that my children will live and breathe this security in the house as they grow. Perhaps Helen saw, from the beginning, exactly what I needed; if so, she was more perceptive than I would have thought at the time I married her. She was lively, flighty, scatty. I plodded in her wake. From coffee bar to rehearsal (she did a good deal of acting before we married) to parties, rather rowdy and jammed with people of whom I scarcely approved; I didn't conceal this from Helen, any more than I had ever concealed my disapproval of Ruth's erratic friends—for they were much the same, at least similarly casual to the point of being downright destructive in their personal lives. (I may be too harsh; my attitude may be too coloured by first impressions. Nowadays I can recognise that they, as the first real friends Ruth ever made, signalled the possibility of change in both our lives; perhaps I would have resented them whoever they were.) In this sense it is true that Helen's circumstances, before we married, were not so unlike Ruth's. But it is not fair to myself, or to Helen, to make too much of similarities. Or to Ruth, either. Where Helen was always slightly diffident, Ruth was impertinent and thrusting. After all, Ruth is herself and has always been. The woman is not so different from the girl, or from the child. Perhaps—and this is the terrible, frightening thing—she will never change.

So that evening, months after Ruth's departure, I stood puzzled before the painting which now hung in my study. Helen, of course, was right. Paintings obviously did need to be changed around regularly, seen in a new context. For I had stopped seeing this one a long time before. That night I looked at it, really looked at it, for the first time in years. The children murmured sleepily in their bedroom, Helen clattered about in the kitchen, and I stood frowning before a painting I seemed never really to have seen before.

It was not a painting I had ever liked particularly, for like so much of Ruth's work it seemed to have very little to it; it lacked depth, in every sense of that word. There was a flatness, a lack of any perspective, in the scene—a fragment of seacoast, rocks and water and lumpy hills vaguely crowded and barely separable, a red dinghy drawn up on pale sand; it could have been, and possibly was, a memory of one of the many places where we spent our childhood. What I saw for the first time, though, was not detail familiar enough—but the strange, almost unearthly light which filled the frame: I could have sworn that it had not been there before; that it was something which had sprung magically from oil and canvas as it aged. Vivid, timeless and dancing, it was impossible to place, and difficult to connect with any sunrise, sunset or noon that I had ever known. On the other hand, and this was perplexing, the flawless light seemed not at all unfamiliar to me; there was a tinkle of response, coming and going faintly, in some distant delta of my mind. I listened, but heard no more. What I saw clearly was that I had somehow missed the point of the painting before; the light *was* the point. And the detail, into which I had earlier peered without success, seeing no depth or perspective, was in fact there only to give the light depth and perspective; or at least to indicate that the light was of this time, this place. Yet the light itself, its source, still escaped explanation. I stood there puzzling until the children quietened, and Helen called me to dinner. Looking at my small blonde wife across the table, observing her tired and rather harassed face, I resisted an impulse to thank her for having shifted Ruth's painting: she might have sensed irony, which I certainly did not intend. For a while we ate in uncustomary silence. Then, as if stirred by guilt, we spoke simultaneously—I of the office, she of her family. The family won, naturally; or perhaps I should say unnaturally. Never having known normal family life until I married, the intrigues of Helen's family, even the most trivial, still fascinate me; with some wealth and little common sense, it has more intrigues than most. Helen had just had, that day, a telephone clash with her mother and another, for good measure, with an unmarried sister who was running wild with a bass-player in a jazz band.

'Be tolerant,' I advised.

'Tolerant?' she cried. 'That's just the wishy-washy sort of thing I'd expect you to say. That bitch thinks she can get away with anything.'

'Perhaps she can,' I suggested. 'Anyway let her find out. You can't affect the issue.'

'God,' she said, 'sometimes you're hopeless. You just don't want to see.'

'She'll settle down,' I predicted with confidence. 'Just give her time. After all, you had your fling. Why shouldn't she have hers?'

'It's different,' she said. 'That's why. Besides, she's been carrying on like this for years. If she's not careful she'll finish up like—' She hesitated.

'Yes?'

'Well, if you must know—like that sister of yours.'

'Like Ruth? But Ruth's different.'

'Of course. She has to be, doesn't she?'

But, as usual, Helen was content to leave it at that: she had no wish to make a frontal attack. The main thing was that she reduced me to silence. Perhaps that is the only way I can defend Ruth, by way of silence. It was unusual for Ruth to lurch into our domestic conversation, and interesting to observe the fact that she had that night in particular; it confirmed all I felt about the shift of the painting.

When Helen called me in my office early next morning to say there was a message, a telegram, from Ruth, I was not as surprised as I should have been; my sister seemed once again central in my life. Yet this was one of the few communications I'd had from her in my married life, certainly the first urgent one.

'Yes?' I said.

'It arrived a few minutes ago,' Helen said irrelevantly. 'I would have redirected it, but I thought you might be out of your office. So I took it down over the phone.'

She sounded strained and nervous.

'All right,' I said, impatient. 'So what is it, what does it say?'

'It's your father,' Helen said.

It seemed my father was dead. *Our* father, Ruth's and mine. After I replaced the receiver I sat in my office a few minutes longer, trying to feel things I did not feel. I could summon up regret but no grief; it obstinately refused to rise to the occasion. I suppose I am still a stranger to real grief: my mother died when I was young, too young to know or remember, and I have had no other close bereavement. It was, I thought, useless to pretend that my father had been anything but remote to me, to either of us. It wasn't that he denied us affection, in his way. It was just that patience and sympathy for the young, and any real love, were missing; we were a sad encumbrance, constantly reminding him of the love of which he had been robbed, and which he no longer wished to remember. He appears to have turned in upon himself, to have become remote from the world entirely, after our mother's death. It might have been easier for all three of us if he had put down roots there and then; but he was apparently unable to do this, and in any case it was partly in the nature of his work—he was an engineer, a man licensed to tug the earth apart—to travel from place to place, job to job. Even so, there was something frantic in his wandering; I imagine that often he must have walked off projects half-finished. It was as if he were determined to bury all memory beneath the tumbling soil and rock of landscape after landscape. There was never any question of his marrying again, and he had few friends. At some stage in my childhood I overheard a conversation with one of the few who remained.

'You can't mourn her for ever,' this friend said. 'It's not right. You've got to snap out of it. You owe it to yourself.'

'I owe nothing to myself,' my father said. 'Nothing.'

'Well, to your kids, then.'

'Am I in debt to them?' he demanded. 'I do my best.'

That was undeniable. He did his best. When he had seen us both through school and packed us off to university, his relief was perceptible. And when we were independent in every sense, he turned from engineering to work menial and manual. Eventually he became the odd-job man of the tiny seaside community into which he retired. There is something awe-inspiring and humbling about a grief which can persist across the years and blight a lifetime. Love, like happiness, is something which can best be defined in its absence; I should be grateful to my father, then, for having in his life taught me the meaning of both, even if his death could teach me nothing of grief.

So our childhood, at least in appearance, was an unsettled one, With its spasmodic shifts from place to place. In this I suppose we were only a little more extreme than most New Zealanders, an itinerant people always pulling themselves up to see how deep their roots have grown; the shallowness of growth can't entirely be explained by the fact that our seed falls in hardened ruts rather than on virgin ground.

When I was young, Ruth was the only constant and settling factor in my life: housekeepers, tired and bulky middle-aged women, flicker faintly across my memory; towns, valleys, rivers, bush and beaches; and my father's haunted face looms now and again. I seldom have the impression that he was even with us physically, though in truth he was never far away. But this doesn't mean our childhood was miserable. It was never that: it was always exciting and full of promise. Perhaps because no adult, and almost no other children, intruded upon our shared imagination. As children we were seldom in one place long enough to make real friends. Our imagination was our world: each move, each new scene, was grist to the mill and fuel to the fire. There was never loss of continuity. Ridiculously, some people called us lonely children. We were never that; we had each other. It rarely struck us that this might end, any more than it struck us that childhood would end. 'Always' and 'for ever' were favourite words in Ruth's vocabulary, and thus in mine too.

'Do you think this summer will go on for always?' I remember asking—perhaps one day when we lay naked and browning in deep dry grass by a riverside, tall trees and taller hills around us, and cicadas singing thick in the afternoon heat. 'I mean, do you think it would if we wished hard enough?'

'If we really want it to,' she said, 'it will go on for ever. In our minds, I mean. That way we can stay warm in winter. Just remembering.'

She was perhaps sixteen then, large and long-limbed, and her answers just a step ahead of my questions in sophistication. But she wasn't impatient with me; that didn't come till later. Possibly that was the last year we were really ourselves. Like summer, childhood had an end, even if we might later warm ourselves with the memory.

Something of all this raced through my mind while I sat at my desk looking at the telephone. I picked it up again, booked a seat on an afternoon flight to Auckland, and then went home to pack. It was May, with Wellington's winds already wintry; my work wasn't pressing, and since it was the middle of university vacation I should miss no lectures. There was nothing to stop me staying away as long as was needed. 'All the same,' I explained to Helen, 'I shouldn't be away too long. There can't be much to tidy up. I imagine his affairs are pretty simple and straightforward. But obviously I can't leave it all to Ruth. She just wouldn't be interested. After the funeral I'll stay till everything's tidy.

It'll save another trip later.'

There was concern on Helen's face. 'Are you sure—' she began.

'I'm sure it'll be all right,' I told her. 'There's no need for you to come along too. After all, there will probably only be Ruth and myself at the funeral. And you hardly knew him anyway.'

Though I made my coolness plain, Helen insisted on treating me as if I were shrunken with grief. While waiting for my flight number to be called at the airport she gave me a comforting hug and an earnest kiss, then placed the palm of her hand gently against my cheek and said, 'Look after yourself, darling. And don't—'

She hesitated.

'Don't what?' I asked.

'Well, don't stay away too long. Remember we want you back.'

'But of course I'll be back. What on earth are you worried about?'

Her smile trembled. 'Nothing,' she said finally. 'I'm just being silly. You know me.'

For a moment I wondered if I did.

Our actual farewell, when the call came from my plane, was more sedate: a quick passionless peck and I walked across the tarmac. I might have been off on a business trip.

I'd sent a telegram ahead to Ruth, and she was waiting for me when I arrived after the flight at the airways terminal in Auckland. In her habitual jeans and sweater, with a duffel-bag slung over her shoulder, she was conspicuous, at some distance, among sleekly clad citizens of that city. She looked subdued, and was silent as she placed a welcoming hand on my arm. We walked together to the baggage counter.

'What are you planning to do?' she asked.

'There's only one thing we can do. Rent a car and get up there as soon as we can to make arrangements for the funeral.'

My father had lived some seventy or eighty miles north of Auckland all his retirement; a rough road in the later stages meant we had more than a two-hour journey ahead.

'Someone up there is making arrangements. A friend, the one that rang me up. A Mr Slegel.'

'Well, that's something. It hadn't even struck me that there might be a friend to do all that. Knowing Dad.'

'It was all sudden. No sickness, nothing. He died in his sleep.'

I felt guilty: I realised I should have asked about that in the first place. The fact that he was dead had been sufficient for me.

'I see,' I said. 'Well, I'm glad it was easy.'

Ruth was quiet.

'Come on,' I said. 'Let's see about that car. We'd better get moving if we want to be there tonight.'

The car was quickly procured.

'We've still a couple of hours of daylight,' Ruth observed. 'Let's run home to my place. You can straighten yourself up with some coffee while I fetch out some clothes for the funeral. That's going to be a job. To find something to wear, I mean.'

I made no comment, and concentrated on getting through Auckland's dense and noisy traffic. Ruth lives just outside the central city area, in a flat off Parnell Rise. It is part of a decrepit house among ugly warehouses, but overlooking the city and sea and sidelong to the sun. The front part of the house swarms with two large families of Samoans. The back part is Ruth's. It doesn't seem to me an ideal situation for her. But she insists that she likes the noise, the life around. Her flat consists of a small and cluttered kitchen-living room and a combined workroom and bedroom.

'Brother mine,' she instructed, 'park yourself in a seat while I get you coffee.'

'Don't worry about that. Hurry up and find those clothes you're talking about.'

'It was only ten days ago I went up to see him,' she said.

'Him?'

'Dad. A friend ran me up there in his car for the weekend.'

'I didn't think you saw him often.'

'I didn't. Not until recently, at least. But I seem to have got up there to see him every two or three weeks lately.'

'Since your trip to Wellington, you mean?'

'I'm vague about dates. I suppose it is since then. I saw a lot more of him than usual, anyway.'

I sat puzzled. I supposed I had seen my father, on average, once every year or two; Ruth, who lived so much nearer him, hadn't seen him much more often. Why the change?

'Did he have very much to say?' I asked.

'No more than usual.'

'Then why the sudden interest in the old man?'

'I don't know,' she said, clicking switches and planting the coffee percolator on the stove. 'Perhaps I had a premonition. I just felt like seeing a little more of him, that's all.'

'Did you have something you felt you wanted to talk to him about? Was that it, then?'

'Not really,' she said, and disappeared into the bedroom to look for clothes. More puzzled than ever, I sat at the bare board table in her kitchen, looking out of a dusty window at the haze on the Waitemata harbour and the neat blue crater of Rangitoto rising beyond. I thought briefly of the bleak landscapes visible from our window above Wellington, and Ruth's obvious enjoyment of them. There man still perched precariously on an island's spiny edge; here where everything was so much gentler, so much milder, man overwhelmed. Even the hills were shaped by ancient Maori settlement, and now pale houses were scattered in clumps of green around; native trees, tropical palms, and Norfolk Island pines planted back in missionary times. One could still feel warmth in a May sun; summer was never too far away. It never seemed far away in childhood either, for this was more my part of the country. For the sake of a career, for the sake of my family, I'd gone among colder hills.

No matter how I tried though, I couldn't get it out of my mind that Ruth's belated interest in her father had something to do with the failure of her visit to Wellington. And more, with some failure of my own. But how had I failed her, and why should she have turned to him?

The percolator began working. Ruth appeared, still in jeans and sweater, swinging her duffel-bag. 'I thought you were getting dressed,' I said.

'No point in that. Not till the funeral tomorrow. And there's the car trip ahead. I always feel sticky after a car trip, don't you? Nothing seems clean. I've got all I want there.' She slapped the duffel-bag. 'Clothes for tomorrow, toothbrush for tonight. How's the coffee?'

She poured from the percolator into two chipped cups. 'Brother mine—' she began.

'Why do you keep saying that?'

'Saying what?'

'Brother mine. It's something you haven't said for years. It sounds quite odd now.'

'I didn't realise. Sorry. If it upsets you, I mean.'

'It doesn't upset me. I said it sounds odd. After all this time.'

'Does it? Well, now. Fancy that.'

'It would sound just as strange if I began calling you "sister mine" again.'

'Would it? I hadn't realised.' She passed me the coffee. 'Stir with the spoon in the sugar bowl.'

'You're not offended?' I asked. 'I mean, I was just pointing the fact out.'

'Why should I be offended?'

There was a silence between us as we sipped the coffee. I was still trying to adjust to the ground again, after the flight, and after being torn so abruptly from my life in Wellington.

'I must say,' I said after a while, 'that we don't look a particularly grief-stricken pair. But it's no use pretending, is it? We hardly knew him, really.'

'I think I was getting to know him,' she said slowly, as if measuring each word for weight. 'I feel I was, anyway. I think it was a question of approaching him on his own terms. And not expecting him to be other than what he was. Which we always did. We wanted a father like other fathers. Wouldn't you agree?'

'But even then—' I began, and faltered. I remembered my own visits, on holidays, with Helen and the children. I had hoped grandchildren, the idea of grandchildren, might produce some response from him. He was kindly enough, true; he picked them fruit from his garden, patted them on the head, walked with them down to the beach near his cottage. But there was something missing all the same. I felt that, so far as he was concerned, they could have been any children. Just as Helen, say, could have been any woman; not a daughter-in-law. 'I think you're simplifying,' I went on. 'I think there was a little more to it than that. After all, fathers don't come in a special mould. They're not all alike, I mean. Speaking as one myself.'

'Well,' she sighed. 'Perhaps I'm wrong about that. But I feel I was getting to know him, all the same.'

'In what way?'

'I told you. In his way.'

I was perplexed and unreasonably irritated, as if I had just found her cheating me of something.

'We must talk some more about this,' I said, and rose. 'It's time we were moving.'

We used the last of the daylight on the journey and travelled the last twenty or thirty miles with the headlights flashing over fern, gorse and rutted road; inland places had the chill of coming frost, but the air was warmer as we neared the sea. Ruth smoked steadily and had little to say.

'Where to?' I asked, as we drove into the settlement. Drawn-up boats and ramshackle cottages, deserted by their summer residents, rose pale in the headlights. Few windows were lit up anywhere.

'His place, I suppose,' Ruth said. 'I mean we'll have to spend the night somewhere.'

'I was thinking in terms of a motel,' I said. 'Something like that.'

'Why pay money? His place is there. And it's ours now, anyway.'

'That hadn't struck me, I admit. I mean, it doesn't seem right that his place should be ours. But what about—' I hesitated.

'The body, you mean? An undertaker's looking after it all. That's what Mr Slegel said. The man who rang me up. He found the body early this morning and he told me everything was being taken care of. He must have told me that at least four times. It seems he expected to spend the morning fishing with Dad.'

More boats, more darkened cottages. Above the engine noise we could hear the sea, the beat of surf, off to our right. A couple of shops floated through the headlights, then pale sandhills and marram grass.

'You sure we'll be able to get into the place?' The more I thought of it, the less I liked the idea of spending the night in my father's house.

'Mr Slegel said everything would be taken care of.'

Lights were even fewer at the north end of the beach. I slowed the car and changed into low gear as the road deteriorated. The last few yards were very bumpy. When we reached the beginning of my father's drive I was startled to see lights burning beyond his sub-tropical jungle of banana trees, passion fruit and paw-paw.

'Someone in occupation,' I said.

'Probably Mr Slegel. Waiting for us.'

'Who is he, anyway? Never heard of him.'

'A friend. I told you. Probably Dad's only friend. A German Jewish refugee, retired now. He got out of Germany with his wife just before the war. But his wife insisted on going back to fetch some relative. He never saw her again. She died in Auschwitz, Belsen, one of those places. He was interned himself as an enemy alien for a while. He bought himself a place here with compensation from the West German government. Dad told me the whole story.'

'I'm surprised he could get so interested in someone else. I really am.'

'You're bitter, brother. Too bitter. Don't let it rankle. Not now.'

'All right,' I said. 'Any further instructions?' On that note I stopped the car. We climbed out and made our way along the winding, rising path to the house. The place was at the extremity of the beach, against a hillside and above rocks washed by surf. In this sheltered place, on volcanic soil, his plants had flourished. We ducked beneath banana leaves heavy with dew on our way up to the house. The surf was very loud now.

A waiting figure filled the doorway and, when we approached, a hand was thrust roughly into mine. 'Slegel,' a thick voice said. 'I thought you would be here tonight.' He guided us through the door.

The inside of the house was warm. Logs blazed in the fireplace. 'You have eaten this night?' Mr Slegel said with concern.

'We had a bite on the way, thanks.' We hadn't really eaten, apart from a toasted sandwich with coffee at a roadside stop, but I didn't want to put him to any more trouble. It was obvious he'd slaved to get the place ready for us. Everything was prepared, neat and comfortable. Miraculously he seemed even to have tidied away the idea of death. The only thing missing, really, was my father himself. I half expected him to walk out of the bedroom to greet us, and then to sit with us before the log fire.

'So long as you are all right,' Mr Slegel said. 'That is the main thing. Anyway, if you want more, your sister knows where to find food in this house. There is a fish in the refrigerator which your father caught yesterday, a twelve-pound snapper of which he was proud. His last. I weighed it for him.'

He hesitated, a heavy and rather clumsy man who apparently found even the shortest speech an effort. It was then I realised, having just grown used to the light, that his eyes were red and puffy and still faintly damp. He'd wept as he waited for us. Perhaps wept all day. I cringed from this grief of a stranger, and perhaps Ruth did too, as we stood there fresh-eyed from the city.

'Your father was good friend to me, so good I can never tell. Life is not worth so much to me today. Perhaps tomorrow we will talk more. For is not the time, this night. Main thing now is that you are comfortable. In the morning we will speak again.'

Before I could reply, thank him for everything, he ducked out of the door.

'Well,' I said, and Ruth and I were left looking at each other. Ruth moved slowly towards the fire and warmed her hands.

'I think he was rather like Dad,' she observed finally. 'I mean they were much of a muchness, lonely here, and they got along together. They kept to themselves. I don't think they even talked much between themselves. They just liked to be with each other.'

'I see.'

She looked into the fire for a while. 'He'll miss Dad,' she added.

'Obviously.'

'Hungry?'

'I suppose I am. It's been a long day. Everything's starting to catch up with me. I mean, a lot has happened in the last twelve hours or so. I think I must have eaten, at some stage, but it's hard to remember.'

'I'll get something,' she said, and turned from the fire.

I looked at her. My voice seemed to strain across the stillness and quiet of the house. 'I suppose this is an event,' I said. 'Back in my father's house, and my sister cooking for me again. How long has it been?'

Ruth sighed as she went through to the kitchen. 'Let's not count the years,' she called over her shoulder. 'Just for once.'

I took her place before the fire and tossed a couple of fresh logs into the grate. Mr Slegel had left us plenty of wood. Then I relaxed in a chair. I felt my father's presence more strongly than ever: our old familiar furniture; his books; the photograph of the fragile stranger who was my mother, on the mantelpiece. Though I had never actually lived in this house, it could have been any one of a dozen places I had known in childhood. Ruth was right: there was no point in counting the years. For it was as if the years had been banished. My father could have been out on a job, late, while Ruth and I fended for ourselves, as we often did, in the absence of regular housekeepers.

The fire crackled; I was lost in the thought.

Ruth appeared from the kitchen. I looked at her, she looked at me. For a moment she said nothing. Then she asked, 'Why are you looking at me like that?'

'Like what?'

'So strangely.'

'Things are strange all of a sudden. I can't help it.' It was as if Helen had never existed, nor my children; as if I didn't have a warm house, warmth of any kind, waiting five hundred miles away. All my adult life seemed to crumble and vanish. 'Don't you feel it too?'

'In the sense that Dad is gone,' she said, 'yes.'

'No,' I began. 'I mean—' But I faltered and finished, 'It's too difficult to explain. Just now, anyway. What were you going to say?'

'I came to ask whether you'd like meat, or that fish Dad left.'

'What do you think?'

'I think I'd prefer to leave the fish. If you would. Perhaps Mr Slegel might like it. Not that there's anything wrong with it. It's just that—'

'I know,' I said.

Ruth went back to prepare the meal, humming softly to herself. My insecurity ebbed slowly; I felt the return of older warmth, older certainties. As a child I had often been utterly dependent on Ruth, on her Judgement. She had stood between me and the world. Her presence at the funeral would make it all so much easier. Perhaps she would even know what to say to Mr Slegel.

'How about a drink?' Ruth called. 'I couldn't rely on Dad having anything, so I put a bottle of sherry in my duffel-bag. You might get it out of the car.'

I went out into the chilly evening. The surf was noisy, the stars bright. A light wind rattled the damp foliage in the garden. I paused beside the car and looked back to the lighted house. It seemed to me now that the place strangely enclosed all the half-forgotten perplexities and mysteries of my life: if I was still alien, it was because I felt alien to myself. I fetched our bags from the boot of the car and carried them inside.

I uncorked the bottle and poured the wine. Ruth came to sit beside the fire while the food cooked. We raised our glasses.

'I'm not sure what we can toast,' I said, 'except Dad's memory.'

'To us, then,' Ruth said decisively. 'To our futures. That's simpler.'

The sherry was cheap and faintly metallic. It soothed, though, and warmed. Ruth kicked off her shoes and placed her bare feet close to the fire.

'So Dad's brought us under the same roof again,' I observed.

'I was under your roof a few months ago,' she said.

'That doesn't count somehow.'

'All right, so that doesn't count. What does count?'

I shrugged.

'My dear sweet brother,' she said, 'I don't expect some gnomic utterance. Just a simple answer. What does count with you?'

'Doing my best, I suppose. Doing my best, in every sense.'

'You think you've done it?'

'How would I know?'

'Don't be so coy. Really, you're very pleased with yourself, aren't you? And proud of your good safe job, your pleasantly tamed wife, your happy family? Isn't that so?'

'Well, I suppose I've reason to be. Proud, I mean. I refuse to be ashamed, anyway.'

'Good Lord,' she said. 'Who's asking you to be ashamed?'

She padded barefoot back to the kitchen and began serving the food. I set the table for the meal: that had always been my job. Then I fetched and refilled my glass and leaned in the kitchen doorway, watching Ruth set out the food on plates. I realised I was still a little afraid of her. My elder sister had always seemed to know best.

'What do you want me to do?' I challenged.

'To be yourself for a change. To be a little less stuffy.' She looked at me sharply; her hair drifted lightly over her vivid eyes. 'To be a little less bloody pompous.'

'Fair enough,' I said. 'So what am I supposed to do now? Run round in jeans? Be a thirty-two-year-old beatnik?'

An oblique attack seemed to me the best form of defence. But she didn't bite.

'Anything,' she said, 'anything but the way you are now. You were such a bright-eyed kid. Sorry, but I can't help remembering.'

'And I can't help feeling you're unfair,' I said. 'There should be room for all kinds in this world. And if there's not room for your kind, and my kind, then it's a poor look-out. That's all I can say.'

'You enjoyed life,' she went on. 'You really did.'

'How do you know I don't still enjoy it?'

'How could you?' She shrugged. 'That house of yours, it's a living death. Really. No honest emotion could survive there five minutes. It's the kids I feel sorry for most of all, though. They just haven't a chance.'

She couldn't have surprised me more if she had struck me across the face.

'What do you want them to have? A childhood like ours? Is that it?'

'They could do worse. A lot worse. All things considered.' She gave me another sharp glance, then took up the two steaming plates of food and carried them through to the living-room table. As we sat down, she added, 'We didn't do badly. We were pretty lucky, in fact. Not many have a childhood as rich as ours, and you ought to know that by now.'

'I've thought about it,' I confessed.

'We ought to be grateful to Dad.'

'For ignoring us?'

'For leaving us alone.'

'What's the difference?'

'The difference between oversight and insight. I've only come to understand some things lately. As I've come to understand Dad himself. It's true that he was stunned when our mother died. And it's true that he didn't seem to know we were around for a while. But when he tried to acknowledge our existence again, he found that we didn't acknowledge his any more. We didn't need him. We'd grown self-sufficient in the meantime. And he seemed to think we were better for it. So he withdrew, and left us alone. Deliberately. It might have cost him a lot, for all we know.'

We began to eat in silence. The surf seemed to move closer to the house.

'That may be so,' I said reasonably, trying to sum up, but I still think there's a certain failure of imagination on your part if you think my kids are unhappy. You think everyone should be like we were.'

She didn't acknowledge the point. 'Then there's your wife,' she said.
'Helen? She's happy enough.'

'That shows a considerably greater failure of imagination on your
part. A more insecure girl I've never seen.'

This time Ruth had gone too far.

'That's bloody ridiculous,' I said, 'and you know it. A sense of
security is the one thing that Helen has got. She has precious few
worries—with the house, or with the kids. I've seen to that. I've worked
for it.'

''I'm not talking about that kind of security.'

'Then pray tell me what you are talking about.'

'She's not secure in herself, in her own mind. Don't ask me why. It's
an impertinence to explain someone else's discontent. I felt it as soon
as I walked into your house. In fact I was on the receiving end. She took
it out on me. For a while there, I was a kind of whipping-boy. I don't
suppose you noticed that Helen and I didn't get along.'

That assumption irritated me even more. 'I'm not altogether blind,'
I said.

'Well, then,' she went on, 'if you saw she wasn't easy in mind, you
might have wondered why. After all, she is your wife; the subject must
have some interest for you.'

'I did wonder why. I've tried to talk to her. Without much success,
I admit. But I have tried.'

'Great. So you've tried. And, having failed, did you draw the only
possible conclusion?'

'I concluded that she didn't like you much.'

'That's a fact, not a conclusion. You didn't go very far, did you? Or
were you afraid to go too far? The only possible conclusion, it seemed
to me, was that she was jealous.'

'Jealous?' The word, usually so hard and angular, suddenly become
rubbery and meaningless; it seemed to slither away from me. 'What in
God's name has Helen got to be jealous about? Why should she be
jealous of you?'

Ruth shrugged. 'I suppose I could list any number of reasons none
of them good ones, mind you. But then people are seldom jealous for
good reasons, are they?'

'Go on, then.'

'Well, one could simply be that I'm your sister and in this situation a kind of mother-in-law. That I belong to part of your life, a good part of it, which is still much of a mystery to her and which she resents not possessing too. But that's only half a reason, isn't it? It doesn't explain anything really. The real question is why she, or any human being, should crave total possession of another, when it's so impossible.'

'Perhaps life's like that. Perhaps love's like that. And perhaps you wouldn't know.'

She took that coolly.

'We can always fall back on love, can't we?' she observed with a faint smile. 'The best whipping-boy of all.'

'All right,' I said. 'Anything else?'

'Another thing could be that she feels she's missing something. Something she imagines I've got, because I haven't married, and she lacks because she has. She may resent being tied to house and children, and may resent even more a woman who is not tied down. Can't you see?'

'No,' I said stubbornly. 'It's no use bringing the children into it. Helen's perfectly happy with the children.'

'But you admit she wasn't easy in mind—'

'That may just be you. You're an upsetting influence.'

'All right. Please yourself.'

The meal moved to its end in prickly silence. I found myself remembering the incident of Ruth's painting: the way it had vanished, after so long a time, from the wall of the living room. I decided to say nothing about it. I would interpret the incident for myself; I wasn't going to supply Ruth with ammunition.

Afterwards we sat for a while in front of the fire. Towards the end of the evening, since Ruth was taking my father's room and bed, she made up a bed for me on the couch in the living room. By that time the long day had caught up with me, and I was hazy with exhaustion. Ruth made herself a last cup of coffee and stood sipping it before the diminished fire. I lay flopped in a chair. She lit herself a cigarette, and flipped the packet into my lap.

'Thanks,' I said. 'I've stopped, but I still like one now and again, when the occasion demands. It certainly does demand today.'

The cigarette, though, only complemented my sense of strangeness;

I felt a little giddy. I looked at Ruth, half silhouetted against the firelight, and realised what a lean and handsome woman she had become. It had always been difficult for me to see Ruth other than as a sister. But men must surely have found her disconcertingly attractive. In figure and manner there was an animal economy, a natural elegance of movement at odds with the erratic life she led. They must have been drawn to her. Suddenly, with a faint twinge, I was sure they had. There must have been many men, many, who had sought purchase on those firm breasts and thighs. But what had happened to them? Had there never been one who meant more than others?

'Ruth,' I said suddenly, startling myself, 'why haven't you settled down?'

'I'm perfectly settled, thanks.'

'But your life, it's so untidy.'

'As far as I'm concerned, it's perfectly tidy. Everything in its proper place.'

'It's never seemed that way to me.'

'That's because you're not living my life.'

An unsatisfying answer. I blamed my own reluctance to be direct.

'Well, marriage, then,' I said. 'Marriage and children. Hasn't that ever appealed to you? Tempted you?'

'Once it might have.' She shook her head. 'I really don't know now. I really don't know at all.'

I felt close to her again, for the first time that evening; her answer was disturbingly honest. As if scrub and undergrowth had parted to reveal a tall, clean-limbed tree.

'You mean you put temptation behind you?'

'It put itself behind me. Suddenly it wasn't there any more. It just wasn't an issue.'

'I see,' I said, and brooded.

'Well,' she said, 'I suppose we've another big day tomorrow.' She washed the coffee cups, said goodnight, and went off to her bedroom.

Though I was probably even more tired, I remained some time longer in the chair before the fire, still puzzling. Eventually I rose.

'Ruth,' I called. 'Just one more thing. Something I've always meant to ask you, but never have.'

The bedroom door was open. I went to stand beside it. In an

undergarment luminously pale against her very brown skin, Ruth was in the act of climbing into bed.

'Yes?' she said.

'Why did you walk out on my wedding breakfast? You remember?'

'Of course I remember. I walked out because I just couldn't stand it.'

'Couldn't stand what?'

'If you must know, I couldn't stand watching my brother make a clumsy clown of himself, before a lot of drunken idiots. I don't care if they were your wife's relatives, I don't care if it was expected of you. I just couldn't stand it, that's all.'

'You were disappointed in me, then?'

'Since you've said it, yes.'

'Well,' I said, 'I suppose I've always known that, in a way.' I hesitated, and realised there was nothing more I could say. 'Goodnight, then. See you in the morning.'

'Goodnight, brother mine.'

I shut her door, and began the long night. Though I was tired and the couch comfortable, my body twisted painfully in search of sleep; after an hour of restless turning I was as far from it as ever. I blamed the strangeness of everything. The strangeness of our arrival, the lights burning eerily beyond the trees in a dead man's house, the weeping stranger at the door; the strangeness of being in my father's house again, beneath the same roof as my sister, alone with Ruth for the first time in years.

And there was the unfamiliar thud of surf outside.

I realised I should have rung Helen. Her voice would have reassured me and I wouldn't have felt so vulnerable. And I might have had some sense of continuity instead of a sense of a widening crack down the middle of my life. I felt gusts of doubt, and doors creaked open on strange places in my mind. My father's face danced dimly before my closed eyes, then Ruth's; finally the puffy-eyed Mr Slegel's. All seemed, in some way, accusing. It was absurd.

Then Ruth again, but younger and different. She was slight and lean in a swimming costume and running ahead of me down to the sea. The water was silver, the early sunlight vivid on sand-dunes and stumps of bleached driftwood. Ruth plunged down from the dunes, skidding, laughing. She looked back at me and cried, 'Come on, slow-coach.' Breathless, I followed. We skimmed like gulls together over the sand.

There was a savage and piercing pain in my foot. I cried out and tumbled forward. Ruth was suddenly beside me, tender with concern.

'Why don't they leave us alone?' she said angrily. She was biting her lip and weeping. 'Why don't they?'

My foot was sliced open, and my blood bright on the sand. When Ruth lifted my head I saw for the first time the ugly half-buried glass of a broken beer-bottle.

She bandaged my foot with a torn strip of towel and, leaning on her shoulder, I hobbled home.

Restless on that couch the night after my father's death, twenty years later, I could still feel the shredding glass in my flesh. I could still twitch with the agony of it, yet feel at peace with Ruth's gentle hands and tender voice.

It was no use. Sleep was hours away.

I rose, switched on the light, and heaped some fresh wood on the fire. Then I heated the coffee and helped myself to another of Ruth's cigarettes.

Remembering how we had bickered so fretfully all evening, seeking to wound in tender places, I wanted to cry to her shut bedroom door, 'Look what they've done to us, sister mine. Just look what they've done to us.'

But I didn't. Instead, wide awake and tense, I hunted along my father's bookshelves for something to read, something to pass the night. But it was hard to find anything appealing. It wasn't really the time to begin an exploration of my father's collected classics, or to examine the works of Karl Marx, Daniel De Leon or Edward Bellamy; socialism had flowed strongly in my father's thought and speech when he was younger, when he could still see all mankind's problems as moral and economic. After my mother's death, an event which may have given his views some cosmic qualification, his interest and involvement in the affairs of men became more academic: Trotsky's *Revolution Betrayed* stood alongside Winwood Reade's *Martyrdom of Man*; Koestler and Deutscher beside William Morris and Thomas Paine. Certainly he didn't argue or attend meetings any longer. His views became so much his own they were vague even to his children. And now—as I passed

over a two-volume work on ancient Egypt, Gibbon's *Decline and Fall*—
his books served still to conceal rather than reveal the man. I could not
associate them with the father I knew.

Was that my fault? Should I, like Ruth, perhaps like Mr Slegel, have
made some effort? My frustration at not finding something ephemeral
to read merged into something larger. Even at this late stage, it seemed,
I would never be able to see him clear. I would never be able to assign
him a place in my mind and say: Yes, that is, that was, my father. He
would always perplex me.

And there wasn't even a magazine. In the cold night foliage from
warmer climates rubbed and rustled against the house, as if craving the
heat within. I sat by the fire, drank coffee, listened to the surf, and
smoked more of Ruth's cigarettes. It was clearly too late to search out
my father, set him straight in my mind. But what had he made of us,
Ruth and myself? In one way, at least, we must have disappointed him,
for neither of us had taken more than a mild interest in things political;
we were like passengers insulated in a ship, trapped placidly, listening
now and then to faint and distant storm surges. Yet in our different
ways we were children of a world he and men like him had made as
surely as we were children of a country he had made: he had seen
society tugged apart as well as landscape; in his lifetime the socialist
idea may have faltered here and failed there, may have been stalemated
by its own successes, may in desperation have assumed grotesque and
fearful shapes, but nothing had been left unchanged by it, no country
and no person. Had there been satisfaction in this for him? It was
unlikely. I could see that, easily enough, but what I could still not see
was how Ruth and I, in our separate lives, must have appeared to him.
Had he been amazed that we should remain indifferent to his late
urgencies, or had he been able to make some imaginative and
compassionate leap into our world? For actually we weren't so much
indifferent as perplexed and powerless, seekers of refuge. Had that
been at all plain to him?

I would, of course, never know. An hour or two later I put out the
light and tried sleeping again.

I must have slept—for a time, at least—before I became aware once
more of the surf's din. The darkness was perhaps less dense beyond the
windows, but dawn still some way off. Then I became aware of what

had woken me: the light was on in the kitchen, and I heard Ruth moving round there. I could smell cigarette smoke, as if she'd just been standing beside my couch.

'You're up early,' I called.

'I couldn't sleep.'

'You too.'

'Coffee?'

'Thanks.'

A minute or two later she came to sit beside me on the couch. We sipped our coffee in silence. 'I suppose I must have slept for a couple of hours,' she said blearily, pulling up the lapels of my father's dressing-gown against the morning chill. 'Then something woke me—a tree scratching on the window—and I couldn't go back off again. I seem to have been awake, thinking, for hours. I'm sorry if I was unpleasant to you last night.'

'You weren't unpleasant. Just blunt.'

She seemed pained, uncertain of herself. She fidgeted a new cigarette out of a flattened packet, lit it, and then ran a vague hand through the hair which streamed over her eyes.

'I seem to remember being unpleasant, all the same. It wasn't a particularly nice way to behave on the night after Dad died. I'm sorry if I hurt your feelings. I didn't mean it. All that stuff about the wedding breakfast—'

'It was true enough, wasn't it?'

'Half true. Let me put it that way.'

'What's the other half, then?'

'You're being difficult.'

'Come on. Otherwise I will be hurt, after all.'

'Let's face it, then. We were pretty close as children.'

'That's no news.'

'No, when I say pretty close, I mean pretty close. I mean pretty incestuous in fact. If I have to spell it out.'

'Well, I wouldn't go so far as to say that.'

'I would.'

I shrugged. 'Please yourself. Perhaps I'd better have one of those cigarettes too.'

'I think it's best to be honest with ourselves. I mean, it's easier that way. My trouble is, I've never been able to make up my mind just where incestuous regard ends and sisterly concern begins. You see?'

'No. Not really.'

'Naturally you could object that you've not seen sisterly concern much in evidence lately, anyway. Fair enough. Blame that on my suspicion of the first. My suspicion of myself.'

'Ruth, you're taking yourself much too seriously.'

'I have to, you see. So when I look back on something like your wedding breakfast I wonder if I haven't just been concealing the whole truth from myself. About why I walked out, I mean.' She paused. 'I suppose Helen is so right to be suspicious. I don't blame her.'

'Now you're trying to dramatise everything.'

'Trying? I didn't think I had to try.' She laughed bitterly. 'We're adults now, for God's sake.'

The windows were brightening to pale grey. Ruth sighed, rose, and carried our empty cups back to the kitchen.

'Ruth,' I called after her, 'there was nothing wrong with our childhood, with us. Nothing unnatural.'

'No. That's just it, I suppose. That's just it.' She ran a tap, washed the cups, and then walked past my couch on the way back to the bedroom. 'Feel like a walk? I'm going to have a look at the sea while I've still got a chance today.'

I swung my feet gingerly to the floor and dressed quickly. Ruth didn't take long either. Then we let ourselves out of the cottage into the keen morning. Dew dipped slowly from frond and leaf; the sea in the east was pale and bright. The air was perfectly still. Below us, the land sloped sharply to rocks patchily black with mussels and tangled with shiny kelp: the tide was out. The beach began with a wide curve into the land and then swept away in a straight line until it was lost in spray-haze and distance. Banked up behind the beach were silky white dunes. Islands floated upon the first light of day. The sky was clear.

'A pleasant enough day for a funeral,' I observed. 'Even if I can think of better uses for it.'

Ruth walked slowly and silently ahead of me. It required some effort to walk slowly down that slope to the sea. A yellow scarf trailed about her neck and her hands were thrust deep in the slit-pockets of her windbreaker. She held herself very erect, as if deliberately pacing out the correct distance to the beach. For myself, it was all I could do to keep from breaking into a jog-trot and hurtling past her on the way to the sand. Once we would have careered down this slope in an instant, skimmed over the beach, thrown ourselves into even this wintry sea. We had never walked together so sedately before.

We reached the sand by way of the rocks at the end of the beach. It was a slight scramble, and the surf kicked spray over us. The razor-edged rocks were slippery, and once Ruth lost her poise and teetered dangerously above a deep crevice filled with foam. I grabbed her and helped her the rest of the way.

'Thanks, brother mine,' she said, when we reached the actual beach safely.

We separated again, and trod the sand carefully, almost tenderly, a yard or two apart, as if there were glass underfoot; as if our feet were unshod.

The sea was green and uninviting, the spray fresh on our faces. The sand squeaked underfoot as we walked in silence. Once more Ruth seemed to be pacing out the distance between one point and another. At length she paused beside an amputated tree-trunk which some spring tide had flung into the dunes with such force that it had actually pierced the hirsute cover of marram grass, between bulging flanks of sand.

'Let's just sit here,' she said. 'And watch the sunrise.'

We hadn't long to wait. The cold silver of sea and sky vanished; there was spurt after spurt of colour above a reddened sea. Before long the light, diluted to pale yellow, was touching our faces with a faint promise of warmth. Lean gulls swayed above the rising tide.

'It's nice to know it's still there,' Ruth observed. 'The sun, I mean. It's about the only thing you can rely on.'

But she shivered, all the same.

'The only bloody thing,' she went on, 'and even then only sometimes.'

She hunched forward, hair falling over her face and with a stick began drawing in the sand. Once she looked back up at our father's house, perched at the end of the beach.

'It'd be nice to stay here, though,' she said. 'Everything unimportant stripped away. Why don't we?'

'You're not serious.'

'I couldn't be, could I?' She paused. 'Just the same,' she added dreamily.

'Ruth, please—'

'Oh, of course I'm not bloody serious. Don't panic.' She stood up. 'Let's go back. We've had our free time for today, children. Now back to the business of life. Or isn't it death?'

She gave me her hand, and pulled me to my feet. We faced each other for a moment. Her eyes searched mine.

'You forgive me, don't you?'

'For what?'

'Everything.'

'In that case,' I said, 'there's nothing to forgive.'

She laid her head silently on my shoulder, then lifted it again. We walked back to the house. On our way we gathered enough mussels for breakfast.

* * *

The funeral was straightforward and almost painless. A retired clergyman, for whom my father had done odd jobs, conducted the service. He made brief reference to my father's professed agnosticism, dismissing this as altogether irrelevant. With the exception of Mr Slegel, all the faces at the graveside were strange; there were about twenty people present, all from the village. Only Mr Slegel wept. Ruth all but wept, I suppose; as the coffin dipped into the earth she shivered, and I slid an arm about her waist. When the service ended, I helped her along a muddy track to the car. Then I went to thank the clergyman, and shake hands with all the pleasant strangers who had attended my father's funeral. It wasn't as difficult as I expected to say the right things, since they had very little to say themselves: none of them had really known my father well. But when I looked for Mr Slegel, he had gone. I went back to the car and sat in silence beside Ruth. She lit a cigarette, and placed it between my fingers.

'So that's the end of it,' I said at last.

'The end of what?' she asked softly.

'Of something. Of him, of us, of whatever we were to each other and whatever we weren't.' I paused. 'Listen, Ruth,' I added, 'I've been thinking about things this morning. It would save a whole lot of trouble if you took over Dad's place.'

'You're not serious.'

'I am. Perfectly serious. Otherwise we'd only have the problem of selling it and dividing the proceeds between us. It's hardly worth it. I doubt if Dad's got any other asset to speak of. Another thing, I'm quite settled. I've got a house, all the security I want. You haven't. With a place like that, even if you use it only as a weekend cottage, a holiday place or a workplace, and let it to other people when you don't need it, you'll have some stability.'

'And you won't need to worry about me?' she said shrewdly.

'If you put it like that, yes. I'd worry less about you, anyway.'

'All right,'she said. 'I'll think about it. And just what is Helen going to think about your brotherly generosity?'

'She can think what she likes. It's my business. In any case she should be able to see that it will solve a lot of problems. About what to do with all Dad's possessions—his library, for example. I can put the whole thing in the hands of an Auckland lawyer and fly straight home to Wellington.'

'Ah,' Ruth said, 'I see. The truth, at last. You want to fly straight home.'

In the distance a solitary gravedigger was heaping the last clay on my father's coffin. It was just noon and there was warmth in the day: the wintry sun was gentle on the small cemetery, the straw-coloured grass, the headstones gripped by convolvulus. Beyond a line of peeling bluegums the sea was very blue.

'Why not? There's no point in spending more time away in the north than I need to.'

'Are you tired, brother? Are you tired, depressed, miserable, uneasy, in fact bloody awful? Try Wife, then. Try Wife, the friendly all-purpose remedy. Back again in standard sizes or in our special flip-top box. Watch for the trademark and beware of substitutes. Obtainable today from—'

'For God's sake,' I said.

'Superior to all other brand names,' she went on. 'Get with it, be in the swim. Tests show that nine out of every ten men prefer Wife. And the others are probably homosexuals anyway.'

'Shut up.'

But she was weeping; she had her face buried in her arms. I put the car into gear and drove back through the village to the house. Ruth went quickly inside, through to the bathroom, to wash her face and brush her hair. I fell heavily into a chair and looked beyond green growth to the sea. After a while she reappeared.

'Sorry about all that,' she said calmly. 'I didn't mean it.'

'I know. You never do.'

'True enough,' she agreed. 'I never do.'

She went into the bedroom to change. Then we packed, tidied, and ate a quick lunch. Ruth defrosted the refrigerator and removed the fish for Mr Slegel. As we moved to the door, I paused and said, 'Well, there you are. It's all here, all yours, if you want it.'

'Yes,' she said. 'All right.'

'All right?'

'I'll take the place over. And if you and Helen and the kids ever want a holiday here, I'll move out—if I'm in residence, which probably I won't be, often. It might give us some sense of continuity after all. If there's something to be salvaged, I suppose that's it—some sense of the importance and relevance of the past. We may need that more and more. I don't mean just us. I mean people in general. If your children are ever going to have a sense of continuity, a sense of family, we might as well start here as anywhere, if we're going to start at all.'

'And your children?' I said.

Ruth shrugged, and we went out of the door together.

* * *

I am in my home. It is evening. The lights of Wellington glitter far below my study window. In another room the television has just been silenced and now Helen is reading to the children. I am familiar with the story she is reading them. It is about a comical, clumsy, well-meaning elephant. Whatever he touches, he seems to damage. When he tries to play with other animals, he inadvertently hurts them. But—since this is a story for children—he manages to do the right thing in the end; it all ends happily. I can see myself briefly in the story, at least my clumsiness. Have I done the right thing in the end? The fact is, I've tried to buy off my sister; tried to buy her off my conscience. I may

actually have done the right thing by Ruth. As for myself, I cannot tell.
I just wish I felt happier in mind.

Before we left the village we sought out Mr Slegel, thanked him for
everything, and presented him with that fish we hadn't been able to
bring ourselves to eat. He was delighted to know that Ruth would be
returning to the house regularly, and promised to look after the place
for her, and tend the garden.

'Your father,' he told us, 'was a good man, good and gentle. And I
can see, for it is easy to see, that he had two fine children of which he
was proud. I know that always he dreamed of only the best things for
his children.'

Was that the truth? Or was he just saying that for something to say?
I couldn't be sure. It left me uneasy.

'I think,' he went on with a sad smile, 'that he would have liked the
house kept. It would have done him good to know that he had not
made a home there for nothing—not just for himself, but for his
children too.'

I was glad to say goodbye to Mr Slegel, for he disturbed me—I felt
drawn to him; I suppose that was the simple truth of the matter. I felt
drawn to him as I had never been to my father. And I was sure at last
that it was my fault, not my father's.

It was too late in the day to see a lawyer and catch a plane home
when we got to Auckland. I spent the night with Ruth—again it an
improvised bed on a couch, this time in her untidy kitchen. She had
greater assurance on home ground again. We talked of her work, which
sells moderately well in Auckland galleries, and I looked over some of
her newer paintings. I was interested to see again, in painting after
painting, that curious light which had perplexed me. I was about to
remark on it when there was a noise, then knocking, at her door.

'Oh God,' she said. 'Visitors. I was afraid I'd have them tonight. I
just had a feeling.'

Four friends, three men and a girl, swamped us. They planted a
dozen bottles of beer on the floor and arrayed themselves around
Ruth's bedroom-studio. With glasses supplied by Ruth, they quickly set
about emptying the bottles. They all seemed to know Ruth well: I had
the impression that they might be as close to her as anyone she knew.
They examined me without great curiosity when I was introduced, and

went on talking to Ruth. She didn't explain my presence, or mention the death in the family, until the beer was gone and the gossip exhausted.

'It's midnight,' she said wearily. 'And my brother and I have had a funeral today.'

Even that didn't particularly shake them. It simply caused a new outbreak of talk, and they didn't leave for another hour or more. Since I had little to say for myself, I had more than enough time, that evening, to sort them out as individuals; it helped keep me awake. A lean young man with thin bristly moustache, apparently some kind of writer or journalist, certainly an art critic, treated Ruth with particular deference: I guessed he was having, or had had, an affair with my sister; Ruth seemed edgily polite when she spoke to him, so I imagined the affair was of the past. The other two men were bearded, and wore tight jeans; they were difficult to separate until I learned that one with dark hair was a sculptor, one with brown an artist. The girl, who in some ways might have been Ruth ten or twelve years younger, remained totally in the background and anonymous. Small and fair and frail, she curled into a corner where she smiled mysteriously to herself now and again. She gave me the impression she had heard most of the conversation before. Perhaps she had. Aside from gossip and character dissection, it mostly concerned the founding of an art magazine.

'Money,' the lean young critic said. 'Lots of lovely money. That's all we need. With a wealthy backer we could go ahead tomorrow.' He swung round on me abruptly. 'You know anyone in Wellington?'

'Me?' I shook my head.

'It's no use looking south, anyway,' the sculptor intervened. 'The further south you go, the more barbarous this country gets. God help us, they're still assimilating French impressionism down there.'

'It's not quite as black as you suppose,' I said. 'There are islands of enlightenment in the capital.'

'It's not enlightenment we're looking for,' observed the artist. 'But cash. And plenty of it.'

'Mind you,' said the critic, 'I feel sure we could pull in enough money to cover expenses on prestige advertising. Once we got started. It's just a question of getting started. There's money around all right. If only we could get our hands on it.'

'You would receive a regular salary as editor, of course,' Ruth said.

'Naturally. The thing should be done professionally, or not at all.'

'Wait till we're all rich, then,' Ruth said, 'and we'll all put money up for your magazine.'

'No,' said the critic. 'The point is that it's got to be done now. To create the climate, can't you see? To give you people a place in the sun. Damn it, I want to make you rich.'

Wherever the conversation travelled, it always seemed to circle back to the same point: money, or the lack of it. Even some new exhibition was discussed in terms of inflated prices which had or hadn't been paid; I didn't quite get the drift of what was said, because by that time I was too depressed to listen—but quite unreasonably depressed, it seemed to me. After all, there was no good reason why artists shouldn't worry about money as much as other people. In fact I—a philistine in their eyes, I supposed—should have been relieved and impressed to know they were much the same as other people. That they weren't so unworldly as one might expect. Had I needed to imagine, for my own peace of mind, that Ruth existed on a different plane from the rest of us? Well, there it was: prices, patrons, dealers, prestige advertisers; my life in the actual world of commerce began to seem positively academic and monastic. Had I needed to imagine also that Ruth lived in an interesting world, with exciting friends? Well, there it was, or there they were: the critic, artist and sculptor, and muse for good measure. As people they didn't exactly dazzle me.

When Ruth finally revealed that it was our father we had just buried that day, appropriate things were said and apologies made. Someone launched into an account of a strange funeral he had recently attended while Ruth, in despair, made black coffee to hasten the evening to its end. In my melancholy I felt the bleakness of Ruth's flat as a grey oppression; in my tiredness the electric bulb above our heads seemed to become dimmer and dimmer, and the figures around me more and more shadowy and remote, Voices rose and merged into one long monotonous and meaningless sound.

The next thing, Ruth's hand was on my cheek. The room was empty. The visitors had vanished.

'Hello there,' she was saying gently.

'Sorry,' I said. 'I've disgraced you. Falling asleep like that.'

'Don't be silly. It was all I could do to stay awake myself. Besides, it worked wonderfully well. I mean as soon as they saw you were asleep they all cleared out.'

'These people,' I said, 'they're really friends of yours?'

'Yes,' she said. 'Why not?'

'No reason. I just wondered. I mean I couldn't really make up my mind whether they were good friends or not. Though I supposed they must be.'

'They're good friends, all right. As good as I'll ever have, I suppose. And they're very loyal.'

'I see. Well, time for bed, I guess.'

'Something worrying you, brother?'

'Not especially.'

'Come on. Tell me.'

'It's nothing I can tell.'

'But something's worrying you. What is it?'

'I suppose I'm worried about dying. That's all.'

'Dying? What on earth—' She knelt beside my chair, took my hand affectionately, and looked into my eyes with concern. 'Is something the matter? Really?'

'No. I just had a sudden vision of myself dead. You too. That's all. No reason. Except the funeral—and that's not it really. I'm just tired. Perhaps that's why. I need—' I shook my head helplessly. Then I knew what I needed. I needed to get home, the sooner the better. 'I need sleep badly.'

'That's no problem. I've just made your bed up on the couch.'

'Sorry. Rather a morbid way to end an evening.'

'But natural enough, considering. The shock about Dad is just filtering through to you, that's all. It's just starting to register.'

'No,' I said. 'It's something different, something more. I can't explain it.' I stood up, as if to shift the weight of my depression. 'Ruth,' I went on, 'you will look after yourself, won't you?'

'What do you say that for?'

'In case I forget to say it when I rush off in the morning. You will, won't you?'

'Of course. But why?'

'You mean a lot to me, that's all I'm trying to say. Without you, I wouldn't have any past, and I mightn't even be able to weigh my future. Without you I wouldn't be myself. That's probably what I mean. I'm not saying it very well. I'm too tired. Sorry.'

'Brother mine,' she said, and smiled. 'I think you've said it very well.' She reached up and ran a hand through my hair. Then she kissed me lightly on the cheek. 'Sleep well tonight.'

She started to turn away, but I didn't allow her to escape. Without considering why I pulled her head clumsily against my chest and held it there. Her body, her shoulders, breasts and thighs, rested inert and almost weightless against me. Yet she lived, and breathed, and possessed warmth; it seemed I needed to know that, to be reassured. Then, as if to confirm it even more, something like a sigh or a shudder shook her body. It seemed she needed reassurance too. I lifted her head and covered her lips with mine. I was sure I could still taste salt on her lips and smell sea in her hair, something of the lost day and lost summers, and I had a sense of wintry space around us.

Again her body shook. Abruptly she pushed herself away, and held me at arm's length.

'If that,' she said, 'was all I wanted, don't you think I could have got it long ago?'

Her eyes were strange, her smile thin.

'You would have been easy,' she went on. 'Dead easy. After all, I've slept with enough men. A brother here or there wouldn't make a great deal of difference.'

Astonished, I realised at last that she was trying to be brutal. It was just that for once she wasn't very good at it.

'No,' I said. 'I suppose not.'

She relented. Her hand gripped my arm tightly.

'Now turn around,' she said, 'and don't look back. Sleep well tonight and hurry home to your wife and children tomorrow. But don't look back. Don't ever look back, ever again.'

'That's your privilege?' I said.

'Mine,' she agreed. 'Goodnight, brother mine.'

The couch in the kitchen wasn't particularly comfortable. I sat on it for a while, before I tried sleeping, and smoked a cigarette in the dark and looked out Ruth's window at the lights trembling on the harbour; the fact was that I was wide awake again, at least in thought. My mind and body were fighting in separate directions. I remembered the cold beach that morning, Ruth walking silently on the sand; then the coffin descending into a dry clay hole, and Mr Slegel's stricken face.

I put my head down on the pillow but it was no use. My mind continued to race in a fever; it unreeled image after image of its own accord, as if it were searching for something. Then, as its progress steadied, as the images became less frightening, I began to understand that it was really travelling in the same direction as my exhausted body. It was collaborating, after all. Now I was wandering with Ruth, along a rocky creek, beneath huge fern; now pulling at the oars of a dinghy, while Ruth trailed a line from the stern; now lowering my rifle and bending to lift a shot rabbit from the tussock while Ruth hid her eyes; now swimming beside her in sunlit water, and the wild spray danced silvery from our bodies. Then I came, as I knew I would, to that beach: Ruth leapt ahead of me over the sand dunes, skidding and laughing and calling back. I plunged after her, down on to the beach. I prepared myself for the impact of that half-buried glass; I could not avoid it. Tensed, I knew exactly the pain to expect; exactly the moment to call out to Ruth. The colours of the world swam gently in the hazy early light. Then, miraculously, I was still running. Running on, after Ruth, over unblemished sand, and diving with her into cool water.

Light was in my eyes, and it was morning; Ruth was in the kitchen, cooking an omelette over a primus. 'I can't let you go home to Wellington half-fed,' she announced. Half an hour later, dressed and shaved, I set out to find my life again.

* * *

The house is quiet now. The clumsy elephant has made his peace with the world, the children are asleep; and Helen, whom I can hear now and then as she moves quietly about the kitchen, is preparing dinner. She has just, without saying a word, set a glass of sherry on the desk beside me. Ruth is in another city, four hundred miles away; but she might as well be in another country. I find it hard to imagine what she might be doing at this moment; possibly eating, or preparing to go out, or waiting for friends to call. For she could, I suppose, be anticipating an evening with friends like the one I remember enduring. That is her way; fair enough. She finds my way a living death, I find hers intolerably bleak. We do not share much in our lives, except the past; but that, when fanned in memory, can still glow so as to make the present seem lustreless and the future drably predictable. Of course I understand that the logic of that past dictates that she should be as she is, and that I should be as I am; we really have had no chance for escape. It is not a matter for regret, nor even for speculation. For Ruth was, of course, wrong when she said we were self-sufficient as children: she was speaking only for herself. Without Ruth I was always incomplete; as incomplete, say, as I am without Helen now. Perhaps that is something Ruth cannot understand. And yet...

Love; she tried to make that an explanation. It wasn't good enough, really. For it explained everything and nothing. This is the paradox I still contemplate on sleepless nights when I rise disturbed from my marriage bed and sit solitary with black coffee in the kitchen.

Again I wonder what she is doing at this moment. At last I find a satisfying picture. She is at home, in my father's house, at the beginning of a lonely evening. She is settling down to work she has neglected, painting her way slowly and thoughtfully into a new scene. Of course; that must be it. To imagine her at work reassures me. My eyes flick up to the painting above my desk the red dinghy on pale sand, and that strange haunting light. The light no longer baffles me. It is perfectly obvious, perfectly familiar. That serene light flows in and out of our childhood, leaving no shadows: could there ever be glass beneath that sand? All things melt beneath it—even the dinghy is insubstantial, a brittle stick to fuel the incandescence, as it speaks of this time and this place; every time and every place. Unreal? Of course. As unreal as her belated explanation of love, her romantic's rationalisation. She is in love not with me, but with what we were and can never be again. More than that, she is in love with what we never were. But who am I to say? That light speaks eloquently where she and I cannot.

I do not see my sister often. But I recall that once, confused travellers at a junction, we met, or almost met, before we fell back into our separate journeys towards—

Well, where else? Towards the extinction of light.

Dove on the Waters

Great-Aunt Alice's memories of Walter Dove were crumbling by the time I panned them for gold. It had been Alice's hope to chronicle Walter herself. Finally she confessed herself unlikely to make anything of her recollections. This was another way of saying that her ninetieth birthday was now behind her. Nevertheless she had no intention of allowing me to meddle negligently with such of her past as involved Walter. She dismissed my complaint that I had too few facts to fill gaps in his story. If I pressed too hard, for too much, she grew terse. 'You,' she reminded me, 'are supposed to be the writer. A few missing facts should exercise your fancy. Where's this famous imagination of yours?'

Well, where was it? And where is it now?

At the beginning of the 20th century Walter Dove was a respected New Zealand lawyer, a mild-mannered and mostly unobtrusive citizen of colonial Auckland. Fastidious to the point of leaving his clients frantic, he never missed a slipshod clause in a contract. Scandal never attached to him, nor alarming aberrance. His wholesome reputation was enhanced by the fact that he scrupulously avoided work involving marital hostilities. Moreover, he never took a criminal case unless he saw a fleck of grace in the alleged malefactor. (Sporadic church attendance would do.) When representing wronged women, he left robust jurymen moist-eyed. These shows of virtue discomforted associates; on the other hand he left cynical laymen persuaded that lawyers were not necessarily rogues. According to Alice his later notoriety came from a cloudless sky.

In 1900 Auckland was home to five hundred gas lamps and fifty thousand people. A city in name if not yet in earnest, it was barely past its frontier beginnings. A canyon of robust stone buildings now hinted at permanence. Astride a lumpy isthmus, lapped by the tides of two large harbours, this unpretentious outpost of Britain remained wedded more to nature than man. ('Last, loneliest, loveliest, exquisite, apart,' romanced Rudyard Kipling on his one reconnaissance.)

The city's legal fraternity was negligible in number, parochial in outlook and clubby in character. Uncomfortable with shop talk and unpractised in gossip, Walter rubbed shoulders with few in his profession and fewer outside it. On occasion, when vocational rites demanded, Walter allowed himself to be seen in the company of colleagues at the vine-wreathed Northern Club, a stocky three-storey building in an enclave of colonial architecture just a short walk from the courts. (Globe-trotting Anthony Trollope had stayed there and praised its surprisingly civilised amenities.) Such social occasions confirmed that Walter was an indifferent mixer; he was often seen heading for the door after one drink and two or three handshakes. On the other hand he was the kind of endearingly eccentric Victorian gentleman relatives delight in recalling. For much of the 20th century no New Zealand living room was complete without a forefather like Walter heroically attempting a smile from a silver frame on an antique sideboard. In life Walter Dove was a man who smiled sparingly and laughed reluctantly. An unhappy man? Alice never offered her thoughts on the subject; she found the question both irritating and irrelevant.

Alice met Walter when the first of her four husbands died young, leaving her with tiny twin daughters, Lucy and Jane. Her husband's confused affairs were in Walter's hands. There were unwise investments and callous creditors. Walter's distress was apparent. There were tut-tuttings and hisses of breath as he laboured through documents. 'There might,' he reported, 'be enough left to pay for the funeral.'

There wasn't. Though Alice didn't learn so till later, Walter picked up the undertaker's bill. He also arranged the sale of Alice's house and settled her in a dwelling suiting her reduced circumstances. One way and another her husband's estate was cleared of claims. Finally Walter gave her employment too.

Women were still an uncommon sight in legal offices. Responsible solely to Walter, Alice proved a competent clerk. She was also, by the measure of any era, an eye-catching one: surviving photographs show a shapely, stylish and warm-eyed girl. (Her undisguised regard for Walter made for rumour, but it foundered on the fact of his rectitude.) Familiar with Walter's concerns, she could be relied on to discourage visitors when his left hand was conferring with his right. In intermittent form, these solo tête-à-têtes possibly predated Alice's appearance in the office. They became an institution, however, after her advent. At two on Friday afternoons Walter's door closed and his working week ended. He emerged from retreat three hours later, clapped his bowler hat on his head, picked up umbrella and briefcase, wished Alice a happy weekend with Lucy and Jane, and caught the 5.30 ferry across Auckland's Waitemata harbour to the marine suburb of Devonport.

There public knowledge of the man stopped. Walter's domestic life was a mystery. Some recalled his wife visiting the office on her way to a funeral. They remembered a tall and haughty woman with hair heaped high under a veiled hat. She spent fewer than five minutes in her husband's office before speeding him away. This vignette suggested that she found Walter's legal exertions of little interest. It was also possible to deduce that she found her husband poor company. Aside from this somewhat phantasmal visitation, little was known of the woman. It was understood that there were no children of the marriage. Something might be made of that. But as Walter pointed out to juries, suspicion is not evidence.

There were portents. Alice later confessed that she preferred not to examine them. One Friday, for example, Walter failed to close his office door at the customary hour. Perhaps the catch was defective; perhaps it was uncharacteristic carelessness. Alice didn't have her eye on the office clock that afternoon. Seeing his door ajar, and imagining there must be minutes to spare before two, she burst into his office with an urgent document. What met her gaze was breathtaking. His office floor was carpeted with maps. All the world's continents were there in their oceanic setting. Walter was on his hands and knees among the maps. Shoes and socks had been discarded, and his trousers were rolled up his lean shanks. Jacket and tie were absent too. And there was a handkerchief knotted around his neck in seafarer's fashion. Altogether absorbed, he was pencilling a note in the vicinity of the Cape of Good Hope. Then he became aware of intrusion.

'Alice,' he said.

'Mr Dove,' she said.

They looked at each other in astonishment.

'I imagine you have something to say,' he decided.

Poor Alice was dumb; she was still trying to reconcile workaday

Walter with this unseemly apparition on all fours. The urgency of Alice's document was lost on her employer. He rose from the floor and arranged himself more respectably. Finally and briskly he rolled up the maps. Alice remained mute.

'You were not meant to see this,' he said.

'I imagine not,' Alice said.

'Nor is it incumbent on you to say you have,' he added.

'You have my word,' she volunteered.

'Lest you wonder, I have always placed great store in the cartographer's trade.'

Alice was not sure she heard right. 'The cartographer's trade?' she said weakly.

'Few of us are without some form of vice,' Walter informed her enigmatically. 'For some it is alcohol or tobacco. For others, gambling on horses or cards. Mine is the magic of maps. Maps, Alice. In maps are dreams. A hundred lands and a thousand dreams.'

Alice accepted this. She had to. A minute later she was at her desk and Walter behind a secure door. It was never again ajar at two on Friday.

That was in 1901. Though Alice did her best not to notice, further symptoms of flux became apparent. When entering his office, even if she knocked, Alice frequently discovered Walter in daydream, his back to the door, gazing through a window with a wide marine view. His hands together as if in prayer, he appeared to be meditating on Auckland's busy harbour and the breezy Pacific beyond. On such occasions she had the impression that he couldn't look her in the face. She learned to live with this. In Alice's charitable view a little idiosyncrasy improved lacklustre males as they aged. A few homely peculiarities made them vastly more interesting. In his middle forties, Walter was hardly old. His unruly mane of white hair, however, made him look more than fifty.

His work was not noticeably affected by his lengthy musings; he remained as punctilious as ever in matters concerning his clients. Alice wondered whether she should say something to one of Walter's partners, lest his condition was signalling mental disorder. In the end she thought not. If his work could not be faulted, why tell? It could be construed as disloyalty. Alice was never less than loyal. And his partners were unlikely to deduce more than she did.

Shaking off such a spell, he once asked abruptly: 'What do you think, Alice?' He was evidently conscripting her for some interior conflict; anyway she was at a loss to reply.

'About what?' she finally said.

'Do you see me as a decent sort of fellow?'

'That is one way of putting it, perhaps.'

'How would you put it?'

'I would see you as worthy. Principled. And honourable.'

This was insufficient for Walter; he wasn't angling for commonplace compliments. 'What I am asking,' he explained patiently, 'is whether I play fair by the world.'

'By the world?'

'Exactly.'

'I should think so,' she said with emphasis.

'Then let me phrase a different question,' he went on. 'Does the world play fair by me?'

Alice found this even more baffling. 'I imagine you are the best judge of that, Mr Dove,' she said.

'Perhaps it has to be spurred along a little,' he mused. 'What do you think?'

'Spurred along?' she asked.

'Pricked and prodded,' he confirmed. 'What do you think?'

Alice failed to determine what she was thinking and, more to the point, what Walter was.

That conversation preceded Walter's land purchase. Alice learned of it when papers relating to the transaction crossed her desk. The purchase was mystifying. For one thing it was ludicrously small, three or four scrubby acres threaded with tidal shallows and powerfully scented with marine decay. His on payment of five pounds, it was nevertheless no steal. Bordered by mangroves and murky water, the property was some miles up harbour from Auckland. There were no roads and no near neighbours. Access was by bridle path or flat-bottomed dinghy. Beefy pioneers with axe and saw had earlier pitched camp there, levelling the forest which once grew primevally sombre about the upper harbour. There were the remains of a mill which once turned venerable New Zealand kauri into honey-coloured timber. Silence was now the most conspicuous feature of the location. Crabs were audible, people never. There wasn't a dejected client in sight, and distinctly no woman.

Then there was the boat. Alice likewise learned of this when papers concerning its acquisition fell on her desk. A forty-foot, gaff-rigged cutter with sleek line, it had been built as a harbour racer in the 1880s. It bore the unpromising name *Albatross*. Doubly skinned with kauri, fastened with copper rivets, it was at least in seaworthy shape. But what did Walter want with a sailboat? If nothing else this venture helped explain his land transaction. 'To catch a bird,' says a proverb, 'first find a cage.' His half-submerged land was the cage; *Albatross* the bird. The boat was delivered up harbour, moored in his private archipelago, and eventually lifted into wooden cradle for a refit. Tradesmen camped nearby were soon sheathing its hull with copper. This was the customary protection against worm damage in tropical waters. But *Albatross* wasn't resident in tropical waters or in danger of worm damage. What was he up to?

The mystery didn't last. An indifferent prevaricator, Walter finally admitted his intention to the intrigued tradesmen in his employ. One presumably passed the news on. Whatever its source, the story sent a ripple through Auckland's boating community. The fact that Walter had no standing in that salty brotherhood made the matter even more curious. The ripple reached further. The *New Zealand Herald*, one sunny Monday, led off local news with the headline: AUCKLANDER PLANS SOLO CIRCUMNAVIGATION OF THE GLOBE: CITY LAWYER REFUSES TO SPEAK. Walter's secret was out. He was quoted as saying that the proposed voyage was a personal matter; that there was no more to be said. But of course there was. Otherwise I should not be struggling to get this down on paper more than ninety years later. Unsurprisingly perhaps, Walter was late for work that day. The delay may have been due to his being as engrossed in the report as any *Herald* reader. He might also have been notifying Mrs Dove of a pleasing reprieve from matrimony.

Everyone in the office was privy to the news by the time Walter arrived; there was a simmering circle of people about an already crumpled copy of the *Herald*. The group dispersed. Desks were reoccupied swiftly, with discreet shuffling and coughing. With mumbled greetings to subordinates, Walter went to his room. There was an awed pause. Finally a bell tinkled. This bell sat on his desk. It meant Alice was needed in his office. Aware of resentful whispers to her rear, Alice presented herself to her employer. 'Close the door,' he ordered. This Alice apprehensively did.

He was quick to the point. 'I daresay, Alice, that you, like most of Auckland, are aware of the tidings in this morning's newspaper.'

'It is impossible not to be, Mr Dove,' Alice said.

'I imagine you may also have an opinion on that report.'

'Not until I hear such news from you,' she explained. 'The report might not be accurate. It might be based on a misunderstanding.'

'It is tolerably truthful,' he informed her.

'In that case,' Alice said, 'I prefer to believe that you know what you are doing.'

'I trust so too,' he said.

He did not make conversation easy. Finally he said, 'Feel at liberty to refer to the subject in my presence. Let me put one fear to rest. Your employment will continue. You will share responsibility for my personal affairs, especially those involving Mrs Dove. These duties will not be demanding. On my return all will be as before.'

'That is most generous,' Alice said. After a difficult pause she added, 'There is one matter which troubles me.'

'And what might that be?'

'What, Mr Dove, if you fail to return?'

'But I shall,' Walter said.

Alice heard unwarranted confidence. She protested, 'It is a dangerous world.'

'Danger is all in the mind,' he told her. 'One cannot see it. One cannot taste or touch it.'

'But the world is real enough,' she argued.

'That also remains to be seen,' he replied.

In the course of the morning his two partners marched into his office. Raised voices were heard. 'Since when did you know the difference between port and starboard?' one challenged. The atmosphere in the office had an electric crackle; the sound of pens on paper could not have been fainter.

Within a week, though, the firm of McDowell, McDonald and Dove began to live with its implausible delinquent. Without hoisting a sail Walter Dove had become a celebrity. Journalists remained intrusive. He was pointed out as he walked in the street. Fellow passengers on the Devonport ferry nudged each other when he boarded. As he tidied his affairs and put the minds of valued clients to rest, his absences from the office became frequent and long. Much of this truancy had to do with lessons in seamanship; he was paying an old salt to supervise him as he excursioned up and down the Waitemata harbour. This proved extremely profitable for the crusty veteran. Another ancient mariner patiently put Walter through a course on the sextant, throwing in every wisp of navigational knowledge he could muster. This conscientious fellow judged rightly that Walter needed all the seafaring wisdom he could win. An inquisitive spectator fleet began following Walter as he took his tutorials. There was laughter sometimes, and unkind jeers. Many wagered on Walter succumbing to the inoffensive Waitemata before he made the acquaintance of the cold-hearted Pacific.

Alice remained fearful, more so when Walter, after months of meditation, announced a departure date: September 21, 1902. He couldn't disavow the project now without losing face. Nor did he mean to disappoint entranced fellow citizens. Walter nosed *Albatross* down harbour with modest competence and moored her on the Auckland waterfront, at the foot of Queen Street, then as now the city's main thoroughfare. There it rocked lightly while Walter stowed provisions and hard-wearing sails aboard.

His audience was now to be numbered in the thousands. Walter's critics became even more vehement. They pointed out that *Albatross* had been built for speed in sheltered water; that it was never designed to duel with ocean. Its sheer was such that there was little more than a foot of freeboard amidships. So frisky a vessel would never survive the Roaring Forties, the perils of which continued to leave Walter unmoved. The enterprise, they asserted, was more than just foolhardy; it was a fancy form of suicide.

Optimists, however, prevailed over pessimists. Most Aucklanders saw a tale likely to bewitch their grandchildren. To enrich their fireside sagas and cheer their favourite away they thronged the waterfront on September 21.

It was a bright spring afternoon. Whatever their reservations about the venture, the city's leading citizens refused to let the occasion pass without prolonged oratory. The mayor stressed that the 20th century was in its infancy and still sadly short of heroes. The mayor also recalled great British voyagers of the past, from Francis Drake to Captain Cook. Walter Dove, he argued, was of the same courageous stuff. Nor was the father of solo voyaging forgotten: Joshua Slocum's classic, *Sailing Alone Around the World*, had only just been published. His companionless triumph was fresh in memory. 'Let it be known,' the mayor said, 'that our little land has its own Joshua Slocum, a man second to none in determination.' Had Walter Dove been inspired by Slocum, as many suspected? If so he wasn't saying. Whatever his inspiration Walter was to be no South Sea facsimile of the sea-hermit Yankee; he was to provide an even more engrossing spectacle. (Not until later was a cynic heard observing that the New Englander and the New Zealander had unsympathetic wives in common: their shrewish womenfolk, it was said, must have made the sea's discomforts seem slight.)

There were few daylight hours left for *Albatross* to clear the harbour for its baptismal brush with the Pacific. There were final handshakes. Legal colleagues were among those gruffly extending good wishes. The notable absentee was Mrs Dove. Alice substituted for Walter's missing spouse with a kiss and a bouquet of roses. 'Come back,' she whispered in his ear.

'I mean to,' he said with impressive conviction.

On the mayor's call, there were three booming cheers for the daring Aucklander. Mooring lines were cast off and recovered by Walter. Sail was hoisted as *Albatross* drifted out from the wharf into uncluttered water. Observers noted that his footwork aboard was not altogether nimble. Reticent to the last about his course, Walter was away.

A flotilla of cordial yachtsmen trailed him for a time. Alice was aboard one of the craft which kept Walter company as far as North Head, the onetime Maori hilltop fortress which overlooks the entrance to Waitemata harbour. There were spectators along the shore, women waving scarves and handkerchiefs. One by one, as they met chilly breeze and choppy water, his waterborne well-wishers melted away. Shoreline spectators thinned too, until only one was visible. It was a middle-aged woman, walking the Devonport seafront as if attempting to keep pace with Walter's vessel. It had to be Mrs Dove, and was. There was no fond call across the water, no arm lifted in farewell. She was seen walking slowly homeward.

Daylight was ebbing as Walter pointed *Albatross* away from Auckland and into the Pacific. Her sails filled auspiciously; waves cracked over her hull as she found wind. The first mile was behind; the most optimistic assessment said there were 23,999 more before he saw New Zealand again. Walter was at last alone with the earth's heaving waters. Alice said she found her heart filling her throat. 'He looked so little and the world so large,' she remembered. Sixty years later a tear slowly formed and suddenly fell.

No one expected to hear from Walter in a hurry. Increasingly many did not expect to hear from him at all. Months without a word were therefore no surprise. These were the days, it needs to be stressed, when there was no radio, no marine bands, no earth-circling satellites ferrying information to seafarers. Those abroad on the ocean had to win intelligence from cloud and horizon, wind and wave. Should they misread the messages therein, there could be no SOS, Mayday call, or last words to loved ones. They would descend mute to their death.

Any communique from Walter in the short term was unlikely. He had last been seen heading east, perhaps toward South America. There is no land of significance between New Zealand and the Americas. Walter's rudimentary knowledge of navigation ensured that he had small chance of locating the little which did. There was virtually nowhere to off-load letters to Auckland. Perhaps, shunning caution, he had simply hurled himself south into the Roaring Forties; perhaps he was still contemplating the dramatic silhouettes of Tierra del Fuego, or battling with towering waves and treacherous icebergs in the vicinity of Cape Horn. For optimists there was always the possibility that some vessel calling into Auckland might set ashore a bruised, heartbroken and skeletal Walter, lately and luckily retrieved from the Pacific's jaws. Such a return would not be altogether ignoble. At least his survival would confound his critics; at least he would be alive.

Nervous Alice made her first call on Mrs Dove the day after Walter's departure. She took a ferry across the harbour and found a modest Victorian cottage on the seafront. Sinister ceramic gnomes leered from pansies in the front garden. Climbing roses wreathed the door. She anticipated a weeping wreck of a woman within. This was not the case. Mrs Dove was composed, dry-eyed, even cheerful. Alice found this difficult to manage. Serenity seemed callous with Walter just a day gone; Alice herself was still shaky. Sensing this, Mrs Dove benevolently poured her visitor a sherry.

'Well?' she said. 'Do you think he'll be back?'

'We must pray so,' Alice said.

'*You* may pray,' Mrs Dove said. 'I fear I cannot.'

Alice, a good Anglican, was shocked. 'Cannot?'

'Should I need to fall to my knees, the Lord will hear no plea for Walter's well-being.'

Alice began seeing a monster.

'My one prayer,' Mrs Dove disclosed, 'would be that he is satisfied.'

'Satisfied? In what sense?'

'In the sense that he has what he needs. Naturally I wish Walter well so long as he remains lost to view. His needs do not include me. They never have.'

'I see,' Alice said.

There was a significant silence. If there was grief in the woman, she had buried it deep.

'You are fond of my husband,' she suggested.

'I am not alone in that,' Alice replied evasively.

'But you, I think, especially,' Mrs Dove said. 'Your face says it all.'

Alice tried and failed to rearrange her current expression. 'I am much in debt to Mr Dove,' she allowed. 'I have never met a man I respect more.'

'Not even your late husband?'

Alice was slow to answer. 'Not even he,' she admitted.

Mrs Dove decided her point made; she changed course a few degrees. 'It has been difficult for everyone,' she said. 'And most of all Walter.'

'I thought him remarkably assured, these past months,' Alice said. 'He refused to hear mockery and laughter.'

'Why should he?' Mrs Dove asked. 'He is now free.'

'Free?' Alice queried. 'My impression is that he has made himself slave to wind and water.'

'I am talking of the strain of seeming worthy. I daresay you have never considered what it might have cost him to win the esteem of others.'

This was true. Alice hadn't. The notion was new. Wordless, she began seeing Walter afresh.

'Nor,' Mrs Dove added unkindly, 'were you to be aware of his weakness for a pretty face.'

Quick to her feet, now unable to leave soon enough, Alice explained that she would visit Mrs Dove regularly and see her comfortably in pocket. Mrs Dove had surprisingly little interest in the monetary details. 'So you will come again?'

'Once weekly,' Alice promised.

'Good,' Mrs Dove said. 'I mean to play bridge with friends on Monday, Wednesday and Friday. Otherwise I shall be available to visitors. Walter, you see, is not the only one free. I imagine the wicked old fake expects me to be grateful.'

'Wicked? Mr Dove?' Alice was not up to larger protest.

'Your innocence is most moving,' Mrs Dove observed.

Such was Alice's version of the encounter. Nothing suggests that she failed Mrs Dove.

More months passed, then all of a year. There was still no whisper from Walter. Not from South America, North America, or anywhere else on the globe. One spurious tale had him dwelling half-naked among the mighty icons of Easter Island. Another as absurd had him revelling with the descendants of Bounty mutineers on minuscule Pitcairn. The first anniversary of his departure—or disappearance—was marked by a newspaper article under the heading: THE MYSTERY OF THE ALBATROSS. This argued that there was still room for hope, but not much. It soon seemed that Alice alone had faith. The virtually unanimous view was that Walter had perished. Boating authorities were quoted at length. Most heartlessly asserted that Walter had courted disaster; that he had himself to blame. Dilettantes, they said, had no place on the great waters of the world; Walter Dove's ill-starred voyage served best as a cautionary tale. Nevertheless there was a crowded memorial service in the Anglican cathedral, followed by a wake organised by onetime legal colleagues in the Northern Club. Walter was recalled with respect and frequently with affection at these functions. He was too long gone for tears. And though a dark-dressed Mrs Dove was present in the cathedral, she made no attempt to play grieving widow. Nor did she exchange words with mourners more saddened. She was last seen scuttling off to her ferry.

The second anniversary of his enterprise arrived with an article headed in lesser font: NO SIGN OF CITY SEAFARER. This curtly recorded what most now knew. Optimism could no longer be justified. Not a paragraph appeared on the third anniversary: it had all been said. From time to time, when mystery wreckage was reported—on the New Zealand coast or elsewhere in the Pacific—Walter Dove was newsworthy again for a week. None of the wreckage, however, could be identified as fragments of *Albatross*. Nor did the occasional castaway seaman, uplifted from sub-antarctic island or equatorial atoll, answer to the name Dove. The lawyer was now lore.

Six years later, or the year after Walter was determined dead for legal purposes, and his will put into effect, that was still the case. Auckland's population had doubled to a hundred thousand. The city now possessed a tall town hall and the largest single-span arch bridge in the world. Suburbs were grabbing up free land. Orchards and vineyards were sweetening unkempt outskirts. By 1910 Auckland was barely recognisable as the city Walter Dove had left. Mrs Dove, no longer reliant on her husband's hand-outs, now with considerable capital of her own, lived in a grand house on the Devonport seafront. Her bridge parties had become famous. So had the accumulations of empty gin bottles put out for rubbish collectors. Alice and her daughters were also beneficiaries of Walter's will. This meant a new dwelling and a modest income. She resigned her job, when it became tactful to do so—that is, when Walter was lawfully dead and Mrs Dove no longer in need of a weekly visitor. Never lacking men friends, Alice once or twice contemplated marriage. On balance she felt widowhood desirable until her daughters were adult. With time on her hands, however, she turned back to law. She enrolled at Auckland university and became one of the first New Zealand women to win a law degree. Uncomfortable male colleagues swiftly perceived her as a menace to their profession. They were right. If women were to be allowed the run of a courtroom, no male citadel was safe. Where might it end? With unseemly feminine laughter in the precincts of the Northern Club, perhaps.

On a summer day in 1910 two teenage canoeists, in search of adventure, were paddling their leaky, home-made craft through the upper reaches of the Waitemata. That day they had more drama than they bargained for. Squeezing through mangrove forest, forcing aside stiff foliage, they found themselves in an unfamiliar stretch of water. Magically sequestered there was a vessel of substance. They cruised closer to investigate. Its name, barely legible among peeling paint, meant nothing to the boys. They had more interest in the apple, plum and peach trees set back from the tideline and generously screening the approach to the boat. The boys beached their canoe and crept stealthily into this appetising oasis. At that point a discharged shotgun made their day memorable. No matter that the shot was directed at predatory birds. They paddled off fast.

One of the boys, at family dinner that night, reported their discovery.

'A ship up there?' his father said.

'An old cutter,' the boy confirmed

'A wreck?'

'Almost sunk. And there's a guard with a gun.'

'It could be stolen. You notice its name?'

'*Albatross*,' the boy remembered.

His father was thoughtful. 'That,' he said, 'rings a bell.'

With his son as guide and a friendly constable as companion he rowed up the estuary the next day. When they ran out of tide, they abandoned their dinghy and floundered through knee-deep mud. After more turns in the maze, however, they found themselves viewing a mirage-like vessel all but high and dry among mangroves. There was a second surprise, this time in the form of a deeply tanned man of middle years with a magnificent head of white hair. Shirtless, with ragged trousers rolled to the knee, he was viewing his visitors with a whimsical eye. 'Welcome aboard, gentlemen,' he said. He directed them to a gangway and courteously extended a helping hand to each. 'You aren't unexpected,' he informed them.

'Us?' the constable said.

'Someone was bound to be along,' the fellow insisted. 'If not in one year, then another.'

'It seems to me that explanation is in order,' the suspicious constable said. 'To the best of our memory a vessel named *Albatross* went missing, with its skipper, some years ago.' The constable deduced that the matter was far from trivial. The mangrove-dweller might be a murderous felon who had cached himself away after disposing of his skipper. A pirate, no less.

'Missing?' the fellow said mildly. 'This boat?'

'Indeed,' the constable said.

'Unless appearances deceive,' the fellow went on, 'it's still doing honest service here.'

'You agree, then, that we are talking about one and the same vessel?'

'I imagine we are,' the stranger said.

'Then perhaps you could favour us with your name.'

'Guess,' Walter Dove said.

'A cheerful old cove,' the constable reported to a superior.

'And where's he been all this time?'

'Afloat, he says.'

With wind of a sensation, the press raced into conjecture. FORGOTTEN VOYAGER'S SHY RETURN, announced one breathless journal. MIRACULOUS SURVIVAL OF MODEST AUCKLANDER, declared another. Their editors would soon rue every word.

Alice remembered the world coming to a halt when she read the news. Neighbourhood noise faded. Birds became songless. Walter had done it after all. Walter, as promised, was back. She sat down slowly, newspaper in hand, and (I surmise) wept. She found it impossible to speak to her two lively daughters when they bounced in from school.

For a time Alice knew no more than any other inhabitant of Auckland. She thought it prudent not to contact Walter until uproar ebbed. Meanwhile the tidal reaches of the upper Waitemata filled with cruising sightseers hoping for a glimpse of *Albatross* and the man who sailed her. Many went aground; most returned foiled, soiled and profane.

The few who did find her had much to puzzle over. Oysters flecked her hull. Rust and rot were rife and rigging frayed. Further, a few furled shreds of mildewed canvas seemed to be all that was left of the vessel's sail. In short, there was much to suggest that *Albatross* was not newly ensconced in the estuary. This meant one of two things. That Walter had survived with unprecedented help from Providence; or that he had never cleared the New Zealand coast.

Cries of foul began drowning cheers. More so when a rural storekeeper, a mile or two inland, identified Walter as an occasional customer for years. As scepticism mounted Walter preserved a stiff silence. There was no reason for him to contribute his twopence worth to the controversy. No word of a lie had been uttered nor deceit intended; he had been afloat these past seven years, and no one could say different.

There was one further headline before Walter faded from the newspapers: YACHTING RIDDLE IRKS AUCKLANDERS. It continued to vex many, though never Alice. After some indecision she wrote a note to Walter and hoped some resourceful postman would seek him out. She had a reply after four tense days. 'Please come,' he said with urgency.

Alice had a male friend willing to arrange an overland excursion to Walter's domain. First there was a smoky train. Then there were plodding horses. Finally they came to Walter's orchard. Nay-sayers had pointed to the well-established trees—lemon and grapefruit, as well as pear, apple and peach—as evidence that Walter had been stationary for almost a decade. On high ground there was a garden where peas, beans, spinach and pumpkin flourished. Everything, in fact, a mariner might need to fight off scurvy. Now the most suspect vessel to have sailed New Zealand waters, *Albatross* sat flightless nearby. It was rolling lightly on rising tide; light rippled on its discoloured hull.

Walter rose beaming from the serene vista. As Alice told it, his seven years of shipboard life had agreed with him; he seemed not to have aged a day. He had an armful of apples, which he spilled on first sight of Alice. He gazed at her speechless as the fruit scattered. Was he thinking on how time had treated her? The apples continued to roll, slowly enough to be counted as lost years of their lives.

'Alice,' he said with unhidden pleasure.

'Mr Dove,' she said.

At this stage in her story Alice became suspiciously reticent. 'You don't need to know everything,' she protested.

'I do,' I assured her.

'People are entitled to privacy,' she claimed. 'Even if decrepit or dead.'

She was in the first category; Walter by then in the second. I assumed she was unwilling to confess that their reunion was an occasion for tears, perhaps even for sobs.

'If you won't tell me,' I warned, 'I'll make it up. Fancy might be more irritating than fact.'

'Don't threaten me,' she said angrily.

'All I want,' I pleaded, 'is a clue to what was said that day.'

There was a thoughtful silence. 'Very well, then. There was more unsaid than said.'

'I can imagine.' I said sympathetically.

'Can you? I think not.'

'Go on,' I urged.

Finally she said, 'There were business matters of course. He was literally back from the dead. His estate had been divided and dispersed. As you know, I was a beneficiary. I offered him all I had left of his legacy. My house too. He wouldn't hear of it. He said that the Walter Dove who dictated that will was long deceased. Heaven knows what arrangement, if any, he came to with Mrs Dove. She remained the wealthiest woman on the Devonport seafront. Her bridge parties became bigger still, giving her even more of a chance to show off her jewellery. Walter on the other hand scrimped and scraped, selling his fruit and vegetables and somehow managing.'

'So it's a sad story,' I suggested.

'If you're talking money,' Alice said.

She didn't volunteer more. Finally I asked, 'Is there anything else I am permitted to know?'

'Just that curiosity killed the cat,' she said.

'I don't see the point of that proverb in present circumstances,' I claimed.

'No?' she said with indifference.

'No,' I said, feebly standing my ground.

'Then a timely reminder seems in order. Even as an infant you were inquisitive to the point of gross impudence. I see no improvement.'

'Can we get on with it now?' I asked in desperation.

'Very well, then. He asked after Lucy and Jane. He wanted my girls to holiday with him.'

'Why Lucy and Jane?'

'You know perfectly well,' she asserted.

'Remind me,' I appealed.

'After his years of solo voyaging he was weary of his own company. He needed crew. First Lucy and Jane. Then you, when you came along. Of course you remember.'

'Not much,' I claimed. 'Just a half-naked old man shouting and racing around the deck. There was always pandemonium.'

This wasn't fair. Nor was it true. To part Alice from her memories, however, I was obliged to sham having few of my own; I had to be provocative.

'It is my understanding,' she said, 'that commotion is not infrequent on the high sea.'

'Alice,' I said patiently, 'we all know his voyaging was fantasy.'

'That, young man, is your view,' she said. 'It is also a libel. I regret Walter isn't here to put you in your place.'

In danger of losing her goodwill, I called that interview off. We never again divided on the authenticity of Walter's voyaging.

On that September day in 1902, after the civic farewell, Walter pointed *Albatross* out of Waitemata harbour and watched floating sympathisers and waterside cheerleaders diminish astern. Even Mrs Dove had flown. What happened then may have been spontaneous. Did second thoughts of heartstopping character win the day? Or was the manoeuvre long planned? There is evidence to support both propositions.

The outcome was the same. As light began to dim, he modified his course dramatically, tacking away from open sea and doubling back up harbour toward swampy solitude. There was no one to witness this inspired U-turn. Walter must have been careful not to quarrel with moored freighters and harbour ferries along his route. One presumes he dropped anchor at a distance from prying eyes as dusk cloaked Auckland and street-lamps were lit.

With dawn's first glimmer, the city's citizens still dreaming, he would have let the tide carry him the last miles up harbour until he sweetly eased *Albatross* on to something approximating terra firma. As the tide rose higher (by chance or choice September 21 coincided with one of the year's largest tides) Walter roped himself to *Albatross* and towed her foot by foot, inch by inch, yet further into seclusion. There, in a cloud of foliage, he moored her forever. There he remained for the rest of his life. That is, for more than four decades. End of story? Never, Alice would say. Never.

'You always did miss the point,' she added.

The point she was making, and I was missing, was that Walter was no fraud. An illusionist perhaps, an escape merchant who made Houdini look mediocre. But a fraud? Never.

Walter's marshy Eden was soon a second home for Alice and her daughters. Lucy and Jane were with Walter for school holidays. They bunked in the foredeck; Alice, when aboard, in the stern. With female company, Walter camped under canvas on the deck; he also wore clothes, not always his custom.

No matter that the vessel seldom moved more than inches, that never a sail filled with breeze. Walter delighted in playing Captain Bligh, roaring orders into high wind as ocean foamed around them. There was no mutter of mutiny from his crew. They loyally survived polar tempest and tropic hurricane; they drifted in equatorial calms under starlit sky. Lucy and Jane were soon reading charts, familiarising themselves with perilous shores, and determining their next port of call. When the pirates of the Celebes Sea weren't menacing, and whale herds no hazard off the Falklands, Walter left the girls with the helm while he prepared nourishing meals on the kerosene stove in his galley. His no-frill cuisine was based on vegetables from his garden and fish netted from neighbouring creeks. His originality in the galley was reserved for enterprises with rotten apples. Years before the world heard of penicillin, Walter persuaded himself of the life-enhancing properties of mould. He ate only blackening morsels of apple, discarding anything remotely rosy. He even let his porridge grow fungus before devouring it with relish. Jars of vegetable matter, in advanced states of disrepair, filled galley shelves. From these he devised remedies which people later swore by. Hardy Walter was testimony to his own medication. He simply ceased ageing, especially with Lucy and Jane aboard.

How often did they circumnavigate the globe with Walter in those spellbinding years? Even Joshua Slocum managed it only the once. They lost track after the first score circuits. There was an end to it, of course. Lucy and Jane soon left adolescence behind; they were suddenly young ladies with another life on land. Male friends began to make an appearance. Two turned into husbands. Then came babies. Difficulty of access meant the girls visited less and annually at most. So passed the 1920s. In that decade middle-aged Alice judged herself ready for matrimony again. She finally exchanged vows with a banker of sober and practical disposition, a man seemingly both safe and solvent. The flaw in the arrangement, not detected until after their nuptials, was that he was as opinionated as Alice. In other respects too he fell short of expectation, not least when he expressed his wish that she abandon the courtroom for the kitchen; he couldn't have associates saying that he lived off his wife. The end, never far off from the first day of marriage, finally came when he raised objections to her continuing concern for Walter. He couldn't see what she saw in the failed imposter. Later in life, in response to my impudent query, she failed to recall how her second marriage happened. Her one attempt at explanation was not especially persuasive. 'I rather think I felt sorry for him,' she decided.

'You?' I said. 'Sorry?'

'Men are quite as entitled as women to have someone feel sorry for them. Life isn't easy for them, as I daresay you know. Not the least of their woes is that they are obliged to put up with women. I wouldn't change sex for all the tea in China, not even all the coffee in Brazil.'

'This is revolutionary, coming from you.'

'I see no reason why I should withhold my sympathies from half the human race.'

There were times when Alice left me speechless. This was one of them. My silence lengthened.

'You were asking to explain my remarriage,' she reminded me.

'I was,' I agreed, leaning forward with anticipation.

'As you may or may not be aware,' she informed me, 'wedlock was once rather the fashion.'

Marital estrangement allowed her freedom to visit Walter more often. Seeing him despondently solo again, she rummaged among relatives for children who might serve as a substitute crew. 'I was a one-woman press gang,' she explained. 'I was like those navy recruiters, in Lord Nelson's time, who biffed unwary men on the head in dark alleys and carried them off senseless to serve their country.'

Alice didn't loiter in dark alleys with the intention of rendering junior relatives unconscious. Nevertheless she had an unsympathetic response from the parents she approached. They had no intention of allowing their little ones to holiday with a lunatic in a waterlogged vessel parked in unlovely swamp. Walter was a proven liar and possibly a paedophile. They were unmoved by Alice's assertion that Walter would broaden the horizons of their offspring as no school could. The answer was always no. Walter remained crewless.

That was still the case when I was born. My young brother bawled into the world soon after. My mother had an enfeebling time of it with his birth. Her condition was compounded by a malevolent spot on her lung. That meant a sanatorium.

With sons to feed and clothe, my father required rescue. Alice stepped in. She announced that she would take charge of my year-old brother. As for me, she knew just the place for a weepy four-year-old. She was, of course, killing two birds with one stone. Walter had a first mate and I had a third parent. And we cruised off together. This had disadvantages. My landlubber parents were soon people in a foreign port of call, speaking an unintelligible tongue. My father was preoccupied with my ailing mother and visited me seldom. My mother was the feeble woman Alice fetched me to see once a month. 'My poor little boy,' my parent would say, beginning to sob.

Poor? Me? Her tears were incomprehensible. I was literally having the time of my life. Huck Finn's adventures with Nigger Jim on the Mississippi, or Sancho Panza's with Don Quixote, were as nothing to mine with Walter. It was a relief to escape the inhospitable sanatorium to rendezvous with Uncle Walter, as he allowed himself called when not at the helm. (On watch he had to be addressed Skipper.) He always arranged an arduous itinerary after a sanatorium visit. My mother's tears would be forgotten as we cruised close to Africa's shadowy shore in humid twilight. 'Smell the wild jungle flowers,' he urged. 'Go on. Smell them.'

I did, and the blooms of Borneo and Tahiti too.

Though memory makes it longer, it seems I crewed with Walter less than two years. I was suddenly of an age for school. My mother was out of the sanatorium. It was time to pack my nautical kit-bag and pick up my seaman's papers (testifying to my competence under sail and recommending me to future employers). As my father and Alice whisked me off in a car (a road having at last breached Walter's fastness) my late skipper stood on the foredeck waving farewell. I imagined I might be back when school and parents permitted. Walter knew better. He knew it was over, his voyaging as much as mine. The decades had taken their toll of ship and skipper. Rot had dug still further into *Albatross*; leaks were many and the deck unsound. As for the skipper, a doctor had diagnosed another kind of decay. In early 1938 Walter Dove disappeared a second time. This journey didn't allow for a U-turn. Obituaries were brief and contradictory. One journalist, confused by old clippings, went so far as to say that Walter Dove had been the least celebrated solo voyager of all time. This was not altogether erroneous. Had Alice or I been asked, we might have said much the same. Meanwhile suburban scavengers boarded and plundered *Albatross* for what it was worth. They found no more than timber and metal.

In the late 1960s, not long before her own life ended, I had an enlightening and sometimes exhilarating week with Alice. I was just back from Europe, after several years away. During those years, to no one's surprise, I materialised as a novelist. Through childhood, adolescence and youth I had been seen by friends and relatives as a resourceful liar, a shifty teller of tales tall enough to overshadow my many shortcomings. My first book, just published in London and New York, confirmed that my storytelling tic was likely incurable.

What did I want from Alice? The makings of a novel? One which drew on a luminous episode of childhood? Though I was never to write it, I must have had one in mind. I had still to admit to Alice that my journeys with Walter continued to colour my life. Perhaps she knew so already. Perhaps she knew, long before I did, that one yarn-spinner had handed the helm to another.

Meanwhile I sat patiently with Alice until she thought to surrender a fact or an old woman's fancy. She delighted in delaying matters. She especially enjoyed outwitting my tape recorder with long pauses and inaudible mutters. Though she wished Walter on record, her feelings were mixed. She had to be persuaded that I would do Walter justice. It worried her that I pried more than seemly. She was, after all, still an Edwardian woman.

'There's something missing,' I complained.

'Like what?'

'Motive,' I said. 'I have no motive for Walter. Nothing to suggest why he did what he did, lived as he lived.'

'No?' she said rather coolly.

'No,' I insisted. 'There has to be more.'

'Authors are a pestilential species,' she announced. 'Why fret about motive? Why prey on the man? He wasn't a murderer.'

'Motive might light my way a little,' I suggested.

She wasn't impressed. 'Was he or was he not a success in what he did?'

'One could argue so,' I said cautiously.

'Then argue so,' she urged. 'When you have lived as long as I have, young man, you realise that human beings, both wise and foolish, seldom make sense. The miracle is that now and then someone does.'

'Meaning Walter did?'

'He did,' she said.

This had finality.

'But there *is* more to it, isn't there?' I persisted.

There was a lengthy silence.

Finally she said, 'Why don't you drive me out there? To Walter's old hideout?'

Though suspecting that this might be a ploy to put me off the scent, I did. Finding the right estuary wasn't easy. The city's population was now a half million and promising to double yet again. A tall bridge now spanned Waitemata harbour. Waterside land had been bulldozed for new suburbs. There were loops of road and patches of low-cost housing. Blundering from one cul-de-sac to another that warm afternoon, we finally sighted familiar contours.

'Here,' she said with authority. 'Stop.'

I parked the car and helped her out. We didn't walk far. Alice wasn't agile enough to descend to sea level. We looked down on the serene backwater where *Albatross* once sat, where Walter Dove whipped up hurricanes, strange lands and high adventure. Alice's one concession to age was a walking stick. She used it with spirit that afternoon, pointing out half-lost landmarks. A few arthritic fruit trees persisted where Walter's orchard and garden formerly prospered. Alice also drew my gaze to scraps of timber, all that was left of *Albatross*, and for that matter of Walter, among aromatic mire. We sat in the shade of a roadside tree and drank tea from a thermos. The day was peaceful. The sound of traffic was indistinct in the distance. There were silent yachts down harbour.

'He's still about,' she decided.

'In a way,' I said tactfully.

There was a long silence.

'What do you have to starboard?' she asked.

'Africa,' I told her. 'Wild jungle flowers. Smell them. Go on.'

She sniffed thoughtfully. 'Indeed,' she decided.

'What do you have to port, then?' I asked.

She was reluctant to say. 'I am not,' she replied, 'going to make this easy for you.'

'I never imagined you were,' I said.

'Good,' she said. 'Ask what you want while I'm tolerable company.'

I plunged in. 'All right,' I said. 'I'll tell you what I think. You tell me where I'm wrong.'

'Very well,' she sighed.

'You were Walter's motive.'

'Me?'

'You.'

To my surprise, she received this in silence.

I went on nervously, 'Walter, from the time he took you under his wing, and into his office, found his longing for you more and more excruciating. And all but impossible to hide.'

'Longing?'

'Lust, then.'

Alice protested, rather weakly, 'Must you? Must you see sex in everything?'

I found the courage to continue. 'I might,' I admitted, 'have said affection. But I think we are talking lust. It would have been Walter's word for his difficulty. It went against the grain of his life. A wife without respect for him made matters even more dire. His marital situation was hopeless; his feeling for you impossible to acknowledge. Aside from anything else, you were in your early twenties, he in his forties. He couldn't have taken advantage of you had he lived a hundred years. I also suspect that, having found the philanderer in himself, he may even have been suicidal. But rather than cut his throat he bought a boat and charted a course to nowhere. It was an enterprising response. Some might say honourable.'

I looked to Alice for confirmation or correction. I found neither. A lone tear drifted down her face.

'I suppose you think yourself smart,' she said.

We sat on the roadside as the afternoon cooled, as silvery tide found a path through amphibious trees. Alice didn't speak. At length I did.

'There is,' I began, 'something else I shouldn't ask.'

'I can't imagine what it could be,' she said tersely.

'I rather think you do,' I suggested.

'Go on, then. Ask.'

'Was there ever anything between you and Walter?'

'Anything?' she asked.

'Of an intimate nature.'

There I stumbled. There I stopped. Alice, with startling generosity, came to my rescue.

'Make love?' she said. 'Is that what you're asking? Did we ever make love? Is that it?'

'I suppose it is,' I replied weakly.

'The world belongs to the imaginative. That, you may recall, appeared to be Walter's belief.'

'That isn't an answer.'

'Let me put it another way, then. You said there was more to the story. More than you could see.'

'True,' I agreed.

'There was more,' she confessed.

An old woman's hand felt shakily for my chin. She tilted my face upward until my eyes met hers. She was smiling.

'What do you mean by more?' I asked.

'A splendidly libidinous week in the Caribbean,' she said.

The Simple Life

A health warning first. This is a 1960s story. Those who see the decade as solely noxious may stop reading here. Those who persist are promised that the Beatles won't feature in this narrative. Nor will marijuana, rock festivals, flower people, carnage in Vietnam and anti-war mayhem around the globe. In respect of cacophony, New Zealand was a match for most countries.

Don Fox acquainted Rex Heath with his vision at an otherwise forgettable Auckland exhibition in 1967. Both cut a dash in the art world. Don was a dealer, Rex an art historian.

'You ever thought about land?' Don asked confidentially.

'Land?' Rex said, briefly baffled.

'Owning some.'

'Me?'

'Not necessarily solo,' Don said. 'In company with others.'

Rex continued to stare blankly. 'What prompts this?' he asked.

'I'm thinking about picking some up,' Don explained.

'You?' Rex laughed. 'Land? What the hell for?'

'As an antidote to urban ills. The simple life isn't to be sneered at. It might do your soul good too.'

Don's overture was not especially startling, not in those years. Environmental movers and shakers were on the march, the banners of the small-is-beautiful brigade floating above; communes urban and rural were multiplying. Those struggling to stay abreast of the times sometimes shook off cosmopolitan comforts to reappear as barefoot gurus or solemn disciples of same.

Don's proposal, however, stopped short of modish extremes. 'I've got a secular retreat in mind,' he divulged cheerfully. 'Nothing too showy. A few acres and a farmhouse, preferably near water. And no television or telephone.'

'You mean a weekend place?'

'More than that.'

'How much more?'

'I'm thinking of a site where some of us can kick ideas around informally. An open-ended symposium in which disciplines could be shared. A syndicate leavened with selected guests.'

'Hang on,' Rex asked. 'Are we talking a commune here?'

'Not of the unkempt kind currently favoured. No drugs. No orgies. Music strictly of a non-psychedelic kind. Nothing immoderate.'

'You're serious?' Rex said with some awe.

'I've been giving it thought,' Don admitted.

'And why are you telling me?'

'I see a possible accomplice.'

'Wrong man. I milked too many cows when I was a kid.'

'You?'

'On my father's farm. I had a talent for warming my feet in fresh cow dung on frosty mornings.'

'Let me set your mind to rest,' Don said. 'No cows. I promise.'

'So what are you on about?'

'A second chance to make sense of ourselves. A connection with our pioneer beginnings.'

'It still sounds suspiciously like cow turd to me.'

'So see it as an investment. Something solid underfoot. As Mark Twain said, no one's making any more of it.'

'Any more of what?' said a female voice to their rear.

The eavesdropper was Janette, Rex's blonde wife, rather giddy with wine.

'Don's got a plan for spiritual resurrection.'

'So what's new?' she said.

'He thinks we've lost our way,' Rex explained. 'He wants us back on the land.'

Janette shrieked. 'Marvellous,' she said. 'Do we leave tomorrow or when?'

But Don had to be taken seriously. Impressed by rumours of a colourful initiative on the cultural front, several Aucklanders involved with the arts were volunteering interest in the project. While they consulted bank managers, Don looked over land north and south. Though he remained laconic, Rex kept Don company on these dusty excursions. At Don's insistence Janette came along too. A recently rehabilitated sexist, Don nobly held that women should have a say in the project. Since Don was between marriages, without even a casual companion, Janette was a useful presence. With his wife standing in for womanhood, Rex was entangled too. His wry view of country life counted for nothing. It might help, Don said, to have a sympathetic cynic aboard.

Their search for a property ended on a warm Saturday in September. After a long drive on a rough road they looked down on a river wandering between mangroves into a sprawling harbour called the Kaipara. Its fretted shore was meagrely populated with perhaps a half-dozen rooftops nested among surviving fragments of forest. According to Don's guide book, the highly tidal harbour had been settled a century earlier by a dour religious sect hoping to shame and eclipse ungodly Auckland. When this ambition faltered, the strait-laced migrants prospered by toppling the trees of the region and shipping out timber. Then they burned their way across the hills, scattered grass seed, brought in livestock and bred robust children. A few of their original homesteads survived attractively among blossoming apple groves.

Elation dawned on Don's face. 'Something tells me this is it,' he announced.

There was no doubt about it: the locale magically conformed to Don's original prescription. Taking hazardous bends with care, he pointed the car downhill.

Janette, in the back seat, thought it time to have her statutory say.

'It looks a little on the quiet side,' she complained.

'That's the idea,' Don said patiently. 'We'll put the world's bedlam behind us.'

'Famous last words,' Rex was tempted to say, familiar with the poignant history of communes. He failed to say it. He failed to say anything. He was almost as impressed as Don.

Don parked alongside a once handsome homestead with ornamental turrets and verandahs framed with elegant woodwork. The cavernous dwelling had been the country retreat of a colonial politician who piously championed the rights of small farmers; his show of virtue, however, had been blighted by fraudulent land transactions and a shotgun suicide. His forsaken realm was fringed with straggling pines and an elderly orchard. Sheep no longer grazed the surrounding hills. Smashed windows confirmed that there was no one resident. There was a weathered For Sale sign among weeds. Breakneck competition for the locale wasn't evident. The sign had a sad lean.

Don was fast inside. His fellow adventurers were quiet as they moved through the building, gingerly sidestepping rat droppings and brushing cobwebs aside. They marvelled at splendidly panelled interiors and decoratively plastered ceilings, the legacy of Edwardian craftsmen. Windows, when forced open, were rich in vistas of sea and sandbank, harbour and headland.

'Is this it or is it not?' Don asked with a grin of triumph.

Rex found the last of his reservations melting. Nor did Janette disclose further qualms. The price of the property was comfortably within range. Space wasn't an issue either; there were enough rooms for a dozen or more people to bed in privacy. With partners recruited, dollars counted and documents signed, they took possession before spring gave way to summer.

'So what do we do with ourselves now?' Janette asked.

Don enlightened them. What they did was forgo summer's languid pleasures in favour of drudgery. The homestead rose afresh through din and dust. The kitchen was soon sanitary. Even the antique toilets were flushing reliably. Most energetic of the toilers were Jim Frost and his wife Sally. Jim was an Aquarian-age architect who mixed mantras with the materials of his calling. Seasoned hitch-hikers on enlightenment's highway, home after a term in the monastery-studded Himalayas, Jim and Sally saw potential in Don's colony. To the relief of less metaphysical companions, Jim proved a fastidious handyman. They were soon followed by the novelist Mike Piper and his longtime consort Charlotte, a poet of willowy form and waspish disposition. Mike was currently warring with a writer's block. It was Charlotte's belief that a little hard labour, and a little less literary suffering, might be the making of him. More charitably, she pointed out that weekends in the Kaipara Collective might provide him with material sufficiently entertaining to kick-start his career. The project deserved a candid chronicler.

'To blow the whistle on it?' he asked.

'Satirically,' she suggested.

'What do you think I am?' he asked.

'A novelist,' she smiled sweetly.

Mike took a long walk.

At this point a serpent was due to put in an appearance. Nothing reptilian did. (New Zealand has no snakes anyway.) Nor did their maiden misfortune derive from adjacent humans: their near neighbours were few, quiet-living and tolerant. Though they wondered at the urban newcomers—the long-haired men in stylish denim and leather, the women vivid in kaftans and bandannas—these conservative country folk were never noticeably hostile. Nor did the collective's inaugural woe emanate from their informal domestic arrangements. Though opportunity was seldom lacking, no one stumbled into the wrong bed. Their weekends remained civilized. There were picnics and parties and envious visitors from the city.

One midsummer weekend the place was left empty. Everyone in the syndicate had reason to remain in Auckland. Rex and Janette didn't arrive in until the following Friday. A burglar had been busy. Everything of value, and much that wasn't, had been carried away. There was mindless vandalism on the side, human excrement on the floor.

Their associates were as sickened when they arrived in.

'I blame myself,' Don announced. 'It's just that this place seemed so tranquil, so far from the city. I should have thought.'

'We all should,' Rex insisted.

This was at a downcast conference.

'There's only one question to be asked,' Jim Frost said. 'Do we stick it out or call it quits?'

'That's drastic,' Rex suggested.

'Our situation is damn drastic,' Jim argued. 'We'll always be easy pickings.'

Don was unable to hide his dismay. Janette had gone to weep in a corner. Sally was trying to salvage trampled flower beds. 'Perhaps it was too good to last,' she sighed. Charlotte was content to observe events with a cool eye.

Rex saw the enterprise foundering. The spineless group view favoured giving up without a fight. Mike, with frequent obscenities, was already packing away books and manuscripts which had survived the uncivilized blitz.

'Did they make off with the masterpiece?' Charlotte asked. She meant Mike's constipated novel.

'Just a chapter the bastard commandeered for toilet paper,' he reported.

'Ah,' Charlotte said. 'Not just a burglar. An enlightened critic.'

'It's no time to parade personal grievances,' Jim said. 'Try a little meditation when you're tempted.'

Charlotte's expression said that meditation wasn't on her agenda.

'What we need,' Rex decided abruptly, 'is some kind of caretaker.'

'Caretaker?' Mike said. 'Who? Some local?'

'Perhaps.'

'A kindly neighbour wouldn't be enough,' Jim pointed out. 'The place would still be vulnerable most of the week.'

'So use your imagination,' Rex challenged.

'Like how?'

'We have a barn which could be made comfortable.'

'For what? For who?'

'The right person. Someone happy to caretake in our absence.'

'In exchange for rent-free accommodation?'

'You're getting the idea,' Rex said.

'And who is the right person likely to be?'

'I think we'd all feel better if it was someone needy.'

'Would we?' Mike said dubiously. 'It's news to me that we're running a charity.'

'As a matter of fact, an indigent painter or writer might serve circumstances best. Someone we think worthwhile.'

'Whoever it is, we'd have to take a vote on it,' Mike insisted.

Don and Rex were off on another tack.

'Eddie Moorhouse,' they said as one.

'Eddie?' Mike said.

'He might be our man.'

'That doomy bugger?' Mike said with disbelief. His feuds with Eddie were classics of their kind. There had been serious fisticuffs at a recent gallery function.

Rex thought it time for his two cents' worth. 'Beggars can't be choosers,' he pointed out. 'Besides which, no one can argue that Eddie isn't worthy.'

'Try me,' Mike said.

Eddie Moorhouse's reputation remained a source of anxiety. Another was that both Don and Rex had a vested interest in their nominee. Don was Eddie's dealer. Rex was writing a book on Eddie's paintings. Eddie, however, had been faltering as a painter for some time. Long the despair of dealers anyway, he was in a creative slide which didn't promise a soft landing. Once-ardent buyers of his enigmatic paintings, often on unfashionable biblical themes, now saw them as a poor investment. The possible publisher of Rex's book had begun backtracking. Though loyal friends and sympathetic connoisseurs continued to think otherwise, Eddie's icons were now often written off as quaint and anachronistic and lacking cool. In short, said some, it was time that Eddie got real. Such naysayers gave Eddie reason to remain sour and silent. It was Rex's view that a therapeutic move to the country might modify Eddie considerably. Rural New Zealand wasn't rife with distractions. Save for visits from female friends—of whom Eddie had notoriously many—he should have little but his work to contemplate.

The vote, with Mike abstaining, was for an approach to Eddie. It was also felt that prudent Rex was the man to make the overture. Diplomacy was needed. After all, they weren't offering Eddie much. In return for playing sentry he would have a barn big enough for a studio and living quarters. Draughts were few and leaks inconspicuous. Eddie had survived worse.

'I hope the bugger's grateful,' Mike said.

Gratitude wasn't evident the day Rex drove Eddie north to the Kaipara. Pleasantries weren't Eddie's forte. Nor was conversation beyond a few surly sounds. Tall, lanky and wispily bearded—as melancholic as some accident-prone Old Testament luminary—Eddie was unlikely to terminate his feud with the world on the strength of a helping hand from either a dealer or a wordy commentator on his work. Eddie made no secret of his conviction that dealers were crooked and critics corrupt. Even his public was suspect.

Wandering this way and that, Eddie saw all he needed in no more than ten minutes.

'Pretty grandiose for a weekend place,' he observed.

'Generously proportioned,' Rex acknowledged.

'And all this land too?'

'All this land too,' Rex agreed.

'You got plans for it?'

'As I've been trying to tell you.'

It was plain that Eddie hadn't heard a word.

'For some of us it was love at first sight,' Rex persisted.

'It's a sweet piece of real estate,' Eddie agreed with unusual warmth. 'You reckon you're up to making more of it?'

'We wouldn't be here if we didn't think so,' Rex said.

Eddie was silent for a time.

'All right,' he said suddenly.

'All right?' Rex asked.

'I'll take it on,' Eddie said.

It was too easy to be true. 'We'd like you to be sure of it, Eddie. Would you like time to think?'

'I've thought,' Eddie said with impatience.

With Eddie about, if seldom visible, the amiable atmosphere began to erode. Privacy was gone, liberty lacking. Charlotte was first to complain. 'He seems to be watching us all the time from his window,' she said.

'He isn't a sex maniac,' Don protested.

'I wouldn't put money on it,' Charlotte said.

Charlotte now sunbathed at a distance from the homestead. Janette and Sally tended to take long walks. Their menfolk didn't permit themselves to be inconvenienced. They turned their backs, drank beer and built a brick barbecue pit to Jim's design. Don's freewheeling seminars weren't the same either. Those contributing could never not be aware of Eddie nearby, perhaps eavesdropping unseen in the dusk and mocking them silently. He had let it be known that symposiums didn't turn him on; that he had more on his mind.

Rex and Don took this as promising. Was Eddie hinting that he was contemplating paints and brushes again?

Winning Eddie's goodwill was Rex's chore. No one else found the nerve; even Don soon lost it. When in weekend residence, Rex sauntered over to Eddie's renovated barn to say hello; he usually returned no wiser.

Don would be waiting anxiously on Rex's report.

'Any signs of activity over there?' he asked.

'Nothing conspicuous,' Rex said. 'Not even a drawing?'

'Not even a drawing.'

'So what's he doing with himself, then?'

'Thinking,' Rex reported.

'Thinking?'

'He does a lot of it,' Rex explained.

On one level Eddie was a useful acquisition. There were no further burglaries. On another the cure began to seem worse than the complaint. Mike and Charlotte were the first to become irregular weekenders. This was not entirely due to Mike's differences with Eddie. Sensitive to loss of privacy, Charlotte's unease continued to mount. She and Mike began finding it convenient to stay in town and take in a movie. Jim and Sally weren't slow following their example, though their preference was for gatherings of fellow seekers of spiritual truth.

Rex saw a messy altercation coming. Jim Frost stirred the pot. Never at a loss in matters otherworldly, Jim believed Eddie's unnerving gaze held the clue to his condition. 'The Greeks know how to manage the evil eye,' he said.

'The evil eye? Eddie?'

'Who else? Note how he watches us. The Greeks carry blue glass and say *ftou ftou ftou* three times to ward off danger.'

Rex was baffled. 'Three times?'

'Or more,' Jim said.

Rex was unable to express himself usefully.

Minus blue glass and *ftou ftou ftou* in triplicate, Rex risked a repeat call on Eddie. The supposed proprietor of the evil eye was benignly planting out tomato seedlings in freshly turned soil. A potato patch already prospered nearby. As a voyeur Eddie seemed to find the reproductive feats of plants more engrossing than Charlotte at her provocative best.

'This is a surprise,' Rex observed, and meant it.

'Land isn't for lazing around on,' Eddie replied mysteriously.

He left it to Rex to decipher this. Otherwise his conversation was mostly to do with peas and beans and the horrors of pesticide. He impressed Rex further with a fish smoker conjured up from corrugated iron and wire netting. Two fat mullet coloured aromatically within.

Don, as usual, was waiting on news.

'His garden's well away,' Rex reported.

'Garden?' Don said. 'What garden?'

'He's not doing badly for fish either.'

'Bloody hell,' Don said. 'You see anything resembling a brush in his hand?'

'Think on the bright side,' Rex said. 'At least he's not in crucifixion mode.'

'It's no joke,' Don protested.

Rex was soon to agree.

A family funeral in the south took Rex and Janette away from the Kaipara collective for two weekends. On their midweek return there was a telephone call from Don's gallery. Don was aggrieved. 'You're a great bloody help,' he grumbled. 'Where are you when we need you?'

'What's wrong now?'

'Eddie again. He's running sheep on our property. Sheep, for God's sake. Most of a hundred ewes and an extremely promiscuous ram. There's even a dog yelping infernally around. Eddie's hard to find. It seems he's out clearing scrub and repairing fences most days. I hardly need remind you that he's making free with our acres.'

Rex took this calmly. 'It's not the end of the world,' he suggested.

'At the moment it's a pretty fair likeness.'

'Come on,' Rex pleaded.

'It changes the character of the place,' Don grumbled. 'When we put our money up, we weren't investing in a Shangri-la for bloody sheep.'

'I recall you having something to say about the virtue of the simple life. It should be gratifying to know your message hasn't fallen on deaf ears.'

'Don't remind me,' Don groaned.

'So what do you want me for?' Rex asked.

'Protection. In the event that Eddie doesn't see reason.'

'Now?' Rex said.

'Now,' Don said urgently.

'Can't it wait?'

'Not until next weekend. By then he might be getting off on goats too.'

'All right,' Rex sighed.

Don drove north at considerable speed, dust billowing behind.

As they left the car and approached the homestead, there were unfamiliar sounds. The most prominent were from sheep picturesquely grazing hillside. Then a rooster crowed close to hand; there was a chorus of hens. Rex looked at Don with a silent query.

'You hear right,' Don informed him. 'In case you haven't noticed, there's already shit on your shoes.'

Eddie proved more sociable than usual, which wasn't saying much. Don was nervously silent. Rex did his best to explain their visit.

'We feel that you're taking too much upon yourself,' he told Eddie tactfully.

'Too much?'

'Of a menial nature. Well beyond the call of duty.'

'What's that supposed to mean?'

'There's no need to work yourself into a lather on the property. The idea was to give you freedom to paint.'

'Was it?' Eddie said with indifference.

'Come on, Eddie. You know it was.'

'I know who gets a 33 per cent commission on my paintings. And who wants a book out of me. No one's doing me favours.'

'Let's stick to the point,' Rex proposed.

'I am,' Eddie claimed. 'Someone has to set an example. It's a hungry world. It's a sin to leave good land barren.'

This left Don speechless. Finally he said, 'We're a collective, Eddie. We take votes. It might be that a majority wants things much as they are.'

'So what are you telling me?' Eddie asked.

'To take it easy. No one begrudges you an outdoor interest. But not to excess.'

'Nothing gets done without a bit of excess,' Eddie argued.

Rex and Don were soon on their way back to the city.

'There's a word for this,' Don said. 'Hijack.'

'Too extravagant.'

'So how would you describe it?'

Rex shrugged silently.

'We'll have to think again, Don judged. 'I could lose Eddie from my stable.'

'Possibly,' Rex allowed.

'Especially if we give him his marching orders. We could be the laugh of Auckland.'

Don remained thoughtful for the rest of the ride.

Another weekend neared. Rex watched its approach with apprehension. A messy showdown looked likely. Tireless on his gallery telephone, Don ensured that all in the syndicate would be present. On the Saturday morning there was anguished debate. Jim Frost was unusually resonant. He saw months of sweat down the drain. His current enterprise, a gazebo rich in astral symbols, might soon be mired in a earthly tide of animal waste. Finally a vote was taken. The resolution was to the effect that, though Eddie's pastoral toil was appreciated, he was to stop tampering with the land until pros and cons had been considered. Yet again Don and Rex were thought best qualified to bear this message. As they were reminded, they were accountable for the current impasse; they had backed Eddie as caretaker.

Rather than argue, the two set off in the direction of Eddie's barn. The door was open; there was no one at home. They headed inland, following a creek. They heard chopping, vegetation falling. 'Eddie?' Rex called. 'Eddie?'

Finally Eddie rose from scrub on the far side of the creek. He had a slasher in hand, a grubby hat on his head and sweat on his brow.

'What is it now?'

'We have to talk.'

'We've talked,' Eddie pointed out.

'Not to lasting effect.'

'Let me guess. You want me out.'

'It's not gone that far. But it could.'

'I just might get difficult,' Eddie warned.

'What's that mean?' Don dared to ask.

'This,' Eddie said. He gathered stones near his feet and began firing them off efficiently. Don was too mesmerised to move. The first missile bounced off his shoulder. Rex ducked beneath the second.

'Eddie,' he pleaded.

'Think of your book,' Eddie urged. 'This might be the best chapter.'

Rex didn't hear. He and Don were leaping left and right as more stones flew.

'He what?' Mike said with disbelief.

'Heaved a rock or two at us,' Rex said. He was already making light of the episode.

'Sweet Jesus,' Mike said. 'What next?'

Jim favoured a truce. 'Let's cool off for a week. At least until we see where we're at.'

'With stones flying out of the wildwood?' Charlotte sniffed.

'No one's seriously at risk,' Rex claimed. 'We just happened to be in the way.'

'You could say that about the population of Hiroshima,' Don said.

'Come on,' Rex said. 'Let's keep things in perspective. It was just a couple of pebbles and a boyish bout of bad temper. Eddie will soon be over with an apology. He's on to a good thing here. He's not going to ruin it.'

'No?' Charlotte said.

Eddie made no appearance with an apology, not that weekend, nor the one following. On that weekend the atmosphere at first seemed serene. Rex saw an unfamiliar car parked under shady trees. A fluttering feminine laugh confirmed that Eddie had a city visitor. That was hopeful. A sympathetic woman might persuade Eddie that there was more to life than masquerading as a wronged peasant.

There was another landowners' meeting at the homestead. Rex was again pushed to confer with Eddie. Still in shock, Don declined to provide Eddie with a target a second time. After an eloquent nod from Charlotte, Mike Piper reluctantly volunteered to keep Rex company. 'Let me make one thing clear,' he said. 'There's nothing in this for me.

I didn't boost the bugger. He was your problem.'

'We're getting the message,' Charlotte informed him. 'You're about to become the man of the hour.'

Brushing greenery aside, Mike and Rex took the meandering path to the barn again. Though the day was cool with approaching autumn, Mike was fast in a sweat.

'Eddie?' Rex began calling.

Foliage parted and Eddie stood exposed. He was much as Rex had last seen him, with one difference. This time Eddie had a double-barrelled shotgun over his arm. Mike couldn't take his eyes off it. Nor, for that matter, could Rex. No one was in a hurry to speak.

'No,' Rex whispered. 'No, Eddie.'

'Yes,' Eddie insisted. He took two cartridges from a pocket and loaded both barrels of the firearm. 'It keeps birds away a treat,' he added. 'It might do the same for two-legged interlopers.'

To demonstrate, he discharged a barrel skyward. Birds scattered. Humans weren't slow either. Rex and Mike covered thirty yards before they heard the second barrel fired. Soon afterwards there was the sound of engines revving and vehicles departing. Two collided in the race for the road out. Their drivers didn't stop to determine the damage.

With enough miles to their rear, there was a roadside council of war. The shotgun was still ringing in their ears. Some less hazardous strategy was needed. Voices were shaky. Women were still disabled with fright. Don was smoking one of Mike's cigarettes. Don hadn't been seen smoking in years.

'We've got to shut up about this,' he said.

'You mean keep it a secret?' Jim said.

'No one wants to advertise it, surely,' Don said.

'The law's on our side,' Mike protested.

Rex weighed in. 'Nothing else will be,' he said.

'What's that mean?'

'Only Eddie will come out of this clean.'

'Eddie? How?'

'The role's written for him,' Rex pointed out. 'The persecuted prophet. The beleaguered artist. The culture hero shrugging off philistine shackles. We won't look pretty.'

'I played no part in provoking him,' Charlotte informed the assembly. 'My conscience is clear.'

'That's a relief to us all,' Mike said bitterly.

'It'll leak out,' Jim said. 'It can't be a secret for long.'

'We don't have to hurry it out of hiding either,' Rex suggested.

'Hang on,' Jim said. 'There's more to this than keeping it quiet. There's also the money we've invested in the property.'

'That's true,' Rex sighed.

'Well? Are we going to walk away from it?'

'It may require negotiation,' Rex allowed. 'In the end the fine print is on our side; it says we own it.'

'Negotiation? With that bloody madman?'

'There must be an alternative,' Jim argued.

'There is,' Rex agreed. 'We buy shotguns and cartridges and attack at dawn.'

It didn't come to that, of course. Not before time (that is, a week of heartburn later) Rex recalled that Eddie had a brother of quiet and conventional character, an Anglican clergyman. Estranged from his embarrassing brother, the Reverend Henry Moorhouse, when contacted, proved difficult to shock. Years earlier he had succeeded in remaining silent when Eddie's paintings were denounced as obscene and blasphemous by fellow churchmen.

'I don't wish to upset you,' Rex finished. 'But this could end badly. Not just in court. Even in prison.'

'And he actually menaced you with a firearm?'

'He made sure we saw it. And heard it too.'

'Deplorable,' Henry Moorhouse muttered.

'It remains a stand-off,' Rex explained.

'And as for the land, there's no question of its ownership?'

'None. With owners gone, Eddie is now squatting. He has already been informed so in writing. He has also been acquainted with the fact that the property is back on the market. No doubt Eddie will do his best to discourage buyers. As for moving him, a bulldozer may be necessary.'

'And what am I to do about it?' Henry Moorhouse asked.

'You're his brother.'

'But not his keeper.'

'We also have the hope that you might shed a little sweetness and light on proceedings.'

'You're asking a miracle.'

'Of sorts,' Rex had to agree.

The Reverend Moorhouse pointed himself in the direction of duty. He contacted Eddie by letter and proposed a date for a reunion. Eddie, in his terse reply, raised no objection.

The day didn't go well. Unfamiliar with the region, the cleric managed to lose himself several times. It was dusk before he saw the homestead in his headlights. Eddie made a morose appearance. 'Where the hell have you been?' he said. 'I've got better things to do than wait on you all day.'

'My apologies,' Henry said meekly.

'What is it you want in my neck of the woods?' Eddie asked.

'An overdue encounter,' Henry said evasively. 'It's years since we saw each other.'

Eddie grunted. 'But why now?' he asked.

Unwilling to tell the truth, also to lie, Henry found it difficult to come up with an answer.

'Have you got someone on your back?'

'I'm unsure what you mean.'

'You know what I bloody mean,' Eddie said. 'Has anyone been getting at you?'

'In respect of what?' Henry said feebly.

'In respect of me,' Eddie said.

Henry was silent. A lie was of no use now.

'I should have known,' Eddie decided. 'Rex Heath, was it, or Don Fox?'

'Eddie,' Henry pleaded, 'I'm exhausted. Can we forget this till tomorrow?'

'Provided you brought some booze,' Eddie said.

Sensitive to his brother's needs, Henry hadn't arrived empty handed. Eddie was even more difficult sober.

Their evening meal was meagre, a stew lumpy with half-cooked carrots and a shredded substance resembling fowl, though it may have been fish. Henry, with fatigue growing, and wine quick to his head, retired early. His sleep was deep. He woke to sunlight and Eddie shaking his shoulder.

'You know what the time is?' Eddie was saying.

Henry didn't much care.

'Eight o'clock,' Eddie said.

Henry failed to see this as a cause for grief.

'I've already put two hours in,' Eddie added.

'Two hours?'

'Clearing scrub. While you slept.'

'I'm sorry, Eddie. I appear to be missing the point.'

'The point is that visitors earn their keep here. No layabouts. No playboys. If you aren't up to life on the land, bugger off fast.'

Within the hour, without breakfast, the Reverend Henry Moorhouse buggered off fast.

In reporting the failure of his mission, Henry provided Rex with an arresting item of intelligence. Eddie now occupied more than a mere barn. He had commandeered the homestead and, save for his indifferent cuisine, had begun residing there in style. It was clear that Eddie's notion of the simple life didn't involve a monkish existence. Observant Henry had seen a woman arrive as he was leaving. Her station wagon was packed with foodstuffs and other necessities, certainly enough to see out a siege. As for rustic matters, Eddie's woolly flock looked ready for shearing. Yes, and there were now pigs grunting too.

There may be a point to this story. Thirty years on, Rex Heath has yet to get its drift. Fine print and fluent lawyers failed to persuade Eddie to move. In the end a knotty monetary deal was made. Legal title would eventually pass to Eddie in return for agreed monthly sums. Eddie was scrupulous in respect of these payments. The malicious might say he could afford to be.

Don Fox was never heard commending the simple life again. As anticipated, he ceased to be Eddie's dealer; he now trades in antiques, which present fewer hazards.

Mike and Charlotte parted company soon afterwards. In hope of the last word, Charlotte came up with a novel. Borrowing abundantly from life, it was only fitfully a work of the imagination. ('It wasn't meant to be cruel,' she explained to intimates, some of whom believed her.) Written in rather headlong prose, it dealt with the tribulations of a kamikaze clique of city-dwellers crash-landing in Arcadia. Mike refrained from reviewing the novel. His shock was such that his writer's block went into recess overnight. Choosing to suffer in silence, Don managed not to read the book at all.

Remote from cultural skirmishing, Jim and Sally continue to pursue primal wisdom, the secrets of the cosmos and a highly organic lifestyle; they dwell in a dome house, deep in the forested New Zealand interior, among mists and alpine streams. The virtue of the location resides in the fact that no sane individual could have designs on it. Jim wears a beard to his waist; Sally, still with a headband, and hung about with beads and bangles, scuffs around in muddy Roman sandals. Jim pans for slim amounts of gold and, when it thins further, throws pots for the tourist market. (Sally is better known for her weaving.) Who knows? Around the year 2020AD a film team may begin searching for survivors of the 1960s. As they track down the world's last hippies and record their reminiscences, these chroniclers of a lost time might find wrinkled Jim and grey-haired Sally the highlight of their quest.

Though Rex Heath bravely tried to stem the tide of tales about the incident, the Kaipara clash was never a secret long. Folklore soon enshrined it as a brutal battle. Dozens claimed to have witnessed the happenings of that day. There was even a ballad sung beside the campfires of the counter-culture. Eventually, however, colourful fictions sputtered out. It never ranked with Vietnam's Tet Offensive anyway. There was no body count.

Rex? Though he remains a respected art historian, he never came up with his book on Eddie Moorhouse. Colleagues saw this withdrawal from the field as making commercial sense. Eddie's work had begun bobbing in a critical backwater, a cultural curiosity. No one saw him wielding a brush, other than when brightening the homestead's exterior. In other respects he remained reasonably fecund; he managed to marry and father four children. Reports say that he pleads ignorance of his past as a painter. It may be so. It may also be true that his time is coming round again. The fickle critical view—three decades after he abandoned his brushes—is that there might be something to be said for his work after all. Not that Eddie welcomes such tidings. Innocents attempting to enlighten him find him strangely deaf.

Near neighbours know Eddie as a model farmer. He is especially helpful to newcomers. He makes no secret of the fact that he was once a raw novice himself. Now and then, in the long shadows of later afternoon, he can be seen patrolling his hilly acres on horseback, an obedient dog padding to his rear; he has the weathered appearance of a man long of the land. The sun sets. The day dims. He rides on.